PRIDE'S
Fancy

THOMAS H. RADDALL

DOUBLEDAY & COMPANY, INC.

1946

Garden City *New York*

PRINTED IN THE UNITED STATES
AT
THE COUNTRY LIFE PRESS, GARDEN CITY, N. Y.

FIRST EDITION

PRIDE'S FANCY

FOREWORD

THIS is a romance, of course. But I think I should mention the background, which is fact. Any good library can give a list of the history books involved. What I want to say here is that I live in a small Nova Scotia seaport which in colonial times had a great deal to do with the West Indies. More than one garden blooms actually in West Indian soil, brought north as ballast in the days of the Caribbean trade. Street corners are marked by half-sunken cannon, muzzle down, which once upon a time spoke sharply for their owners in the Caribbean waters. Other relics are carefully preserved, and tales of the old wild days survive in family legend as well as in letters, diaries, logbooks, and other documents of the time.

The pistol of one privateersman lies at my elbow as I write. In my bookcase is the log of a Spanish brig, brought north as a prize in 1798. I have before me a battered pilot book, well marked by tarry thumbs, the end papers scrawled with notations of latitude and longitude, jottings of laundry sent ashore in friendly ports like Barbados and St. Kitts, and suchlike matters, and bearing on the flyleaf in a bold fist:

Francis Kempton is my nam
Seaman is my stashon
N. Scotia is my dwelen plas
And Ingland is my nashon

That might have been written by the immortal Billy Bones himself. It was written by a simple trader captain of my town who fought as a privateersman in the Caribbean from 1798 to 1801 and lived to pass the book and the tale to his descendants.

During the long wars which followed the French Revolution a good many seamen from my town cruised in the Caribbean under letters of marque issued by the governor of Nova Scotia. A few got rich. Most of them gained nothing but a romantic experience, the risks being more than the rewards. Some perished in battle, some of yellow jack in the islands, some by the common hazards of the sea. Fortunate ones survived the wars and lived out their days as seamen, woodsmen, farmers, or merchants in the long peace afterwards. One of them struck up a friendship with the black king Christophe, after the passing of Toussaint and Dessalines, and for years enjoyed a semimonopoly of the coffee trade out of Haiti. Another (my wife's ancestor) founded a prosperous timber-and-shipbuilding firm and died a deacon of his church. At least two served their province in after years as members of the legislature. Another built a college and a temperance hall, and his widow bequeathed the land on which our town hall stands. And there was one who founded a bank and died the richest man of his time in British North America.

But all this was afterwards, and these were the exceptions. Most of the Nova Scotia privateersmen were men of simple trades and humble destinies, and I write here of a time when they were young and looking for riches and finding nothing but adventure and sore bones. Of such men and such matters is this tale.

THOMAS H. RADDALL

Liverpool, Nova Scotia
May 1st, 1946.

Chapter 1

IT BEGAN on the night we thought all was ended—the night we left Hispaniola for home, with the town of Cap François burning red behind us and the smoke alive with the flicker of the fires, and the darkness wild with shots and cries. I remember how feverishly we pushed off the boat from the stinking mud of the foreshore, with the French planter Dolainde and his small daughter on the stern sheets and three chests of polished mahogany thrown in all anyhow. And I remember the faces of those others, pale and beseeching, wading out with torches after us, calling on us in the name of God to take them into a boat already down to her gunwales; and how I cursed myself and them and turned my back, snarling at the oarsmen to pull, pull like mad if they hoped to make old bones in Nova Scotia.

Long ago, and I am old bones now. But I can see the houses burning and the savage dark faces swarming through the streets athirst for blood, the quick bright spurt of firearms through the jalousie slats, the black fists clutching their polished yellow clubs, beating on doors and then on heads and faces, and the cruel sugar cutlasses rising and falling. And I hear the screams of the townsmen, of their women and children, high above the roar of voices mouthing the war cries of Africa there in the white town under the Caribbean mountain; and I hear my own voice, hoarse and strange, urging the seamen onward as we half dragged, half carried Dolainde and the small girl and the wooden chests down to the water. And then I feel the night wind cool on my sweat-sodden shoulders, the moist breath of the mountains wafting us out to the little brig in the roadstead and whispering in our ears, "Never come back again . . . never . . . never . . ."

Ay, on hot nights of summer when the house is still and the crickets cheep in the garden, when a faint air stirs the tops of the pine trees and a flood tide mutters on the shore, when the oil in the lamp is low and it is time for bed and the tang of the buttered-rum nightcap warms my throat—then the old memories come back with that picture of hell, where Satan has a face as black as night, and howls a mixture of French and Fulani, and shows a glitter of polished teeth and staring bloodshot eyes in the light of the fires, and breathes forth a reek of Hades—or Haiti if you like, or Hispaniola, Saint Domingo, it has many names.

Chapter 2

WE WASTED no time, I tell you. I had a whim to kneel and kiss the *Sally's* deck, but there were other things to do. We set the headsails and slipped our cable, leaving a precious anchor to the ooze. Titus and Black Boston swarmed aloft and let fall the topsails, and we sheeted them home with a will, but without song or shout. There was noise enough ashore. The brig began to move. Monsieur Dolainde and his child stood at the tafferel gazing towards the anguished flutter of those torches on the foreshore. She stood very still and erect in her fine silk gown and petticoats, a little woman of fourteen, and suddenly stretched a hand.

"Maman!" she said, not loudly, but it wrung my heart. Dolainde said nothing. God knows what agony he suffered then. God knows what gentle lies he had told her since he fled with her in his arms, that little sallow man who looked as if he could scarcely carry a doll from a garden, who had carried young Lia-

Marie from the Haut du Cap to the town on that night of terror when the blacks rose on the plantations.

Alas for *Maman,* that beautiful creature! Madame Dolainde was from the old Spanish colony at the far end of Hispaniola, a spirited woman with black hair and moist black eyes and a smooth and pallid skin, like one of those flowers, fragile and passionate, that flourish in the shadowy courts and walled gardens of the Spanish creoles. And now she was dead like a flower plucked and torn and trampled in the ruined garden on the Haut du Cap.

There was a cold knot in my stomach when I thought of that.

I found Hosea Biggar in his berth where I had left him, ill of the yellow fever. There was a dreadful change in him, the long face gone yellow as a lemon and drawn to skin and bone. The nose stood out from his features sharp as a knife, his lips were covered with ulcers, and there was an ooze of black blood from the mouth corners. His head was shaven and bound with a cool plantain leaf, and over that a wetted handkerchief, and there was a pannikin of brandy and water by the berth, and a palm-leaf fan. Black Boston, the cook, had tended his captain with a woman's care, but it had gone for nothing.

Hosea opened his eyes and regarded me with hot yellow eyeballs, the pupils wide as a cat's at dusk. A puff of night air came down the wind sail we had rigged through the skylight for his comfort.

"Nathan?" he muttered. "Where is Dolainde?"

"Safe aboard, with his daughter."

"And Madame?"

"Dead."

"Eh? What's that?"

"The devil's to pay—and hot pitch aplenty. The plantation blacks have got into the town, three thousand or more, led by that wild fellow Macaya." He stared at me wildly. "Up anchor then! Make an offing while ye can."

"I've slipped the anchor. We're under way now."

He raised himself on his elbows and in a harsh rustling voice exclaimed, "Slipped!" And then, "Bedfast . . . and an anchor gone . . . and my ship amongst the reefs . . . in the dark . . . in the hands of a shaveling . . ." He fell back on the berth like a lean yellow corpse. After a time he rolled those feverish eyes at me and sneered.

"So it's captain now, eh? At last! Captain Cain!"

"Well?"

"A hand to the spreet, and one to the fore-topmast. Watch for the white grounds. . . . Is there starlight?"

"Ay, and the town afire for a beacon."

"Picolet Point . . . range along Picolet . . . at a musket-shot distance, no more . . . and keep the point south . . . sou'-sou'west at most, mind . . . till ye see the white grounds o' the first reef. You hear me, Nathan . . . Captain Cain?"

"Ay, and I know the rest," I said impatiently, for the deck was my place now.

"A spar marks the channel with a flag on it . . . but God knows what they may ha' done with that. . . . Leave the spar to larboard if it's there and then haul up nor'west . . . nor'west a quarter west and be sure . . . take ye clear o' the long reef . . . then make your offing whilst the land breeze holds. Keep Picolet well south the whole way out, mind. . . ."

"I know, I know."

Black Boston was rapping gently on the open skylight and calling, "Mistah Cain, sah! Mistah Cain!"

Captain Biggar uttered a long rattling sigh and closed his eyes. I thought he was dead and turned to go, but as I jumped for the cabin stairs I heard him say very distinctly, "Who's to bring the cow from pasture, Jenny?"

His mind was home in Nova Scotia, sixteen hundred miles by sea to the north, and five up the bay and one up the river, where his old wooden house stood by the water, and he was singing a country love song in a high cracked voice when I cleared the last of the stairs.

A dark departure. What is worse?—except it be a dark landfall, and in such a place. Hispaniola is a sailor's nightmare at the best of times, with an ocean about it bottomless to a common lead until you are close in, and then a sudden jumble of reefs and cays in the very shadow of the mountains. We were mad, stark mad, to venture the passage out of Cap François without a pilot in the dark, but the mad town gave us no choice, and there was in all our minds a shaking horror of the forty-eight hours past that left no room for ordinary fears.

And so we sailed, with a leadsman busy in the chains and our topsails set to give us steerageway in the chancy places, and Boston the cook, who could see like a cat in the dark, perched in the fore-topmast crosstrees watching for the shimmer of the shoals. Behind us those hell sounds fell away and the fires sank to a red glimmer at the black foot of Picolet Mountain. As we drew off to sea the land breeze fell lighter and lighter until it was only a fitful breath that set the canvas grumbling and fretting at the sheets.

"Well, Nathan, we are clear—thank the good God," said old

Lot Mayes. "And morning will bring the trade wind and the passage home. How is Hosea?"

"Bad. The black vomit has begun."

Lot clucked his tongue. "You'll be master, then?"

"I shall take her home."

He nodded in the glimmer of the binnacle, knowing how the matter stood. No man, not even the owner's adopted son, could say he was master of a Pride ship until Amos Pride said so first.

"Lord, what a wax o' things!" Lot muttered, looking back towards the land, to the tall black shape of the mountains hard against the stars. "Who'd ha' thought it, eh?"

Ay, who? The richest colony in the Caribbees, the pride of France and envy of the world, swallowed in a tide of black humanity that only a few months back was singing and laughing in the sugar fields!

Our seamen lay about the deck like dead men, the strength, the very sap of life gone out of them after the struggles and terrors ashore. I had no heart to stir them. Let them sleep. There would be hard labor and short commons in the days to come.

"Where's Boston?" Lot Mayes asked.

"Gone below to fit my berth for Dolainde and his child. I'll share yours, Lot, on the voyage home."

"Home!" His harsh voice lingered on the word. "I wish to God that you and I were home abed, and all that"—a mute gesture towards the land—"something dreamed o' mince pie and hot grog. What pictures for a Christian man to carry in his mind!" And then in the wheedling voice I knew so well, "Your mouth must be as dry as mine, Nathan. Ay, it is, I know, and a tongue like an old woolen stocking. A sup then! A sup o' that French rum in the captain's berth, to stave off the fever if nought else."

"No!" I snapped, for a mouthful of tafia now would knock him senseless and I wanted one wakeful man on deck beside me. He uttered a long whine through his nose like a mournful dog.

"Well," I said, "a sup then, but no more."

We went below and met Boston outside the captain's door with an awed look on his sweating black face and the whites of his eyeballs gleaming.

"Nathan, sah, he's daid!"

So! As quick as that! The whole burden of the *Sally* and her people on my shoulders in a moment. Boston saw the pannikins in our hands.

"Nathan, sah, we got to put him overside."

That was true. In such a climate dead men are ill company, and God knows we had ill company enough with yellow jack aboard. We nerved ourselves with stout drams at the keg and then rolled Hosea—or what the fever had left of him—into a piece of old thin topsail from the canvas locker, and carried the limp long bundle to the deck.

I had not loved Hosea Biggar: he was too harsh a man, and jealous somehow of my presence in the *Sally*—"the owner's mate," as he often called me in the hearing of the crew. A bitter old man and may Davy Jones be gentler with him than he ever was with me.

It was flat calm, the sea a pool of pitch and the vast darkness all about us one hot and prickling silence. Our stumbling feet rang loudly on the deck. The least whisper carried far. When one of the sleeping seamen stirred there was a rustle and thump you could hear the length of the brig. We found a plank of pine saved out of our southward cargo for some petty repair, and balanced it on the rail, while Boston went to the hold and fetched a stone from the ballast to carry the dead man down.

We had shipped our ballast from the stony beach outside Fish Point at home; and it was strange to think of those awful depths beneath us where the sea of Hispaniola goes down a thousand, some say two thousand, fathom at a leap, and Hosea Biggar lying on the bottom there in the eternal night, in the dark wet bowels of the sea, with God knows what beasts and fish and queer old ships and foreign men to keep him company, and a bit of old Nova Scotia at his feet forever.

It did not take us long. Lot muttered a prayer—he was a pious man at home and a great singer of psalms in the meetinghouse before the drink set him to leeward of the elders. The big stone took the captain down all standing, which was proper, for he made no splash to speak of. But the inky dark brought out the phosphor in the water so that it broke into sea fire as if aflame, a wonderful thing to see at any time and awesome now, and the dim shape went slowly down aglow like a corposant.

Boston uttered a squeak of dismay, but Lot cried out in a deep voice, "So! So! Hell's flame can have no terrors for thee, Hosea, sinful man—an ye pass it wet enough."

"Belay that!" said I through my teeth.

"A cheerful Christian word in the passing——"

"I said belay!"

I could hear Boston gibbering. And below in the captain's berth waited the little keg of tafia. Down we went with one impulse and a rush as if pursued by ghosts, and drank and drank. I was a sad example to my men that night, but they were past knowing or caring. Dolainde and his little girl were shut up with their sorrow in my own berth. They made no sound. Perhaps they slept. And all through the night the *Sally* drifted on that silent sea.

I woke with a rough tongue and an aching skull to find the sun strong through the skylight and the topsails flogging noisily.

I lost no time in getting to the poop and found Lot Mayes at the wheel stark sober, with a look of virtue on his lean face fit to charm the angels. The land wind had sprung up again as sometimes it does in those parts in the morning, a last flourish before the sun can suck the life out of it. I bawled, "All hands!" and those dead men about the decks came to life.

I put young Simon Dawkins at the wheel, and Black Boston came up from his fire, where he had been making coffee and stirabout as if nothing had happened. The big Negro was a freedman of Mr. Pride's, a sea paragon who could hand, reef, and steer, and cook into the bargain, the most useful man in the ship. He swarmed aloft with Swann and Bowles and the other seaman, Nash, and they had the harbor furl out of the fore and mainsails in three shakes.

We sheeted the big sails home with a will, Lot and I pulling and hauling and yo-hoing with the rest, for we had found our voices again. Then we set the royals and braced all to the wind. The *Sally* heeled and the water began to speak under her forefoot. Behind us the gutted and reeking town of Cap François had sunk below the sea's rim in the night, and the great mountains of Hispaniola stood shrouded in the morning mist. We fled away from them with the wind large and our faces hopeful to the north.

Lot Mayes now was mate by my order, as he had long been in fact; for I was mate in name and little else if you come to the fine point. Hosea Biggar never tired of reminding me that I was a stripling of twenty with three years at sea, no more, whilst Lot, rising sixty, had never set foot to shore three months on end since he was out of frocks. Of course I had a good deal of book learning and knew the mathematics of navigation where Lot had only the thumb rules, but there was no jealousy in him, and he had taught me a vast deal of sea knowledge not to be found in my books.

Now there must come a time when the pupil knows more than his master, or thinks he does, and I thought I did. And I had that charming and arrogant belief in myself which is the special property of young men at twenty. So I set the course nor'east by east, and Lot came to me growling in his throat.

"What folly's this? Keep her off, boy, keep her off for Inagua and the Crooked Island Passage. The long road home's the best one, this side Monte Cristi anyhow."

"And take home nothing but the ballast? What would Mr. Pride say?"

"Damme!"—swallowing his quid and his piety at a gulp—"he'll be lucky to get his brig home if ye don't look out. Dolainde can witness that his cargo for the *Sally* had to be left in the warehouse at Cap François. What could Pride expect at such a time?"

"He'll expect me to use my judgment and pick up a cargo where I can. There's the Caicos Passage and Turk's Island, and a lading of salt for next summer's fishery."

"Turk your grandmother, Nathan! Why, you're mad. You'll fall upon the Caicos Bank with your damned judgment, and that will be the end of us. How many times have I told ye the land winds hereabouts die in the middle o' the forenoon, and then ye must reckon with the trades?"

"I've reckoned with 'em, Lot. Turk's Island, I tell you—if we have to tow her there with the boats in the teeth of the trade."

He gave a great snort at that, but he said no more. He was confounded. The land wind held large at the south, and when it died at last we got a slant of the trade wind from the southeast and made good weather of it into the Caicos Passage. Lot's eyes were quizzical, and I could see what he was thinking—fool's luck and nothing else. He was filled with old forebodings, having tried once upon a time to reach Turk's from Cap François, caught the trade full in his teeth, failed to make Sand Key, and gone afoul of the great hidden bank to the west of the Passage.

And so we took a salt cargo at Turk's, a burning place in late June. The salt pans blazed in the full stroke of the sunshine, cruel to the eyes, and the windmills pumping sea water into the vats spun their foolish arms in the steady rush of the trade like men gone crazy with the heat. I paid for the salt with a draft on Mr. Pride's agent in Jamaica, and felt pleased with myself, though Lord knows it was poor enough business. A salt cargo from Turk's Island was the last resort of empty bottoms bound to the north, and Mr. Pride would be expecting a handsome lading of rum, coffee, and sugar from the Dolainde estate in Hispaniola.

When this was done, in a further show of self-confidence I stood the brig across the passage to Anse à l'Eau, within the Caicos reef, a snug little cove where I knew the Providenciers came to water; and there we watered for the voyage north, boating our casks between the *Sally* and the shore. I expected to see Lot's pigtail stand on end as the little brig jogged amongst the shoals, but he disappointed me, chewing his cud and humming psalms and wearing on his bony face the resigned smile of a martyr at peace with God.

Mr. Dolainde watched these affairs morosely from the shade of a small awning on the poop. He showed no interest in life, and small wonder when I thought of poor Madame Dolainde and the great white mansion above the sugar fields, the luxury and happiness that had seemed destined to go on forever, all snuffed out like a candle in the night.

The small girl moved about the deck, a lively creature with her mother's clear pale skin and glowing black eyes, and Dolainde's yellow hair, a contrast very outlandish to our northern minds. We called her Mam'selle respectfully, for after all she was the daughter of our owner's richest customer in Hispaniola. She spoke a little English, and all of us had a bit of French and Spanish, which were her native tongues; and so we conversed in all three, with a great waggling of hands and pointing of fingers, and understood each other perfectly in the manner of children and sailors everywhere.

'Twas not long before she mastered the queer names of our crew, Lot and Simon and Titus and Comfort and Lathrop. She shrank a little from poor Boston at first, haunted no doubt by those black faces in the nightmare just past, but he was smiling and gentle, waiting on her, running at her slightest whim, singing bits of creole songs and twisting rope ends into marvelous knots and patterns for her amusement.

Me she called simply Capitaine, with a grave politeness. I could not unbend like the foremast hands, even to a child. I was very conscious of my dignity in the flush of my first command, and for the first time I knew a captain's loneliness.

Chapter 3

ON THAT voyage home I heard myself called Lucky Cain, a change, for most men in moments of conviviality called me Red. The change was a quip of Lot Mayes', meant for my hearing, that caught the fancy of the crew. That dour old dog could not forget the fortune of the winds that took us to Turk's Island so handily, or the brig's adventures in the white grounds off the Caicos which have wrecked so many ships and scared good seamen out of their wits.

I resented the title and the quip, for I was carried away with my own importance—as who would not have been in my shoes in those days?—and I credited our success to a cool head and good seamanship when Lot vowed it to be nothing but foolhardiness and Providence. He was right, of course. I had all the world to learn, and the sea is a bitter schoolmaster with many a rod in pickle for a fool. But at bottom he was wrong.

There is something more important than experience. On the sea a man must believe in himself or he is nowhere. I have seen men all their lives at sea, ay, and in command for a good part of it, who were not worth their owners' pay. There was always a devil of doubt in them. Such men lose more money for their owners than the ship is worth, and sooner or later lose the ship itself for failure to take a stout chance at some place or moment where there is no time for pondering. Well, I seldom suffered doubt in those days, whatever else my sins. Lucky or not, I followed my own rash head—and live to tell this tale.

So we came north by the Caicos Passage and reached across the trades for the fair current of the Gulf Stream. There was a patch of doldrums, but abreast of Hatteras we picked up the first bluster of the westerlies, and from then on it was plain sailing, a soldier's passage all in all, though we were nigh starved at the end of it. There had been no chance at Cap François to stock the lazaret. Salt beef and biscuit was our fare, and that in meager quantity.

We made a landfall in late August and gazed upon the familiar sands and dark trees of Cape Sable with the famished eyes of wolves. It was blowing a gale, and the wind had the first bite of autumn. Dolainde and Lia-Marie went below shivering, with faces as desolate as the long gray seas.

By night we were up with the west head of Gosport, the brown bluff and the high trees wrapped in rain and the first candlelight twinkling in the fishermen's huts on Bear Island. The wind was westerly and promised a long beat up the narrow bay in the dark. The sensible thing was to jog off the headland till daylight, but we were hungry for home in all ways, and had we not come blind out of Cap François? So I ordered the helm down and the seamen cheered—even Lot Mayes had a grin. Black Boston alone was silent, staring at the dim headlands in the dusk and rain, his eye whites flickering.

I had an anxious time of it after that, for all my confidence, and so had everyone, with incessant labor at brace and sheet and tack. I had to stand the *Sally* over from shoal to shoal along the estuary, taking all the room there was. The rain beat hard in our faces, coming in thick squalls that hid both shores, and all about us the sea birds wheeled and hovered, crying dismally.

Once the brig hung in stays and my heart was in my mouth, for the froth of Neal's Ledge showed white in the dark not a biscuit toss away. Lot was at his station forward with the best of the seamen, Comfort Swann, watching the flutter of the head-sails, and I thought grimly, "Pray now, old dog, or ye die wet tonight!" But she came over, the yards aswing, the canvas booming out like cannon shots, and dim figures springing to brace up the after yards. In a few moments we had the mainsheet aft, and eased our patched old spanker to leeward, and then I was roaring, "Let go and haul!" in the voice of an angry bull.

Even then 'twas a touchy business. Boston let go the weather forebraces promptly, and Bowles, Nash, and Simon Dawkins hauled in to leeward, old Lot lashing them with his tongue. And I shook my fist at the smother to starboard where the ledges waited, and slapped the *Sally's* rail again and again with my tarry palm, crying, "Up, Sally! Up, my girl! To windward if ye love me! Ah, take hold! Take hold!"

I heard a small sound at my back, and there was Dolainde in his thin West Indian garments, wet and shivering and wild, fetched up from the lurching cabin by the shouting and scurry of feet above his head. Beside him stood young Lia-Marie, slim as a withe in her drenched nightgown, pigtails blowing, eyes enormous in the faint glow up the cabin stairs. There was no fear in her face, only an eager curiosity, watching the seamen leaping about the deck, glancing aloft at the taut rain-drummed canvas—and regarding me with astonishment as I caressed my ship. I dropped my hand, growling, "Get below, monsieur. There is no danger, and the night is wet and cold." He took the girl's hand and vanished.

Thus we came up the harbor of home, straining our ears for the boom of the shoals and our eyes for the steep wooded shores. I was thankful when we made the shelter of Fish Point and dropped anchor at last. The tide was past the flood and no getting over the river bar till morning. The lights in Ma'am Hackett's tavern on Fish Point showed that the town was not yet abed, and I was too restless for sleep in any case, so I ordered the gig manned and went ashore, telling Lot I would come off again at daybreak.

With the boat hauled up on the beach I gave my oarsmen leave to go home, and off they went with yelps like boys out of school. There would be tousled wives by morning. I set off in their wake along the muddy street, walking quickly. The hour was not much past ten of the clock. The wind brought a smell of wet pinewoods down the river. I threw back my head and snuffed it eagerly. Tomorrow I must see the brig warped over the bar and up to the Pride wharf; but after that I would take my gun and seek out the partridge on Great Hill, and pause awhile on the shoulder of it, looking back over the harbor and the masts of ships along the river, and the wooden roofs of the town swimming in ash and elm and poplar trees, and to the northward the low flanks of the river valley, thick-forested and blue in the autumn haze. That was a sight I had loved always, and loved now better than ever. I would not give one acre of Nova Scotia in early fall for all the riches of Hispaniola.

My foster father's mansion stood on a knoll overlooking the basin where the river mingled with the tide. From its four white walls a battery of windows commanded the two Pride wharves and the dock between, the warehouses and the busy store where half the business of Gosport was done, the Pride shipyard where the Pride ships were built, and across the water the rocky face of Moose Hump, with its crown of pine trees, the beginning of the Pride timberlands which ran far up the river past the Pride sawmills and the long pond full of Pride logs.

Each of those logs at the sawmill bore in clean white ax strokes the Pride mark, so that no petty woodsman could mistake them for his own in the mingled rush down the river each spring. And there were some in our town who said that Amos Pride had put his mark on everything worth having in Gosport, indeed the whole of Queen Charlotte County.

It is no land of milk and honey, our Nova Scotia, and rich men are not loved in a poor country. My foster father was a merchant and a stirring one, with a hound's nose for an opportunity and the courage to reach out and seize it, often at a risk that frightened lesser moneybags. But his fist was tight as well as bold, he did mean things by instinct, loving money for its own sake. That men found hard to forgive.

The great three-storied house, square as a box, with its gleaming white clapboards and green shutters, with its four doors, one each side, the front door having a pillared portico, and with its great chimney clusters at each end of the roof, and the widow's-walk, railed and floored, that ran between the chimneys and gave a view of all Gosport—the big house, I say, was a mark of Amos Pride's rise in the world and the citadel from which he ruled his small empire. Gosport folk had called it Pride's Fancy in the silly way folk have with ambitious men's houses, but they had lived to see its owner rich and the house a symbol of his foresight.

I had seen it first as a boy of nine, an orphan child from some village down the shore. Mr. Pride had sent a sloop to fetch me and my small belongings, and Mrs. Pride received me in the west parlor, a short plain woman in a huge mobcap figged out with ribbons of three colors, and a hooped gown that hung in flounces and reefs and bunches that made me think of a ship's mainsail hanging in the clews. I had never seen anyone so grand or so be-draped. And beside her, partly concealed by the wide fall of her mother's dress, stood a small girl of about my own age, dressed very much like her mamma.

"So this is Mary Kelland's boy," Mrs. Pride said primly.

"Yes, ma'am," I said.

"Do you know you're to live with us, to be one of Mr. Pride's family?"

"Yes, ma'am."

She was silent a moment, regarding me with a pair of blue eyes in which I could see no affection and no welcome, only a gleam of curiosity or anger, I could not tell which.

"Do you look like your mamma?"

"I don't know, ma'am." My mother died when I was born, but somehow I could not tell this strange cold woman that.

"Um! Well, from now on, Nathan, you must look upon me

as your mamma; that is Mr. Pride's wish." And in a strained tone, "Do you know why?"

"No, ma'am."

She looked at me very hard for a moment or two, sucking in a great breath until I thought her laced and ribboned bosom would surely burst. Then she said, with a long sigh through her nostrils, "This is your foster sister, Mr. Pride's child and mine. You must be very nice to her, indeed to all of us, and grateful, too, I hope. Speak up, Felicity dear."

The little girl regarded me with eyes the color of brandy, larger and much brighter than her mother's. Her lips were struggling with something she was supposed to say and could not, or had forgotten perhaps. Finally she announced flatly, "I think you are a very dirty little boy. And ragged, too!" and ran out of the room.

Mrs. Pride clucked her tongue, but she said no more. She stepped to the wall and pulled on a tasseled bell rope. A maid-servant came and curtsied and led me off upstairs—two flights of stairs—to a small chamber in the top of the house. There she paused and looked me up and down with a grin on her broad Irish face, saying, just like Mrs. Pride, "Well, d'ye know why you're here?"

I did not feel abashed with her as I had with Mrs. Pride, I suppose because Betty Boyle was more like the fisherfolk I had lived amongst.

"Because I've got no father nor mother now, that's why."

She gave a snort and a chuckle. "Psha! Well, it's the only way Old Pinch will ever get a boy now, I'll warrant. And herself!" Another chuckle. "Her nose is out o' joint, I venture. She's only got to look at ye."

With that she departed, leaving me standing in the middle of the chamber floor and digging my toe into the drugget. I went over to the wall and inspected myself in the looking glass that hung there, wondering why these people looked at me so. All I saw was a thin face brown with the summer's sun, a short freckled nose, and a pair of serious blue eyes, the whole surmounted by a shock of thick red hair.

Chapter 4

THAT was eleven years, an age ago. Betty Boyle was gone long since, dismissed for some impertinence or other. Mrs. Pride had become a still, silent creature in spectacles, much occupied with religion, and Felicity had grown to a slim young woman very cool and pleasant with the world and me. And I?—I was simply part of the Pride property, I guess. I had been taught my manners by Mrs. Pride, a notable task, and my letters and figures by a succession of Gosport schoolmasters, the drunken misfit men who wandered up and down the coast in those days selling education at sixpence a day. And I had learned that God looked with special favor on the Congregational folk, of whom the Prides were chief, and none of this New Light nonsense.

At seventeen I had been sent to sea in a Pride ship to learn my trade. Before the mast, of course. Mr. Pride had instructed his captains to treat me no better nor worse than the rest, a course they followed faithfully, knotted rope ends and all. Last year, at nineteen, I had been sent to the *Sally* and Captain Hosea Biggar; to be mate, if you please, but no privileges. And now for the space of a voyage I had been the *Sally's* master. As I walked up the carriage drive to the big house in the elms I wondered what Amos Pride would say.

There was a dim glow through the dense red velvet curtains of his library, but the rest of the house was dark and abed. The doors were bolted, I knew; there was a strict regimen at Pride's Fancy in such matters. No need to arouse the house, I thought. I stepped over the wet grass to the library window and tapped upon it gently. No movement within. I tapped again, and the light went out as if at a quick hard puff. Suddenly the window swung wide the full length of its rod and my foster father's voice said, "Don't move!"

In the dark I could see nothing, but I knew he had a pistol in his hand.

"It's Nathan, sir," I said.

I heard a sharp click of tongue against teeth. "Must you come creeping about the windows like a thief in the night?"

"The *Sally's* just home. I didn't want to waken the house."

"Ah! Well, swing yourself in, sir." I put my hand on the sill and vaulted inside. I could hear the *chick-chick-chick* of a tinder-box. A light flared, and presently the candles revealed the room. We regarded each other. Mr. Pride was a tall man and gaunt, with blue-shaven jaws and a sallow skin, the queer yellowy-brown skin you see on men who have spent years in the tropical seas and then come north and indoors. He had begun life as a seaman in the West Indies trade, like so many Nova Scotiamen, and the mark of it was on his features like a dye.

His nose was long and pointed, a questing nose, a thrusting nose, and the lips beneath were very thin and set so firmly together that they gave a little smack when he spoke, as if reluctant to part with his words. And this habitual set of his jaw had drawn hard puckered lines about the mouth corners, like those you see at the clews of a tight-drawn sail. His eyebrows were black and straight, with no gap over the nose. He wore his hair cut loosely at the nape. There was hardly a gray hair in those dark and oily locks.

In his prime he had followed the fashion, and I remembered

a time soon after I came to the big house when the Prides entertained Governor Parr, a dapper little pomposity whose appetite for wines and good dinners—and perquisites of every kind—were famous in the province. Mr. Pride had worn his hair long then, curled about the temples and pigtailed behind, and dusted heavily with the dull pink powder then in vogue with the Halifax bucks. He had a scarlet coat and gold-embroidered waistcoat, white breeches and silk stockings that clung to his lean legs, and a pair of pumps with gold buckles, a very fine figure indeed. He was a rising merchant then, a little rajah of the outports, and had felt the need of impressing his worth upon the king's governor.

But all that was past now. Amos Pride's worth was well established even in the little provincial court at Halifax where Governor Wentworth now reigned, and he could afford to dress in such things as the sober blue coat and snuff waistcoat and the gray pantaloons in which I saw him now. But I have not mentioned the feature of my foster father that struck you at first sight and gripped you and possessed your most secret thoughts then and thereafter. That feature was his eyes, of a pale yellow, greenish in some lights, clear and bright and bold as a tiger's, that looked you through and left your mind naked and betrayed. Under the thick black brows they gleamed transparent and lit within like round yellow jewels. Those eyes were upon me now, with curiosity in their cold stare.

I felt abashed. I had not stopped to shave the red stubble from my jaws. I had cut off my pigtail last year when I was promoted from seaman's rank, and now wore my hair roughly clipped, with a thick chestnut fall at my neck. And I was rigged in a seaman's checkered shirt, a blue pea jacket and a pair of nankeen trousers, all smudged with the fires of Cap François.

He laid the pistol in a drawer amongst a scatter of small paper cartridges and a delicate little powder horn. "Well?" he said.

"Captain Biggar died of yellow jack in Hispaniola. I've brought the brig home."

"Oh? Ah! And you beat up the bay tonight, in a foul wind and the dark. Is that your notion of handling a Pride ship?"

"We were nigh starved, sir, and I couldn't risk being blown off the coast. Besides, I've important news for you. The revolution in France has spread to Hispaniola. There's the deuce to pay."

"Dolainde?"

"Came away in the *Sally* with his daughter. Madame is dead—murdered."

He looked startled, and I felt a twinge of satisfaction. He sank into a chair behind his writing table and motioned me to another before it.

"What happened? Tell me the whole of it."

"Well, sir, you knew the trouble in France since '89—all the people up in arms—seizing estates—the King and Queen in prison—all that? Well, the tale of it reached the French colonies, and there was a rumpus in Hispaniola."

"I know all that," impatiently. "Some fools in Paris—what did they call 'emselves? —*Les amis des noirs?*—shipped a lot of tri-colored cockades to the island and told the niggers that Sambo's as good as his master. The blacks kicked up a dust for a time. It came to nothing. Dolainde kept me informed."

"Dolainde was blind like all the planters," I said bluntly. " 'Twas easy at first. The white troops in the Saint Domingo colony were loyal to King Louis, and so were the well-to-do planters. The mulattoes rose and armed themselves, talking very high about liberty and equality—and looking down their noses at the blacks. The white troops put 'em down. The mulatto leader Oge was tried and beaten to death in the public square at Cap François for an example. I was there in the *Fair Wind*, unloading, and saw the whole thing from a tavern window on the square. I went aboard sick as a dog."

"Well?"

"That wasn't the end. The parliament in Paris sent out republican troops, a wild lot, with some rough greasy fellows who called themselves 'commissioners,' to rule the colony. You can guess what the regular troops and the rich planters thought o' that. High words first, then blows and musketry. With the whites at outs there was an end to law and order everywhere. The mulattoes rose again, and presently the blacks. Now the whole of Hispaniola's one big dog pit, the whites at each other's throats, the mulattoes fighting the whites, and the blacks fighting everybody. Between Cap François and Jacmel the devil is king, most of the plantations up in flames, the planters murdered or driven out. When we got away from Cap François the blacks were into the town itself, and the streets afire and running blood."

"Umph! What are the planters doing about it?"

"Some are hiding, hoping it'll blow over. Most are getting out for their lives, to Jamaica, Georgia, Carolina, anywhere they can. I heard talk of calling in British troops—declaring Saint Domingo a British colony."

"Ah!" My foster father drummed his long fingers on the mahogany. His clear topaz eyes were on mine, but he was not seeing me any more. He was looking down the sixty-fifth parallel of longitude, that stroke of the geographers which runs straight south like a road from our Nova Scotia to the Caribbees, and seeing men and things in those far places and turning them to his account.

"Those wild fellows in Paris," he said softly. "They've chopped off their King's head and declared war on England—did you know that?"

"Yes. The commissioners at Cap François were for seizing the

Sally as a prize of war, but Dolainde greased their palms and no more was said."

"Hispaniola? There's a prize!" He was thinking aloud. "Some British troops in Jamaica. More at Halifax to draw upon. They'll need transports, munitions, supplies of all kinds. Must write to Quarrell at Jamaica. See the commissary general at Halifax. Um." His gaze came back from the Caribbees. "These planters . . . if they call in our troops it means they hope to get back their estates under British rule, eh?"

"That's what Dolainde thinks, anyhow."

"Um! A shrewd move. A smart move. Give 'em credit. A man's wealth is bound to prove more precious than his nation when the pinch comes. A sharp lot, those planters, though wasteful as tinkers with their money. Dolainde used to spend half the year in Paris with his family and a train of black servants, living like a king. A lot of those creoles did the same. It got to be a byword there—'Rich as a Saint Domingo planter.' Well, they'll have to trim their canvas closer now. Dolainde—did Dolainde save anything besides the child?"

"We carried three chests aboard."

"Money, I dare say?"

I shrugged. "I don't know. A mahogany chest's a heavy thing of itself."

"Um!" He nodded several times and said in a satisfied voice, "Well, Nathan, Mr. Dolainde shall have shelter here as long as he wishes. This storm will pass. I've seen wild days in those parts myself, long ago. A fool I was, too, for in those days a man might have had all the land he wanted there for the taking. But I was a young seaman just like you, and could see nothing in Hispaniola but parched earth and mountains and the long road home. Blind!—for there was Africa full of idle niggers, very easy had by the Middle Passage, and those rich plains back of

Cap François and Port-au-Prince wanting nothing but the bush cleared off and a few canals dug to bring water from the hills. Fellows like Dolainde saw it well enough. In twenty years they were as rich as princes, the whole land turning to sugar and rum and coffee and indigo under their eyes, and nothing to do but loll in a fine villa with blacks to wait on 'em hand and foot, and all the pleasures of Paris in the summertime to think upon."

'Twas queer to hear the pleasures of Paris on Mr. Pride's tongue in that tone of whimsical regret. Suddenly his voice was sharp.

"What's your lading?"

"I picked up salt at Turk's Island."

"Damme! D'ye mean to say——"

"Mr. Dolainde's sugar and coffee and indigo had to be left ashore. We were lucky to get free with the brig and our lives."

He regarded me in a gloomy silence. It was a blow—the goods that were to pay for our southward cargo lost at the very quay-side; especially the pipes of Western Islands wine, a gift from Mr. Dolainde, selected carefully at Madeira and carried first to Hispaniola for the benefit of long rocking in warm seas, and mellowed there and ready for shipment to the north—all gone down those yelling black throats at Cap François.

"Umph!" he said at last. "The red shed's full of salt now, enough to pickle all the fish from here to Halifax! Why didn't ye go down the Windward Passage to Jamaica for rum and molasses?"

"Because the Windward Passage was swarming with privateers flying the French republican flag or anything else they fancied. At Cap François we had Dolainde's protection—till the blacks rose, of course—but once outside, the *Sally* was easy game for any picaroon with a gun and a few cutlasses. Aside from the French privateers there's a swarm of craft manned by rebel mulattoes out of Jacmel, Jérémie, Tiburon, and Aux Cayes, seizing anything that comes along. They've captured a number of slavers, amongst other ships, and turned a rabble of black cannibals ashore to join the revolution."

I met the yellow eyes squarely as I rapped this out, for my blood was up. I suppose the late voyage in the brig had given me a sudden rush of manhood to the head. Besides, I was weary and on edge, and hungry as a wolf, and I thought I had deserved well for bringing safe home his brig and his best client, with a cargo of whatever sort.

"Hearsay, boy, hearsay! I don't doubt Cap François was humming with wild tales, but the war's too new for the French to have many privateers abroad. As for ships manned by niggers and half-breeds, tsha!"

"The French traders out of Port-au-Prince have manned their ships with Negroes and *sang-mêlées* for many years, and very good seamen, too. I've seen a mulatto shipmaster who could figure his latitude and longitude—especially his longitude—better than any skipper of ours, sir. And come to fighting, I've seen Negroes swinging cane knives in the streets of Cap François and the whites going down before them like a sugar field at harvest. I wouldn't want to be boarded in such a fashion, and nothing in the *Sally* but a couple of cutlasses and Hosea Biggar's old fowling piece."

"Ha!" he snapped and looked his contempt. "Well, get to bed, Nathan. The tide makes at seven tomorrow, and you must look sharp to get the brig over the bar. I want her warped up to the wharf here. The river's high with the rains, and the men will have a long heave-and-pawl of it. Tomorrow's the Sabbath, so mind the men don't chantey about the capstan. We can't have 'em singing and yo-hoing all the way up past the meetinghouse when everyone's at prayers. Give 'em leave to go home as soon as she's fast to the north wharf, and pay 'em off prompt in the morning to save wages. A dead loss, the whole voyage. No fault of yours, of course. Good night."

I closed the door upon him in a grim disgust, my high mood gone, and made my way up the familiar stairs in the dark like a small boy sent supperless to bed. The wind stormed about the house, and the rain beat on the panes. I had got the brig up to Fish Point before the weather set in thoroughly for the worse, a chance well taken, but I could almost hear the anchor watch saying "fool's luck," and I knew these blasts about the eaves must set my foster father thinking on my recklessness.

I slipped my shoes off and crept across the landing of the second floor. The fine walnut staircase with its carved newels and sweeping handrail ended there. A simple stair of pinewood led to the servants' quarters and my own. But as I set my foot on the first worn stair a door opened softly and a shaft of light fell across the darkness of the landing. I turned and saw Felicity standing in her chamber door. She had some sort of wrapper over her nightdress, a pale silken thing, with her dark hair spread about the shoulders.

She said quietly, "I thought I heard your voice down there with Father, Nathan. Have you made a good voyage?"

"No," I said. Felicity had her father's eyes, and they gleamed like his in the light of her candle with the same cold curiosity, or so it seemed to me. Perhaps it was just that I was out of sorts with myself and the world of Amos Pride that night.

I was in the habit of bringing small things home from a voyage, walrus ivory carved by Eskimos at the Labrador fishing posts, a fan or a bit of basketwork from Madeira, beads and shellwork or a few oranges or tamarinds, or a little pot of ginger or of guava jelly from the Caribbees. These I presented to Ma'am Pride and Felicity. They received the gifts calmly and pleasantly, and I cannot say that I presented them with any more sentiment than a sailor's desire to please a relative ashore. There never had been much outward affection between my foster mother and me, nor with Felicity. Mrs. Pride treated me with the same brisk manner she used upon the servants, and Felicity was just the scornful little girl of my first hour at Pride's Fancy, grown tall and eighteen.

Well, I was still a very dirty and very ragged young man, come to think of it. And I was thinking of it, of my rough dress and unclean jaws and hands, when she said, "What have you got for me, Nathan?"

I turned towards the garret stairs. "Nothing," I said brusquely, "except a pair of strangers you must find houseroom for tomorrow."

And away I went, hearing the little sharp slam of her door.

Chapter 5

THE Sabbath was kept holy in our town in those days. The French wars, which were to last so long and to change so much in our life and the life of the world, had just begun. In that year 1793 some of the Gosport founders were still living, the dour psalm-singing Yankee folk who came to Nova Scotia before the war of independence and hewed the first clearings in the forest by the river, and built the first wharves and ships, and took the first cargoes of fish and timber to the Caribbees. The American revolution had flung a number of exiled loyalists into our midst, but many of these were from New England also, and in thought and speech and to all outward appearance Gosport remained a Cape Cod settlement transported across the Bay of Fundy, and so remains to this day.

In '93 our Nova Scotia folk were pious, and rested the seventh day, and praised God loudly in the meetinghouse. But all recognized that ships and property were sacred in their fashion and no more to be neglected than Jehovah—and there was the *Sally* lying outside the bar, and it was the time of the southeasters, the gray wet hurricanes that come roaring up from the West Indies in the fall and give our rocky coast a dying lash of their tails. By the Lord's grace we had got home with sound spars and whole canvas, and who were we to stretch His providence over a week's end in the hurricane season?

And so we warped the brig over the bar and hauled her slowly up the river past wharves and sheds and taverns—and the meetinghouse—while the good folk of Gosport went about their prayers.

'Twas a long job, as Mr. Pride had foreseen. The rains had raised the river, and the spring tides were ten days off. We were the better part of a day at the capstan bars, tuneless like a lot of marines, lest we offend the elders with our lewd sea songs. When we got to the Pride wharf at last the men sank dizzily to the deck, their heads spinning after tramping round the capstan for so many hours on end. The day was hot and still after the wet gusty weather. The sunshine burned on the quiet harbor water at full tide. Not a leaf stirred in the dark woods on the far side, or in the elms about the Pride house, or in the young elms, maples, and poplar trees which lined the street along the river.

From the cobble beach at Fish Point, from acres of brushwood flakes along the waterfront, and from the flat roofs of warehouses came the strong clean smell of split codfish drying in the sun. It was good weather for making stockfish—the sun a mite strong perhaps, and after dinner some careful men had jostled the Sabbath a little to cover up their cod, lest it turn brown and lose the best market. Sawing had begun the past week at the falls up the river, where the mills had been silent through the summer's drought; there was a drift of sawdust on the river, and the ground behind Mr. Pride's dock was stacked with new-sawn boards, filling the air about them with the pleasant cut-pine smell.

From within the warehouses came whiffs of rum, of molasses, sugar, coffee, dyewood, and other pungent matters of the southern trade. The shipyards gave off a mingled smell of shavings, tar, and oakum; the smithy, a reek of scorched iron and Spanish River coals, gone cold in Sabbath idleness. The sail lofts had the dry sharp smell of virgin canvas. From the ropewalk came that scent of new hemp which always smelled to me like sunned hay. The tannery up the river sent down a smell of hemlock bark and soaking hides.

The town marched along a low slope between the forest and the river, its few streets crossed by lanes and alleys running down to the docks. Pride's Fancy was the biggest house in it, imposing on its hillock by the water. The other merchants' houses lay along the eastern end of Fore Street, painted white or yellow or Spanish brown. But most of the homes in our town were simple story-and-half things, with steep pitched roofs to shed the snow, and dormers and squat brick chimneys in the manner of Cape Cod. A few of these were painted, a few were daubed with limewash. For the rest the bare wood only, shingle or clapboard, weathered to the bleak tint of a winter sky. Since hodden was our common wear, the town and its people seemed clothed in one universal gray.

Such was our town of Gosport, and such the look and smell of it on the sultry afternoon when Etienne Dolainde and his small daughter came down the *Sally's* plank and looked upon their refuge in the North.

It did not take long to whip their baggage out of the hold. I set Lot and the cook and a hand to look after the drying of the sails, and saw the fenders hung and the fasts secure on the wharf bollards, and then set off with my passengers, Lia-Marie holding tight to her father's hand, and three seamen ahead, each trundling a mahogany chest on a wheelbarrow.

As we approached the pillared portico of the house the great front door was flung open by the black manservant Julius, all figged out in pewter-buckled shoes, a blue coat with brass buttons, and a pair of tight white smallclothes in very nice contrast with his bare black shanks. Then appeared the family; Ma'am in a great looped gown of lilac silk, her thin mouse hair piled high and powdered in a style twenty years out of fashion, Felicity in a light sprigged muslin thing that showed her pretty ankles, and my foster father in a long tight-waisted green tailcoat, white silk tights, and tasseled Hessian boots.

They made a mighty fine group, framed by the white pillars, and I thought with some dismay how shabby we were—Dolainde in the thin linen coat and trousers and torn shirt in which he had fled from Cap François, Lia in the once-fine gown and petticoats that made her look a little woman at fourteen, and I in my rough seaman's rig topped by the only decent thing I had, a glossy beaver bought in Cap François before the trouble started.

The seamen halted, sweating at their barrows, to let us pass, and we came uncertainly to the steps, where Julius made a tremendous bow and Ma'am Pride performed that elaborate curtsy and swirl of petticoats on the floor which was known in Halifax drawing rooms as "making a cheese." Felicity gave her mother an amused look and inclined her head first to Dolainde, then to the child, in the manner of a princess not quite sure of her company. Mr. Pride bowed a little stiffly, for it was many years since he had practiced arts like these.

I could see his yellow eyes inspecting Dolainde, ignoring the small girl and me, but he smiled very pleasantly and cried in his harsh voice, "Welcome, monsieur—and you, too, child—you were not born when I last saw your father. Monsieur, let me present my wife . . ." Another cheese by Ma'am Pride. A deep and graceful bow from the haggard little Frenchman. ". . . My daughter, Felicity . . ." A more gracious nod from Felicity, a no less graceful bow from Dolainde.

Mr. Pride's bold bright gaze was no longer on his guests; he was regarding the three chests with a remarkable intensity—it would have given me little surprise if that yellow gaze had gone clean through the hard wood like a ray from a burning glass. But now he recalled his gaze and his manners, breaking into French, the patois of the islands, learned in his younger days, and sweeping the Dolaindes into the house in a torrent of words and gestures that surprised me and I think astonished his wife and Felicity.

I hung on the step uncertainly, wondering what to do about the chests; but in a moment or two Mr. Pride returned. The smile of welcome still hung on his gaunt features, but it was not for me or my men; he was looking at the chests.

"Come! What are ye waiting for? Bring in Mr. Dolainde's baggage. Careful, now! They're heavy, I dare say. Can ye manage, two men to a chest?"

"We can manage," I said sourly. Half a dozen of us had managed them all the way from the plantation to Cap François, stopping to beat off the swarming blacks here and there with cutlasses and belaying pins, and what was the staircase to any part of that?

The seamen carried their freight along the hall and up the stairs to the big west chambers kept for guests. Mr. Pride dismissed them with a wave of his hand and turned to me.

"See to the discharge of the crew at once, Nathan."

"The sails must be dried first, and——"

"Ah! So! Well, keep a couple of hands till tomorrow and let the rest go. And—um—wait a moment, Nathan. This war—the West Indies will be a cockpit for a time—no place for peaceful traders. Have the *Sally's* sails unbent tomorrow and stowed in the canvas loft. Get the salt out of her and sweep the holds, or the bolts will rust. We must bide our time. Something will come —yes, to be sure—always a dollar to be turned when nations take to powder burning. Never failed yet. Mark my words."

He turned away, pursing his long lips.

It was well past suppertime when I returned from the wharf, and it suited me very well, for I had no mind to prink for the family table, and that bit of pomp at the welcoming of Dolainde had given me a notion what the evening meal would be like. I went around the back way past the stables and carriage house and the jumble of other outbuildings, and so into the kitchen, where I could eat to my stomach's content with no time out for manners. All the gathered hunger of the voyage north was gnawing under my belt.

Diana was there, the lean black woman, Boston's wife, and I suppose he had told her something of our hard fare in the brig, for she had a great spread prepared for me—a cold roast shoulder of mutton, new potatoes boiled with mint leaves, turnip, cabbage, corn bread, country butter fresh from the mold, all this with good Burton ale to wash it down; and then an August-apple pie, the deep dish swimming in sweet juice and the whole covered with a rich brown sugared crust, a plate of arrowroot pasties filled with plum preserve, and half a bottle of south-side Madeira.

Much of this was left over by the solemn company upstairs,

but 'twas none the worse for that. I looked at it and kissed Diana's black cheek and swore she was beautiful, which set her cackling and flapping her great loose hands. And I swore her slatternly daughters were beautiful, and bantered them about the coachman and the gardener and the warehouse Negroes, which set them tittering and pushing at one another until Diana boxed their ears and sent them flying to their chores. But chiefly and urgently I ate and drank and ate again until my stomach could hold no more (to my vast regret), and then, in high peace and well set up amidships, I made my way to the hall and up the stairs.

Candles burned in both parlors, but there was no sign of anyone, and I supposed the Dolaindes had gone to bed, glad enough after their long discomfort on the sea. Ma'am Pride retired early, for always she was up at daydawn setting the servants at their tasks. Felicity often sat late in the south parlor playing her spinet softly, but she was not there now. And Mr. Pride's nightly habit was to sit in his library scratching letters, for he trusted very little of his correspondence to the clerks.

As I gained the first landing there was a buzz of voices from the big guest chamber on the west, where the door stood ajar. I suppose my step had been heard on the stair, for the door was jerked wide and Mr. Pride's voice called sharply.

"Nathan!"

"Sir?" I turned with a wry mouth. The notion of bed after the long day was a very pleasant thing, and my head was in no state for business.

Within the room stood Dolainde with a look of distress on his sallow face and Mr. Pride all thunder and lightning. A shaggy man, one of the shipwrights from the yard, was arising from his knees, a hammer and chisel in his hands. In the midst of the floor, and broken open, I suppose, because the keys had been lost in the flurry at Cap François, stood the three chests with a mass of women's garments, satin and linen and paduasoy and lace, heaped and tumbled over the sides and on the carpet.

I don't know quite what I had expected to see in them. I knew the chests were not full of golden doubloons, as Black Boston devoutly believed, for in that case we could not have carried them at all. But there was some notion of valuables in my mind—bundles of deeds and other documents of that magical sort which turn to money at the owner's whim, and Madame's jewelry, a fair amount of money, of course, and some of those beautiful little madonnas, each with a crown of gems, which stood in niches in every chamber of the Manoir Dolainde—well, things of that sort, snatched up in haste and flung into the chests.

I stared at the clothing stupidly. Back to my mind came that picture of the great pillared portico at the Manoir littered with these chests and a dozen others exactly like them, each of polished mahogany, each with an oval silver plate set in the lid bearing the name of Etienne Dolainde engraved in the metal—the travel chests of the family, taken to Paris every spring until this anxious year, and now hurriedly crammed with cherished things of all sorts for the flight to Cap François. The portico was lit very brightly by the blazing outbuildings across the road, where the field Negroes capered and howled. They had not molested the Manoir so far, held back, I think, by Madame's courageous presence more than the pistols of Dolainde. A dozen house servants remained faithful, and these were dashing in and out of the house, bringing forth all manner of things, clothing, tapestries, paintings, even furniture, flinging them down and running back inside, shouting in their high voices and showing on their dark faces a mixture of pleasure and fear—pleasure in the excitement, fear of that raging multitude on the far side of the lawns.

This was the scene we came upon, my seamen and I, as we

hurried up the carriage road from the town. Strangely enough we had not been attacked, although every villa and mansion along the way was either burnt or besieged, and the whole night over the plain was lit with flaming sugar mills and distilleries.

It was after we came that Dolainde's blacks worked up their rage or courage to the point of attacking the Manoir itself. They came rushing and screaming across the lawns and from behind the burning stables and the long carriage shed, a full two hundred of them armed with sugar cutlasses and *cocomacaques,* those polished three-foot clubs, yellow as mustard and hard as iron, which the Hispaniola Negroes make from the monkeynut tree.

Dolainde fired both pistols into the thick of them, and one shot told. A tall rawboned Bambara man in the front of the rush dropped his club and began to dance on one bare foot, clutching his other leg and howling dolefully. If he had dropped dead the mob would scarce have noticed him, but in this state he became at once the center of all interest. Like children the blacks paused and drew a little away from him, as if he were accursed, and we could see the roll of their eye whites as they shifted their glances from the wounded man to our resolute little company on the portico steps.

Then began a curious harangue in patois between one of the house servants and several of the mob. The upshot of it was that they consented to let us go down the road if we went at once. Their hands itched for our blood, but more they itched for the loot of the big house, and so as we began to move off there was a rush of blacks up the steps. 'Twas a touchy moment, but had we drawn clear quickly all would have gone well. This was not to be. Madame was resolute. She pointed to three of the chests and would not budge without them. Dolainde had snatched up the child and was on the lawn already, urging his wife to come.

I and Lot Mayes and the seamen turned back and caught up the chests, stumbling away towards Dolainde, when behind us there was a cry. We never knew exactly what happened. The beautiful and imperious woman standing her ground, the naked blacks rushing past, all dissolved of a sudden into a nightmare of dark shapes. There was a flourish of *cocomacaques,* a cane cutlass flashing for a moment in the fire light. A savage shout went up. We saw the body of Madame tossed off the portico like a bundle of old petticoats that fell and rolled and disappeared under the stamping feet. At the foot of the steps a knot of them drew apart, howling hideously. An object appeared above their heads, caught on the point of a makeshift spear. It was the head of Madame Dolainde.

My foster father's voice cut through these dismal memories and broke harshly on my ear.

"You fool!" he was saying in a stony sort of fury. "You and your crew of dolts! You brought away the wrong chests!"

Chapter 6

AY, WE had carried off a treasure right enough, but it was the treasure of Madame Dolainde, the hasty choice of her wardrobe: gowns, petticoats, stockings, shoes, linen, laces, the trumpery women love, the stuff that had meant more to poor pleasure-loving Madame than her very life.

And so we brought Dolainde and his daughter away from Hispaniola penniless, and planted them in the bosom of a charity as cold as any to be found on God's green earth. Dolainde did not know that, of course. Whatever illusions he may have had about his old friend were to be shed in the time to come. For the present he witnessed only the cold rage that possessed Mr. Pride whenever he saw some value lost that might have come to his hands.

Dolainde was to learn slowly, with what agony of soul I can guess, for he was proud, that Amos Pride despised a pauper with a contempt that amounted to hatred; that the refugees remained on sufferance alone, regarded by Ma'am Pride with a pious tolerance ("Papists!") and by my foster father with a chill politeness tempered somewhat by a hope that sometime, somehow, all this black nonsense in Hispaniola must come to an end and Dolainde would return to his estates.

Felicity alone was warm to them, especially to the child Lia, and I did my clumsy best to show Dolainde the pleasant side of life in the North, taking him with me on fowling expeditions along the shore, or up the river by canoe to hunt moose and caribou. Not that I had much time for sport. Mr. Pride found me tasks about the warehouses, checking over the goods in store with the warehousemen, scratching a pen in the countinghouse for hours on end, or tramping up the river to inspect the sawmills, to help his surveyor run off new timber lots or to blaze fresh range marks on the old ones.

He hated the sight of idleness, and there was plenty of it now about the town, with his own five ships and the ships of the other West India merchants laid up on account of the war. Gosport was full of trade-fallen men without a pennyworth of work.

There was some excitement that October, a scare of French invasion, and it brought some employment after a fashion, for

Governor Wentworth summoned the militia of the whole province to Halifax. Most of the regular garrison had gone off to the West Indies, on what business no one knew. Every man between sixteen and sixty was liable to militia duty, and I went up to Halifax with the Gosport company, in which I was made an ensign, though I had no sword to wear and scarcely knew the exercises well enough to give commands on parade.

Halifax swarmed with militiamen from the country like ourselves, without uniforms, armed with our own hunting guns, a strange army, farmers and sailors and fishermen for the most part, despised by the regulars and the butt of Halifax. We were sadly out of our element at military maneuvers, and the best work we did for the defense of the fortress was with mattock and shovel on the citadel and batteries. Our company was quartered in old fish sheds on an island in the Northwest Arm, traveling back and forth by boat. We were heartily sick of the whole affair by the time the governor got over his alarm and sent us home.

But I learned something there in a tavern on Hollis Street, a snatch of conversation between two officials of the commissariat engaged with a bowl of punch. I passed it on to Mr. Pride when I returned to Gosport.

"English troops in Hispaniola!" he cried. "What! So soon?"

"Some of the Jamaica garrison. They landed at Jérémie in September."

"What about those regiments that went south from Halifax?"

"They're for an attack on Guadeloupe and Martinico in the spring, according to the gossip. They say Prince Edward himself is to have a part in it."

"Guadeloupe and Martinico . . . tsha! What about Hispaniola?"

"Nothing but a handful of regulars from Jamaica. As I overheard it, Hispaniola's not in the plans—for the moment anyhow.

The governor of Jamaica simply sent over a few troops at the urging of the French refugees."

My foster father closed one eye and looked at me, and I saw his mind. He was thinking of Dolainde, pondering on the prospects of a restoration of the estates under British rule. Restoration could mean the old trade in full swing again—and you must understand that the old trade with Hispaniola was a very pretty thing for men like Amos Pride. It was not merely the timber and fish cargoes south and the rum and coffee and sugar cargoes north. There was something else.

The Spaniards had always kept a very close fist on trade with their colonies along the Main, and that was a very rich trade indeed, with a monstrous appetite for manufactured goods, and gold and silver to pay for it, a state of affairs that invited smuggling. Now smuggling direct to the Spanish Main was a risky matter on account of the swarming *guardacostas,* and certain shrewd Yankee merchants and Nova Scotiamen like Mr. Pride had worked out a neat way of doing it through the French in Hispaniola. It had been going on a long time when the French republicans upset the cart.

Southward we took not merely timber and fish but quantities of English hardware and dry goods for the Spanish trade. These were transshipped at Cap François through influential creoles like Dolainde and taken to a little port called Monte Cristi, up the coast in Spanish territory. There small Spanish vessels took the stuff aboard and sailed for their home ports on the Main. If the coastguard there was curious, why, the ships had been to the Spanish end of Hispaniola and had papers to show for it. It beat the old assiento to a rope end, and all cash business, too. Many a chest of Spanish dollars had come this way to Amos Pride's hands; indeed there was a stream of dollars coming north for years. In Gosport, ay, in Halifax itself the Spanish piece of eight was standard currency—often the very garrison was paid with it for lack of English specie, a clear proof of the volume of the trade.

All this was in my foster father's mind as clear as print. The revolt in Hispaniola had shattered the business at a stroke and left our merchants pawing at the air. Here was a piece of news that might redeem the whole thing.

"Expeditions to Guadeloupe and Martinico!" he said pettishly. "Don't those fools in London know that Hispaniola's the richest of the Caribbees?"

"And the biggest, next to Cuba," I said thoughtfully. "Monstrous hard to fight in, I should think. All those mountains and forests and ravines."

"Pooh! The French troops, those republican fellows, they're all on the coast, you say, huddled in half a dozen of the ports."

"Ay, sir, but the whole country behind 'em is swarming with freed slaves."

"You say they're at each other's throats . . ."

"So they are. But an English invasion would bring 'em all together—whites, griffes, quarterons, métis, any other mixture you can name, and all the blacks. That means half a million blacks, many of 'em lately out of Africa, savages accustomed to the heat and the bush and the air of the fever swamps. They're strong and warlike and would make good soldiers, properly trained and armed—and you may be sure the French would see to that."

Mr. Pride's lips twisted. "Nathan, my dear boy, you seem to be in great awe of that affair at Cap François, a bad enough business, I grant ye—but d'ye doubt the chances of British regulars against a lot of slovenly French republicans and niggers? Half a dozen regiments of redcoats under a good commander could overrun the whole of Hispaniola in a month. Why, tsha! with five hundred determined men, well armed, I could take the northern province and set myself up king at Cap François!"

And as he said this the old tiger came into his eyes, and I could see that he was thinking again of that adventurous time in Hispaniola when the blacks were few and docile and the white inhabitants no more than a parcel of cattle hunters, when a handful of reckless men with sword and pistol could write their will upon the whole coast. Those times were as far as the moon, and as dead.

We were standing in the west parlor, with a brisk fire warming our backs, looking out upon the empty shipyard and the river. A cold November rain was thrashing the last red leaves from a lone maple by the shore. A few shreds of scarlet hung on bravely, fluttering in the wind and wet, but the end was certain. And that was the way I saw the redcoats in Hispaniola . . . and Dolainde's hopes . . . and Mr. Pride's.

Chapter 7

THE cold came early that winter, and soon there was three feet of snow in the woods, and the town half buried at times by white storms blowing in from the sea. After New Year the river froze hard, clean down to the Pride wharves. It gave me a pang to see the *Sally* at her moorings in the stream, gripped by the ice and crusted to the trucks with snow. Her naked spars pointed stiffly to the gray winter sky like the legs of a dead beast.

I put on my skates and went out to her frequently, as if to break her loneliness, and sometimes Felicity came with me, and young Lia. I found it pleasant, skating with Felicity, her hands in mine and our legs moving in perfect unity as if we were one being, with the ice flying under our feet and the cold air rushing past.

On sunny afternoons we went right up to the falls, nigh on two miles, and then the two miles home again with the wind at our backs and the white banks and the forest swirling by. The cold put a rich glow in Felicity's pale cheeks, and she laughed a good deal. Her eyes seemed less like her father's and more like spoonfuls of some golden wine.

For Lia I got one of the shipwrights to rig a chair on runners, and we skated along the river, pushing her ahead of us, and sometimes sent the thing flying and spinning just to hear her shriek with delight. It was all new and marvelous to the little creole. Soon she demanded skates, and I had a pair made for her with slim iron runners well curved at the toe, and set in polished maplewood shaped to her small feet.

She fell a good deal at first, too eager to stride like Felicity and me; but there was grace in her movements nonetheless, a poise that came of her mother's blood, the gift of a dancing race. Before long her skating was something to watch. She liked to stride hand in hand with me, but often she preferred to play alone. She invented and mastered all sorts of intricate whirls and loops, very foreign to us but delightful, and I had a feeling sometimes, watching her, that all she needed was a pair of castanets and a fandango tune to be completely happy.

In fact Lia-Marie had taken to our harsh northern climate like a young otter to a slide. She would get down and roll in fresh-fallen snow like any of our red-cheeked Gosport youngsters, and she was forever building castles and snow men in the carriage yard where the sun fell warm enough to make the stuff pack well, or snowballing merrily with the house servants on errands outdoors.

And always when I went to inspect the loggers up the river she was waiting in the thick green skirt and the scarlet jacket, cut in a military fashion with gilt frogs and blue lapels, which

Mrs. Kemp, the sempstress, had made for her, and with a little fur cap pulled over her yellow hair. Away we would go in the sleigh with a bearskin tucked about us, jingling up the river road. She sang little creole songs, French and Spanish.

She was learning English from Felicity and spoke it quite well by the turn of the year, but with an accent that seemed to me very droll, and a queer turn of phrase sometimes that made me laugh. She did not like this and would sulk for five or ten minutes until some turn of the road brought a change of scene. She could never quite get over the beauty of sunshine on snow, on a clump of pines hung in white by the riverside, say, and would exclaim in delight, putting forth her mittened hands and opening and shutting them in a gesture that was charming, as if she wanted to take hold of these things and keep them forever.

I had no tunes but sea songs, few of them fit for a child's ear, but she liked one that chimed with the motion of the sleigh rising and swooping over the uneven white road. We sang it together:

"Haul the bowline,
The bully ship's a-rollin',
Haul the bowline,
The bowline haul!"

And I taught her to shout the last word mightily, as seamen do when they use this chantey for a last long pull on a rope. It startled the horse always and sent the nervous beast tearing over the snow, ringing a wild tune on the harness bells, and the girl and I hanging on and laughing. Those were happy days, and I think of them with a glow at the heart even now, when so much has passed and I am old and glad to keep the fireside. To be young and without a care, to be in Nova Scotia in the keen bright winter weather, to feel the blood tingle in the flesh, to come to the table ravenous and leave it with a tranquil digestion, to sleep like a child as soon as the head falls on the pillow, and to wake with a feeling of worlds to conquer—those are gifts from God, each marvelous, and Lia and I like spendthrifts enjoyed them all at once.

Dolainde, poor man, could not abide the cold and spent the winter close against the household fires with a shawl about his shoulders, pinched and miserable. When he looked upon the snow outside, it was with desolation in his face, as if he had gone to a hell where everything was topsy-turvy and men were consumed with frost instead of fire.

"Monsieur," I said to him one day, "the world is ill arranged. If we had some of your Hispaniola sunshine, and your country had some of our Nova Scotia snow and ice——"

"We might use some of it to cool our wine," he muttered with a thin smile.

"And surely your climate?"

He looked at the window and shivered. It was a bitter February day, and the blaze of stoves and hearths all over the house had melted a round bull's-eye in the frost of each pane, no more.

"How savage it is, this land!" he said in French. "This land where one must live besieged half the year!"

It astonished me to hear him say that, for all my memories of his island, even before the revolution, were of a savage and threatening wilderness. The beautiful villas of the planters and their prosperous fields had seemed to me besieged the whole year round—by the mountains, the forest, the damp and choking heat that lay upon them night and day, and by something else I could not name, a sense of doom perhaps. Perhaps it was the mountains alone. Such heights should bear snow upon their summits as mountains do in Mexico and suchlike hot places, but in Hispaniola the palm trees grew to the very peaks, wrapped in a steamy heat arising from the sugar plains, and in a vast and terrible silence broken only by vast and terrible thunderstorms. In those mountains I seemed to see a brooding spirit of the land, dark and monstrous, awaiting a time—for what I did not know.

These conversations of ours were a matter of daily routine, for Mr. Pride had decreed that I should learn French and Spanish from the planter during the long winter. 'Twould be useful, he said, for trading in the islands when peace came again. I knew, of course (and Dolainde understood), that this whim of my foster father's sprang chiefly from his hatred of idleness and from a frugal notion that Mr. Dolainde would be glad to earn a little of his keep.

So there was a whimsy in our eyes and in our voices as we talked. Spanish came hard to me, I know not why unless 'twas that my dull red head had room for no more than one thing at a time. In French I made fair progress. Dolainde tried to teach me formal French, the French of his Parisian summers in the old golden days; but he had difficulty there, for his tongue was alive with colonial expressions, the language of the islands, of the creoles.

There was another kind of French, the patois of the Hispaniola Negroes. This I learned with surprising ease from young Lia on our rides and expeditions. She could imitate them perfectly, pouring the slurred French and African off her lips with childish gusto, chanting their cane-field songs and waggling her shoulders in the Negro fashion, very comical to see. She enjoyed this mimicry and so did I, and on the whole I think I learned more of her patois than I did of Dolainde's French.

She called me Roux—my red hair amused her very much—and once Mrs. Pride reproved her, saying solemnly that Monsieur Nathan was a grown man and a captain, to whom nicknames were not becoming from a child. Lia curtsied and looked meek, and after that I was Monsieur Nathan, with a vicious little emphasis whenever we were in the house.

My foster father in these times was like a caged lynx. Trade was at a standstill, or at best an enormous risk with little reward. One or two Gosport merchants sent vessels south with boards and fish for the British islands. One captain sold his cargo at Grenada and got sixteen dollars per thousand for boards and three dollars per quintal of barreled fish—a mighty poor return for the risk. Another was taken by a French privateer and his crew flung into prison in Guadeloupe. The French privateers seemed to be everywhere. The Caribbean fairly swarmed with them, and now they were reported off our own coast and hovering about Cape Cod.

Insurance on cargoes to the West Indies demanded a premium of 16 per cent—that was the Halifax rate—and Mr. Pride, who commonly underwrote cargoes himself or went snacks with a group of other Gosport merchants, began to charge 20 per cent. There was no profit to be had in voyages at such a handicap.

Mr. Pride sat long at his desk, sipping a little wine and staring at nothing with those fierce yellow eyes. At times he would arouse from these grim silences and scratch off letters by the dozen, to Halifax, to Boston, Philadelphia, Baltimore, Savannah, and Jamaica—especially to Jamaica. I knew what was in his mind there—a commissary contract with the British forces going against the French islands. And then without waiting for a reply from anywhere he would be off in the packet schooner to Halifax, to harry the governor, the admiral, and anyone else he thought might be of use.

Whatever the result of these visits, he would return more like a caged beast than ever. His long nostrils twitched, as if he could smell the money to be made out of supplies to the forces in the Caribbees, and his long fingers twitched and snapped, as if the money were just beyond his grasp. There would be long sittings again over his accounts, and the letter bag, and the newspapers that came in the coastal packets.

Then on a sudden he would leap up and shout for me, and we would set off up the river in the sleigh as far as the sawmill road went, and then into the woods on snowshoes, hunting up ship timber and the like as if he had a naval contract in his pocket. I can see him now, striding amongst the trees with a long green coat blowing about him and the ends of his wool comforter flying, an old cocked hat jammed down over his ears, gazing and pointing here and there, and I at his snowshoe heels.

Or it would be the sawmills at the falls that worried him. Away we would go regardless of weather, to tramp about the icy dam and the silent mills with snow drifted along their floors, the water wheels frozen fast in their pits, the long saws in their vertical frames, all useless till the spring sun and the melting of the log pond. The sawmill foreman had gone over these matters with care, greasing the saws against winter rust and so on, but when the fit struck Mr. Pride he would see for himself and stand there in the chill gloom of the mill, with frost sparkling on the walls, busy with schemes for another gang saw here or there, and bigger water wheels and a higher dam.

Or it would be his notion of a "railroad" to carry the boards and timber to the ships at Gosport, with long wagons fitted on wooden rails and drawn by teams of horses or oxen. As things stood, the stuff was floated down the river to the Gosport wharves in rafts, made up and piloted by men who worked for a shilling a day, mostly in rum and corn meal and suchlike necessities from the Pride store; a cheap enough method, all considered. But Mr. Pride was never satisfied with "cheap enough."

Then it would be ships. He would call in his master shipwright, and they would pore over designs, with two or three Pride captains standing by to answer questions—never to ask one. In the midst of these deliberations he would thrust back his chair and gaze over our heads with the look I knew so well.

"A short war or a long?" he would say, as if anyone knew. "A short war's only a nuisance—upsets trade and provides no substitute. A long war—there's another matter. Trade becomes the war itself. Fish—humph!—might as well leave it in the sea. Market in Hispaniola's gone. The British islands—planters feed dry cod to their niggers—at a beggar's price to us—and that in rum and molasses—no money, never any money. The forces? I've tried to talk fish to the commissaries at Halifax—ye might as well talk fish to the moon. His Majesty's soldiers and seamen must be fed on salt beef from England, salt pork from Ireland, half of it rotten in the barrel, because it's always been the custom, because the forces won't eat anything else, because—here's the truth on't—the rich contractors in England and Ireland must have their profit if it means ramming their salt junk down the throat of King George himself.

"Well, timber, then. Something in that. Takes timber to build barracks and wharves and suchlike matters. Army and fleet in the Caribbees—a part we know right well. But consider this—why take our timber abroad when we can build it into ships here at home and man and sail the ships ourselves? War means traffic on the seas. The wider the field the longer the haul, and the longer the war the fatter the freights. We've only pottered at shipbuilding in this country—ships for the fishery and the southern trade, for our own small purposes, you understand?—schooners and fat little snows and brigs and pinkies that 'ud do the work or carry the stuff, and time no object.

"Too early to see clearly yet, but I've a good notion this war will be a long affair, the way it's going. Those kingdoms of Europe are rotten and ready to fall at the shake of some vigorous and reckless people like those French republicans. Give 'em the run o' Europe and the French'll take some putting down, and there's the sea at their doors and other tunes than Rule Britannia, eh? They build good ships, the French, and make good sailors. They're swarming the Atlantic already. Another year and they'll be all about the world. England might have to build a navy such as no one ever dreamed of. And armies sent here and garrisons there, and supplies everywhere . . . ships! . . . ships! . . . a long war means ships any way ye figure it. That's what I see.

"Now! What sort o' ships? Nothing like we've built aforetime." Mr. Pride thrust aside the plans and sketches of the master shipwright with an impatient sweep of his arm. "They'll have to carry cannon—that means we'll have to strengthen the decks. Stout bulwarks, too. Gun ports. Hatches and all other deck furniture must be laid out so as to give room to work the guns. Important, that. I'm not proposing to build warships, mind. That's a matter for the royal dockyards. What we'll want is a cargo ship that can fend off a privateer at a pinch and run from anything heavier. Speed! Sacrifice cargo room for speed . . . the high war freights'll pay the difference, once the campaigns are under way. Means a long hull and a lean one, and tall spars and mighty square yards and lots o' canvas. D'ye see? Something new from the keel up, designed for the purpose. Take away these"—another poke at Job Eames's plans—"and bring me the kind o' thing I want."

Thus he talked and thus he moved . . . and thus we moved

at his bidding. Gosport said he was mad, and mad he seemed to me; but it was money-madness that possessed him, always and all ways. He looked upon the world as a bone to be picked, and he did not care how small the pickings.

I remember riding with him down the main street of our town one winter day and seeing him pull up suddenly outside Goody Owen's tavern to stare at something on the beaten snow. I had some difficulty in stopping my nag, for I was a typical sailor ahorseback, never at home in the saddle. And as I turned my beast a ragged fellow ran out from the lee of the tavern, where he had been sheltering from the cold wind, and stooped to pick up something from the road. 'Twas a shilling. As the man straightened himself, pleased with his prize, there was my foster father leaning over the saddle with his long mittened hand outstretched.

"I'll trouble you to give me that," said Mr. Pride.

"Why?" said the fellow.

"Because it's mine," replied Mr. Pride.

The fellow gave him a mournful look. But he handed over the shilling, and as we rode away Mr. Pride turned to me with a chuckle.

"I saw it first anyhow," he said.

Chapter 8

THE news of the war in Europe was bad, and worse from season to season, with the French beating the Dutch and scaring the Prussians into peace, and the Spaniards throwing in their lot with the French and declaring war on England. But on our side of the Atlantic matters seemed to go right well. An expedition from Halifax captured the rocky islands of St. Pierre and Miquelon, where the French pursued the Grand Bank fishery.

In the spring of '94 the soldier son of King George, Prince Edward himself, arrived in Halifax from the Caribbees, reporting triumph everywhere—Guadeloupe, Martinique, St. Lucia taken from the French, and British forces pouring into Hispaniola.

Later we heard a different tale—the French had retaken most of their islands and set up the guillotine for the planters who had called in British aid. Nevertheless in Halifax the times were gay, with ships and troops coming and going, and Prince Edward installed there with his little French mistress, and French prizes up for sale, and French prisoners wandering about the streets.

I remember taking the *Sally* up to Halifax with a lading of timber for the garrison, and seeing amongst the throng on Granville Street the Negro Bellegarde walking with his family. He wore the uniform of a French general and carried himself with a fine military air that made some of the people laugh. I saw nothing to laugh at. Bellegarde had been captured in Martinique, commanding a black brigade in the French republican service, and I thought of Hispaniola, seeing a vast army of such men drilling and arming for a time when they would drive the British back into the sea.

I mentioned this to Dolainde on my return, and he looked grave, but Mr. Pride only pursed his lips and snorted. And the war went on, with the French fighting their way across Europe and the nations going down like ninepins year by year. By '96 it was clear that the struggle had only begun. We were quite sure that England would survive, whatever happened to the rest of the world; but none of us guessed, not even Mr. Pride, that the war was to go on for nearly twenty years.

One of things we soon came to accept was a multitude of French prisoners in our midst, crews of captured warships, privateers, and merchantmen, and soldiers of fallen French garrisons in the West Indies, and poor bedeviled common folk, men, women, and children, torn away from their homes in St. Pierre. Most of them were ready enough to give parole; indeed there was not prison room in Nova Scotia for a tenth of them, and they were permitted to wander about the province, finding a living any way they could.

Some came to Gosport. One Galibrand, an elderly army officer, taught French and dancing and fencing to the sons and daughters of our merchants. But the most popular of our prisoners was a man named Victor Brule, who set up a hairdressing shop in Fore Street. Long hair and wigs were out of fashion, but our older gentlemen still clung to them, and I and many another of the town's young men went regularly to Monsieur Brule to have our hair clipped loosely in the mode.

Brule was a stocky active man of thirty or so with a dashing mustache, lively blue eyes, an olive countenance, and very black hair cropped close to his skull in the republican fashion. He proved to be a man of parts. He had been captured as a petty officer in a small French corvette to the southward and was full of droll tales of the republican service. He kept a violin hung in a green baize bag on the wall of his shop and would scrape queer French airs for us or fiddle a jig that set our heels aclatter on the floor. He would play English airs like "How Stands the Glass Around?" and "Would You Know My Celia's Charms?" and flattered our patriotic notions with "God Save the King," played slowly and with great feeling; but always he ended these impromptu concerts with a wild republican thing called "Ça ira" that had a fine lilt to it and set us whistling it about the streets.

Often in wintertime I took him rabbit hunting in the woods behind the town, a comical sight, muffled against the cold in an old watch coat and floundering along on snowshoes. He was good-natured and joined in my laughter whenever he tripped over the things and came up plastered with snow. He made jokes about himself, about the rabbits, the forest, the weather, the war. You could not help laughing with Victor Brule. The fishwives young and old adored him, for he had a habit of strolling amongst the drying flakes of a summer evening when they were covering the split cod for the night, and more than one found herself giggling in the cool grass and tickled out of any virtue she possessed. Indeed his success with women was amazing in a town like ours, where the tombstones of the Yankee founders still cast a very long shadow and the Cape Cod conscience hung like a chill fog in the streets.

Brule was the merriest man in Gosport, just as Dolainde was the saddest, and I suppose it was inevitable that they should meet. Dolainde went with me one day to the shop in Fore Street to have his wig combed and repaired—he was an old-fashioned man and wore about the house a great two-tailed thing of the sort they affected in Paris in the days before the revolution.

I said in my best French (for I liked to air my doubtful accomplishments when I could), "Brule, my friend here is a countryman of yours, M. Dolainde." Brule gave his head a quick little bob. Dolainde bowed stiffly—the royalist to the republican—and produced the wig from under his arm, explaining in curt tones what he wished.

Said Brule politely, "One does not see many of these nowadays, monsieur."

"That is because you have cut off the heads that wore them," snapped Dolainde. Brule shrugged and turned to place the thing on his wig stand.

"I wear it, me, not for the sake of the old time, but to keep my head from freezing in this cursed climate," Dolainde added in a bitter voice.

Brule said casually, working delicately upon the wig with a

comb, "The Negroes in the West Indies wear turbans about their heads to keep them cool, monsieur."

Dolainde gave him a long hard stare. He said no more. But as we emerged from the shop he muttered, "I have seen that man before."

"Where?"

He shrugged. "One meets a world of people in a lifetime."

It was about this time that Dolainde began to visit Halifax, going up in one of the fishing schooners or the packet, staying a few days or a week, and returning with a red eye and a somewhat raffish air that sat very queerly upon him. He said little or nothing of these visits. For that matter he kept a close lip on all his affairs, a silent man, a small, shriveled ghost of a man lost in the past. Town gossip said he had a woman in the capital, but I found that hard to believe.

Then he made a trip to Halifax with me in the *Sally* and invited me to his lodging for a glass of wine. It was a tall, narrow, slatternly house in Barrington Street, and very soon I came to know that he had found in this place a little colony of Frenchmen, some of them royalist exiles from old France, the others refugees from the West Indian plantations like himself. A strange society. The planters, clad in cheap and sober clothing purchased or given them here in the North, the royalists in shabby silk and brocade, never without their sword canes, wigs, and snuffboxes; and there was one old buck whom they called the Chevalier, a lean and dissipated goat of a man who wore powdered hair and a patch on each cheek, rings on every one of his snuffy yellow fingers, and reeking of perfume from head to foot.

The aristocrats used a lofty tone towards the planters, and the planters addressed the others with a cynical air, as if to say, "Ah, my dear fellows, we're all in the same boat now, and, after all, whose fault is it? Not ours!" At first I thought they clung together for the simple sake of speaking their own tongue in a foreign land, but one evening I called at Mrs. Jessop's with a letter from Lia for Dolainde, and the woman ushered me into a long room at the back of the house where I found the Frenchmen busy at cards and wine. The windows were covered with heavy velvet curtains of a faded green, the candle flames seemed to float like will-o'-the-wisps in a fog of tobacco smoke, and there was a heavy smell of claret, of burgundy, of cognac mingled with the reek of the planters' cigars, the perfumed snuff of the shabby dandies, and the flowery scents of the Chevalier.

They did not look up. They were absorbed in their gambling, and there was a silence broken only by the *flick-flack* of cards, an occasional exclamation of pleasure or disgust, and the chink of money passing back and forth. I stared. The French wines I could understand, for there was a brisk and profitable smuggling trade with France in spite of the revolution and the war. But where did they get the money, these outcasts?

Dolainde sat coughing over his cards. He was tipsy, but he acknowledged my presence with a nod, took the letter and thrust it into a pocket and in courtesy came with me to the door. There an odd thing happened. It was a fine summer evening, and there was still a goodish bit of daylight in the sky. Barrington Street was thronged with folk returning from the after-supper stroll towards Point Pleasant and the Kissing Bridge, a daily rite in Halifax in the warm weather; redcoats, sailors, trollops, apprentices, sober townsmen and their wives and youngsters, prisoners on parole, countrymen up to town to see the sights of wartime, idlers of every sort, including many of the Maroons—the half-wild Negroes of the Jamaican hills, gathered up in hundreds and sent north to work on the Nova Scotia defenses—and a long procession of the carriages of the gentry.

I stood on the step with my back to the throng while Dolainde murmured a few polite nothings and gave me a greeting to take back to his daughter. A voice at my shoulder said, "Monsieur Dolainde, *voici le don . . .*" French was common speech in the streets of Halifax by that time; still there was something about the voice, the queer twist on the words. I turned my head idly and saw a tall powerful Negro putting a bare foot on the step. I had never seen him before. I took him for one of the Maroons at first, but they wore castoff uniforms of the English regiments in garrison, and this one was dressed in the coarse blue denim clothing issued to prisoners of war.

It all happened in a moment. The Negro thrust something into Dolainde's hand and turned and ran away into the passing crowd. A messenger, I thought. The prisoners turned a penny in all sorts of ways.

Dolainde cried out sharply, staring at the object in his hand, and then dropped the thing as if it were red hot. It lay on the sill in the light of the door lantern, and I bent forward as if to pick it up. I saw that it was nothing more alarming than a bit of plaited horsehair perhaps three inches long with a pellet of clay molded to one end.

"No!" hissed Dolainde. He kicked at the thing, missed it once, twice, and then sent it sailing into the street, into the dust where the passing feet tramped and the carriages rolled in the twilight. His face, always sallow, was dull white in the queer mingled light of sundown and the lantern. His eyes glowed like coals. For a time he stared over my head at nothing. Then he uttered a sound meant for laughter that rattled like a pea in a gourd, and swung away on his heel.

I sailed for Gosport at daylight. Felicity came down the wharf in a hired chair at the last moment, returning from one of her visits to the capital with her usual clutter of baggage and parcels. She was dressed in a light blue thing in the latest fashion, of very thin stuff caught taut about her bosom by a ribbon tied beneath, and the rest of it hanging free with no hoops and clinging to her figure in the wind. There was a small scoop bonnet on her head. The gown was cut very low, and her arms were bare nigh to the shoulder except for a pair of long yellow gloves drawn loosely to her elbows. She carried a fur muff and had an absurd little fur tippet about her shoulders.

She stood beside me aft as we went down the harbor. The wind was nor'east with a bite in it, a breath of the icebergs on the Banks, the sort of wind that makes a mockery of June along the shore.

"Aren't you cold in that rig?" I asked.

"Don't you like it?"—with a tilt of her bonnet.

"There's not enough of it," I growled, feeling a family concern not so much for her health as her modesty. The seamen were inspecting her slyly, and I remembered many a merry tale of Victor Brule about this new fashion of republican France which all the idle ladies of England and the garrisons were aping. Frenchwomen had thrown away any modesty they possessed along with other notions of the old time and went all but naked under these flimsy gowns in proof of their liberty. It was foreign and indecent like everything else the French were doing, and I said so.

Felicity's voice went cold as the wind. "You seem to like it well enough on some of us—on Major Sherring's lady, say."

I was taken aback at that. Mrs. Sherring had been mighty nice to me, these past three trips to Halifax. I had gone to the major's house on some business about the cargo—timber for the fortifications—and she had asked me to come again and entertained me handsomely. She pointed out to me that Halifax was a horrid place for gossip, and though she was very eager to learn about the sea, it wouldn't do for a woman of fashion to hold public conversation with a young captain from the outports. And so I had made my visits by the back door, all unseen—or so I had thought.

Mrs. Sherring was a lively woman very different from our sober Gosport dames and hospitable in the extreme, begging me to taste this wine and that, and plying me with little cakes and dainties, and having me to sit beside her on the sofa, where she lay against the cushions. My red hair amused her, and she had a way of pushing her fingers through it and exclaiming, "La! It tingles just like fire!" and laughing very merrily, and asking me if other women had not found it so.

As for Mrs. Sherring's dress, it looked well enough on her, what there was of it, and there was not very much. She would ask me, "Do I show, Captain Cain?" and when I confessed she did, she would shrug her white self under the cobweb stuff and inform me 'twasn't every woman that could show as well, and she could name twenty ladies of high fashion in the town who daren't show at all for dread of their own bones and bad skins. Then she would close her eyes and invite me to talk to her, saying how nice it was to know someone with whom she could be lazy and at ease.

I said to Felicity, "Mrs. Sherring is fond of the sea, and I tell her tales about ships."

Felicity laughed in that way women have when they wish to call a man a liar without saying so.

"Poor Nathan! Do you remember the time I caught you at the preserve closet and tattled to Mamma? There was jam all over your face, my innocent."

"Well?" I kept a hard gaze on the helmsman's face. The fellow was out of earshot, but I wanted his attention where it belonged.

"If you could see your own face now!"

"Shall I send a hand below for your cloak?" I said through my teeth.

"A tarry sailor rummaging in my things?" Off she went with her quick sure step to the companionway, and so below. She did not come on deck again until we were crossing Gosport Bar in the late afternoon. She paced up and down impatiently, wrapped in a woolen mantle, and when we reached the wharf she went off to the house without a word.

Felicity and I had got along very well since I came to the big house, friendly enough in the casual way of most brothers and sisters I have observed, and with as little interest in each other's doings. But for the past year it seemed to me that Felicity's manner had changed somehow. I felt her eyes upon me when she thought I was occupied. Sometimes I caught her in this inspection, and when our eyes met I seemed to see a gleam of curiosity, as if it were I who had changed and taken on some queer significance—as if I had grown a pair of horns, say, or turned into a Chinaman. And there was something else in that yellow gaze of hers that was so like her father's and yet so different, a glint of malicious humor that puzzled and irritated me, as if she knew some secret of my future and wondered how I would behave when the unpleasant moment came.

She was her father's confidante in most things. I wondered if it had to do with the Pride ships. She knew I hated this petty coasting, that I wanted a command in foreign voyages, and she knew how bitter I had been when John Colt went off as master of the *Venture* in a West Indies convoy, and young Harry Bowden in charge of the *Fair Wind* on a voyage to Britain. The Royal Navy now was furnishing protection to merchant ships in a huddled sort of fashion, but there was still much risk, and Mr. Pride nursed the rest of his vessels for the sure time coming when each freight would bring a fortune. What were his plans for me? I was tempted to ask Felicity, but I knew what she would say, and I would not give her the satisfaction of saying it.

I suppose it was this quizzical behavior of Felicity's that made me sensitive to every look and gesture in my foster father's house, for about this time I noticed a difference in Ma'am Pride. When I was a boy she had taken a stern hand with my lessons and such-like things, and scolded me often, and despaired of me aloud, but always in a stony sort of way, as if she did it all for duty's sake and did not really care a whit. I had never forgotten that strange quizzing when I came to Pride's Fancy, and felt a stranger in her presence all my boyhood years. After I came to my teens and Mr. Pride took over the order of my life, she seemed to withdraw; there were days and weeks on end when she did not seem to see me at all.

Now I was aware of a sudden attention on her part, and it was nothing affectionate. There was an air of resentment about her, a renewal of the manner in which she had regarded me when I first came to the house, but with something added, a sharp anger in her voice and in her eyes.

All of this increased the restlessness that had come upon me with the war, the outcome of monotonous coasting trips and other odd-jobbing and time-filling, and having to ask Mr. Pride for money for my simple pleasures, and feeling in the big house like a lodger who has fallen to leeward of his bill. The trouble was my own ambition, I suppose, for I was longing for a ship of my own and deep water, and in this feckless longshore existence I was moody and fancied slights of every kind.

But the root went deeper than that, I know now. The root was loneliness. As one of the Pride household I came under the suspicion if not the dislike of the town. Men were careful of what they said in my presence, and their frugal women were silent. And within the household I felt trapped and watched by my foster mother and Felicity, an object of cold curiosity, like a tadpole in a bottle that has begun to put forth legs and breathe. Mr. Pride offered no companionship, a harsh and calculating god who ruled the house as he ruled the town, and would like to have ruled the world.

Dolainde? Dolainde had never been intimate with me or anyone, not even with his daughter, and nowadays the morose little man spent most of his time in Halifax with his French cronies and his cards.

As for young Lia-Marie, she had been friendly enough as a child, but I had seen her grow into a coltish and uncertain creature, more and more silent and withdrawn, resenting the charity of the Prides, I knew, and occupying herself in ways I did not know. Yet that is not quite true. I saw one way she amused herself, and it was the end of our old friendship.

Chapter 9

IT HAPPENED on a wet night in the late autumn of '97, with rain flooding down the panes and splattering from the eaves spouts, and an east wind, the last breath of a sea gale, sobbing in the chimneys in a mighty mournful way. I had worked late in the wharf countinghouse going over the bills of lading for the next sailing to Halifax, and came home chilled and dull in mind and wrapped in my stained old boat cloak.

I went in the main door and paused a moment in the hallway

by the east parlor entrance, where Mrs. Pride sat knitting and Felicity at her pianoforte, a beautiful thing brought from Halifax in the *Sally's* last trip to replace the familiar old spinet and its thin, ghostly chords. A smart fire crackled on the hearth, and Ma'am Pride sat close by it in her high-backed red damask chair. The big room was ever a drafty place, especially on a night like this. The flame of the piano candles in their polished brass brackets trembled at every gust, and Felicity sat with a shawl across her slender shoulders.

She turned her head at my step in the hall and gave me one of her whimsical looks, running her fingers idly over the keys. Ma'am Pride said in her thin voice, "Good evening, Nathan. You've worked late. I suppose we should all be abed, but throw off that wet thing and stay awhile by the fire. You haven't heard Felicity's new toy, have you?"

It was unusual, this word of welcome in my foster mother's voice, though it had no warmth at all. I put aside the cloak and stepped into the room obediently, glad enough to get my back to a fire, but chiefly wondering what was in the pantry belowstairs. Felicity turned to her music again, or rather to her aimless finger-capering, and Mrs. Pride said in a prim tone, "Now, dear, play and sing one of those little things you do so well."

Felicity paused, looking straight at the music before her. She was wearing something brown, well cut but of sensible stuff, not a bit like those gauzy things she wore on her Halifax excursions, and which I suspect she kept secret from her straitlaced mother, not to say Mr. Pride. It came to me that Felicity was a prisoner much as I was, and with the same longing for the world outside.

The difference was that Felicity had plenty of money for pleasure when she got leave for a holiday. Mr. Pride's hard fist seemed to slacken very readily in that direction. I suppose he thought it good business, for she visited the daughters of his merchant friends up there in the provincial capital, and had the entry of Government House and other places where young officers dined and danced, and where a rich or titled husband might be caught. That was the view of Gosport, at any rate, and it seemed a sound one. Why should the Halifax girls make all the best marriages?

Felicity began to play and sing "Early One Morning." She had a rather sweet voice, clear and true on the high notes, though there was not much strength in it, and the song had a lonely sound in that big room. After a few lines she stopped with a crash of keys and swung herself about on the stool.

"Nathan, I don't want to sing for you, and I'm sure you don't want to listen. Why should we be polite and suffer?"

"Felicity!" Mrs. Pride raised her delicate brows.

"Pooh! Nathan's notion of music is 'Haul Away My Billy' and suchlike things that his sailors rant about the deck. Who's to blame him?"

"Felicity's quite right," I said to Ma'am Pride quickly. "I haven't much ear for chamber music, ma'am . . . and I'm hungry, if you don't mind." I ducked my head at each of them and stalked away belowstairs gladly. I liked Felicity's music well enough, but I did not enjoy the look in her eye or the mysterious half smile on her lips. In another moment she would have asked me how the tune of "The Major's Lady" went, or some such thing, and I'd have looked the fool I felt.

The passage to the kitchen was dark, and I had to fumble my way. At this hour the servants were abed—the Gosport maids to their homes or their narrow quarters in the garret, and Black Diana and her daughters away to Boston's hut. But as I drew nigh the kitchen door there was a sound within that set my heart a-beating. I paused. Suddenly those old wild memories of Cap François came flooding back. It was the sound of a Negro drum. Not one of those great things the size of a beef tub that go booming through the hot hills in the night, but the small kind you see black men strumming with fingers and palm outside their huts of an evening.

I opened the door with the care of a thief, the chink slowly widening until I could see within. The only light was a small flicker on the great hearth. I could make out the shape of hams and bunches of garden herbs dangling from the beams, and near to the floor the forms of Black Boston, Diana, and their daughters Rosamund and Lavinia crouching on stools, sharp against the firelight.

The long tables had been pushed back to the walls, and the Negroes gazed intently towards a part of the kitchen beyond my view. Boston was playing the drum, a thing the size of a gallon pot, gripped between his knees, striking the stretched skin softly and quickly, now with his finger tips, now with the heel of his hand.

Their eyes glistened as they followed a mysterious movement in the far part of the kitchen, and beyond the drumbeat I was aware of other sounds, a soft patting and rustling, a panting of breath that did not come from the Negroes. Then a figure moved across the firelight with arms flung wide, long hair flying, skirt whirling about a pair of ivory legs that writhed and stamped to the beat of the little drum. A fall of coals on the hearth revealed the dancer's face, drawn and serious, the lips parted, the dark eyes wide and flashing. It was Lia-Marie Dolainde.

I came nigh crying out in my astonishment. She was dressed in the style of black girls dancing in the hot Hispaniola nights, nothing but a thin chemise and short petticoat, arms, legs, and breast bare. Her blond locks hung to her shoulders free of combs, butter-golden in the hearth glow. Her skin gleamed. It was not her dress or the strangeness of the scene that impressed me; it was that Dolainde's child had grown into a woman.

I suppose all men are blind in this respect. When the girl child of the house is in her early teens you think of her still as a child and address her so; and by the time you have come to see her as a shy young colt, all feet and mane, she has in fact passed eighteen and is something else again.

It was only four years and a little since we plucked young Lia-Marie from that hell on the Haut du Cap, a thin and frightened creature of fourteen, yet here was a woman grown, not tall like Felicity or petite like poor Madame Dolainde, but well formed, with round breasts swaying now with her exertions, and full white arms and shoulders, and strong and finely turned legs. I had a guilty feeling as if I'd come upon a strange young woman at her bath, but I could not take my eyes from her and did not try.

The drumbeat changed, and Lia ceased her flitting and stood full in my view, bending her left knee until the toes barely touched the floor, bringing it back again and at the same time thrusting forward the right in the same manner, caressing her round knees together in a peculiar movement that seemed to ripple up her legs and body, swaying her young hips and bosom. It was like those wanton dances I had seen in frowsty dens in Cap François, with a roomful of drunken seamen and planters, a smell of rum and sweat and *maccouba,* tallow candles drooping in the heat, and brown girls naked on a platform setting the men aroar with their movements.

But there was a vast difference, too. The tavern girls of Hispaniola had laughed and squealed in the drunken faces, alive to all they did and why. The look on Lia's face was that of a dreamer, serious and absorbed, the dark eyes wide but seeing nothing. Her bare arms were at her sides, the fingers plucking the petticoat high for the better movement of her legs, her whole person governed by the little drum, now beating faster and faster.

Diana spoke suddenly and the spell was broken. The drum ceased. Lia's limbs paused and her face came to life, anxiously. Diana grunted, "Ain' right yit, Miss Lia. Feet's wrong. Show her, you Vinny, how it go wid de feet." The gaunt slattern Lavinia leaped up, and Boston began to beat the drum again. Lia stood relaxed but with eager eyes, watching the black girl perform those strange, exciting movements. And it seemed to me, watching them, that Lia could never match the boneless quality of the young Negress, something born in her, savage and of the jungle, the movements of an animal.

Lavinia ceased at a signal from her mother, and Lia tried again, this time watching her feet, and I saw Boston wagging his head slowly and Diana frowning and grumbling that it was not right . . . not right . . . not right.

Black Rosamund cackled, "Ah, Miss Lia, no use—*chica* dance for black gals, not for white gals. This for you" and she sprang up, mincing back and forth before the fire, holding the edge of her cotton gown between a bony thumb and finger, sweeping an imaginary fan with the other hand and cocking her woolly black head from side to side in a droll imitation of a lady in the country dance.

Lia put back her golden head and laughed merrily, and Boston and Lavinia chuckled, but Diana growled in her deep voice, "Stop dat! Ain' for you make dance like white folks! What Miss Lia t'ink? Miss Lia want learn *chica*. All right. Miss Lia, you make *chica* 'gain now. Boston!"

Again Boston struck that queer slow beat on the drum, gathering speed as Lia threw herself into the movements, her face rapt, the red lower lip caught in her teeth like those of a child at lessons. I was just as rapt, for I let the door swing slowly wide and edged forward until I was standing inside the threshold. None of them noticed me, none even glanced my way, and presently Diana and the black girls began to clap their hands softly with certain of the drumbeats. At that moment Lia, as if by instinct feeling an unwelcome stare, stopped and gazed full at me, ay, and past me, with a look of wild surprise and anger. From behind me came the voice of Mr. Pride, harshly.

"What the devil does this mean?"

I shall never forget how Boston rose from his stool and dived through the other door and vanished into the yard, drum and all; or how lean Diana, after one frozen moment, set about her daughters, cuffing their ears and crying loudly, "How many times I tol' you git to bed an' stop your foolishin'?"—or how they fled, and their mother after them shouting fainter and fainter across the yard and down the slope in the rainy night. And I shall never forget how a shadow in the far kitchen corner leaped and stood in the light—the figure of our jolly barber, Victor Brule, with glittering eyes and a face of stone.

Lia remained very erect before the fire, her small fists clenched against her sides, breathing stormily and giving Mr. Pride and me such a look of contempt and defiance as should have shriveled us up.

Mr. Pride stepped into the kitchen like a wrathful Jehovah, so tall he had to stoop to clear the lintel.

"Well?" he demanded, ignoring me and staring from Lia to Brule.

Lia-Marie drew in a great breath. Then the words came. In four years she had learned our tongue so well that she spoke it almost without accent; but she was in a passion now, and all the French and Spanish in her blood seemed to rush to her lips and struggle there with the English speech. The result was an accent beyond my pen, but this is what she said:

"So! You spy on me! You—you Prides! Who sent you here? I know—Madame and that girl! How I hate you, all of you! You want to know what I do here? I tell you. Here is the only warm place in this big cold house. I do not mean the fire, I mean the heart. Ah, you cold people! I come here because here is the warm heart under the black skin. I come here because it is like home to me, it is like the old days at the *manoir* when I was small and went to see the black people of my father, and they danced for me and made music and sang, and we were happy. You want to know why I dance? I tell you. When I dance I think I am there, I feel the sun, I smell the cane and the lemon trees, I hear the crickets singing, and the little song of the pigeons. I hear the parrots crying in the wood. I see the fireflies under the genipa trees when it is night. That is why. You understand? But no, you think I am a bad. You think I am a bad because I dance, because I do not like to sing through my nose on Sunday, because my father comes to you for money, because——"

She ran out of breath then, and my foster father said coldly, "That's quite enough, miss. I think you are a 'bad' because I find you sporting like this, half naked, before the servants and this barber fellow and what's worse, before my son. I shan't ask how long it's been going on—long enough for mischief, I dare say. I'll speak to your father next time he comes from Halifax, but in the meantime while you're in this house I'll thank you to keep away from the black people and from Nathan—amuse yourself in other ways."

He gave Brule a look. "As for you, sir, I don't want to see you here again. Stay where you belong, with your scissors and combs, or you'll find yourself back in the hulks at Halifax."

He turned to me. "I've something to say to you, sir! Not here."

He moved away into the passage. I hesitated. I wanted to explain, to tell Lia how I came to be there, and that I had not known my foster father was behind, and that I thought her dancing was a charming thing. But the words would not come to my tongue. I felt the cynical gaze of Brule, and Lia regarded me with the same sullen anger she had given Mr. Pride. Under that gaze what was a man to do but mumble, "I'm sorry, Lia," in a sheepish voice, and go?

Chapter 10

I FOLLOWED my foster father to the library, where the table held its usual litter of letters and newspapers and the fire and candles had burnt low. Outside, the rain had dwindled to a few scattered drops flung on the panes by the gusty wind. He was pacing the carpet with his hands clasped under the long blue tails of his coat, but he stopped as I entered. We faced each other.

"Close the door," he said. I closed it with my foot, not gently. I was in no mood for one of his nasal sermons on the folly of wickedness, still less for one of his towering furies. In my younger days this room had been the place of punishment for household crimes, and many a time Ma'am Pride had marched me there with a tale of my mischief and turned me over to her husband and the long Malacca cane that stood behind the door. I was afraid of him then. I was not now.

I said harshly, "Well?"

He inspected me with the watchful eyes of a cat.

"Just what are your relations with that young woman, Nathan?"

"I don't know what you mean." I did, and the truth was simple enough, but I seemed to feel the scornful gaze of "that young woman" upon me still, and I would not explain.

"Umph! I'm not blaming you entirely, Nathan, you understand? I was young once." He took a turn up the carpet and came back again. "The little creole's a pretty thing, but after all she's Dolainde's daughter, a guest in the house—a charge of mine and yours. Not to mention her father. That man's too busy with his gambling friends at Halifax."

"How did you find out?" I said. I had not breathed a word about that shifty group at Mrs. Jessop's.

A sour smile. "Where d'ye think he got his play money? He's come to me for money all this time—and I've let him have whatever he asked, knowing full well what he was doing with it. Not for old friendship's sake, I may say, but for a very rich security and a very pretty rate of interest—to compensate me for my risk, of course." He went to the table, pulled out a drawer, and waved a packet of scrawled slips of paper.

"Those shabby compatriots of his have robbed him handsomely these past two years. Here are Dolainde's notes of hand for close on ten thousand pounds, with all his properties in Hispaniola for security. D'ye know what they're worth today?" A snap of his lean finger and thumb.

"Why?" I asked dully.

"The republicans have outlawed all the planters who left the island and seized their estates—Dolainde's with the rest."

"But you said yourself 'twas only a matter of time before the British forces——"

"Ay! That's what I gambled on—and I was wrong. Don't say, 'I told you so,' Nathan, for you were just as blind yourself on the other side. You thought the French and blacks 'ud drive our forces back into the sea inside six months. Well, they tried hard enough by all accounts, but it was something else that beat our forces in Hispaniola. Yellow jack. I didn't believe the tales at first. Fever, of course—there's always fever in the islands. But who'd ha' believed a regiment of sound young fellows fresh out from England, or from a healthy garrison in Nova Scotia, say, 'ud see half its strength on the sick list in a month, and most of 'em dead as herrings in six? Whole regiments have gone like that, all through the campaign, just holding onto half a dozen ports. Since '93 the British army and fleet ha' buried close on twenty thousand men on the shores of Hispaniola—and for what? Nothing but acres of graves about the ports! If England knew the whole truth there'd be the deuce to pay in Parliament—and the Army knows the debt's past due. I've private word today that the British forces are to be withdrawn, come spring, and the country left to the niggers and mosquitoes—for the French troops are perishing just like ours. And that means the end of everything—our old trade with Hispaniola, Dolainde's estate, and all the money I've lent him on the strength of it."

He looked at me gloomily. I should have felt some sympathy, I suppose, for I knew how much he loved a guinea, but I was thinking of Dolainde, poor devil. What was to become of him and that furious young creature in the kitchen? My foster father read my thoughts, for he put up his long jaw and said coldly, "That girl of Dolainde's—you must have nothing more to do with her."

"For what reason?"

"For one thing because I say so. For another because she's deep in some kind of affair with that hairdressing fellow Brule, and I leave you to guess what sort of affair it must be that takes her to his lodgings so frequently. What, are you surprised? Brule's her countryman, after all, and you heard what she thinks of us people. She'll run off with him one of these days, and I say a good riddance to both."

"How do you know all this?"

"Ha!" He looked at me with a severe expression. "I know a

good many things, Nathan. I know, for instance, you've been dallying with some woman in Halifax, the wife of a major on the prince's staff—one of those high-nosed fellows who'd shoot ye down like a dog if he caught a breath of it, and see my timber contract canceled into the bargain."

"Has Felicity . . . ?"

"Felicity had nothing to do with it. I have my own sources of information that may affect my business or myself, and very good ones, too. Felicity? What made ye say that? Felicity thinks too much of you, my boy. Oh, to be sure, she keeps her affections well guarded from the world and you, but—tut! You ought to know better."

While saying this he walked around the table end and sat in his favorite morocco chair, gripping the arms of it with his long hands and regarding me with an intent yellow stare.

"Be seated, Nathan. That chair, there, where I can see you by these miserable wartime candles. I've a matter to put before you, something I should ha' said long ago, I suppose—something of the very greatest importance to you and to me."

I sat, wondering, and feeling a sudden tightness in my stomach.

"I should ha' told you this when you turned twenty, Nathan, but I've waited, hoping things would come about in the—ah—natural way. Well, I might ha' known better. Matters that count in this world don't come about, they're brought about. Listen to me, boy. For a long time I've looked upon you as a son—my son that nature didn't bless me with—and although I may seem a hard man, Nathan, there is in me a great affection for you, ay, the same father's affection that I'd have for my own flesh. I rescued you from the overseers of the poor—they were going to bind you out for an orphan. I gave you over to Ma'am for your schooling and such, and when you turned sixteen I sent you off to sea, before the mast, as I went myself at that age. To make a seaman of you, understand? Ay, and to give you a knowledge of ports and the business that draws ships back and forth. That was my own apprenticeship, and very well it's stood me in the time gone by. I learned the hard way and turned my knowledge into money through the years. You know what I mean; the ships, the warehouses and wharves, the store, the shipyard, the timberlands and mills and . . ."

He picked up the little bundle of Dolainde's notes, twisted his lips wryly, and dropped it again. "A hard loss there, I suppose, but I learned long ago that a man must take a long risk sometimes for a profit. Well, I've plenty of notes of other men, all sound and secure, a number of very good mortgages besides, and a mighty pleasant sum in bankers' credits at Halifax and abroad. A little empire, Nathan, all of one man's making in a lifetime. But there's the rub—the lifetime. Nathan, I'm sixty-nine."

He paused, and I saw in his lined face a look of savage regret, of helpless anger, as if he were indignant that a man could not hoard his years like so many guineas.

"I'm a vigorous man—have all my teeth but three—and my mother lived to ninety-odd. But there's no telling. At sixty-nine a man must consider what's to become of his family and his properties when he's gone. Common sense, that. Many a pretty fortune's gone to the gutter—and the man who gathered it hardly cold in his grave—for the want of a bit o' timely thought. Well, I'm a forehanded man by nature and I've thought on this a good few years, and now I've put my hand to paper while I've strength to hold a pen."

He turned to the drawer where he kept his pistol and drew forth a document, folded but not sealed, and sat there tapping it on the chair arm and looking at me. I sat stiffly, an image of bewilderment. He tossed the thing across the table.

"Read it, Nathan."

I opened the sheets awkwardly—my fingers had gone to thumbs, it seemed. The date was three days back. And I read:

> In the name of God, amen. I, Amos Bradford Pride, of the town of Gosport in the province of Nova Scotia, merchant, being of sound mind and body, and having a firm faith in Christ and my salvation, and knowing the certainty of death in the flesh, do hereby devise and bequeath unto my beloved adopted son Nathan Cain my worldly goods entire, as follows:

There followed a long list, sheet after sheet, of his possessions, but I could read no more. I raised my head slowly, with a mist before my eyes and it seems to me a smile on my lips, the trembling smile of an idiot. I felt like the poor boy in the fairy tale who steps through the witch's door and finds himself enchanted in a castle, with fine clothes awaiting him, and servants bringing rich food and drink, and the air full of wonderful music, and a beautiful princess in the offing.

All paupers dream of such things, I suppose. But I had fancied nothing like the document before me. There had been nothing to prepare me—no, not a word, not even a kindly look in all the years. My foster father had been harsh and aloof, absorbed in his affairs; and from the time I set foot in the big house Ma'am had never let me feel that I was part of it. I had been rescued from the overseers and given a comfortable home and a pious upbringing, but I had felt a bound boy nonetheless, with chores to be done for my keep, a cot in the garret, a footing with the servants, and a notion that I must be grateful for these things.

"You're surprised," he said.

I nodded and gulped. It was strange and wonderful to see the taut lines of his mouth and jaw gone slack like old rigging, a whimsy in his countenance where I had never seen anything but restless energy, a benign and even sentimental look where I could remember nothing but greed. Looking back, I can see that there is sentiment in all men, good, bad, or the common run, and that from time to time it must come to the surface to be seen, if only for a moment, like a chip in a whirlpool. I was young then, and my eyes must have been very wide, for it seemed to me that I was seeing Mr. Pride for the first time, and I felt a sting of reproach that I had been so blind.

He bent forward eagerly. "You see what it means, Nathan? You've been restless, lately—wanted a ship of your own, haven't ye? A ship and deep water under ye, and trade to seek in the far foreign places—eh?"

"Yes," I cried. "That's what I want!"

"Ah, but here are ships! Ships! Ships and God's plenty besides, a score of busy matters, all yours when the time comes. This is your place, Nathan, here with me in Gosport—your hand beside mine on the tiller—and one day all of it yours. Think, boy, think! The great man o' Gosport, ay, and one o' the half dozen men whose word is law at Halifax—and that means the province. Governors asking you to wine and dine. Merchants, bankers, commissaries, high-and-mighty officers of His Majesty's forces glad enough to hold a word with you, to be seen with you, to be known as a friend o' yours for their credit's sake if nothing else. Why, there's Prince Edward himself, commander o' the Nova Scotia garrisons, the younger son to a king—and less to look forward to than you, come to the fine point."

He paused. Then, abruptly, "Well, Nathan?"

I called up a voice from my boots that did not seem to belong to me at all. "It's—wonderful, sir. What else can I say? I never dreamed——"

"Ha! I'd no intention you should! I've seen too many sons o' rich men spoiled with dreaming. Well, I've bided my time, and now ye know. No fear of it turning your head—a man grown—brought up seaman fashion—discipline—a taut hand and a frugal mind—seen a bit o' the world, ay, and the flesh and the devil, I don't doubt. Time to settle down—give over these little flirtations—face your responsibilities—um! Ye haven't read the rest o' the will, Nathan, but no matter."

He plucked the sheets from under my nose, folded them neatly and returned them to the drawer. "There are one or two conditions you must observe, of course. The will requires you to adopt the name of Pride by proper legal process—a thing that can be done very easily now that you're well past twenty-one. It requires you also to make a decent provision for Ma'am in case she should survive me. You'd do that anyhow, I know. And there's another provision—the last. But you'd best hear that from the person most concerned."

"And who is that?" I asked easily, feeling like a prince already.

"Felicity."

Chapter 11

WHAT a change in my world after that midnight conversation! The little wooden town beside the river seemed to shine, to put forth towers and spires. The idle shipping in the roadstead merely awaited some golden adventure. Even the hardwood clumps on the hillside, leafless and dripping in the autumn rains, put on a mysterious charm. It was only in the big house that I felt like my old self. This may seem strange, seeing that I was Amos Pride's heir, and this great ark of a house which had seemed so long a prison to me was in reality the palace of the storybooks.

But Ma'am Pride preserved that air of hostile watchfulness which had puzzled me so long and was now so very clear. And

Felicity kept her distance. I felt a guilty sympathy for them—I, the orphan boy, the red-haired interloper to whom someday they must look for something close to charity. I wondered how long Felicity had known. I guessed that Mr. Pride had told her last year, on her twenty-first birthday probably. I ransacked my memory for little incidents and still could not decide. Mrs. Pride of course had known, or had a foreboding, ever since I came to Pride's Fancy.

As for my foster father, he had plunged back into his affairs and put on his old face and manner as if nothing had happened, as if that revelation which changed all our lives were nothing more than a stroke of simple business, planned, matured, made known to the interested parties, and done with.

But from this time on there was plenty to take his mind—and mine—for business began to move in a way that was heartening after four uncertain years. And soon there was something else. I had returned from another dull trip to Halifax and was busy with the bills of lading when Mr. Pride came striding down the wharf and into the *Sally's* cabin with a look of triumph on his face.

I sprang up, capsizing an inkpot over the ship's papers in my surprise, and swallowing the round sea word that came to my tongue.

"It's come!" he shouted. "At last! And a fine long time they've been about it!"

"What?" I muttered, regarding the ruin of the papers.

"London—the Lords of Admiralty. Oh, I dare say they've had troubles enough—the French rampaging over Europe and the seas, and England short of everything to fight with. But what did I tell ye? The thing to do was to strike at the French and their allies wherever they could be found—and by sea, the way we know how. Take their ships, destroy their commerce, shut 'em off from their colonies and the world. Strangle 'em—ain't that what I said?"

I could remember him saying no such thing, and I was tempted to say so, but I put my tongue in my cheek.

"What about our own commerce?" I asked.

"That! We've had to trust the convoys so far, huddling up and down the seas like sheep, ay, and scattered and lost like sheep whenever a gale blew and those French sea wolves closed in. D'ye wonder I wouldn't risk more than a vessel or two? Talked of fast ships and fat freights, and the devil with His Majesty's escort—didn't I?"

"Yes," I said, still watching in dismay the drip of the ink, the black stain spreading like the armies of the French. "You said that."

"Ha! But there was one thing wanting. That was guns. Guns! We had to have 'em and we couldn't get 'em! Not a cannon to be had for love or money, up and down the coast. Hounded the governor, set all those pettifogging officials at Halifax by the ears, pestered the Navy—Admiral Vandeput, that bad old man—ay, and tackled the prince himself one day in his love nest on the Basin shore. No good. Cannon enough for the Navy, cannon galore for the Army—Prince Edward's got the woods about Halifax chock-full o' guns, throwing up forts and barracks and batteries as though the whole French nation was at Sable Island bent for Canada. But not a gun, not so much as a pistol for the merchant ships that keep alive the trade o' the province!

"But now—aha!—all's changed. Somebody in London woke up. Some high cockalorum got to thinking. There's those idle colonists in Nova Scotia, seamen all and old hands at the Caribbee trade; and there's the French West Indies and the Spanish Main to be harried for all they're worth—and they're worth a pretty penny. So! Write the governor at Halifax—encourage the fitting of private ships o' war—letters o' marque for the asking—guns from the naval stores—ammunition, anything they want, so long as they pay for it. And there you are! A blow at the French and Spanish that won't cost His Majesty a penny—everything to gain—profit for shipowners—prize money for seamen—fat fees for the vice-admiralty courts and lawyers—huzza!"

With energy (and no little danger from the deck beams overhead), my foster father performed a few steps of the hornpipe, learned in his youth, I suppose. I looked at him with some concern and so did my mate, who thought him gone quite mad, and later so informed the crew. 'Twas weird, I confess, to see that grim old man grinning and capering like a boy out of school.

Privateering! Nothing new, of course. There had been privateers sailing out of Nova Scotia in the old wars, and from time to time since the present war began there had been talk of renewing the game, but, knowing the sentiment of the Royal Navy in this matter, I had put the talk down to Halifax tavern-pots. His Majesty's sea officers went into a fury at the mere notion of private ships of war, calling them pirates and suchlike, and talking loudly of "giving 'em the stem" if any appeared and the chance afforded. It irked them to think of privateers reaping prize money that might otherwise have fallen to the fleet—and every post captain saw in the present war his chance to make a fortune.

"Come!" Mr. Pride snapped. "Let the mate straighten up those papers. There's more important things to be done." Off he went up the companion, and I clapped on my hat and followed him. On our way from the wharf to the house we were joined by Job Eames, coming on the run with a bundle of drawings tucked under his arm, and in a few minutes we three stood about the familiar table in the library, studying the vessel Eames had evolved from those restless conferences of '94 and '95.

Once again I had to admire Mr. Pride's foresight. There was nothing much to argue now. The size had been agreed long ago —two hundred tons or so—and after a long wrangle we had come to an agreement on the rig. The older Pride captains had been all for a full square rig on both masts, having in mind the handy little ten-gun brigs of the Royal Navy. Younger men like me had plumped for a schooner, thinking of its handiness for windward work in the islands. In the end we had come to a compromise, a brigantine, or what the older sailors called a hermaphrodite brig. I remember Lot Mayes growling at this mating of brig and schooner rig, declaring no good ever came of it—"nothing but a seagoing hinny mule, having neither the nimble feet o' the dam nor the strength and beauty o' the sire."

But Mr. Pride's voice had decided the matter. "Brigantine? Um! Square canvas for'ard, very useful running down the trades . . . and there's the jibs and stays'ls and a good big fore-and-aft mainsail for spanking her into it. Six men and a boy could handle her while the rest fight . . . a clear view for'ard once the fores'l's clewed for action . . . no fores'l boom to clutter the deck and get in the way of a swivel gun . . . ay! The sum comes right, I say. It comes to a brigantine."

And now she lay in plan and scale before us. Job Eames would set to work on her molds at once. Her timbers were still growing in the woods, but we knew exactly where they were. There was not a Pride timber lot within ten miles of Gosport and handy to the river that Mr. Pride and I, or I alone at his bidding, had not cruised with an eye for spars and frames and suchlike since the war began. This was easier than it sounds, for it was the custom of our woodsmen in logging for the sawmills to leave standing any likely-looking piece of ship timber, against a future need in the yards.

As for the masts, they were really chosen for us by His Majesty.

For many years the very best mast trees near tidewater had been selected and marked with the King's broad arrow by deputy surveyors of Governor Wentworth, who went about the province reserving such timber for the Royal Navy. Timber owners who took the King's mark seriously grumbled a good deal, for it amounted to a tax, payable on demand. But Mr. Pride always winked when the King's surveyor went his way, and said with a thin smile 'twas mighty nice of Johnnie Wentworth—hunting up our finest spars and marking 'em so a busy man could find 'em when he wanted 'em.

And so I and my crew of axmen had no trouble to find the spars for Mr. Pride's privateer. Two tall slick pines for the lower masts stood on the riverbank half a mile above the town, each with the broad arrow and the bold JW of the governor cut deep in the white wood. We felled them on the bank, trimmed them carefully, and floated them off to the mast pond at the shipyard.

For topmasts we took a pair of lean spruce near the gristmill brook and hauled them down to the river with chains and three yoke of oxen. Whenever I saw them afterwards, smooth and glistening in their places aloft, I thought of that pleasant spot beside the brook and the day we felled them in the lovely Indian-summer weather.

So it was with all her timbers. When she was built, the brigantine seemed to me like one of those models that sailors make of foreign woods and bits of old wrecks and such mementos, each piece with a tale. A thousand miles from home a man could look at her and call up, scene by scene, the lovely countryside of Gosport in the autumn by the river.

The timber for her keel we hewed from great yellow birch in a hardwood grove near Indian Point, with the fallen leaves rustling underfoot. The stem- and sternpost we cut of oak on the east ridge, and I remember the sound of our chopping brought up a big bull moose to see what was afoot, as the sound of chopping often does in our Nova Scotia woodland in the fall. He stood a full minute in a break in the trees, with the sunshine gleaming on his wide brown horns, a sight to make a hunter's mouth water, and none of us with a gun.

The brigantine's frames we hewed of white spruce, which is tough and full of life and keeps its quality in hot climates; and these we cut in the gloomy wood below the river falls, a notable haunt of owls. The lean red spruce for her yards and boom and bowsprit we got farther down the slope, where a sound of water rattled through the woods. That was Rocky Brook. More than once in springtime I had played the truant there and caught a basketful of trout—and later a taste of Mr. Pride's Malacca.

For the rest of her we went above the falls and floated the logs down to the mill there—yellow birch for the floor timbers, spruce for the deck beams and kelson and the topside planking. We had an argument over stuff for the garboard planking, some insisting on birch, some on beech. The birch men vowed that beech would rot too fast at the waterline. The beech men pooh-poohed and said the shipworms in the southern seas ate birchwood like so much biscuit.

We held a solemn debate in the woods, squatting on our heels, while chipmunks skittered up and down the trunks about us and a fat black porcupine crawled out on a branch and dropped hemlock twigs on our heads. In the end we took beech, for the shipworm was more to be feared than rot or the cannon balls of the French, and later I had to go over the argument word by word for Mr. Pride's benefit, and for the sake of his nod.

We cut logs of red pine to be hollowed for the pumps, and some good clear white pine for the deck beams and for the inside finish. The paneling of the captain's cabin was to be sawn from a butt of bird's-eye maple, laid away in a shed at the mill long ago for just such a purpose. Finally we took our oxen to a sedgy meadow at Long Stillwater and cut and dragged to the riverbank the material for the brigantine's knees, stanchions, and trenails, all of hackmatack, the tough, rot-defying wood of the swamps.

From first to last we chose nothing but the best our forest could afford, and we were satisfied. You may talk of hard pine and southern oak as much as you please, and your teak-built ships and your heart-of-oak ships and the rest. Give me our northern pine, spruce, hackmatack, and hardwood, and a man like Job Eames to build it, and there, sirs, is a ship!

Chapter 12

ALL this took the labor of many men, and I drove them hard, as Mr. Pride drove me, but snow was flying before the last log was in the river, and then it was a race with the weather. The first cold snap would freeze the log pond, choke the water wheels with anchor frost, and put an end to our sawing for the season. Apart from this the shipyard soon would be drifted deep in snow, with a pinching wind along the river ice, and all the work put over until spring.

Job was anxious to get the new vessel set up in frame at once, so that the wood might season in the winter months before the plank went on. That way we could avoid any rot between frame and planking later on. And for the rest of her, we wanted every bit ready to hand when springtime came.

And we did it. The keel was laid on a dark November day with white specks flying on the wind and the river ruffled in cold gray chops. In two days more Job and his shipwrights got the frames up. The keen wind carried down to the house the sounds of ax and adze and hammer and saw, and the sound of men singing at their work. From the early days of the Caribbee trade a dram or two of rum had been part of every Gosport workman's wage, and today, considering the weather aloud, Mr. Pride ordered an extra round from time to time. Some captious folk murmured at this, seeing in it nothing but a cheap way of getting the men to work harder, and maybe they were right; but it seemed to me fair enough to toast the first bones of the privateer in ripe Jamaica, having in mind her destination and the trade she was to ply.

Lot Mayes was there with other Pride seamen, helping the shipwrights to raise the heavy frames. He grinned at me as he tipped his pot.

"Nathan,"—he smacked his chapped lips—"this is the stuff for a man alive! It has a good short manly name and should be taken as spoken—a gulp and a snap of the lips together."

I kicked the keg lightly. "Why not mount the devil's pulpit with your text?"

"Watch your feet, man! I'd as lief see blood spilled as the good brown stuff. Tsha! You're a seaman and ye know the good quick bite of a dram in a cold watch coming north. Eh? It has the Caribbee sunshine in it, man, and call it what ye like."

Some of the townsfolk had braved the cold to see the raising of the frame, and a little apart stood a group of Indians from their camp above the falls, eying the keg thirstily. I offered a dram to old Moise, the chief, and he drank with pleasure. He looked on the work with pleasure, too, for our Micmacs have no fear of the sea and go upon it in their bark canoes, and the frame of a canoe and the frame of a ship are much the same, and call for the same skill in the making.

"Cain," he said, "why you make this *kweedun* now? See!" He stabbed a brown finger at the gray sky, where a flight of wild geese was passing over the river, swift and high, belated on their journey from the north. "Winter comes. The Frost Giant shoots his arrows to the south."

"So shall we, come spring," I answered. "This is a war canoe."

"So?" he muttered, turning his bright eyes to me. "Who you fight, Cain?"

"Our old enemies the Wenjoo [French]—and another people you have never seen, Moise. We call them Spanish."

"Espanij!" He could not get his tongue around the word. "They are far?"

"Very far. Many days. We go where the sun goes in winter."

He raised his eyebrows. "How shall you find the home path on the Big Water?"

I laughed. "We shall find it, Moise."

The old man considered gravely. "Cain, I am too old for such a journey. I must keep the wigwam now. You take my son."

I shook my head. An Indian in a ship?

"He is strong, Cain. And he has been upon the Big Water in his small *kweedun* as far as Oonamaagik [Cape Breton]. Cain, you take my son. Young men must go to war. When my son returns he shall tell us of the sun's home in the south."

"That is for Pride to say, Moise. I have no say."

"But you go?"

"That also is for him to say."

"Um. He will say go, Cain. You are a young man and his son. When Pride sends you to the war, you take my son. Yes?"

"Yes," I said.

The winter played a game of frost and thaw until a week before Christmas, when it hardened suddenly and covered the river, the sawmill ponds and all the lakes and swamps. Then came a snowstorm from the sea, and on its heels another. Our town sat in a white flood, in many places almost foundered in it, with drifts higher than the fence tops. In the stark cold that followed we set about our winter's work, logging for the common run of sawmill stuff to be sawn in the spring and shipped mostly to Halifax on Mr. Pride's military contracts. We had several camps in the woods upriver, cutting on various timber lots, and all had to be kept manned and supplied and directed, and there were accounts to be kept, and so on. Much of the directing and accounting fell to me and kept me busy.

I spent Christmas Day in the woods with a logging crew whose fare for the day was stirabout and fried codfish cakes. (Salt fish, as Mr. Pride said, was very cheap and nourishing, and so it formed a staple of the camps.) Of course Christmas had never been a festival in our town, where the settlers were Yankee folk from the Massachusetts coast, suspicious of all that smacked of "Popery." Time had mellowed those old notions to some extent, however. Young women decorated the meetinghouse with fir boughs for the Christmas prayers, young men and boys paraded the streets on Christmas Eve, firing guns and knocking at doors for pies and sweetmeats and singing not carols but sea chanteys for the most part, while merchants and shipowners held feast in their homes on roast wild geese and puddings and Western Island wines. But none of this was like Thanksgiving, our one true feast, the high day of the year.

On New Year's Day I came to town on snowshoes, weary from much traveling and famished for sleep. I went up the back stairs, having no wish to meet anyone, least of all my foster father, who would want a long account of the woods work. I had a week's beard, and my face was grimed by the open fires of the logging camps, which were built after the fashion of Indian winter houses and like them full of smoke always. And I was dressed in my woods rig, moccasins, buckskin leggings, an old patched pea jacket, a draggled raccoon-skin cap—a walking scarecrow. And so when I met Felicity on the landing I gave her a quick hello and passed on towards my chamber, but she called me back.

"Nathan, we haven't seen much of you lately."

"No. There's a lot to do in the woods this winter."

She laughed. "You look like a wild man of the woods. That beard of yours! No wonder Lia used to call you Red. You're thin, too. You work too hard. That's Father's fault, I know. I'll speak to him."

"I'm all right," I said.

She wore the brown gown I have mentioned before, with a bit of white lace at the throat and wrists, and her hair was done in a long curled fashion new to me. She regarded me with her clear-brandy eyes.

"Nathan, there's something I have to say to you."

"Some other time——"

"Now, Nathan. Tomorrow you'll be off again somewhere." She looked about her and motioned towards a little sewing room with an oriel window that looked upon the snowdrifted garden. Obediently I followed the softly swishing tail of her gown, and she closed the door. It was cold in there with no fire in the grate, and when she spoke a small wisp of vapor hung about her lips.

"Nathan, I won't beat about the bush. It's too cold here for one thing, and I'm not the bush-beating sort, nor are you. Father tells me you've seen his will."

"Not all of it," I said.

"So he warned me. There's a provision about your inheritance affecting me, and I'm to tell you. I've known his mind since last year—a great surprise, too, Nathan. I suppose I should have guessed long ago, as Mamma did, though she said nothing all this time."

I blurted out, "Let me say, before you go any further, Felicity, that I never guessed at all. The notion of such good fortune never crossed my mind."

"I know that, Nathan. But you see——"

"I want you and Ma'am to know that all this is strange and wonderful to me. I can't yet realize it. What have I done to deserve Mr. Pride's fortune? When he told me I was taken aback —I want you both to believe that—but since I've thought it over I feel very strongly that it's most unjust to you and Ma'am, though of course it's all plain business in his eyes. Better to divide the properties——"

"Ah, but he wants the properties kept together in one hand, Nathan. That's the point. And what better hand than yours?"

I looked at her quickly, suspecting some mockery in this.

"Nathan, you're to take the Pride name."

"I know."

"Do you know you're to marry me?"

My heart gave a single mighty thump. There was a long silence. I stared out of the window, swallowing. A pair of oxen dragged a sled laden with birch firewood along the lane past the foot of the garden, with a slow dull clink of brass bells and the teamster walking ahead in the snow, flourishing his little whip and calling over his shoulder to the melancholy beasts in that queer language of ox teamsters which I dare say was spoken in the Ark. I watched them out of sight in the pink snow glow of the winter sunset.

"Well, Nathan?"

"I don't know what to say."

"Don't you think I'd make you a good wife?"

"I've never thought of you in that way."

"I confess, Nathan, that I never gave much thought to you in any way—until last year. You were, well, a brother—not a very handsome brother, nor a gay one—not any sort of young man that a girl might find affection for."

"And what do you think of me now?"

She hesitated, looking out upon the snow as I did. That was the way we talked, unseeing, like two people talking through a wall.

"Nathan, I've always been very close to my father. What he wishes, I do. I've never liked the notion of marriage much, unless I could meet a man like him. You're not. But I like you well enough, as well as I'd like any man, I dare say. I wasn't made to flutter at the touch of a man's hand or to swoon at the sound of his voice or anything like that. We've been good companions sometimes, you and I. After Father told me, last year, I set out very dutifully to make you think of me in a more romantic fashion. Do you remember my poor little batiste gown that you found so indecent?"

She turned to me, laughing, and I responded with a most uneasy cackle. I was trying to picture Felicity as my wife.

"I've got a figure, Nathan, as I hope you saw. I'm a woman of quite good parts, believe me—much better than Mrs. Sherring's."

I ground my back teeth at that, feeling the fool I doubtless was, while she stood cool and self-possessed and I think enjoying my discomfiture.

"Would you mind telling me," I asked in a surly voice, "what brought all this to pass, just now of all times?"

She pursed her lips in a whimsical way and shrugged. "Father knew about Mrs. Sherring, of course. And it seems that lately he found you dallying with some Gosport wench—he didn't say who or where. You're quite a gallant in your quiet way, Nathan, aren't you? Father seemed to think it quite natural—men always do, Mamma says—but he decided it was time you had a wife to put an end to your nonsense. 'To settle him,' he said. And I'm to be the wife, you see. I'm to settle you—as if you were a pot of hot coffee and I the little dash of cold water. As if . . . well, never mind. I mustn't be indelicate. But it's droll, Nathan, isn't it?"

It seemed very serious to me. I felt deep inside a stir of indignation that Mr. Pride, who ordered all things in our world, should order us to come together like a pair of cattle for his purposes. That, I felt, was the thought in Felicity's mind as well, and it sharpened the barb on her tongue. She was defending her own pride.

"My dear," I said gruffly, "this is a very sudden thing. I wasn't prepared for such a thing. Nor are you, it seems to me. We must have time to think about it."

"I've thought about it," she said quickly, "and I'm willing."

"Because your father says you must?"

She laughed in that cool way of hers. "Oh, come, Nathan, you're not so bad as all that. I like you. I think I could amuse you after my fashion. I'm quite sure I'll be a good mistress for this house—and a credit to you—and Father—and I'll raise my children with a proper respect for money and property—so that Father's name and fortune can go on for ever and ever, amen. That's what he wants. And isn't that what you want, Nathan, when all's said and done? You're ambitious."

"Yes."

"Had you any other woman in mind? To wife, I mean."

"None."

"Well, then?" She stood before me very slim and straight, with her hands dropped and clasped, her clear gaze on mine, a faint smile on her lips. Her manner nettled me, she was so calm and assured, while I was upset with all sorts of notions and an instinct to shy clear of her for careful contemplation, like a seaman making a landfall in an unexpected place. But somewhere inside me a voice was whispering, "Take her, fool! What are you waiting for?" For surely this was the final boon to the poor boy in the tale—the princess, willing and waiting? She was part of the marvelous destiny that Mr. Pride had revealed to me, a matter not to be questioned.

I put out my hands, and Felicity stepped into my slow embrace and laid her brown head against my shoulder. She did not put her arms about me; they hung down before her, the hands clasped, an attitude of submission. We stood so for a bewildered age that probably was no more than a minute. Then she turned her face up to me, flushing a little, and said in a steady voice, "Aren't you going to kiss me, Nathan?"

I kissed her awkwardly, once, twice. Her lips were cool and firm. We drew apart and looked at each other in an odd shame-faced way for a time. Then she walked to the door and paused with her hand on the knob.

"I'll go now, Nathan. And I'll tell Father, shall I?"

I nodded slowly.

"I promise not to ask too much of you, Nathan. It will take some time to grow accustomed to each other—in this way, I mean. Father will understand."

"And your mother?" I blurted suddenly. "What does she think of this?"

"Would you really like to know, Nathan?"

"Yes, of course."

"Poor Mamma hates the very sight of you."

With that she was gone. I heard her small wooden heels on the stairs, going down very quickly and firmly. I turned towards my own chamber, too muddled now for sleep or for anything but long lying and smoking and pondering on that queer betrothal in the sewing room. Gentlemen in books make wonderful speeches at such a time, and young ladies are confused and shy and apt to swoon away. But I was no gentleman—a seaman ashore, smelling very strong just now of balsam and the smoke of camp-fires. Felicity was lady enough, yet I could not imagine her swooning, even at a mouse, which is a very upsetting beast to women. But tsha!—from what I had seen and heard of the world young men and women considering marriage did not talk at all like the books. I venture most of them pledge their troth in some such stiff and silent fashion as the sewing room had just witnessed, a few mumbled words, a smile or two, a frown and a blush perhaps, and a hurrying apart to contemplate the miracle.

We had not mentioned love, of course, but what the deuce was love?

Chapter 13

A WINTER of harsh cold and snow on snow. From Halifax we heard that troops were kept shoveling the drifts along the Basin road so that Prince Edward could ride back and forth in his sleigh between his love nest and the garrison headquarters. Mr. Pride kept me busy in the woods and put another captain in the *Sally*. To keep me out of Mrs. Sherring's company, I knew. And I did not care a fig. There were other matters to mind now, and Felicity to anchor my fancy.

I spent most of the time in the woods from camp to camp, where a sudden shift of Mr. Pride's mind demanded a great cut of ship timber. He talked of having half a dozen privateers on the slips by next autumn, all to be built after the chosen model. At the end of each week I came to town and spent the Sabbath quietly with the family at home and in the meetinghouse. The Sabbath evenings we passed in the long parlor, where Felicity played and sang at the pianoforte and I turned the music and sometimes joined my voice to hers in airs I knew.

'Twas a pleasant way to spend an evening, yet my gaze kept straying to the window and the scene beyond, where the frames of the brigantine stood ghostly in the snow of the shipyard like the ribs of some great beast picked clean and shining under the stars. Just as in the desolation of winter it was comforting to picture the grass green, the trees in leaf, and the river a lively blue where now it was stark and white, so I fancied those bones clothed in plank and paint, the masts stepped and rigged, the yards aloft, and canvas bent to them.

More, I could see her sailing down the stream and over the bar, with the guns snug in their tackles, a swarm of men aloft, the red jack flying from the gaff, and the long wet road to the Caribbees running straight south from the harbor heads. And then the music would stop in a crash of keys, and the dream vanished, and Felicity sat looking up at me with a whimsical displeasure in her face. I had forgotten to turn the page.

Ma'am Pride watched all this in silence from her high-backed chair. But Mr. Pride laughed very heartily—he was always jovial these days with Felicity and me—with a waggle of his long finger and a quip about a dreamy lover making a wakeful husband, or something of that sort; and Felicity's lips tightened, and I in my haste to duty would turn two pages instead of one. Again, she would pause and catch my great paw in her slender one, her fingers very white against mine, and make a little grimace, saying in an amused voice, "Nathan! First it was tar forever on your hands. Now it's balsam—just as black!"

And I would murmur the same old apology, that tar and balsam were necessary things to the sailor's or the woodsman's trade, and that, no matter how much you scrubbed with hot water and soap, the stain remained. And Mr. Pride would add meaningly that a time was coming very soon when Nathan could keep his hands out of such messy matters and play the gentleman.

We played this little comedy many times, for she was ever at her music, her hands flitting and pecking at the keys like busy white birds, and I played the polite lover as well as I knew how. I had no small talk, and whenever we retired from the instrument and sat together our conversation was slow and painful until Felicity —in desperation, I suppose—fastened on a subject and ran off with it, pausing now and again for a jerky word or two from me.

I felt the awkward lout I was, and sometimes wondered if ever I could play the part of Felicity's husband in the way she wanted, or the way Mr. Pride wanted. We were never really alone. If we could have been, our courtship might have been easier. I had my own notion of love-making. But whenever I hinted at it Felicity seemed not to understand.

These Sabbath evenings ended always in the same way. Prince Edward's mania for clocks had set a fashion in the province, and Mr. Pride, no spendthrift and certainly no follower of fashion, followed this one with a princely extravagance. He worshiped punctuality. There was a clock in every nook and mantel of the big house, and he watched them with care and pleasure, making a round from day to day to see that all kept time alike.

And so at the hour of ten they began to strike all over Pride's Fancy, a jangling chorus from the deep slow boom of the tall case clock in the lower hall to the merry tingle of the ormolu thing on the mantel of the long parlor. In this uproar we would rise and troop out to the hall, where a servant had lit and placed the bed tapers. As the last mechanism ground to a stop we all bade each other a solemn good night, and Felicity and I turned to ourselves for a single careful kiss under the eyes of our elders.

Her lips were firm and resolute. Sometimes I fancied a response in them, just as sometimes in her eyes I saw a ghost of warmth, of pleasure, it might have been of passion, that faded just as quickly as it came, and then there was only the faint smile, the lift of her head, and the brisk step on the stairs.

So passed the white months and the long, long spring. In April we began work upon the ship. Although the ice had gone out of the river the wind held cold, and from time to time a snowstorm came whirling in from the sea and put a stop to our labors. But after each storm the wind hauled to the southwest, the clouds broke and the sun was warm, ay, hot in the lee of the sheds, and the snow turned gray and shrank and vanished. By mid-May there was another kind of snow upon the shipyard, of chips and shavings very white and clean against the dull mat of past years' work and the fresh green grass on the hillside.

Job Eames was everywhere, and I his shadow, watching four years' dreaming come to life. I longed for a real skill then with adze or broadax, auger or hammer, plane or saw, filled with a wish to have some part in the actual shaping of her, in the good sound beauty of her. But that was not to be. There were skilled hands aplenty. Commonly Job put a dozen men to work upon a hull and took his time, but Mr. Pride and the times were very urgent, and so no less than thirty cunning-handed fellows, the best in Gosport, swarmed about the frames. Job growled that they got in each other's way and drove him frantic, trying to keep them all busy and seeing that the work was good; but they worked right enough. The vessel grew before our eyes, and she was lovely.

And she was strong. Under her was the yellow-birch keel, hewn to a width of fourteen inches and a depth of two feet, the pieces fitted and scarfed together so cunningly that they were one to the eye and to any rude stress of the sea. There were the stem- and sternposts of clear grained oak; and the white-spruce frames gone yellow in the winter weather, rising in mathematical curves above our heads, measured now with Job's unerring line and dubbed to the mark, a chip here, a fine shaving there, by razor-sharp adzes in the careful hands of his best shipwrights, a joy to watch.

Then the inner sealing of two-and-a-half-inch spruce plank, and on the outboard side the garboard planking of three-inch beech, the topside planking of two-and-a-half-inch spruce, all bored through and through for the trenails. Boring called for a true eye and the arms of a bear, and it was something to see men standing shoulder to the hull, whirling the big pod auger with both hairy hands, hour after hour. Followed the trenails, all of tough hackmatack, driven home with sledge hammers and the ends sawn flush, and each end keyed with wedges of dry maplewood, and these in turn driven flush with hammer strokes.

Then came the turn of the calkers; two strands of oakum were driven deep in each seam by a wide horsing iron under the heavy blows of the wooden beetle, and the final strand tapped in with the small calker's iron and mallet. And a musical sound that was, a fine quick *tack-tack-tack* that rose in chorus and sounded over the river and through the town. Calkers' mallets have a clear hard ring I love. There is only one sound to match it, and that is the tune of coopers at work. More than once on my southern voyages, sick for a sound of home, I have gone into a cooperage and tossed the Negro workmen a coin or two and set them at the cooper's march about a cask, for the fine rolling beat of it that made you want to sing and dance, that always put my mind far north in Jamie Carr's small barrel shop.

On went the deck plank of two-inch pine. When that was calked it was time to trundle the little fire engine down from the town house to the yard and set eight lively fellows at the handles, four each side, pumping water through the leaky leather hose into the spaçe between inner and outer planking, while the calkers went carefully round and round the hull, seeking signs of a leak.

Then came a grave discussion about coppering. A prolonged cruise in the southern seas meant shipworms, riddled planks, and men breaking their hearts at the pumps before the cruise was done. Copper was expensive stuff and hard to get in these times, and Mr. Pride drew a sour mouth at the mere mention of it. Some old sailors were for a good thick coat of hot tar and brimstone, others vowed that a mixture of fish oil and verdigris would do the trick. Old Lot Mayes, with a hot breath of grog in my face, declared any kind of painted stuff worse than nothing. "Why, the worms love it, man! I mind the time we hove down the old *Venture* at St. Kitts; and there she was, riddled like an ant nest in a pine stump, 'spite o' two coats o' hot stuff afore she left home. We had to plug the holes with whittled pegs—hundreds, I tell ye, Nathan, hundreds!—it took us three hard weeks at the careenage in the island, and all hands sickening o' sunstroke and the yellow jack afore we got away. And even then 'twas pump or drown afore we fetched Cape Sable on the passage home."

In the end we decided on a thorough charring of the garboard planking and over that a hot coat of pitch mixed with brimstone. And so while the water was in her and the work safe, we seared the whole of the planking below waterline with torches of oil and rags, and then daubed the stuff on, heated in big iron caldrons over fires of chips and refuse lumber gathered about the yard. For a boot-topping we mixed a paint of fish oil and Baltimore red. The topside we painted black—bulwarks, gunports, and all.

While all this was going on, Job had the best of his carpenters busy at the cabin finish and the forecastle. Then came the turn of the riggers, and it was fine to watch them, too, as they got their sheers aboard and lashed, on broad timber shoes to spread the weight over the deck. They rigged the bowsprit and its bobstays for an anchor to their rigging tackle, and then they swung the mainmast aboard, fastened the standing rigging as it lay, and got it on end.

But before they slid the mast foot through the deck, Daniel Stacey, the chief rigger, came down to Mr. Pride, standing with Job and Simon Dawkins and me in the raffle of the yard.

"Where's the money pieces?" he demanded.

"Eh?" snapped Mr. Pride, as if he did not know.

"Should be a coin beneath each mast—'tain't lucky without."

"Um!" Mr. Pride drew forth his purse and fished amongst the coins. "There's for your whimsy, Daniel." He pocketed the purse and moved away, and a few moments later we heard his harsh voice in the sail loft, railing at Elisha Riddock on some petty point about the canvas for the brigantine.

Dan held Mr. Pride's pennies in his broad brown palm and stared from them to Job and Simon and me. "Should be silver," Job said.

"Ay," said Dan. He uttered an oath deep in his thick throat and flung the coppers far out into the river. We rummaged our pockets. Silver was ever a hard thing to come by in our frugal town, and since the war had well-nigh throttled our old trade with the Caribbees there was an end to the stream of Spanish silver which had been so long our currency in Nova Scotia.

Job pulled forth a few pennies and ha'pence and gun-metal trade tokens of Halifax merchants. Dan found a pistareen in his fob pocket.

"Small, look you, but it'll do for the fore. We should ha' something better for the main." And he looked at me.

I brought out a piece of eight, my last memento of the Cap and the smugglers of Monte Cristi; I had kept it all this time for luck. And so I said, "There goes my fortune," watching Daniel climb the staging to the deck with the coins clutched in his paw. Job gave me a queer look and turned away, saying in a sour voice that he wished his fortune were as safe.

"What d'ye mean by that?" I demanded.

He made a mouth and tipped his tarry old thrice-cocked hat down over his eyes, as if I were the sun itself. "Some say they figgered Pride's fortune 'ud be yours someday, from the time ye came to the big house a ragged orphan without a penny to bless yourself. I didn't think so, myself. But lately everybody's noticed how he's letting ye take more and more of a hand in the business, and now o' course the cat's out o' the bag, with the Prides' sewing woman prattling about a great touse over gowns and linen now that Miss Felicity's made up her mind to marry you, come July. Is it true, Nathan?"

"And if it is?" I said sharply.

He gave me a long look under the peak of the shabby black hat, and all the town's dislike of the Prides was in the small bright eyes.

"Then I wish ye joy of it—all of it, Nathan." He hesitated, and then, "I knew your father. Red-haired like you, a laughing fighting sort o' fellow who'd give anyone the shirt off his back for the asking. He died poor, but well loved."

And with that he hunched his thick shoulders and spat, and went off to the mast pond.

And so the brigantine's masts were stepped on Spanish silver for the luck of it, and raked well aft for speed and strength; and after that the spring stays were rigged and set up taut, and then the jib stays. The topmasts went aloft, and the topgallants, and fine they looked up there, the slim spruce tops that never again would hear the owls hoot in the woods below the falls. And then the yards went up and were slung across, and all the running rigging rove; for Mr. Pride had determined to launch her fully rigged for sea.

And that was the way she grew out of the litter of the shipyard and rose like a flower beside the water, putting forth tall stems and branches towards the sun, so beautiful that sometimes gazing at her from my chamber window in the bright June mornings I felt a lump in my throat and a childish desire to cry, as once long ago I had wept at the sight of morning sunshine on a silver thaw.

But the brigantine was not made for dreaming. When Daniel Stacey and his lads began the running rigging, Mr. Pride and I took passage in the packet for Halifax, to get the all-important letter of marque and to sign for the guns and powder and shot. A dull bit of business, but it turned out pleasant enough; and something happened on that visit to Halifax that changed the whole intent and purpose of the brigantine's cruise to the south.

Chapter 14

HALIFAX was bright and astir in the summer sunshine. The long harbor, blue in the green gutter of the hills, bristled with men-o'-war, transports, dispatch vessels, fleet tenders, escort brigs and sloops, a fine warlike scene. Ashore, the steep wooden town rang with trumpet calls from the barracks, posts, and batteries, the sudden clap of signal guns, and frequently the rattle and squeak of drum and fife and the tramp of a smart red-coated column waking the dust of the narrow streets. Our little colonial capital in these bustling times was a raree show of the finest kind, what with a prince of the blood commanding the garrison, endless funds to carry out his whims, and Halifax the port of the North Atlantic squadron and a source of men and supplies for the West Indian campaign.

I looked with interest at Citadel Hill, whose green cone, surmounted by a rotten blockhouse and a crumbling earthen battery, had so long stood guardian over the town. It was green no more. In the five years since the French war began a multitude of soldiers, militiamen, town workmen, and wild Negro Maroons brought north from Jamaica had fallen upon it like a swarm of ants, sheared the whole top off the hill, and thrown it into the ravines and hollows of the slope, ay, and shifted the very slopes, so that the rough sugar loaf of the old days was now a mathematical pyramid. And now they had built a moated fort on the squat new summit, with walls and bastions of heavy mortared stone, with quarters for two regiments inside, and emplacements for an arsenal of cannon brought out from England at a time when England herself was in great peril of invasion.

"All very fine for the Halifax merchants," grumbled Mr. Pride, as if he had not sold a stick of timber to the commissary general in five years. "But tsha!—what's the good of it, any of it? The French are too busy running all over Europe to bother their heads about North America. All these men and guns should ha' been striking at the French in Hispaniola. As it is, the British haven't force enough in the West Indies to defend their own islands, let alone conquer more, and the fleet's pretty well tied down in convoy work. That's why they want private ships o' war to carry the war against the enemy. Well, we'll not complain so long as they give us what we want."

I had not visited Halifax in his company before, and felt something of his importance when he introduced me to his merchant friends as "my daughter's intended." They gave me a welcome and a deference that was strange when I thought of my coasting-skipper days, wandering friendless about the streets. They pressed us to stay at their fine homes in the upper streets, but Mr. Pride preferred an inn downtown. "It means a tavern bill, of course," he said a little gloomily, "but our business is down here." Then he astounded me, pulling forth a new leather purse and dropping it on the table before me. "Nathan, you'll be meeting people as my son and heir by and by. You should look the part. There's sixty guineas in Bank of England notes and gold—get yourself some proper clothes. There's a gentlemen's tailor in Duke Street rated the best in town. Go there. And mind, nothing but the best."

The Duke Street tailor rigged me out in the course of several days with tight white pantaloons, flowered silk waistcoats in the new short mode, double-fronted things with embroidered button-holes; and a fine green tail coat with clouded buttons, a pink one with gilt buttons, and a stout everyday blue one with brass buttons. And I bought two pairs of Hessian boots with bullion tassels, a wide black hat cocked up at the front and back that caught the summer breeze like a ship's mainsail, a small glazed billycock hat with a curled and jaunty brim that sat much better; and a snuffbox of tortoise shell and a sword cane with a thin and evil Solingen blade concealed in the Malacca. I bought shirts both plain and ruffled, cravats of all hues, a pair of gray kid gloves, and silk stockings, some white, some black, and some with embroidered clocks.

I had never possessed or spent so much money at one time in my life, and I confess I enjoyed every penny and every minute, thinking on the long memory of shabby sailors' slops that went before. And my astonishing foster father seemed to enjoy it even more than I, bidding me turn this way and that while he admired my purchases, and clapping me on the back and crying, "Now, Nathan, you look the part! Now we shall let these people see us and wine and dine us as they wish!"

Wined and dined we were, by merchants and officials all toad-eating Mr. Pride in a manner that tickled my humor, knowing how brusque they were with lesser folk. And whenever Mr. Pride mentioned, with a preliminary scrape of his throat, "the forth-coming happy event," there was a toast to my future happiness, another to the charming bride-to-be, and a third to the continued prosperity of the family.

Several of the merchants placed their carriages at our pleasure, and I remember lolling in the shining comfort of one upon a sunny afternoon when our spanking pair of grays overtook a familiar tandem opposite the Parade. In it sat my Mrs. Sherring with a gallant I had never seen before, a young officer of the garrison. I doffed my billycock with a flourish and bowed as we drew abreast, and she looked at me very hard under her bonnet's brim with curiosity and then amazement in her clear blue eyes. Her lips parted as if to speak, but no words came; and that is the last memory I have of her, openmouthed and staring in her curricle in the midst of Barrington Street.

I was only one of her toys, and I shall never know what turned her fancy to the tarry and red-haired young seaman that I was; but she was generous as she was demanding, she was kind, and she taught me much I did not know about the way of women and the world. I am grateful to her to this day. For a young man, poor and lonely, there can be more comfort in one riggish woman with a heart than in twenty virtuous ones without.

His Majesty's dockyard was a busy place, a world of men with the hard mark of the sea upon them—and the marks of war, for I never saw so many peg legs, patched eyes, empty sleeves, hooks where there should have been hands, or so many scars and powder burns, in one place in my life. It was the practice to find jobs for such poor devils in the Royal Navy's shore establishments; nevertheless I was surprised and a little chilled, seeing how many they were, and realizing suddenly that sea fighting, under the gilt and glory, was nothing but a butcher's business.

We threaded our way amongst gray ironstone buildings with wooden roofs and long rows of peering dormers. The walks were kept very trim, with cobblestone gutters at the sides, and amongst the buildings there were little squares and circles and ovals of mown grass, old figureheads in unexpected corners, a tall flagstaff, and a mighty brass bell in a wooden tower from which a sentry rang the hours and half hours in quick paired strokes, ship fashion.

The long jetty was lined with ships. A big seventy-four lay alongside the sheer hulk, with riggers swinging the masts out of her. A sloop of war was hove down in the careening basin, her royal yardarms touching the grass on the slope above, and the smoke of breaming torches rolling up thick and black about her hull as if she had gone to some nautical hell. Offshore a frigate and a pair of ten-gun brigs awaited their turn at the sheers or the careenage, with bumboats clustered about them and liberty boats plying back and forth.

From all of this, ashore and afloat, arose a mingled uproar that made our modest shipyard at Gosport seem as quiet as the grave—sailors shouting at their tasks, gangs of dockyard workers at theirs, a shrilling of boatswains' pipes, clank of capstan pawls, creak of tackles, rattle of chains, a constant musketry of dropped planks in the timber stores; and all the sounds of all the trades within the gray stone workshops—calkers, shipwrights, blacksmiths, tinsmiths, brass founders, coppersmiths, carvers, painters, gilders, boatbuilders, spar makers, and the rest.

"This is the tune of Rule Britannia," said Mr. Pride in a solemn tone in which I detected a note of complaint. "A very costly music, Nathan, when ye stop to think on't."

The commissioner's quarters lay upon a small point between the boat slips and a huge stone mast house, with the mast pond and canal beyond. The house was an imposing one with a high-pillared portico facing the yard, tall windows, a cluster of mighty chimneys, a belvedere and a railed walk on the roof. We were ushered into a big chamber with cable-and-anchor designs carved in the cornices and about the mantel. At a stout mahogany desk sat a fussy and all-important fellow in blue who greeted Mr. Pride and me with a grudging sort of courtesy, as if he were facing something much against his taste and principles.

The way had been prepared for us by Mr. Pride's powerful connections, not least of them Governor Johnnie Wentworth himself; but the Navy's opinion of privateers was in Mr. Commissioner's face and in the face of the ordnance officer who came at his summons. There was a long document for Mr. Pride to sign, requiring all men to know by these presents—(the commissioner read it aloud, as if we were all men)—that Mr. Amos Pride of Gosport, Province of Nova Scotia, merchant, was held and firmly bound unto Clement Horton Esquire, Storekeeper of His Majesty's Ordnance at Halifax, in the full sum of £920 sterling money of Great Britain—and so on—and so on. And whereas an application had been made by the aforesaid Amos Pride unto Admiral George Vandeput, commander in chief of His Majesty's squadron on this station, to be supplied with ten six-pounder iron guns, and two nine-pounder iron guns, and one long nine-pounder brass swivel gun, and certain other stores set forth in the valuation attached hereto—and so on—um!—redelivery within three months after the conclusion of the war, or in case of their loss or capture the said Amos Pride shall pay the full value thereof—um!

—if all conditions faithfully complied with, this bond to be null and void—um! Sign here if you please!

The attached valuation set forth to a penny the cost of the "certain other stores" we were to have—round shot, grapeshot, bar shot, ladles, sponges, wad hooks, powder horns, muskets, pistols, cutlasses, pikes, wadding, paper cartridges, flannel cartridges, copper powder measures, tubs of match, kegs of powder—everything a warlike mind could think of. I thought of my foster father's mind, and those old sea days of which he spoke so seldom and on which he must have thought so much, and I marveled how he could be so calm and precise now, stooping to sign the documents, complaining about His Majesty's pen, and the value His Majesty set upon his stores, and the scandalous money risks a private man must take who desired to serve his country nowadays, and charging me to see that all these guns and goods were safely put aboard the *Sally* for Gosport when she moored at the gun wharf tomorrow.

We dined that evening with Sir John and Lady Wentworth at Government House, a rambling wooden mansion set in gardens between Granville and Hollis streets just above the market place. I was awed at the great table with its glittering display of glass and silverware no less than by the presence of the governor and his lady, his naval and military aides—a haughty pair, and our fellow guest, none other than Admiral Vandeput himself. Tall menservants in hair powder and livery stood solemnly behind each chair, and a procession of others, chosen apparently for their size like grenadiers, passed in and out with food or empty dishes, as silent and as wooden-faced as Indians.

Lady Wentworth was a dark slender woman rippling and shimmering in a gown of scarlet silk that seemed chosen to chime with her very gallant reputation. She had kept Halifax agog with her affairs for years, one of them with wild young Prince William when he served on the Halifax station; but now she was fifty-odd, a beauty still in a somewhat haggard fashion, with a restless, petulant look about her that made me sorry for Sir John. He was rising sixty, a chunky ruddy-faced man who had spent much time in the forest in his younger years. Both he and his wife were loyalists from New Hampshire.

The aides, a pair of snobs in gorgeous uniforms, looked down their noses at us. Admiral Vandeput, a rough old dog in a wig and a blue coat with the fouled anchor very prominent upon its large silver buttons, devoted himself to the food and drink. He was a noted guzzler and wencher, well hated in Halifax, where his pressgangs roamed the streets; and I don't doubt he had his opinion of Mr. Pride and me, prospective owners of a squadron of privateers, making demands on him for guns and stores, and soon to compete with him for seamen ashore and, worse, for prizes afloat.

Mr. Pride was no table talker, and I was no talker at all; but we were little called upon. The Wentworths held the conversation like a ball, tossing it back and forth from head to foot of the table, and most of it had to do with "this hovel" in which they had to live. While those mum grenadiers of lackeys plied us with turtle soup, boiled salmon fresh from the nets, fried breasts of partridge, broiled chicken, roast beef, a delicious sugar-cured bear ham, and a great variety of confections and wines, we heard a duet of complaint about the mansion—too old, too small, too moldy, too hot in summer, too cold in winter, and (in Lady Wentworth's voice) too odiously near the fish market.

Sir John had been harrying the legislature for years to build a mansion worthy of his high office and his fashionable lady, and now for two hours we heard the dismal story. I was wickedly amused and I confess a little flattered. There was an air about Sir John which said to us very distinctly, "I have done something for you, now you must do something for me." This invitation to dinner, the dinner itself, the presence of Old Put, and all this pointed harangue, were tributes to the power and influence of Mr. Amos Pride of Gosport, in the Province of Nova Scotia, merchant—and I could not help thinking how someday this power and this deference should be mine.

After dinner, in the glum presence of Old Put, and after Lady Wentworth had withdrawn, Sir John presented Mr. Pride with the all-important letter of marque, signed by himself as representative of the King, which gave our privateer authority to seize and make prize any ship of His Majesty's enemies encountered on the seas. Mr. Pride accepted it politely, without looking at it, a picture of indifference, and we took our leave. But in our chambers in the inn he unrolled the thing eagerly and scanned it with a hard yellow eye. He muttered now and then. At the end he threw the scroll on the table and said to me with a sour smile, "Well, Nathan, there's our license to trade upon the French and Spanish—and let's hope His Majesty will find other enemies before the year is out. A mill like ours can use all kinds of grist. Privateering's a business now like any other except that it's hedged about with His Majesty's provisos and whereases. First, we must put up a bond of £2,000—to be forfeit if our privateer oversteps the letter of her letter o' marque in the way of captures on the seas. Second, every prize taken must be brought all the way north to Nova Scotia for the consideration of the Vice-Admiralty Court. That means an admiralty judge at Halifax with a fat salary to earn, and a hundred lawyers and other land sharks swarming about us. Third, when our capture is properly condemned by the court as legal prize, we must sell ship and cargo at vendue in a public manner and after proper advertisement, et cetera, et cetera —a fine to-do. All in all we'll be lucky to rescue a third of the value of each prize we take, and then we must pay the crew's share before we touch a penny ourselves. Well! Give us prizes enough and we'll rub a penny or two in spite of all.

"But, Lord, Nathan, the way they hedge us about with laws and regulations and expect us to do miracles! That's the Admiralty of it: they ask us to risk our necks and fortunes in war against the King's enemies, but they can't abide a fair reward. That's why they put so many sticky fingers in the way of the prize money. Still, it's the only trade open to us now that the Caribbees are crawling with French privateers, and we must make the best of it. Yes, that's it. Make the best of it."

On the following day I saw those Admiralty stores safely aboard the *Sally*. On the next I rode ahorseback with a young merchant named Hartshorne along the shore of Bedford Basin, and saw the lodge where Prince Edward kept his charming *Canadienne,* with a barrack full of soldiers hard by the road to guard his privacy, and what was called a "telegraph," a frantic toy which, as far as I could see, consisted of nothing but flags and pennants and black wicker baskets going up and down a flagstaff in a constant flutter, that somehow kept Citadel Hill informed of all the prince's whims.

We dined at Three Mile House and in the evening attended a theater in Argyle Street, where Mr. Powell's company performed what seemed to me a very dull play indeed, although young

Hartshorne found it marvelous—young officers of the prince's regiment playing female roles in false curls and borrowed gowns, and Powell's thin wife and bulging daughter in the breeches parts.

I returned late to the inn and as I approached our chambers heard a sound of high voices within. The door revealed Monsieur Dolainde engaged in a furious quarrel with my foster father. The little Frenchman seemed more shriveled than ever; the shabby wine-stained clothes hung on his meager frame as if thrown there by a careless chambermaid, and his gesticulating snuff-stained hands were yellow claws. His weak blue eyes were bloodshotten, his tongue thick, his hair wild. He must have come straight to our inn from a bad session with the cards at Mrs. Jessop's.

They ceased their argument as I came in, and for a moment there was an awkward silence—Mr. Pride's face as dark as thunder, and Dolainde gazing at us both with an absurd defiant air, like a drunken little sparrow.

I asked, "What's the matter?" but I knew. The Frenchman had come again for money and been refused.

"I've just told Monsieur," Mr. Pride said, biting off the words with his thin lips, "his notes are worthless. Absolutely."

"You have small faith in your armies, you English!" Dolainde sneered.

"We have less in the chances of you royalists from Hispaniola."

Dolainde threw himself into a chair and lay outstretched, heels on edge upon the floor and his thin body one straight line, with that unkempt head sunk down against his shoulders. In this attitude his chin tuft stuck out, twitching with his muttered words like the tail of a worm-hunting robin.

"Money! That is all you think about, Pride, my friend. Someday you will be dead, and what good will all your dollars do you then?"

"That," said Mr. Pride severely, "seems to have been your philosophy, all you creoles, all this time. You lived like kings—but kings lose their properties and oftentimes their heads."

"I still have mine, *mon ami;* my head—and something better still."

There was something in the way he said this. I regarded him curiously. He did not seem so drunk now as I had thought at first. Into his bleared eyes had come a look of cunning, of desperation, I was not sure what. There was a cynical smile on his lips and a sudden positive air about him where before there had been nothing but despair.

"What besides?" said Mr. Pride sharply.

Dolainde bared his small yellow teeth in a smile that had no pleasure in it. His eyes were watchful now.

"You remember those chests we brought from Cap François?"

"Yes! Full of poor Madame's clothes."

"True. And do you remember, *mon ami,* what you told our young friend here? I can hear you now—'Fool! Dolt!'—that is what you called him—you remember, Monsieur Nathan? 'You have brought the wrong chests!'—that is what you told him—you who think of nothing but money all the time."

"Well?"

"Suppose one told you there is money, a fortune—thirty thousand louis d'or is a fortune, is it not?—even to you, m'sieu, who have so very much—thirty thousand golden louis reposing even now on the Haut du Cap, concealed in the Manoir Dolainde—eh?"

"I'd not believe you," Mr. Pride said, and there was a thin sweat on his face.

"Ah! Then believe this, *mon ami.* Not all we creoles were blind as you seem to think. What, do you think that I, for example, could ever forget that once I was a poor adventurer, a Brother of the Cays like you, yourself, with nothing but my two hands, one to take what I could from the world and the other to guard my head? A man does not forget those things so easily. When I went ashore into Saint Domingo—which you English insist on calling Hispaniola—and found that sun and earth and the sweat of black men could be turned into sugar and rum and coffee, and so into gold—I kept some of the gold. Only a part of it, you understand? I married. We lived well. I built the *manoir*. I bought more slaves each year. But some of the money I put aside. Do you know why? I had no thought of a revolution there, much less in France—Dieu! Who did? What I saw, monsieur, was the blacks, always the blacks, the savages from Africa, like a pot of boiling tar that gleams, that bubbles, that stinks, that someday will boil over into the fire and flare and destroy everything. That is what I saw. And every night I heard their drums talking, grumbling amongst the hills and over the plain, like thunder that is small and far, that might upon some other night draw near and boom and shake the earth and rain down lightnings. Yes. That was it. My poor Luz had no fear of them. Our little Lia loved them. But I—I knew, down in my heart I knew."

I glanced at Mr. Pride casually and got a shock. His yellow eyes that could be so clear and cold and merciless, like the eyes of a hunting owl that sees the coming of night, those eyes were all fire now. In the deep sockets of his bony face they burned like candles in a skull. I knew the greed for gain that drove him by day and filled his dreams by night, so that he had no rest, waking or sleeping. I had seen him angered often, alert always, sometimes even amused. But I had never seen him quite like this. They say that the sight, the sound, or even the thought of gold—the metal itself, I mean, the evil yellow metal with its fat and greasy feel, its dull glimmer and its duller chink—sends some men a little mad. And that is the way my foster father looked to me in the stuffy little chamber of the inn, in the presence of the man Dolainde, in the heart of that night-fallen town where we had come for such cold things as guns and papers and the blessing of King George.

He cried, "You swear, Dolainde—you swear this is true?"

"Swear? I will do more—I will go to Saint Domingo with you, *mon ami,* or any of your captains who will give me passage, and if I cannot show you thirty thousand louis in the *manoir,* let me die! So!" The haggard little gambler sat up swiftly, seized his waistcoat lapels and wrenched them violently apart as if to bare his breast to a dagger, so that the china buttons flew all over the room. In any other man, at any other time, the gesture might have been absurd. But there was a fanatic light in Dolainde's weak blue eyes to match the greedy light in Mr. Pride's. A profound silence. I think we did not even breathe. I was excited with the strangeness of the moment and with something more—perhaps with a sense of what might come of this affair, struggle, fear, pain, wild deeds in wilder places, love, hate, death—ay, who knows?

'Twas relief when Mr. Pride spoke. His eyes had that wild fire but his voice was calm, was cold as ice. "Dolainde, if you think to get more money on the strength o' this pretty tale, you're mistaken in your man. But if you mean what you say, I'll take that offer. I'm fitting a privateer for the southward, a cruise in the Caribbees against the enemies of His Majesty. And if I choose to seek His Majesty's enemies in Hispaniola, who's to say me nay? The Manoir Dolainde is not far from the coast, a few hours' walk for active men; and you shall go for guide, Dolainde. And this shall be our bargain. If my seamen find the gold you promise, I want twenty thousand louis for the satisfaction of your debt, for interest accrued, and for the risk I have run in all these matters. The rest is yours."

Again Dolainde displayed his yellow teeth, his mirthless smile.

"Twenty thousand louis for a debt of ten thousand guineas? How generous you are, m'sieu! When do we sail?"

Chapter 15

WE LAUNCHED the brigantine on a day in June, a burning blue day after a night of rain, with a moist heat wavering over the sodden chips and shavings of the yard. Locusts shrilled in the river pastures. A smell of hot pine forest drifted down the river and through the town. In the garden the apple trees and Felicity's lilacs and Dutch tulips were in bloom. The fields were bright with buttercups and daisies, the forest clearings edged with huckleberry and blueberry blossoms; the swamps in places were a shining living blue of flowering flag.

It was a good day for a holiday, and I think the whole of Gosport came to see the launching. Our preacher was there to give a blessing, supported by the rival preacher lately brought in by the Methody people. All the magistrates came, with old Mr. Frude tottering at their head; and Pearce, the excise officer, that pinched and shabby man, trade-fallen like so many in our town (for he lived on his fees, and there had been precious few these past five years), and all the merchants and shipowners, a score of hopeful captains, a mob of hopeful seamen. Even Victor Brule was there, laughing and pinching the fish-lot girls, spreading a little pool of mirth about him with his agile tongue and fingers. For of course there were many women, old and young, most of them figged out in their best caps and ribbons for the great affair; and a swarm of giggling little girls and a froth of small boys and dogs.

The shipyard lay below the hill on which the big house stood, and the hollow made a natural theater for these crowding folk. The brigantine's jib boom reached clean over Water Lane, so that carts drove underneath, and her twin masts rose and towered high above the sheds and warehouses with bunting of all colors strung from yardarm to yardarm, like tall West Indian trees in flower. She glistened, she seemed to quiver on the stocks as if she knew her time had come and yearned for the water; she was so beautiful that no one, least of all a seaman, could look at her without a lump in his throat.

Her name remained a secret to the very last. There had been a queer little passage on the yesterday, when the family walked about the yard on that last evening of the brigantine's repose. Felicity had said carelessly, "You'll name her after me, I suppose?"

"Of course!" said Ma'am Pride sharply.

"Hum!" said my foster father, halting the little march. "My dear, if you knew how seamen curse their ship, however affectionately, in all seasons and on all occasions, you'd think twice on't. It's always amused me that ladies should so cry to have ships named after 'em—d'ye want to be damned up and down the world? Nunno! She shall have a name that's been cursed aforetime in this town and grown used to it—never mind what. You'll find out soon enough."

"Then let me christen her," Felicity said stoutly.

"Nonsense! A woman christen a ship? Who ever heard o' such a thing? Nunno, my dear. The brigantine is mine, all mine, my dream, my constant thought for five long years; and only the beginning, mark you—the forerunner of a fleet to come. I've put my money into her when every fool in the town was crying ruin and at prayers for peace—as if nothing could be plucked from war! I'll christen her myself."

And so he did. When the great moment came he mounted the scaffold at the bow and turned to the silent people on the slope.

"Listen, you people!" he cried in a harsh high voice that rang in the hot afternoon like a trumpet. "Listen, you nigglers who never yet saw beyond your noses' ends! Long ago when I was only a petty merchant in this town I built the big house on the hill yonder, and you laughed up your sleeves, and said Amos Pride would wake up someday and rue his notion. And you gave my house a name, a name that sticks, though you've waked up yourselves long since. Now I've built a privateer, and all your tongues are wagging once again. Listen then, fools!"

He turned and smashed a bottle of Madeira on the stem with such a force that his knuckles struck the hard oak in a welter of wine and broken bottle glass, and he cried aloud, "I name thee *Pride's Fancy!* Go on, Parson!" And our preacher, poor old man, teetering nervously on the scaffold plank at his side, quavered in a voice that only God could hear distinctly, "Lord, watch upon this ship . . . this ship . . . and all who sail in her . . ."

Skillful axmen had split the blocks beneath her, and with his own sure hand Job Eames had undertaken the sawing of the launching plank, the single piece of pine that like a navel cord still joined her to the place of her creation. The ways had been well greased with tallow and fish gurry. Job had been around the hull full twenty times to see all clear, but he was pale for all that, his broad face pimpled with anxious sweat.

When you have seen a ship conceived, when you have watched her come to birth term chip by chip and stroke by stroke, there is something awesome in the moment when she comes to life and moves. You know the trick of it. You tell yourself it is no more than seeing a new sulky trundled from the carriage maker's, or the first flight of a paper kite. And then—ah, who can describe it, the mystery, the wonder and the beauty of the birth of a ship that takes your breath and stills your heart as if your own life did not matter any more, or the fist-clenching anxiety that grips you from the first faint shudder until the moment when she takes the water and sits safely in the breast of Mother Sea?

Job's saw rasped through the last fiber of the plank, and he remained there in the long clean shadow of the bowsprit, on his knees, a prayerful attitude, staring at her forefoot. For several awful moments nothing happened. Then the hull trembled, budged, began to slide, very slowly at first—my eye was measuring her stem against the corner of the mold loft—and gathered speed with a faint hiss and a growing rumble and a loud and louder groaning of the hard-pressed ways. Women and children, ay, and our preacher, timid man, shrank away then, seeing a menace in this moving mass that stood so far into the sky, as if the whole might topple sideways and come crashing down amongst them like a felled pine in the forest.

Her stern took the water with a mighty splash, shearing the high tide in two waves flung up and outward that looked for a moment like a pair of great scallop shells, curved, fluted, gleaming in the sunshine. We found our voices then and lifted them in a shout as the brigantine shot into the tide the full length of herself and dipped her sprit in a graceful curtsy to the yard, to the floating wreckage of the launching ways, to the waving handkerchiefs and hats. Mr. Pride's words were forgotten, for the moment all the town's hatred of the Prides was forgotten. In the presence of that lovely thing the people shouted and capered, the very dogs barked in a passion of excitement. And every man had worship in his eyes.

A long cable had been passed between her stern bitts and a capstan on a wharf upstream, ready for the launching, and after the first swift surge the gang on the wharf heaved in upon it cheerily, roaring a stave from throats well tuned with Mr. Pride's rum and stamping round and round. But before the warp took hold, and with precious little else to account for it—there was no current in the lower reach of the river at high tide, and on this hot June day no breath of wind—the brigantine began to swing her bow towards the harbor mouth.

"See!" Job Eames cried, all smiles now but sweating still. "She knows the way! An omen! An omen!"

I heard a muttered oath from Lot Mayes at my side and turned to twit him for a breach of his cherished piety—and saw my foster father standing under the now empty scaffolding and wrapping his handkerchief about a hand that dripped red on the shavings at his feet. The flying bottle glass had cut him badly.

"Blood!" Lot said, and his eyes bulged. "There's the real omen, and a pretty one it is, for all the preacher and his calling on the Lord. I say God save that ship and all who sail in her!"

"Then you wouldn't," I said lightly, "given the chance?"

He gave me a hard look and then grinned in a sheepish way. Most of Lot's teeth had gone long ago, and the sunken mouth in the long face gave him a very grim expression in repose; but now the tucked lips opened and the gape was huge.

"I'd give an eye—my right arm for the bare chance, Nathan. Well ye know it!"

That very evening, in the first hot dark, with June bugs knocking like flung stones against the closed panes and flitting in the open ones and dashing at the candles, Mr. Pride put before me the matter of a crew. He saw no need of beating up for men as the privateers' custom had been in the old wars. The town and countryside were full of men without two ha'pence to their names, ready to join anything. Besides, beating up meant an open house at some tavern or other, with the seamen getting drunk and noisy at the owner's expense. And all that silly business of marching up and down the streets with flag and drum—tsha!

I said slowly, "I think it should be done, sir, nonetheless. It's the custom, and the men will look for it—a chance to swagger a bit for the admiration of the girls; and where's the harm in a drink or two and a song together, and a hornpipe on the tavern floor? There'll be small chance of such things in the days to come."

"I trust so, Nathan, anyhow," with a forbidding smile. "I seem to recall that men fight best on short commons and a longish bit o' chastity. Well, we'll beat up, then—but I tell you I'll set a limit on the tavern bill. Two shillings a man, and charge to my account. They'll growl, o' course, but let 'em! They were growling in the yard today—for my hearing, o' course, saying Mister This and Merchant That always stood a cask o' rum at the head o' the slip so the people could drink a ship's success at the launching. As if I hadn't spent money enough on the ship itself, and all their wages and the rest. In these times, too! Well, enough o' that—who's to be captain? Lathrop? He's done well with the *Dawn* in convoy voyages and knows the Caribbees right well."

I made a mouth. "Too safe a man. You want a cut-and-thrust fellow for this work."

"What about Swinney?"

"Too old."

"Carson, then. Or Babcock, say?"

Again my mouth. "Not a word of French or Spanish in the pair of 'em."

"We could get a linguister and sign him on. And anyhow, Dolainde goes in the ship. He speaks——"

"So! But how far could your captain trust a linguister or even Dolainde in such a matter as you have in mind?"

I suppose I was trembling a little. I know my voice shook, for Mr. Pride turned his gaze from the ceiling and looked at me sharply. "Damme, Nathan, what's the matter with ye? Who shall we take, then?"

"Me!"

Up went his thick black brows in bristling arches like a pair of angry black cats. A yellow flame played in the eyes beneath.

"This is no time for joking, Nathan, we must——"

"I'm mortal serious, sir. I'm a qualified shipmaster, I know the Caribbees; especially I know Hispaniola and the country round about Dolainde's estate. I speak French well, and Spanish well enough. What's more, I've learned a good deal of the mixed tongue the Negroes speak in those parts."

"What! How?"

"From Dolainde and his daughter."

"Ah!" His lips looked sour. "I'd no idea you'd pay so much attention to your lessons, Nathan—or to the Dolaindes. Well, the thing's impossible, that's flat. I need ye here. All the other ships to build and fit—and when the prizes begin to come in there'll be business enough with sea lawyers and admiralty courts to drive the pair of us horn-mad."

"I tell you I must go master of the brigantine."

He stared at me hard. He was a judge of men. He must have seen the set of my mind no less than the set of my jaw. His voice took on a querulous note.

"Why, Nathan? Why in the name o' common sense and reason must ye go? Gosport's full o' shipmasters, but I've only one son —for I count you my son now, ye know. My heir, damme! I've risked good money in the ship, and I'm about to risk the ship in a venture to the south, even this venture of Dolainde's—I've taken bigger chances in my time for less and come out square. But not you, Nathan boy. I can't risk you."

I stared him in the eye. "I tell you I must take the brigantine on this cruise. My heart is set on it."

He frowned. "When did ye get this wild notion, Nathan?"

"When I saw her take the water this noon."

"The whim of a moment!" He sat back with a baffled look on his long face. "I confess I find you hard to understand, Nathan. When I told you of your future you were pleased. Your face shone. It did my heart good just to see that look o' yours. And there's Felicity—you're to marry Felicity in July, had ye forgot? She's told her friends—the servants know—all Gosport knows. What'll she think—and what'll the gossips say if ye go traipsing off to the Caribbees a week or two before the wedding day?"

I felt my lips go tight. How could I explain to him or to Felicity that I must go in the brigantine because every plank and timber had been cut beneath my eye, that everything about her down to the last lick of paint was somehow part of me, not to be separated, because she was all my longings put together in one shining beauty, made for the sea—and the sea for both of us? Such things are not to be explained. They are, and nothing's to be said. I could not have told him why, any more than an eel three years upriver could say why it must go down to the sea with the rains and the October moon.

But I knew I must say something. And so, sullenly, I blurted out, "These things you offer me are fine. I want them well enough. But a lifetime's very long to be sitting on a chair and casting figures on paper—and whatever else I must be doing here ashore. I'm young. I know the life of a seaman and like it. I want one fling at the sea before it's all too late. Too late—that's it! I've waited long enough."

"And if I say no?"—in a cold voice, and inspecting the lint bandage on his cut hand.

"Then," I said wildly, "I'll go anyhow—in the brigantine or some other, somewhere, anywhere! Oh yes! You can't hold me—you nor any man. Why should I spend my whole life doing what you say, and nothing to look back on? I'm my own master and I love the sea—and do you think you can moor me to your coat tails with your damned inheritance? Is that it? I tell you——"

"Nathan!" he cried, and there was a sort of whimsical sadness in his eyes that made me put a stopper on my tongue. "Lord, Nathan, how like your mother ye were then! She—— But never mind that. Nathan, I know how ye feel. I was young once myself, ay, and a seaman. I know this crazy longing for the sea, for adventure, for a chance to try your strength against the world. There's nothing in it, boy, nothing but the salt at the bottom of the cask. The rest is a dream that fades and goes with time and sour acquaintance. Hold fast to what's real, what can be touched, ay, taken in the grasp. All else is folly. I know, I tell ye! Didn't I waste good years of my own youth down there in the Caribbees, chasing wild geese with a pinch o' salt? I know, I tell ye! Ah, what wouldn't I give to be you, Nathan, and all my time before me!"

He paused and regarded me solemnly; I said nothing.

"Um! So your mind's made up. There's nothing else for it, then. You're five-and-twenty and your own master, as you say, though I protest you've been a son to me and I'd expected something of a son's obedience, in mind of all I've done for you. Very well, she's yours for the cruise. For one cruise only—that's the bargain, eh?"

"One cruise," I agreed recklessly, feeling a little remorse at the pained look in his face, the tired note in his voice.

"Give me your hand on it, Nathan." He rose from the chair, and we shook hands, a long hard grasp, in silence. And then, all over the house, the clocks began to strike the hour of twelve.

In that medley of whirring cogs and beaten gongs and bells, and the insane cry of a German cuckoo in the upper staircase, we took our candles and went off to bed. I was impatient for the morning and my new command. Who would not feel that life was slipping past in nothing-doing, when time cried so loudly in his ears?

Chapter 16

I NAILED the notice to the tavern door myself, all written out in Mr. Pride's own bold hand with gallant downstrokes and important scrolls, and when that was done I stood back to admire his handiwork:

ALL BRISK LADS

Who wish to Strike a Blow for their Country and at the same time fill their pockets with Prize Money, are Invited to sign articles in That Fast New and Well Built Brigantine *Pride's Fancy,* private ship of war, mounting ten 6-pdr. and two 9-pdr. carriage guns, and One Long Brass 9-pdr. Swivel Gun, and now Fitting for a Cruize to the Southward against the French and Spanish enemies of His Majesty. Captain Nathan Cain will make a rendezvous at the Sign of the Half Moon in Dock Street, between the hours of Nine each morning and Four each afternoon until the muster roll is filled. A hearty Welcome is assured, and rum flip and Stingo for each Honest Volunteer.

GOD SAVE THE KING

The King's Head was our largest tavern, where captains and merchants met to discuss voyages and to underwrite cargoes like a little provincial Lloyd's Coffee House, but I had chosen Mrs. Owen's ordinary in Dock Street because 'twas nearer to the wharves where the seamen lingered, and because the widow needed all the custom she could get. Mr. Pride, remarking that her prices would be lower, had cheerfully agreed.

And so from nine to four I sat at a deal table in her taproom, with the article sheets and muster roll and an inkpot and half a dozen sharp new quills before me, while Goody Owen herself stood at the bar with a new-tapped rum keg at her elbow, a regiment of strong-beer bottles ranged along the shelves at her back, and a pair of small iron loggerheads in the fire to heat the flip.

I had chosen my officers already, ranking them man-o'-war fashion as Governor Wentworth recommended: Lot Mayes for first lieutenant—how his old slack face lit up when I told him!—and Simon Dawkins for second. For gunner I chose Pardon Gardner, who had served his time in the Royal Navy at that rate. These three stood in a group just inside the Half Moon's doorway as the men came in, looking them up and down and tipping me a wink, a nod or a shake of the head as each volunteer stepped to the table.

I had expected some difficulty in filling my roll, for war was a dangerous business after all and the Caribbees a very far cry from home, but men came in a steady trickle all day long. Some of them surprised me—Shanks, the schoolmaster, was one. I asked what he could do aboard a ship. He thought a moment and said, "I play a very fair tune upon the fife." Everyone laughed, but I signed him nonetheless, and a stout boy for drummer, because I wanted music in my ship.

I did not have to look far for a cook; Black Boston was there, grinning all over his broad black face, and with a Negro youth, a nephew of his, to be his mate. For boatswain I took Michael Brady, the giant Irishman who had drifted into Gosport from a man-o'-war and taken up with a Portugee woman on the back road.

At noon I broke my labors, ordered a stiff round of flip for the signed men, and sent them off to parade the streets with Simon Dawkins at their head, a big red ensign tossing on a pole, and the schoolmaster and the boy playing valiantly to the tune of "A

Stout Heart and a Thin Pair o' Breeches Goes thro' the World, Brave Boys."

A rabble of boys and dogs ran beside them and behind, and girls and women came flying to doors and windows along the way; and yet it was a sorry show, the men all out of step, shouting and singing as if they were going to a fair, dressed in the common gray or brown homespun jackets and tongs, red shirts, gray shirts, checkered white-and-black shirts, a pair of greasy leather breeches here and there, or wide canvas trousers cut off at half-mast and exposing the gray woolen shanks; and they wore moccasins, sea boots waterproofed with fish oil, shoes of all sorts and conditions, and hats thrice cocked, or cocked fore and aft, or cocked with a single leather button before or behind, or wing-and-wing like a schooner before the wind—and many had the simple red flannel nightcaps of fishermen.

Yet they must have impressed the beholders in some fashion, for in two days and three parades I had my crew, eighty men and boys, some of them sailors familiar with the Caribbee trade before the war, some of them fishermen, and the remainder hunters, loggers, men of every trade known to the river and the town. Mr. Pride himself had chosen the prize masters amongst them, half a dozen trading captains out of a berth since '94, most of them older men than I and none too pleased to call me captain.

Towards the last, indeed when I had called an end, I noticed a tall young Indian lurking shyly in the doorway. I did not know him, and I was folding my sheets when old Moise put his head around the doorpost, saying woodenly, "Cain! You take my son?"

I told Goody Owen to give the old savage a pot of flip, and motioned the young man to the table. He could not write—nor could half my crew, for that matter—and so I told him to make his mark. He took the quill and drew with surprising skill on the paper a little figure of a fox.

"Is that your name?" I said.

He nodded. "Wokwees," he said.

"Very well, my friend. You shall go in the big canoe and do what I say many days until we come to this place again. You understand?"

"Ayah!" said Wokwees solemnly.

Old Moise grinned and belched approval over his flip.

I returned to the house with the papers ink-splattered and well thumbed, and marched with some triumph into the library. Mr. Pride was there—and someone else, someone I had not expected to see again in the big house. It was Victor Brule, a very earnest Brule with a flush on his round olive face, an urgent set of the lips under that lady-killing black mustache. When I entered he was talking at a great rate in his rapid and strongly accented English, but he stopped and there was a ponderous silence.

"Nathan," Mr. Pride said, "this fellow seems to think he can be of service to us."

"In what way?"

"In the matter of—in the particular matter we have in mind."

"How does he know about that?" I demanded, looking at Brule.

"Precisely what I asked him myself." My foster father gave a thin snort and shrugged. "Well, you might guess. Dolainde told his daughter, and of course she told Brule. Our friend here tells me he is very familiar with Hispaniola—once was master of a small sloop in the trade between the Cap and Monte Cristi—

even knew Dolainde—by sight, of course—in the old days. Tells me he saw the *manoir* in '95, two years after Dolainde fled the place—the house still standing, the fields still worked by Dolainde's niggers in a slipshod fashion—they'd found their liberty and fraternity damned poor stuff to eat, I judge. Ha! Well, it looks to me, Nathan, as if you ought to take Brule along."

"He's on parole," I objected. "Suppose we're overhauled by one of His Majesty's ships. They'd question the crew—the deuce to pay."

"Sign him on as a seaman and warn the crew. It's the truth, so far as it goes."

"And what's he want?"

"His freedom, somewhere about the Cap, when he's served our turn. He wants to get home, that's all. He was one o' the poor whites, the *petits-blancs,* and don't give a rap who rules the country now, French or English, black, white, or half-and-half. That right, Brule?"

"Yes! Yes!" cried our whilom barber eagerly. He fixed an imploring blue stare on me like a dog who wants a run. I had not the heart to refuse, though I did not like the notion much. A French prisoner, after all . . . harmless of course . . . and three long years in our cold country, scraping chins and combing wigs for a pittance. A pilot for our venture into Hispaniola. I thought of those reefs in the dark of Cap François.

"Very well," I said.

Brule burst into thanks, joyful and voluble, with a frantic bobbing of his round bullet head that made me smile in spite of myself. And out he went, the image of a happy Frenchman, caroling all the way along the hall and out of the house.

"I wouldn't trust that man too far," said Mr. Pride crisply, "but I've questioned him and he knows the coast of Hispaniola right enough—has been a smuggler, I don't doubt, afore the republic made him an officer if not a gentleman. Well, I've always held a knowing rogue worth ten honest fools in a pinch."

I nodded, wondering how far we could trust Dolainde, who talked so much, or that strange sullen daughter of his, who hated us all so much. And what was she to Brule? The question troubled me, thinking of the forlorn little creole on the *Sally's* deck that wild night at the Cap, and the way we had let her slip into womanhood, motherless—ay, fatherless, for what care Dolainde had given her—a slender shadow flitting about the house, silent and resentful like a sulky ghost.

Now began a madhouse, the preparation of the new ship for departure—eighty-odd men to be berthed in the confines of a slim hull, the shipping and lashing of guns, the final rigging, the bending of sails; and the checking of stores, the shortages, the demands, the worried quill drivers, the galley firewood, the water butts, the arms chests, the stowage in the magazine; the doubts about the ballast, the questions and arguments and the remaining doubt that only a stiff bit of weather could dispel; the squabble of the prize masters over their berthing arrangements, the discovery of petty shipyard matters wrong or left undone, the last-minute carpentry and joinery.

It dragged on for nearly a fortnight, and sometimes I despaired of getting her to sea, free of all this longshore confusion. But the day came when I sent my quadrant and my plain pine sea chest down to that fine maple-paneled cabin where the sharp smell of new paint hung like a fog, took my stand on the weather side of the poop, ordered the brigantine's lines cast off, and set that eager sprit of hers down the river past the town.

The Pride wharf was a mass of people, many women amongst them, weeping and crying out to men who were too busy jumping under the lash of Lot Mayes's tongue to see or hear them; and there was a knot of folk at each wharf's end as we passed, and a yelling stream of boys and young men and fleet-legged girls along Water Lane, trying to keep abreast of us.

It was not our real departure—but I gave no hint of that. I wanted the *Fancy* over the bar on this day's full tide and anchored well clear of the town as soon as might be; for a number of men, besought by their women or struck with a sudden faintness of heart, were showing signs of quitting at the last moment; and several indignant merchants had appeared on the wharf with the sheriff, his fist full of capias papers, denouncing ten or more of my heroes for absconding debtors pure and simple.

I gave Dolainde the spare standing berth in my cabin and sent Brule to sling a hammock with the prize masters in the afterhold. We anchored in the outer harbor at sunset, well offshore, and after setting the watches I ordered the gig manned, with Michael Brady in charge of it to see that none of the oarsmen thought better of their bargain when the boat touched Fish Point.

I walked alone through the town in the first dark to make my own farewells. I was blithe of heart. I had expected a storm from Ma'am, if not Felicity, when they learned I was to go in the brigantine, what with the putting off of the wedding and all that, but they had taken it calmly enough. Felicity had shrugged and said little, and her mother nothing at all. After all we lived in a seafaring town where such things were commonplace. Courting and wedding and wiving had to wait upon ships always. There were wives in our town, mothers of large families, who had not seen their men two months on end in all their married lives until this war began.

I found my foster father in the familiar setting in which, looking back, I see him best: the windows shrouded now against the night, the lit candles, row on row of books in their cases about the room, the globes on their stands, the mahogany table and chairs, the fireplace swept and empty in the summer weather, the polished brass knobs of the andirons, the conchs at each side, the framed print of Rooke's fleet off Málaga, the cattail rushes and peacock feathers standing out of the Toby jugs on the mantel, the old cutlass on the wall, of which he never spoke, the worn Turkey carpet underfoot.

He was expecting me and had a chart of the Caribbees spread on the table before him, an old thing I had never seen before. (I thought of the crisp new one in my cabin, from the Admiralty stores at Halifax.) His chart was much creased and scored all over with courses plotted long ago, and marked with tarry thumbs at the corners, and the circular stains of grog pots. He gave me a nod and motioned me to the opposite chair, scanning the island-sprinkled sea with his bright yellow eyes and running a long-nailed finger over it.

"There's not much I can tell ye, Nathan—times have changed a great deal since my day in those parts. But here's a point or two. In the first place and the last place, bear in mind that you're a privateer, not a man-o'-war, and don't go flying at anything ye see, like a puppy with a new set o' teeth. Be cautious, don't tackle anything ye can't manage. Steer clear o' warships—ours or theirs. And give French privateers a good berth; they're not worth taking an ye get mauled doing it—dog eat dog and mighty poor business. Remember you're not there to fight if ye can help it. Merchant ships are your game. And even a merchant ship can bear a good look first—some of 'em have nasty teeth, and a waistcloth can conceal a swarm o' men. Never be too sure. But once ye've joined action, fight it out—a faint heart means a lost ship nine times out o' ten. The Hollanders are in the war against us now, so anything French or Spanish or Dutch is legal prize, provided ye can take it.

"You're not likely to meet anything worth while until ye reach the Trades. I'd look about the Bahamas first—the Havana ships have a weakness for the Florida Strait, 'spite o' the British privateers out o' Nassau Town. A week there, say. Then make for the Windward Passage. That's the best hunting ground in the Caribbees, or was in time gone by. Havana ships going southabout, ships for or from the Spanish Main stealing past the Jamaica squadron—um!—take your station off Great Inagua for two weeks—say. Then's the time for your venture into Hispaniola, down there under your lee. Once ye start, don't hesitate. It's all or nothing. The whole island's supposed to be under blockade by His Majesty's ships, but the blockade's a joke—a coast full o' harbors and creeks—too many to watch, and Hispaniola's as long as all Nova Scotia and twice as wide. The republican armies seem to get troops and supplies from France without trouble, and you'll have none if ye mind your eye and pay close attention to Brule and Dolainde. They agree the best chance is to land your party well to the east o' the Cap, somewhere short o' Fort Dauphin——"

"What! That means the whole cultivated plain before us, people everywhere, and a stream or two to cross. The *manoir's* on the slope of the Morne beyond. Why not land to the west of the Cap and climb over the mountain?"

"Think a moment, Nathan, of Dolainde—that palsied sot. Could he scramble over the Morne du Cap? It winds him getting up these stairs."

"Oh!"

"Brule will show ye where to land. From there on Dolainde's your guide. It's only ten or twelve miles by the old plantation roads, flat country, an easy night's journey; a child could make it. Ye won't meet a soul; the plantations were all destroyed in '91 and '93, that whole rich plain's a desert now, I'm told, and the slaves drifted into the town of Cap François or went off to join the black brigades o' the French. Oh, there might be a few people here and there, living in the ruins o' the plantations, but ye know how those Hispaniola niggers are at night—they won't set foot outside a door for fear o' zombies and such heathen nonsense. Take a stout party, Nathan; gold's heavy stuff, and thirty thousand louis is a lot to carry ten miles in the dark. Be sure to reach the *manoir* afore daylight, and keep out o' sight during the day. Make your way back to the ship the following night. Then let Brule go free—but take Dolainde aboard."

"You make it sound mighty easy," I said.

Mr. Pride turned his gaunt face from the chart and gave me a long look. The yellow light was glowing in his eyes.

"I'm a cautious man by nature, Nathan, but I've always believed this—for a bold reward, the bold stroke always, and devil take the man that hesitates."

"And when the gold's aboard, what then?"

"Stow it amongst the ballast or in the cable tier, out o' sight, case a naval boarding party should take a notion to look through the ship. Make sail down the Windward Passage for Jamaiky. In Kingston keep your mouth shut and caution your men, or the admiral on the Jamaiky station'll get his itchy fingers on the money—enemy property, smuggled specie, some such quibble. See Whittendale, my agent there. He'll take it off your hands and send me a bill of exchange on London for't."

"And then?"

"Then?" Mr. Pride exclaimed, hoisting his brows. "Why, go on with your cruise, of course! That's what ye're there for, ain't it? Cruise then, my boy, and show your letter o' marque to any nosy man-o'-war that questions ye. Make for the Mona Passage, say, or down amongst the Virgins and the Loo'ard Isles for a lick at the French trade out o' Guadeloupe and Martinico.

"Watch your weather well in those parts—the hurricanes begin about the end of August, and there's precious little shelter and a lot o' nasty lee. If ye lose a spar or touch ground bad enough to want careening, make for St. Kitts. I've an agent there—you know his name, Ashley, George Ashley—I'm writing him to watch out and give ye any assistance in his power. He deals in ships' stores and can get ye more powder and shot if need be, though I'm told it's hard to come by in the islands since the war began.

"Failing all those places—and mind, it's like trouting up our river here at home, sometimes ye can pick up fish wherever ye cast a line, most times ye've got to try from pool to pool—failing all those, why, go down-wind to the Main and cruise along 'tween Margarita Island and the Cartagena roads. Been famous pickings on that coast in time past. No more galleons full o' gold and silver without escort, like the old tales say. But there's a busy trade along the Main, cargoes o' cocoa, coffee, wine from old Spain, dyewood—don't turn up your nose at dyewood, Nathan, it fetches a mighty good price in Philadelphia or New York; and be sure to save out a few sticks for the fishermen's net pots, here to home.

"Man out your prizes promptly and send 'em off for Halifax. I've given ye six spare masters, that should be enough. Be sure to send along one prisoner in every prize for a davy-man—those blessed admiralty courts ain't satisfied with ships' papers but must have a prisoner's affidavy that she's French- or Spanish- or Dutch-owned, or bound to or from an enemy port. And don't touch neutrals, no matter how fat they look. I stand to lose my bond in such a case." A grim smile. "I've seen the time—but never mind. I think that's all. Is anything not clear?"

I thought a bit. "Hispaniola—what's the state of things within the country, do you know?"

"Um! Well, it's pretty much of a hotchpot by all accounts. The British troops have given up the whole coast except Mole St. Nicholas. They'll try to hang on there, I fancy, to guard the Windward Passage for the sake o' Jamaiky. All the rest o' Hispaniola—including the Spanish part, I'm told—is now in the hands o' the French republican commissioners, who sit at Cap François. Chief commissioner is a radical lawyer from France, a fellow named Sonthonax. But tsha!—the white French troops die like flies in that climate, just like the English died, and the country's really held by black and mulatto armies.

"There's no law nor order anywhere. The south is held by an army of mulattos under a griffe named Rigaud. The rest is pretty much in the hands of a nigger named Toussaint. The French have made him a general, I believe. He used to be a coachman on the Breda estate at the Cap." My foster father snorted. "That's liberty and equality for you, Nathan! Coachmen turn generals, slaves become rulers, and what's the end? France is a madhouse, Europe's a slaughterhouse, and the richest colony in the West Indies is a desert in five years. Mind, not all the whites fled from Hispaniola like Dolainde. A good many hung on, fawning on the republican commissioners—but none o' this concerns us, boy. The point is, the British retreat to Mole St. Nicholas has drawn the French troops towards the nor'west tip o' the island. That's why I say your venture at the Cap should succeed without a shot fired or a blow struck."

I nodded slowly, my head buzzing with these theories and cautions and instructions. I put out a hand, and Mr. Pride grasped it in a way that nipped my bones.

"Good-by, good luck, Nathan, and a safe return. Write from

Jamaiky or St. Kitts, whichever ye fetch first. I'll be anxious—we'll all be anxious—'specially Felicity. She's waiting down the hall to say good-by. Be nice to her, Nathan. It's a blow to her, to all of us—you going off like this."

"Yes," I said, backing away. "Yes of course, sir. Good-by."

"Good-by—good-by—and Nathan——"

"Yes, sir?"

"When ye make port anywhere be sure to anchor in the roads and see the side well guarded lest the men desert—a man's easy tempted from his duty down that way, what with the rum and the mulatto girls."

"I'll have to give the men a run ashore here and there, sir."

"Well, choose some small island where they can't run off. Don't advance 'em money unless they threaten trouble, and keep 'em out o' the dancing houses if ye can. And anchor in the roads, as I say. It saves wharfage bills. And Nathan——"

"Yes, sir?"

"Once you're to sea, muster all hands aft each Sabbath, man-o'-war fashion, and read 'em the Articles o' War. I've furnished the gunner a stout pair o' cat-o'-nine-tails for the punishments—see they're laid on well. And have the men join in prayer for the confusion o' His Majesty's enemies and the success o' this cruise. Seamen should have religion issued regular as beef and biscuit, whether they like it or not. And Nathan——"

I was out of the chamber and part way down the hall. "Sir?"

"Be sparing with your stores; the chandlers' prices in the islands are sheer robbery."

"Yes, yes," I said and turned and fled along the hall.

Chapter 17

I LOOKED into the drawing room. A solitary candle on a side table cast a dim light over the silent pianoforte, the staring portraits, the shapely and uncomfortable Philadelphia furniture, the silken Chinese screen that hid the cold black hearth, the great dull mirror in its frame of Hispaniola mahogany, the sampler beside the mantel which bore the letters of the alphabet and "The Lord Is My Shepherd, Felicity Pride aged ten years, 1786," so very neatly stitched. The single light proclaimed its emptiness, and I was turning away when Mrs. Pride spoke and startled me. In the depths of the great red chair, with its low seat and high back and wings, she sat still and watchful like a small shriveled queen upon a throne.

"Felicity is waiting for you in the garden, Nathan."

"Thank you, ma'am."

"You'll be gone six months, I'm told?"

"It all depends on the luck, ma'am."

"Luck!" sharply. "You think very little of yours, Nathan, your great good fortune—leaving Felicity like this on the wedding eve for some wild business halfway down the world. But you don't care, of course. Men are selfish by nature, and you were headstrong always, and ungrateful. You never loved me, Nathan. Do you love Felicity?"

I could find no simple answer to that. "Love's a thing I don't know much about, ma'am—I never had much in my life that I can recall. Felicity . . . I've looked upon her as a sister for so long that it comes a little strange to think of her as a wife. I dare say she feels the same about me. I think we'll make a happy marriage, if that's what you mean. I find it pleasant to think upon the time when I come back, and she and I will——"

"When you will get your hands on Felicity and the fortune that should have been hers—all hers!" Ma'am Pride's voice was high and shrill.

I pressed my lips together, not liking the words that sprang to my own tongue, and reminding myself how bitter a pill all this must be to her.

She sat stiffly in the great chair, in her plain gray gown and ribboned apron, the great bunch of house keys dangling from a thin chain at her waist, one hand clasping the other in her lap, her small round spectacles in their horn rims pushed up on her lined pale forehead, the frilled white muslin cap set high upon her thin gray hair.

"Go!" she cried. "Go and be damned, Nathan Cain!"

I found Felicity in the garden, standing by the summerhouse that Mr. Pride had copied from one of Prince Edward's at Bedford Basin, a Chinese-pagoda kind of thing, of gilded trelliswork, with several roofs rising one above another like the capes of a traveler's cloak, the eaves of which were festooned with dangling strips of glass and thin brass bells that tinkled in the wind. The wind tonight was small, a mere breath down the river in the dark that failed to stir this trumpery. There was a scent of roses, a mingled smell of garden flowers rising from the earth. A host of small white moths fluttered over the grass. Mosquitoes whined, and I felt on my cheek the hot prick of those tiny biting insects our Indians call No-see-ums.

She made a slim white shape in the darkness, and as I came to her she said plaintively, "At last you've come, Nathan! What a time you've been. I'm near devoured."

I took her hands in mine. I did not know what to say, now that the time had come for parting. I felt some remorse, knowing how proud she was. Women set great store on wedding matters—and on what the gossips say. I knew she must think what her mother thought—that I was dashing off to sea like an ill-bred horse that shies at the first hedge.

"I dare say Father's filled you full of good advice?"

"Yes," I said.

"And Mamma?"

"I took my leave of her."

"What did she say?"

"I'd rather talk about you and me."

"I see." She turned her face away as if in thought. "Nathan, did she say anything about—about you or your people?"

"No."

"Have you never wondered about them yourself?"

"A little."

"Do you know that my father once courted your mother, and that she married someone else?"

"No."

"You're not very romantical, are you, Nathan? Don't you remember your parents?"

"My mother died when I was born. I remember my father a little—a very little. A gloomy drunken man, but kind, and very poor."

"Did he ever mention Mr. Pride?"

I thought a bit. "It seems to me he did. But all that time is very dim. Why do you ask?"

"A woman's curiosity, Nathan. But surely you see why Mamma hates you so?"

"Why?"

A silence. Then, lightly, in her cool even voice, as if she were repeating a bit of amusing gossip about some acquaintances of hers and mine, "Because, my dear Nathan, you were the son my father wanted—by the woman he couldn't have. Mamma was his afterchoice, when he was cold and disappointed; and all she bore him was a daughter—me. So he never forgot your mother and never really loved mine—never—though he loves me—yes, I think he loves me very much—just as he loves you—for somehow in you and me he sees the satisfaction of that old passion of his. Now do you see? No doubt it seems very strange to you, all this—but I've known about that old affair a long time, and I understand. Poor Mamma! I should hate you and Father as she does, I suppose, but I can't—of course I can't! I've always felt closer to Father somehow."

"And how do you feel to me?" I said soberly.

She answered carefully, "I've told you, Nathan. I'm falling in with Father's wish, as you are. We like each other, you and I, in a sensible fashion. I see nothing lacking in that. Love? That's an old wives' word. I don't know what love is. Do you?"

"I don't think so. No."

"I remember Monsieur Dolainde once saying love was a gift that sometimes came after marriage, but never before. The French are said to be very wise in such matters, aren't they? I think it should be good enough for you and me, anyhow. It should be interesting—finding out."

She shivered suddenly. I noticed then that she was wearing the thin batiste thing I had once condemned so rudely. No doubt the night air was chill in such a rig. I put my arm about her and felt her pliant waist go rigid at my touch. She said quickly, "But you mustn't expect too much, all at once, Nathan, when you return and we're married. You must realize—— What are you laughing at?"

"You sound like an old maid of fifty!"

"Oh? Oh! And a fig for me and my qualms, is that it? It's all very well for you, Nathan, you're off to six months' adventure and plenty of other things to think about. It's different with me. Who wouldn't be a man?"

It startled me, the passion in her voice when she said that. I felt a pang, almost of jealousy. She had always been the frigid mistress of herself in all ways, a little amused at the world and me, but otherwhiles indifferent. All women sigh for the freedom of men, of course—or so they say; but I never heard one say it with the passion of Felicity. And it seemed to me, there in the soft darkness of the garden, that Felicity did not want to be a man so much as she hated to be a woman. She wore her slim flesh in the resentful fashion of a girl in a poor family who wears some other's gown: because she must, because she has no choice, because she was born to it.

I thought how she worshiped her father. And I thought how Amos Pride wished she were a man, and how it would have changed his world, and hers, and mine. It was queer to think that if Felicity had been born a man-child she, not I, would be setting forth for the Caribbees and coming back to a golden inheritance. Was this what she was thinking of?

She broke the uncomfortable silence, saying calmly, "Well, Nathan, let us say good-by—I find it chilly here. There's nothing much to say except just that, good-by, good luck, and a happy return. Take care of yourself and Father's ship. You will, I know. Do you know, Nathan, I think of you as a small boy somehow, the boy I saw when you first came to us? I can't imagine you sailing a ship and fighting—such a horrid business; but I suppose such things must be. Write me a letter now and then, when you're in a friendly port. And—well, that's all."

She turned her face up for my kiss, and I felt her fingers lightly on my shoulders. I had a sudden impatience with her metaphysics and clasped her hard about the waist and bussed her soundly. After a moment she put her hands against the breast of my old blue pea jacket, pushing me away and saying in the cool amused voice that I knew so well, "Is that the way you salute your tavern wenches, Nathan?"

"No," I said, "I have a different kiss for them. Would you like to try it?"

She shook her head, a quick wagging of the pale face in the dark, with a sharp outbreathing through her nostrils as if she were still amused, or shuddering, or giving a ladylike snort—I could not tell. She flitted away towards the house, a pale moving shape, like a ghost in the darkness.

I called, "Good-by, Felicity!" but she made no reply and vanished. I heard the slam of the door.

I should have felt ashamed of my boorishness, but in truth I was not a bit. I went gaily down the garden path between the conch shells gleaming like white stones in the dark and let myself into the lane by the wicket gate.

It was a night to remember. Stars, a smell of new-cut hay from the hillside, a mutter of summer thunder far up the wooded valley, the ebb tide flowing silently out of the river, darkly shining, chuckling about the slimy spiles of the wharves, a yellow glow and a snatch of song in the King's Head, houses dark and abed, shops shuttered, a scurry of rats about the warehouses, a late roisterer reeling home, a man and woman embraced and silent in the shadow of a doorway, the velvet dust of the street underfoot.

'Twas a time for reflection, I suppose, since I was leaving all these peaceful sights and sounds for the chances of war and the sea. But—this is the truth of it—the only image in my mind was the brigantine awaiting me off the beach, and how beautiful she was, and how she would not shrink from the touch of a lover but rather would heave herself, passionate, under his caress, and give him all she had and was, no matter the moment, no matter the world.

And so I went through the town and down to the boat, whistling softly and thinking on the tide.

Chapter 18

IN THE gray morning our landsmen looked in vain for a last glimpse of home. The wind had drawn east in the night and fetched the cold fog of the Banks to smother the coast, as often it does in our Nova Scotia in the month of July. There was no shore to be seen; for that matter no spars to be seen above the topsail yard, and no bowsprit when you stood aft.

We fired a gun in signal of departure and heard a flat dull echo in the harbor hills behind the mist like a muttered farewell. Lot set his seamen at the capstan bars and round they went, heaving in the cable. I ordered our fifer and drummer to give them a tune, man-o'-war fashion, but our fishermen and merchant jacks would have none of it, bawling a capstan chantey of their own—and I did not blame them a bit. A good song is worth a whole band of music on a rope or at the capstan bars. In such ways, one by one, we dropped the man-o'-war pretensions the governor and Mr. Pride had urged upon us.

At the yell of "Hove short!" the fore-topsail was let fall and sheeted home, and then the fore-t'gallant; and with so many hands to heave we got the big fore-and-aft mainsail hoisted quickly. And those were good sounds after the weary longshore waiting and argument, the stamp of bare feet and the clack of capstan pawls, the roar of the chantey chorus, the creak of good hemp on the stretch, the slither of well-greased parrels, the chuckle of blocks, the flog of canvas loosed from the yards, the drumming of reef points on taut canvas in the wet sea breeze, the harping of rigging in the wind and swish of water under her fore-foot, and the voice of the ship herself, speaking now for the first time, the grunt and creak and groan of every timber taking the strain as she heeled, and murmuring together as if to say that Job Eames's work was good . . . *good* . . . *good!*

Away we went, spreading sail above sail until the brigantine was fully clothed in 'Lisha Riddock's careful handiwork, and she ran over the long smooth fog swells kicking up her heels like a gay girl off to the fair. The wind was a good one for the southward-bound, and I resolved to make the most of it, fog or none, and so we went bounding away from the coast all blind and not caring, except to keep a man jangling the watch bell and lookouts posted at the sprit and foretop. Lot Mayes looked doubtful now and then, but I ignored him, tramping my side of the poop and whistling for more wind.

Towards night, in the first dusk, there was a sudden yell from the sprit and Simon Dawkins's voice in the waist repeating rapidly, "Down hellum! Down with it!" I leaped to help the helmsman heave on the spokes. And as the brigantine swung into the wind I caught a glimpse of a small hull, a mast, and riding sail going swiftly past our starboard quarter in the mist, and a hand waving a torch—a brand plucked from a galley fire, I suppose—and several faint and querulous voices crying out like gulls in stormy weather.

We had missed them by a hair, and they were past and gone before they or we had time to worry much. Our sails were lifting noisily. I said to the helmsman, "Wipe her off and take your course again."

"Nathan, that was close!"—Lot Mayes at my ear.

"Ay, and past."

"A fisherman, and maybe a dozen others under our forefoot afore we clear George's Bank tonight."

"Keep the bell going then, and fire a gun each turn of the glass."

"What, and doff no canvas?"

"None!"

"But it's night, and thick—black as the devil's pocket!"

"And a fair wind for the south'ard!"

He said no more, pursing his old slack mouth and tramping forward to give the order to the gunner, but I could see what he thought of me.

We ran out of the thick weather on the second evening, and by the third we were tossing in the lumpy sea that marks the edge of the Gulf Stream in northern latitudes. This was too much for some of our adventurers. I heard Lot fall upon them, roaring, "Over to loo'ard, ye lubbers! There! There! Retch away now—you'll feel worse afore this cruise is out. Who wouldn't sell a farm and go to sea?" He came to me, muttering, "Nathan, I'm hanged if I know why ye signed so many landsmen, with good seamen to be had by a little persuasion. All these lubberly trappers and woodsmen, that don't know any better than to puke to windward!"

"They'll have their sea legs when we reach the Trades, Lot. As for seamen, we've plenty. Six men and a boy could handle her, come to a pinch. These 'lubbers' are for fighting."

"Pooh! Show me the seaman couldn't swing a cutlass or push a pike as good as any o' those buckskin fellows."

"And shoot as well? These men can hit a penny at thirty yards and kill a man at two hundred. They've brought their own rifles—and for that matter their hunting knives and tomahawks. I have in mind some work ashore. But afloat or ashore they'll earn their pay, while your seaman with a musket is as clumsy as a cow. That's why His Majesty's ships carry marines."

"Ye seem mighty impressed with His Majesty's ships, Nathan.

All this drum-and-fife nonsense, and calling me a 'first lieutenant' and so on. What?"

"The governor's notion and Mr. Pride's, not mine, Lot. We carry a big crew, a sad temptation to any shorthanded captain of the Royal Navy that might overhaul us. Have you never heard of the press at sea?"

Lot's shaggy gray brows went up. "What? They wouldn't dare! Got a letter o' marque from Governor Wentworth, ain't ye?"

"Ay, but the Caribbees are a deuced long way from old Nova Scotia. And who's Johnnie Wentworth to any of those who-are-ye-damn-ye captains on the Jamaica station? Mr. Pride hoped that if we handled the *Fancy* man-o'-war fashion it might convince His Majesty's captains of our high intents and purposes, and they'd let us alone."

"Gammon!"

"Gammon, and the deuce with it. Our best warrant is a sharp eye and a clean pair of heels. Keep that well in mind."

Monsieur Dolainde appeared to feel sickly from the time we sailed. He lay in his berth in my cabin a good part of the first three days. But after that he was on deck most of the time, snuffing the warm moist air over the Stream and gazing towards the south with the eyes of a hungry dog. And drinking like a thirsty one. The rum for issue to the crew was a raw New England stuff that left a taste of copper in the mouth. I had laid in some right Jamaica for the cabin, with a few dozen Madeira, a case or two of Nantz brandy, and some claret and sack from the Pride cellar.

I made Dolainde free of these because he seemed in pain. He indulged himself well, strutting up to the poop like a shriveled old turkey cock and sitting on one of the after six-pounders, wordless and reeking of spirits, hour after hour, with the sea miles sliding past. Once I remember he cried out to me, stretching a yellow claw southward and singing the words through his nose, "I can hardly wait, Capitaine! I can hardly wait!" But there was no gladness in his face, only a sad drunken gravity that left me pitying and wondering.

All this time and in the days to come I kept my motley crew drilling at their various tasks, especially the gunners. Under Pardon Gardner's hard voice and eye they cast loose the cannon again and again, trundled them in and out of the ports, sweated them this way and that with the handspikes, and went through the motions of swabbing, loading, aiming, firing. Every morning I had a cask tossed overboard for a mark, and the gunners fired upon it with the long brass nine, which was Pardon's special delight, and one or two of the six-pounders in the waist. More powder we could not spare.

And this was how our guns were placed. The long nine on its swivel at the bow, the most important gun in the ship. The two iron nine-pounders stood at the forward end of the waist, one each side, to add their voices to the brass one when we were in chase. For the broadsides we had these and four six-pounders each side of the waist; and for a running fight, in case we had to take to our heels (a very likely prospect in the islands, where three navies prowled), a pair of sixes on the poop. At a pinch the long nine could be sweated aft and fired from the stern windows. A very respectable armament, all in all, and I felt we should give a very pretty account of ourselves when the time for fighting came.

And with our lively trade in mind I kept the hands scrambling to sheets and braces and halyards, and swarming aloft to reef, to furl, and then to make sail again—and again. I had the muskets, pikes, pistols, and cutlasses taken out of the arms chests and cleaned of the heavy armorer's grease, and polished so that they shone like Ma'am Pride's silver on the Sabbath dinner table.

Another matter I drilled thoroughly was the sending down of topmasts and yards in a hurry. And twice I had all the cannon struck down to the hold and there lashed securely, timing the men by my pocket piece and giving them the rough side of my tongue, and thinking of the hurricanes a month or two ahead.

All this made grumbling, as may be supposed. It was observed in the hold and forecastle—and not least in the prize masters' berth—that the new command had gone to young Cain's head, and he would ride the crew to death like any beggar ahorseback.

I grinned when Lot told me, and said that by the devil's grace they should have more to growl about as time went by. Eighty-odd men, three months' stores and water and all the fighting gear and spares, crammed into a lean hundred-foot hull, meant shorter tempers day by day, especially when the sun of the Caribbees drew overhead and turned the hold to a Dutch oven and boiled the very pitch in the planking. If they thought themselves hard-used now, what would they think after three months' cruising in those burning seas, with fighting to be done on short allowance, and wounds and yellow jack and scurvy to be suffered, with a rare foot to shore and maybe a scant share of prize money in the end?

"Cockerel!" snapped Lot. "That's what some of 'em call ye now—Pride's Cockerel, and faith, it fits—the red thatch and the strut o' ye, and this deck your dungheap!"

"Better that than Rabbit."

He shifted a tight knot of tobacco from his starboard cheek to the larboard. "Cockerel suits ye well enough." He laughed his toothless laugh, a wide gape of the old stained lips. "If ye fight as well as ye crow, Nathan, I guess it'll suit us all."

He said no more, and nor did I. A crew that cannot fetch a grumble is little worth. I remembered Mr. Pride's quip about short commons and long abstinence. They would growl more and pull harder as the weeks went by, ay, and fight the better when the time for fighting came.

Old sailors have a catch that warns,

If Bermuda lets ye pass
Then look out for Hatteras!

Our course took us well between those stormy regions, and there occurred two incidents that upset us pretty much, and since one has a bearing on the other I must tell you that the first took place in thirty-one north latitude in a sudden blow that forced us to douse the *Fancy's* royals and topgallants, then the foresail and spanker, and finally both topsails and the jibs.

By night we were scudding along under a storm trysail and the fore-topmast staysail—a pair of handkerchiefs, no more—with a big sea on the quarter and two hands at the wheel. 'Twas a clear night, not a cloud to be seen, with a warm westerly gale whistling along the sea's face under the moon, as if the great sprawling continent of America had turned in its hot summer sleep and said Phoo. We get such wild starry gales in our Nova Scotia latitude in autumn, but the wind comes out of Canada and is bitter cold. This fierce giant's breath under a clear sky was unreal and disturbing after my long absence from warm latitudes. Under a three-quarter moon the naked black shadows of masts and yards moved back and forth across the deck like the shadows of bare trees in a winter wind, now slowly, now quickly, now to larboard, now forward a little, now hesitating, now leaping to starboard, and pausing again, and aft a bit, and so on in a sinister game of hide-and-seek.

I observed this shadow play from the poop along with Simon Dawkins, whose watch it was; for there was some danger of broaching in this wind and sea, and I could not stay content below. The helmsman was a tall fellow with long black hair blowing about his face that gave him the look of a landsman, though he was a seaman right enough, and Simon ordered young Tom Armitage—Adam the carpenter's boy—to lend him a hand at the wheel.

The great wind made a wild outcry in the rigging, and the ponderous lift and hiss of the long seas on the quarter made the boy throw uneasy glances over his shoulder. I heard the helmsman grunt from time to time, "Eyes for'ard, boy! Eyes for'ard!"

Tom was a well-made boy of seventeen, strong and quick as a cat. He had been once or twice to the banks in fishing craft, but this was his first real voyage. He had persuaded his reluctant mother to let him go in the privateer because other lads were going, "and after all, Pa's her carpenter, ain't he?" So she had told me in the street the day after he signed, adding solemnly, "They say 'tain't lucky, more than one of a family in the same ship," and watching my face with her large round eyes. And I had said, lightly—for women past five-and-thirty will risk a husband with surprising good cheer where they are mighty timorous about a son—"Have you never heard of Captain Noah's ark, ma'am?"

And here he was, standing up to the wheel manfully beside the black-haired seaman, in a shirt wide open to the rushing warmth of the night, a pair of petticoat trousers, his calves in long wool stockings knit at home, a pair of broken cobbler's brogues on his feet, and a long flannel nightcap pulled well down upon his shock of hair, fisherman fashion.

The seas were beautiful in a way, all silver on their long slopes where the moonshine fell and cavern-black under their crests where it did not. All went well, indeed there was nothing to fear in such a gale so long as a taut hand kept the wheel, but I went along the waist for the sixth or seventh time to inspect the gun lashings, having in mind that a boarding sea might tear one loose and give us a merry night of it. I was standing by the starboard nine-pounder, near the foremast, when I heard Simon Dawkins bellow, "Lord God! Hold on!" I looked aft and saw a giant sea rising black and frightful against the moon beyond the stern and rushing down upon us.

Simon was yelling to me and the watch, but the boy forsook the wheel and began to run forward, as if he could escape that almighty sea by the speed of his heels alone. And at that moment the first send of the great wave kicked the rudder and flung the dark seaman clean over the wheel, a wild figure, all flying arms and legs, that fell in a heap against the six-pounder on the lee side of the poop.

I remember that, and the moonlit face of the boy, gone mad with fright, and the awful cry he gave as the huge sea closed upon the ship and him and all of us. I ran up the weather forerigging with such a spring in my hands and feet as a man finds only at such a moment, but I had not got far when it struck. I locked my arms about the shrouds and hung on, gasping. I felt the ship lift, I felt her tossed up like a cork, so that it was the crest that broke upon us. But that was a frightful thing in itself. My eyes were wide—I could not have shut them if I wished—and as that mighty rush of water took the ship and set her shuddering in its grasp I saw for a moment the leeward surface of the crest as it passed, curving, toppling, darkly gleaming, like one of those blue ice tunnels you see sometimes in bergs upon the fishing banks.

Old sailors talk of seventh waves, and the seventh of seventh waves that sometimes makes a monstrous sea, but such things have no birth in mere arithmetic, nor in the force of winds. They come of some convulsion in the sea itself, in the depths of it, and maybe Simon Dawkins had the right of it when he said afterwards that ours came straight from Davy Jones, shaking a great fist at the bottom. Many a stout ship and a hearty crew goes missing in such waves, and none to tell the tale, but ours lived, and we had good cause to thank God for our deliverance and Job Eames for a stout bit of shipbuilding.

I felt her lift, as I have said, and that is what saved her, that alone in simple truth. Then she was flung forward like a chip, all in a white smother that seemed to me to cover her from stern to stem as high as the foreyard. Then the wave was past, and I saw it go sweeping on, the long steep back of it all white in the moonlight like a mountain range in winter in high latitudes. It rushed away to the eastward as if it would not stop this side of Teneriffe. An awesome sight, and I clung to the rigging and stared after it, all sodden and beaten and breathless as I was.

Beneath me the ship moved drunkenly, with a mass of water surging in the waist and not a living soul to be seen. I scrambled down the ratlines and heard Simon Dawkins crying, "All hands!" somewhere forward, at the forecastle door, I suppose. The two storm sails were gone clean out of the boltropes, not a rag was left. The longboat and yawl were smashed to flinders and the pieces swashing about the waist. I reached the wheel and found it unbroken but spinning wildly for lack of the relieving tackles and useless for the moment. The brigantine had lost all way and lay wallowing, shaking herself and trembling still, like a stunned dog. The vast weight of water on her deck concerned me more than anything else, but in a few moments the surge of it smashed out several of the gun ports and so freed itself.

By that time men were coming from forward, from below, all

yelling, and there was one voice faint and appealing at my very feet. I looked down and saw the helmsman doubled up against the six-pounder's carriage, his hands still clasping the breech tackle to which he had clung while that great sea passed over him. We got him below, and the schoolmaster, who admitted some knowledge of medicine, took charge of him.

There was no sign of the boy—and no turning back to look for him in that wind and sea. I had a strange whimsy that the running sea mountain had carried him off to Africa, and wondered what I should tell that mournful woman back in Gosport when the time came. The main boom had been torn out of its crotches and was banging to and fro, indeed there were a hundred and one matters clamoring for attention, but I could see no mortal damage to the ship. I ordered the men to set the main-topmast staysail and put a goosewing on the fore-topsail, and in this fashion got the ship before the wind; and when that was done and the steering tackles rigged, and two stout men at the wheel, it was time to see how the crew had fared.

Two men of the watch had vanished with young Tom Armitage, and two we found dead and twisted in the scuppers close against the forecastle bulkhead. They had been amidships, leaning against one of the boats, when the great wave boarded us. No one below was hurt, although the throng in the hold had been shaken up like dice in a box. Dolainde lay drunk in his berth and slept through the whole affair. The helmsman lingered until morning and then died in a frenzy, crying, "Heave, boy! Heave if ye look for dry burying! Heave, now! Heave, or we're pooped and sunk, the lot of us!" His skull was cracked like an egg, and he must have had a great vitality to stay alive so long.

Next day in the forenoon watch we buried the dead that were left to us, all three decently sewn up in canvas with bar shot at their feet, and I saying the prayers as best I could, for in the scurry of sailing day my book had been forgotten. By that time the wind had slackened and hauled northwest, a fair wind to pay us for our tribulations, and I ordered all sail set.

"Ah," cried Lot Mayes, sniffing the wind and spitting a brown stream over the lee rail, "ye don't deserve your luck, Nathan, that's a fact. There we were, tossed in the wet hand of God, and you without a prayerbook. A flight in the face o' Providence, and nothing but two boats and a pair o' storm sails gone, and five men and the boy to pay the reckoning. A miracle, I say, and where's the humble man? Not you, at any rate. Why, you ought to be looking to heaven at this moment——"

"That I am," I said curtly. "Have the watch take a small pull on the lee fore royal brace."

Chapter 19

THERE were glum faces after this affair, to be sure, and much talk of omens and forerunners and suchlike nonsense. I reckoned work the best cure for melancholy and drove them hard, and if they found my medicine bitter it was none the less effective. Then something happened that killed the disease entire. On the second morning after we put those dead men in the sea, we raised a foreign sail and stood chase, and there was such an eager scurry and such a fierce glee in every face that it was wonderful to think upon the change.

The wind was steady at northeast and the stranger hull-down to leeward, with a long blue swell rolling between us that sometimes hid him to the topgallants, but as we bore down we saw that he was xebec-rigged, a Spaniard by the look of him, jogging along in a lazy fashion under his queer lateen lower sails and nothing else.

Lot and I climbed swiftly to the fore-topsail yard and passed a spyglass back and forth, speculating on the stranger's guns and crew. Beneath was a scene to remember, though we gave it scarcely a glance except to see that all went Bristol fashion. At my shout of "Beat to quarters!" the music boy had seized his big red-painted drum and the schoolmaster his fife, and they were marching up and down the waist looking mighty droll, the short fat boy and the long Pictou dominie, all bones and lank hair and sharp red nose, rattling and shrilling away for dear life.

Pardon's gunners had dropped the ports, cast loose and loaded their cannon, and now stood waist-naked to the sun, clutching their rammers, swabs, and handspikes. Michael Brady and his men had hoisted the black canvas waistcloths to conceal our guns and numbers as the ships drew eye to eye. Isaac Yarrow, our master-at-arms, had issued cutlasses all round and placed the pikes in their beckets on the main boom. In the long rack against the after bulkhead stood forty muskets with flints fixed and cartridge pouches dangling. Lengths of match were lit and fuming in the gunners' tubs, linstocks stuck upright in the deck by their spiked butts, and powder boys stood by with spare cannon cartridge in their slender canvas buckets. The narrow racks about the fore and main hatches were filled with ball and grapeshot ready to hand. Water buckets and wet swabs were in place in case of fire.

And grouped about the mainmast and the fore were my landsmen, the trappers and hunters of Gosport River, wearing their fringed gray hunting shirts in defiance of the heat but with kerchiefs tied about their heads, seaman fashion, looking over their long rifles, their patch boxes and cartridges, and settling the hunting knives and tomahawks in their belts. They were lean men, and the seasickness had left them sallow in the face, but they had their legs now and were stepping about the deck in their moccasins like hungry cats, eager to be a-doing.

Lot Mayes was still scornful of them—"no better than a lot o' sogers"—and when I asked him what was wrong with soldiers (as if I did not know), he and Simon Dawkins chanted at me,

"Messmate afore watchmate,
Watchmate afore shipmate,
Shipmate afore a dog;
But any dog afore a soger."

And Simon added, seriously, knowing that I proposed to use these men aloft in any close action, "This shooting from aloft—I never liked the notion, Cap'n. Apt to set the sails afire wi' their damned powder, and what's the good of it anyhow? Ye can't shoot straight from a ship's yard in a seaway any more'n ye could from a treetop in a gale."

I shrugged and smiled and said nothing.

But all these hopes and doubts and preparations went for nothing. The Spaniard came awake to his danger. We observed a scurry aloft, and very soon those tall pole masts and slender yards were sprouting canvas in a disconcerting fashion. The Spaniard's best vantage was before the wind, and down the wind he went, and crept slowly away from us, though he could not shake us, and by nightfall we were making a stern chase of it with his royals still in view from the masthead. Would he try to slip aside in the dark? That was a question. The chances were that he would keep on down-wind, fair for the Florida Strait and the eventual safety of Havana, where doubtless he was bound in any case. We held on with the wind throughout the night.

And that same night a queer tale went through the ship. It reached me last, of course. Lot gave it to me at breakfast in the cabin, in the first light, when I had posted lookouts at both mastheads with the promise of a stiff grog for the first sight of the Spaniard.

"The men are in a great touse, Nathan. Seen a ghost."

"Eh?"

"Last night and the night afore, creeping about the deck. Scared the watch out o' their wits."

"Wits! Grown men frightened by a shadow!"

"Shadow then. They saw the shadow plain enough, for it came and took a swig at the scuttle butt same as a Christian."

"Oh? What Christian, say?"

"Young Tom Armitage."

"Tsha!"

"Young Tom, they swear—plain as day, dressed as he was when he went overboard, long nightcap and all. I'd put no stock in one man's say, nor two for that matter, but it's all the men in two watches now—saw him coming from the bow, just after he'd climbed aboard by the dolphin striker and the spreet, like. He must ha' come out o' the sea—where else?—but this is the terrible thing about him, Nathan, he left the deck bone-dry behind him, not a drop, not a mark, and had his sup at the butt and disappeared for'ard again. Not a sound out o' him, not even a word to his old mates in the larboard watch . . ."

Through the open skylight came a cry from the masthead, "Sail-O!" and away went Lot's story like the ghost itself. We leaped up the cabin stairs and onto the poop, yelling, "Where away?"

"Three points off the larboard bow!"

Up the main rigging we went like a pair of startled monkeys, and there she was, sure enough, the xebec with her outlandish topsails catching the first rays of the sunrise. She saw us at the same time, for there was a quick shift in her course and she began to inch away from us as she had before. All through the day we hung on in pursuit, spreading our stunsails and every other stitch of canvas the *Fancy* would carry—and fared no better than we had before. At nightfall we barely had the Spaniard's topsails in view, three black specks caught in the sunset light on the very rim of the sea.

Again I chose to hold on in the dark and chance that the xebec would do the same. The Spaniard was making for Havana plain enough, and since he had the heels of us with this wind there was no reason to doubt his ability to beat us down the Florida Strait. And from our point there was a certain advantage in the darkness. John Spaniard would not know where we were, and there was a chance of coming up with him by some accident of wind and course before the break of day.

And now as I stood above the break of the poop, seeing the deck all clear for the night, the watch came shuffling aft. Simon Dawkins, stout man, roared, "What's this, ye dogs? Get for'ard where ye belong!"

A seaman named Mudge, apparently their spokesman, cried, "For'ard's no place for men like us, Cap'n Cain—not men that wants to stay right-minded, it ain't, not arter dark, and young Tom's ghost about."

"Tom gammon!" I snapped.

"Ah, gammon is all right for you as sleeps snug in a berth below, Cap'n—no disrespect intended—but there's young Tom whipped over the side like a wig in a hurricane, and no time for prayers, and it black dark, too. Soul can't leave a body that's drownded arter dark, that's a fact, as any old seaman knows, so there's poor Tom a-swimmin' along o' the ship, and comin' aboard by the spreet every night for sup o' sweet water at the butt. I tell ye, sir—and any man here can bear me out—the watch has seed him two nights runnin' now, and third sight's bad sight for all hands. Such sights ain't good for mortal men."

"No?" said I in a rage. "I know what's good for mortal men like you—a stiff catting at the gangway in the morning, to give 'em something healthier to think upon. Ghosts! I don't believe in ghosts, but I know mutiny when I see it, and I know the remedy."

One of the other seamen spoke—Carroll, an honest fellow enough.

" 'Tain't mutiny, Nathan, sir. We ain't refusin' duty—not proper duty, we ain't. We'll bowse and haul whenever ye say. But we wants to be aft here—out o' the way o' that *thing* when it comes aboard tonight—that's all, sir. That's reasonable, ain't it, sir?"

It was nearly full dark now and three hours to moon-rising. The group of faces made a small pale mass at the foot of the short poop ladder, like a parcel of children caught abroad on Halloween. I wanted to laugh, for all my anger, so very still and awed they were.

"Very well," I said, and heard Simon's sigh of relief at my side. "Stay where you are, then—I'll not have a man on the poop that doesn't belong here. You'll be safe enough. And I'll keep the waist myself tonight. Some fool's at play, and I'll have the fellow's hide if I can put a hand on him."

They stayed close about the ladder foot, talking in low voices, while Simon kept the poop with the helmsman. I walked down to the fife rail and slipped a belaying pin into my hand, and began to march slowly and solemnly up and down the deserted waist, whistling softly through my teeth.

Nothing happened. Hour after hour nothing but the hum of the rigging, the faint stretch and creak of sails full-drawn to the steady wind, Simon turning the binnacle sandglass every half hour and calling a seaman to strike the bell, the sharp brassy notes of it ringing along the deck, an occasional shuffle and stir of the watch about the poop ladder, and the binnacle lantern throwing a pale glow, ghostly enough, upon the young face of the helmsman.

At midnight the starboard watch took the deck and the men of the larboard tumbled below to the hold, to the hammocks there —not one would go to the forecastle. Lot Mayes relieved Simon and showed no surprise at seeing me in the waist. Nor did the watch. They took post by the poop ladder as the old one had, and it was clear to me then that the fear had gone all through the ship.

The moon appeared and began its slow climb up the sky in a high run of clouds, now hidden, now shining full on the deck and the sails and the long smooth seas.

When the bell struck three of the watch my legs were weary with tramping up and down. Someone was making a fool of me. Who? My fingers itched for his throat. He had caught me nicely, too. If I quit the deck now, like a sensible man, the crew would say I was afraid. If I faced it out, someday in Gosport it would be told how So-and-so, that merry fellow, had kept young Captain Cain—Red Cain—tramping up and down an empty deck the whole night through like Robin Duff the walking constable.

I sat on the breech of one of the starboard guns and tried to fix my thoughts on the Spanish ship and the chances of coming up with her. Luck! Was there anything in omens after all? Amos Pride had cut his hand at the launching—all the crew were telling it now—and already his *Fancy* had cost the lives of six. But tsha! —what else but luck, the silver pieces under her masts, say, had carried her through that mighty sea at all?

I cannot remember now how long I sat musing and glooming and staring at the breeching tackles of the gun. The moon came out of the clouds again and lit the deck and turned the dim swinging shadows of the sails all black and sharp on the white shimmer of the planking. I looked up idly—and saw it. Yes, by heaven, the figure of poor Tom Armitage, of a well-built boy of seventeen, at any rate, slinking half stooped along the other side of the deck and dressed in the short flapping trousers, the stockings, the shirt, the long drooping nightcap such as the carpenter's son had worn that wild night of the wave.

Not a sound from aft, but I knew they saw *it,* all of them, Lot with the rest. They were staring and gaping as I was—I could not help myself. My courage was gone. It is one thing to laugh at a tale of ghosts and another to see one before your eyes, at night, in the lonely heart of the sea a thousand miles from home. I seemed to feel a cold hand on my heart that stopped its beating and set me shivering as if a cold wind blew. I longed then for the comfort of my kind, to be one of that silent group at the break of the poop, which seemed to have drawn a great distance away. But I fought down an impulse to run.

The scuttle butt was placed on chocks well aft, under the eye of the poop, lest in the hot weather the seamen should drink it dry in a single watch. The figure crept to the butt as noiseless as the very shadows of the sails. I saw it reach for the pannikin that dangled from the spigot. And the pannikin *clinked.*

I came out of my trance then. I came out of it with a leap and a firm grip on the belaying pin. And as I rose, the figure turned swiftly. I saw the pale oval gleam of a face regarding me. Then *it* began to run like a deer—like a ghost if you will, for it did not make a sound—towards the forecastle head, and I cutting across the deck towards it, full split, clutching the pin.

I heard a cry from aft, Lot Mayes I think, a shout of dismay, of warning—I'm not sure, and it matters little—as I cut across the deck. The figure skimmed along the larboard side at such a rate that I could not head it off, but it checked a little at the forecastle steps, and I dropped the pin and threw myself forward, clutching at its waist. My hands grasped firm and living flesh—I confess I half expected them to meet in mid-air—and the creature uttered a small cry and struggled to get free. I shifted my hold quickly, intending to throw the fellow to the deck in no gentle fashion, but my hands closed on warm round flesh and silky skin that sent a tingle through me to the bones. That was the final astonishment of the night. Living or dead, I had no boy in my grasp.

The ghost ceased struggling then and stiffened, saying in a panting voice, "You have me. Take your hands away, please. Please!" It was Lia Dolainde.

I tell you I was dumfounded. I could not have been taken aback more thoroughly if I had found a mermaid in my arms. I dropped them hastily, and she turned and faced me, drawing her torn shirt together with one swift clutch and pulling off the baggy nightcap and letting the confined hair fall about her shoulders. In the moonlight her eyes seemed enormous.

She spoke, in a voice so full of hate that it shocked me. "So, Capitaine, you have caught me! What are you going to do?"

Lot Mayes came running, very bold now, hearing a human voice from my prize. I waved him away.

"What are you doing here in my ship?" I said coldly.

She hitched her shoulders, French fashion, and said sullenly, "You were sailing to Saint Domingo with my father. Do you think I would stay there with those—those Prides—all alone—do you?"

I had a sudden thought. "Brule!" I rasped. "Brule smuggled you aboard! Or was it your father—or both of them?"

She was silent.

"Tell me," I said, "or I'll have it out of 'em tomorrow with the cat as sure as you stand here."

"Beast!"

"Well?"

"If I tell, will you promise not to punish anyone? Anyone but me, Capitaine Cain. You may beat me if you wish."

"All right. I promise."

"*Bien!* My father knew nothing of this. I did not ask him—I knew he would not let me go. Victor—Monsieur Brule helped me. And Black Boston."

"So!"

"You promised not to punish——"

"I know. Go on."

"Black Boston brought me food from the galley. I was hidden in the—what you call it, cable tier?—up there"—motioning towards the forecastle head.

"I see."

"Boston—he had to be very careful. Some days he could not come at all. It is hot in there, in that place. At night I had to come out, to stretch myself, to get a little drink of water. So—you caught me."

"And Brule—did he visit you there?"

"No." A little silence. "Why do you ask that, Capitaine?"

"You and Brule—you were lovers, weren't you, back in Gosport?"

She gave an indignant gasp. I thought for a moment she was going to slap my face. But she threw up her head and declared in a disdainful voice, "Capitaine, that is no business of yours."

"Oh! Then what's your business in my ship, if I may be so bold?"

Again the small heave and fall of her shoulders. "My father is going to Saint Domingo, to our old *manoir*. He told me. He said he would come back, but I did not like the way he said it. I was frightened. I did not wish to be left behind with Madame Pride and those others. I hate them." She added in a vigorous little outburst, "And I hate you!"

"So I see."

I saw, right enough. She wanted to see the old home again, of course. And she hated Pride's Fancy and everything about it. But chiefly she was in love with Victor Brule. That was the core of it. Well, here she was, and no putting her ashore anywhere this side of Hispaniola, as far as I could see.

I said harshly, "I'm hanged if I know what to do with you, miss. This is a ship of war, not a packet boat. One thing's sure—you can't stay in the cable tier. I've half a mind to berth you with the crew, but that'd only make trouble. Come with me!"

Obediently she followed me along the deck, past the gaping men of the watch, to the cabin hatch. As we entered the cabin Dolainde stirred on his berth and opened his eyes, and I shall never forget the astonishment and the wild horror in his face. He sat bolt upright, the skinny yellow man, in his nightshirt, his thin hair and his goat beard all wild, crying out in French, "My God, what is this? Lia!"

In a meek voice she explained, and he stared from her to me.

"She will have to berth here, with us," I said angrily. "There's no choice."

I hesitated. Dolainde was drunk so often that he had to have a berth to sprawl upon. I did not see why I should give up mine to a stowaway of any sort, least of all a sweetheart of Victor Brule's. There were just two standing berths in the cabin, one each side, and a table down the middle, slung from hooks in the deck above. At the forward bulkhead was a low padded locker, a sort of nautical sofa, a touch of luxury not often seen in ships when I was young. I pointed to it.

"Mademoiselle, there is your bed. Here is a blanket to cover you, and another to rig as a screen—a piece of cord will do it. You will stay here, you understand, and take your meals. I put you in your father's charge. You will not go on deck except when I say so."

She pressed her lips together and gave me a look that said Fiddle-de-dee.

"Yes, Capitaine Cain."

"You are a confounded nuisance."

"Yes, Capitaine."

She sat on the locker with the golden hair all matted and tumbled about her shoulders, her face and hands stained with the brown grime of the cable tier, the white breast gleaming where the shirt was torn, dressed like a boy and looking very much a woman—and a willful one, with those dark eyes fixed upon me, lively with dislike.

She must have suffered greatly in that dark hole forward, for the cables bulked large in the tier and reeked of harbor water, and for some days now the heat had been oppressive even on the open deck. And she must have been terribly frightened, that night of the great sea. I thought how much she must love Victor Brule to follow him at such a cost, and wondered what she saw in that stocky dark man besides a merry eye and a mustache.

I turned on my heel and went off to tell Brule and Boston what I thought of them and their passenger. I knew the crew must be agog, and I guessed what they would say. The young ones would consider it a great lark. But I could fairly hear the older men. A woman in the ship! . . . better than a ghost, of course . . . but no good would come of it . . . bad luck to have a woman aboard . . . worse than a horse or a pig by far . . . worse than a bucket capsized on Sunday . . . trouble . . . trouble . . .

Well, women were trouble wherever you found them, and you found them everywhere you turned. What couldn't be helped, we would have to put up with. There was one comfort in the offing. Before very long we should make our venture into Hispaniola, and the problem of Brule and his sweetheart could be solved in a stroke.

Chapter 20

WHEN day broke there was no sign of the Spaniard, and we found none in the hours that followed, search that sun-blazing sea as we would. Late in the afternoon the lookout on the fore royal hailed land, and from the rigging soon after I made out the first of the Bahama cays, a long yellow streak edged white with breakers. No doubt the Spanish ship was well into the Florida Strait and far beyond our grasp.

Nevertheless I stood the *Fancy* over towards the Florida shore, battling the strong set of the Gulf Stream there, then back towards the Bahama side in the last of the light, and so on, slowly traversing the strait throughout the night, a lookout with a night glass in the foretop and a gun's crew ready at the long nine.

The weather now was stifling hot, the very breeze like an opened oven even at night, and through the day, when the heat below decks became intolerable, the men sat or lay about the decks, jostling for the uncertain shade of the sails and talking in listless voices. The landsmen were stripped to their buckskin breeches, the sailors to their wide-legged trousers, which some of them now cut off above the knee, and many wore nothing but a clout of knotted handkerchiefs. A shirt on the back could not be borne—not our coarse Nova Scotia linseys, anyhow—but I made all hands wear headgear of some sort, if only a kerchief, and keep a shirt loose-draped over their shoulders when idling in the sun, lest half of them go down with blisters and calentures.

For a breath of live air in the cabin I had a wind sail rigged through the skylight, and when Lia Dolainde thanked me I snorted that it was for her father's comfort and my own. I confined her to the cabin by day, partly to punish her for this foolish adventure, but chiefly because I reckoned it indecent for her to be about the deck in broad daylight in the presence of so many nigh-naked men. I told her this, and she looked me up and down in her scornful way. I had my own shirt off at the time, for I had prepared to wash and shave, and stood with my feet well apart and my body swaying this way and that as the ship rolled and the looking glass swung, making careful strokes with my razor. Such was the daily intimacy which our close quarters thrust upon us, and which I resented just as much as she.

There was another reason I did not give her. Brule. The Frenchman was allowed the freedom of the deck in the daytime. He made himself useful there, heaving and hauling with the watch and sweating like a short bronze bull, and amusing the men with his fiddle and his droll songs and stories, the most popular man in the ship. He had smuggled the girl aboard for his own amorous purposes, I could guess, and I did not intend him to enjoy them—while the voyage lasted, anyhow. In Hispaniola—well, that was a long way off.

And so after nightfall she came up to the poop—I forbade her to walk in the waist—and took her evening's air between the low forward rail and the tafferel, on the lee side, for she knew the windward side was mine. 'Twas a fisherman's walk—twelve steps and overboard—and we must have looked odd to the watch, she and I walking slowly up and down in the starlight, on opposite courses, one each side of the poop, stepping around the gun tackles and ignoring each other as if there were not another creature in fifty miles.

From his own stock Dolainde had provided her with a cambric shirt and a pair of thin yellow nankeens, very tight in the leg, as the fashion was with the *émigré* gentlemen at Halifax, these in place of the filthy things she had worn in the cable tier; and because she was taller than he, with a notable roundness in the places where Dolainde was most meager and emphasized by her waist, as slim as the *Fancy's* royal mast, the borrowed garments gave her the look of an actress playing a breeches part—and playing it deuced well.

These matters I observed on deck and when we dined together in the cabin, as any man would who had eyes and a healthy curiosity, and I was indignant when from time to time she caught me in these casual inspections and gave me a look of contempt. Indeed in all our relations she wore an air of outraged innocence, so that sometimes I felt an interloper in my own cabin, and once or twice I was on the point of transferring myself to a hammock in the mates' small berth out of sheer vexation. But my pride stepped in there. I would not have it said in the ship that Captain Cain—Cockerel Cain—had been driven from his roost by a little French pullet.

And there were times when her manner irritated me to a point where I itched to box her ears or better still turn her over my knee and spank the taut seat of those flimsy nankeens as I would have spanked an insolent shipboy's. I dare say I looked my thoughts for in one of these encounters she sat very straight on her locker, tossing her yellow locks, and said in a mocking voice that irked me to the teeth, "You wouldn't dare, Captain Cain!"

I was across the cabin in a stride. She flung out a hand to ward me off, but I caught her wrist and threw her across my bent knee. I gave her the full swing of my hard hand once, twice, three times—six times in all before she writhed free of my grasp. She came to her feet in a leap, all flashing teeth and claws, and before I could step back she had drawn the nails of her right hand down my cheek in a quick furious stroke that set it stinging. The ship heeled at that moment and threw her off balance. She stumbled and fell, half on the floor and half on my berth, and lay there gasping, sobbing with rage, and looking up at me with eyes all black fire.

There was a tipsy giggle behind us. I turned and saw Dolainde smirking in the doorway. I felt a fool and worse. What did he think?

"So," said Dolainde in a high voice, "you have found what we all find sooner or later, Capitaine, that women and cats . . . eh?"

I did not like his tone or his manner, but I said nothing. My only desire was to beat a retreat as quickly as I could. Lia spoke.

"Capitaine," she said with a most surprising meekness, seeing what had gone before, "I am sorry that your face——"

"My face has suffered worse in time past, and I lived." I said it in French, I suppose because that language always seemed to me to have more dignity than English, or perhaps because it was the tongue we had always used together when she was younger. I turned then and escaped to the deck, where Lot Mayes opened his eyes very wide and demanded, "Ecod, Nathan, what have ye done to your face?"

"I fell. I fell in the cabin."

"Ye look more like ye'd fell foul of a wildcat!"

"I fell, I say."

He was grinning. So was the helmsman, and I saw the sprawling men about the deck regarding me with sudden curiosity. But chiefly I noticed Victor Brule. That man was staring at me with venom in his hard blue eyes, the fiddle forgotten at his cheek and the bow drooping to the deck. I gave him look for look, feeling a great desire to break someone's bones, his for choice; but he dropped his gaze at last and lifted the bow and went on with his tune.

I returned to the cabin then to wash the guilt from my face, but it was not so easily removed. The thin dried trickle of blood went away with the soap and water, but the looking glass revealed four long scores in the sunburned skin, a damning bit of evidence to every eye.

Lia lay full length on my berth, very quiet now, her face hidden in her folded arms. Dolainde sat on the edge of his berth, opposite, nursing a brandy bottle and regarding me tipsily.

"The brand of Cain!" he said suddenly and shrieked with laughter.

Lia Dolainde shuddered.

My instructions gave me a week to cruise the Florida Strait, and three of the days were gone. So was the Spanish ship. After you pass Cape Florida the strait widens steadily, with the long line of the Florida cays trending off to the southwest and the Bahama bank running on towards the south. I held the *Fancy* to the middle of the strait, reaching over to the Florida coast now and again, traversing slowly towards Havana. 'Twas a chancy business on the landward reach. Twice we got amongst the reefs and could look over the side and see the beautiful but evil corals, red, brown, yellow, some shaped like the horns of a stag and some like the brains of slain giants, with the bright green-and-blue parrot fish swimming all about.

However, the water is mighty clear in those parts, and we picked our way out to deep water again by the swash between the reefs, and thanked our God and mopped our brows and blamed our streaming faces on the heat. On the fourth day we sighted a sail, and then another, apparently in company. There was no need to hunt them, for they came to us, a pair of schooners painted black, with sharp-raked masts and a rag bag of patched sails. I had the drum beat to quarters. They came on, and seeing our red ensign at the gaff—and after a good look at our guns—they hoisted British ensigns themselves. One ran down and spoke us. Her deck swarmed with men, black, white, and all shades between, as villainous a crew as ever I saw. A bearded half-naked fellow hailed us with a speaking trumpet from the stern.

"Brigantine ahoy! Who are you, pray?"

"*Pride's Fancy,* privateer, out of Gosport, Nova Scotia. And you?"

The fellow stared at us in silence for a time. I suppose the notion of our far northern colony sending ships to cruise these seas had never occurred to him. Then, "*Black Tom,* privateer, Providence, Bahamas."

"Just what I thought!" growled Lot Mayes at my side. "A pair o' picaroons out o' Nassau Town and privateer be damned. They couldn't read a letter o' marque if they had one. There's no law in those parts anyhow. A good thing we showed our teeth."

Another hail from the schooner: "See anything of a Spaniard, xebec-rigged?"

"Oho!" muttered Lot. "Say no, Nathan."

"No!" I bellowed.

"We sighted a xebec yesterday running down for Havana. She wore and slipped away from us." A pause. "Where ye bound?"

"For the west end o' Cuba."

A wave of the Providencier's trumpet and a roar to his outlandish crew. They got their square topsails to the wind again and were off, standing to the north.

Lot whistled and lifted his shaggy gray brows. "They turned Johnnie Spaniard back, Nathan. Why didn't we see him?"

"Passed us in the night, no doubt."

"Um! Well, they'll harass this part o' the strait, ye may lay to that. The xebec's got to come this way if he wants to make Havana. Hullo, they're parting company, one's off to the southeast!"

"Ah! They think the Spaniard may have turned along the

Bahama bank by the Santaren Channel. Do you see the game?"

"Havana's not that way."

"No, but once he passed the Cay Sal Bank he could haul his wind and sneak up the Cuba coast."

Lot favored me with an arch look and a grin. "D'ye know, Nathan, there's times when ye seem to make sense. Well—three's a crowd. Let's get to some other hunting ground. Where next?"

"The Windward Passage. We've a mission in Hispaniola."

"Oh?"

"Dolainde."

"Ah—and that fellow Brule, and the girl?"

"And Brule."

He twisted his mouth. "You're mighty close with your plans, ain't ye, Nathan? Something tells me there's deviltry brewing. Hispaniola? That means we take the Santaren Channel ourselves."

"Not quite. Have the watch swing her off to the south'ard."

He frowned. "That'll put us square on the Cay Sal Bank."

"Not if we watch our way. I want a look at Cay Sal."

Cay Sal Bank is a scatter of reefs and low parched islands, a hundred or more, some as big as a ship and many no more than a patch of dry coral. The chief of them have queer names got from the buccaneers long before my time—the Dog Rocks, Elbow Cay, the Dead Men, the Double-headed Shot, and Cay Sal itself, where the Spaniards come from Cuba to make salt.

'Twas only a notion of mine. I knew from the way he handled his ship that the Spaniard was smart as paint. Those Nassau picaroons had turned him back, but he knew we must be coming down the wind, and although the Florida Strait is a hundred miles wide in that latitude there was a fair chance of falling foul of us. No doubt the Santaren Channel tempted him, but he must have guessed that the Providenciers, old hands in those waters, would separate and hunt him there as well. What then?

Hunting ships was a new game to me, but I had hunted moose in the woods at home, and I thought how a moose pursued will run straight into the wind for a stretch and then swing to the right or the left and stand in a thicket, watching the hunters go by. And why not John Spaniard? The trick was as old as the world. And what better dodge hole for the flying xebec than that maze of reefs and small islands to the southward? None of them was high enough to conceal much more than her hull—but I have known a moose to halt in a thin clump of bare hardwoods and fool the hunters just by standing still.

So we went down to Cay Sal Bank, with Lot muttering all the way. He had an old sailor's longing for deep water under him, and when we came out of the great depths of the strait into the sight of white breakers he was like a cat on hot bricks. Yet there is plenty of water amongst the reefs if you keep a good watch and use your lead. We came down between the Dead Men and the Double-headed Shot with six and seven fathoms water under us, and saw nothing worth note until we shoaled our water to a scant four fathoms drawing in towards Cay Sal. There we noticed what appeared to be a flagstaff on the low hump of the island. There was nothing unusual in that, but as we veered towards the east a bit the lone staff became three in line. Suddenly I knew them for the thin masts of the xebec.

I had to admire the fellow's cunning. He had run in close under the island, which is barely thirty feet high, and unbent his sails and even sent down his upper yards, leaving nothing exposed to view but the three slender poles, invisible at a distance. I yelled,

"Beat to quarters!" and Lot spat and gave me a delighted thump on the shoulder. But it was too soon to crow. Would the xebec fight? If so what sort of fight would it be? If we had to shoot her to pieces first, she would make a very poor prize indeed. The notion of defeat, of the shoe on the other foot, did not occur to me at all, in spite of Mr. Pride's careful instructions. The truth is, I was caught up in the wild excitement that gripped us all at the prospect of our first prize, though I tried very hard to keep my voice steady, to speak and move deliberately, to act as though I had been doing this kind of thing for years and wars on end. But I had caution enough to approach the Spaniard under our topsails alone, and felt my jaw tighten as we came into gun range and saw the red-and-yellow flag of Spain run up boldly to his masthead. We could make out several cannon as the xebec rolled in the blazing blue swell, and a scurry of men about the deck.

I waved my hand to Pardon Gardner at the long brass nine—we were calling it Pardon's Delight by then—and the squatty hooknosed man aimed carefully. A sweep of the match in the linstock, a blast that jarred the whole ship, a gush of white smoke thinning on the wind. The ball struck water just this side the Spaniard's stern, and the spray flew. Almost at once there was a puff of smoke from the xebec, and a ball came droning out to us and passed between the masts, a good ten feet above the deck. 'Twas droll to see how all our bravos ducked heads at the sound of it—and I bobbed as smartly as any, and so did Lot and the gun crews on the poop who were well out of the way of the ball in any case. I looked around and saw Dolainde.

"Get below," I snapped, "and tell Lia to lie on the deck. You'll do the same if you're wise." He nodded and vanished with a liveliness I had not seen in him since '93.

I sang out to Pardon, "Try again—and keep your shot low.

We can patch his hull, but there's not a spar to be had this side Jamaica."

The xebec was a graceful thing, now that we saw it close to. She sat the water like a gull, what with her high poop, her long sweeping run, her lateen lower yards cocked like folded wings, and the sharp steeve of her bowsprit. I thought, What a pity to smash her! For smash her we could—there was no doubt of it now. The Spaniard had trusted all to concealment and lay at anchor close inshore with no spring on his cable, unable to swing for good or ill, his broadside useless unless we approached him by the beam.

I did some quick thinking. We could hammer him by the bow quite easily where he lay, a tempting prospect for our broadside gunners. But if we raked him in that fashion the shot would tear away his headstays as likely as not, and so endanger his whole standing rigging and the masts as well. That was the last thing I wanted. We had to sail the prize home a thousand windy miles or more before it was worth a penny to Mr. Pride. And so I chose the stern, a delicate matter enough.

We had to sail close in to Cay Sal to do it. Perhaps the Spaniard had not reckoned on such hardiness, and no doubt I was a fool to risk my ship. I put a man in the starboard chains to sound, and I remember how in the noisy minutes that followed he kept up his singsong leadsman's chant, crying the depths as calmly as though we were inching over Gosport bar.

The gun on the Spaniard's poop was no toy, a long brass eighteen, we guessed by the sound and reach of it, but we rattled him with two nine-pound shot through his cabin windows and another that struck his tafferel and sent the dark splinters flying, and after that his aim was wild and his loading mighty slow. Finally it ceased. By that time we were little more than a cable's length astern, and I was weighing whether to stand on and board him with all hands or to luff and tear him with a broadside, when the men in our foretop began to cheer wildly. I leaped on the main boom and saw the Spanish crew scrambling over the landward side.

There were only a dozen at most, and small blame to them. They had played a chancy game and knew when it was lost. We saw them pull away from the side in their longboat with a great flurry of oars, making for the beach. The gunners at our starboard six-pounders were cracking their teeth for a shot, but I shook my fist and roared, "Hold your fire, there!" And to Lot, "Let go your topsails by the run. We've way enough." The yards came banging down at his yell, and in another two minutes or so we ran upon the xebec's quarter. Simon Dawkins and an eager mob with cutlass, pike, and tomahawk leaped aboard her. In the excitement no one remembered the grapplings, in spite of all our drills, until Lot's harsh voice broke upon them, but before very long we were moored fast to the prize, with the men wandering over and through her like a parcel of curious schoolboys.

My first concern was the cargo. We took a hatch off in a hurry and saw tier on tier of wine casks, neatly stowed bilge-and-guntling with the bungs up. At such a sight what could a man do but whistle and grin, as I did? Our crew did more: they cheered like mad, and suddenly Brule was there with his fiddle and fifty men dancing the hornpipe on the Spaniard's deck as if the mere thought of all that drinking stuff had turned them tipsy.

Abruptly I ordered the hatch put on again, but Lot said, "Wait a moment, Nathan," and I saw the gathering thunder in all their faces. Several voices cried out for their privilege, one old man-o'-war's man insisting loudly on "a hogshead for the lower deck, by God, or we'll take it!" and I knew the old sea custom well enough. I ordered a hogshead broken out of the hold and swung over to the *Fancy.* That was done briskly, and I had Simon Dawkins and Michael Brady stand by it with handspikes, ready to knock down any man who tried to start the bung.

It was time to examine the prize. She was built of some hard tropical wood, a stout thing, though her sails were worn thin and her rigging gone slack for want of tar. Lot stabbed a horny finger at the guns in her waist, six each side, the guns she had never had a chance to fire.

"Quakers!"

I stared for a moment and then laughed, and we all laughed merrily. Quakers they were, neatly fashioned of wood and painted with some glinting black stuff that gave them a look of metal. The only true gun in the xebec was a long brass twelve on her poop. She was armed and rigged for running, not fighting, and her men had left her promptly when the game was up.

Our shot had not damaged her much, though the cabin was a sad mess. Our round shot had entered the stern windows and gone clean through the forward bulkhead, knocking a table to kindling on the way and tearing the whole side off a locker. A little Madonna of painted plaster lay shattered on its wooden shelf in a corner. In the broken locker a row of wine bottles had been bowled over like ninepins in the wreckage of their wooden fiddles, and some were broken, some intact, and three stood neatly severed at the neck as if by the stroke of a sword.

The floor was a litter of papers, with a wide pool of mingled blood and wine and what was left of a slim dark man in white trousers and a yellow cotton shirt. A nine-pound shot had cut him near in two. The captain, beyond doubt. I picked up the logbook, spattered with his blood, and slowly mouthing the words, made out that she was the *Nuestra Señora del Carmen,* forty-six days out of Santander, Spain, and bound for Havana with a full cargo of Rota, Málaga, and Galicia wines. What a prize! In

Halifax, that thirsty garrison town, the stuff was worth in these war times a good five thousand pounds at least.

My mind's eye saw the quick yellow blaze of Mr. Pride's eyes —I could fairly hear his voice crying, "Well done, Nathan, my son!" Ay, I stood there gloating and glowing, with the dead man swaying gently under my feet with the lift and fall of his ship in the swell, and nought in my head but my own success and cleverness, and the praise of that lean man far to the north, and what Felicity would think if she could see me now.

A distant sound of musketry awakened me and took me quickly to the deck. The Spaniards ashore, a scatter of black specks in the white glare of the salt pans, were popping at us hopefully. Some of my bravos were on the poop, tugging at the brass gun, but I stopped them. "We're well out of their range, lads. Besides, there's other things to do."

I set our sailmaker to overhauling the Spaniard's worn canvas and ordered the carpenter and his mate to board off the shattered cabin windows. And I chose the prize crew carefully, seeing what was in the hold. John Bowles for master, a pious man who reckoned drinking sinful, two seamen of the same persuasion, two others sickly and well out of the heat of these seas, a landsman, Enos Bent, who could take a glass or leave it, a fisherman from the West Head, and a good stout boy.

We lacked a prisoner for davy-man, but I gave Bowles her manifest for evidence before the court of vice-admiralty at Halifax, and a scrawl to show that he and his men were a prize crew from the *Fancy,* under letters of marque signed by His Majesty's governor in Nova Scotia, in case he met with questions on the way.

"Shall I make north?" Bowles said. I thought of those Nassau schooners lurking in the strait.

"No. Go down the wind, round Cuba by the west, and haul

up for Jamaica. See Mr. Pride's agent there—Whittendale's his name. Bide your time in Kingston until he finds you a place in a convoy for the north. This cargo's too valuable to risk on a lone run."

He nodded, looked about the deck, then aloft, and gave a resolute sniff. "She's a well-built thing, Nathan. We'll have a bit o' fun in convoy—these xebecs are inclined to be a bit slow in stays. I watched one tacking out o' La Guayra a few years back. But never mind."

I put out my hand and he shook it heartily.

As I walked away there was a splash aft. I turned, wondering, and saw two of my fellows leaving the rail and chafing their palms together noisily, as if to brush off something foul. Just beyond the stern the form of the Spanish captain was slowly sinking, his breast held afloat for a moment by the air in his shirt. Then he was gone, and I felt sorry, thinking on the stout game he had played all down the Florida Strait, and that long voyage from Santander beset by all manner of dangers that he had weathered safely till this last unlucky chance.

I have his old logbook beside me as I write these words, a fine thing of good paper bound inside thick parchment covers with a lacing of rawhide, each page covered with the day's routine in his neat Spanish hand, the calculations of his noonings carefully set forth, and each day ending with a pious "God give me grace"—for was not his ship called Our Lady of Carmen?

There is his name, Francisco Uriarte, inscribed with care at the beginning of the voyage, and there are his queer nautical expressions that sound like poetry, the very sails with names like music—*bela de estai, juanete de proba* . . .

I am an old man now, and know the vanity of that young red-haired fool who stood in triumph on the xebec's deck so very long ago. Let me say now what I should have said then, as I watched his body sink to the coral off Cay Sal. *There passed this way Francisco Uriarte, of Santander in the land of Spain, a good man and a sailor. God give him rest and grant to me a death as quick and clean..*

Chapter 21

WE PARTED company with *Nuestra Señora del Carmen* on the following day, in the Nicolas Channel, with the mountains of Cuba low and blue towards the south. And when our prize was hull down to the west I signed Michael Brady to put the spigot in the wine.

It was time. The men were gathered in the waist, growling like surly dogs, parched with these burning seas and worn with hard lying. They had smelt powder, ay, and blood, for half a dozen of them had been hurt by flying splinters when a Spanish shot struck the capstan. They had taken a fortune, of which their share would be precious small when the lawyers, the vice-admiralty court, and the owner had taken theirs. Now they would have at least a fill of the wine if they had to cut my throat for it.

As for me, I believed in the taut hand, the word and the blow where discipline was in question, for I had gone to sea as a boy and come aft by the hawse, a cruel hard school; yet I knew my men, and I had sense enough to know that there comes a time when the master must stand aside and swallow his discipline, however it ache his belly. Jove, what wouldn't I have given then for a snug cove where the brigantine could lie in safety till the crew had drunk their fill! But there was no safety at Cay Sal of any sort, and the Cuba coast lay hostile all along our lee, and the Bahamas to windward a nest of thieves and worse.

And so reluctantly I took the sea for it, and yielded what I could no longer refuse—what I could not even control. There was order at first, the men in line with their pannikins and awaiting their turn at the spigot in good cheer. I began to hope that all would go well. But once the pannikins were filled, and filled again, the jostling began, and the scrabble about the cask, the oaths, the blows, the singing and dancing, the wild carouse that went on into the night.

'Twas a hot night with an uneasy wind and a long sea out of the Santaren Channel that gave the brigantine a slow swinging roll and set our topmasts scraping at the stars. And such stars! They seemed to hang low in the dark tent of the sky, each burning with a golden glow as if fanned by that warm breeze off the islands. A night for poets and lovers given over to madmen, yesterday's wounded amongst them, guzzling and capering in their bloody bandages. Simon and the boatswain stood aloof with me, but Lot Mayes gave way to his weakness and reeled about with a slopping pannikin singing, "Five Sail Bound for Malago" in his old cracked voice, and boasting of old brawls and wenchings in a way that must have burned the ears of that dry waspish wife of his, all the long miles to the north.

Ay, never so wild a night, never such a hurrah's nest as the deck of *Pride's Fancy* as she swung her patient way down the Nicolas Channel in the dark! Black Boston came to me quietly with a long keen meat knife in his belt and a stick of firewood in his hand. His mate had crept away from those wild sounds and hidden his skinny dark carcass in the forepeak. I armed Simon Dawkins and Brady and the schoolmaster with cutlasses and handspikes, and laid a pair of loaded pistols on the cabin hatch, and fetched up Dolainde and put a cutlass in his hand. And so we five men sober and one fuddled stood guard over the poop and the cabin stairs, while Dolainde's daughter lay below, thinking God knows what thoughts all through those long mad hours.

We took turns at the wheel and prayed the wind to hold small, for there were not steady hands enough to manage the ship if it veered or came on to blow hard. Ay, we steered and prayed with mouths as dry as cinders and a longing for a sup ourselves that withered us down to the toes. The shipboys crouched by the musket rack aft, lost in wonder at the spectacle before them. And in the midst of it all, like a piper in Bedlam, the sound of Brule's fiddle went on and on and on. I thought of those fairy fiddlers of the Irish who dance mortal men to death.

From time to time a man reeled away below or to the forecastle to sleep it off, or fell to the deck and rolled to the scuppers clear of the stamping feet. And at long last we saw a dim form go to the cask and rattle a pannikin under the spigot without result. He cursed the thing and fetched the cask a kick that rang hollow—a mighty sweet sound to me then. Over the side went his pannikin while he roared his rage, and the sound brought others to try the spigot. They combined their drunken efforts to tip the hogshead on its chocks, and got no more than a dribble for their pains. Away they staggered, crying the thing was dry, dry as a sucked orange, and laid themselves amongst their snoring fellows on the deck, muttering and falling into silence at last. I slipped down and rapped the cask to make sure. 'Twas empty as our battle drum. Sixty-three gallons of fine Jerez poured down the throats of threescore men betwixt sundown and some hour well short of daydawn, and still a thirst in some of them!

They lay about the deck, sprawled on the hatches, or sat in the scuppers with backs to the bulwark and heads on their breasts, as I had seen corpses in the streets of Cap François in '93. The ship moved with a proud indifference, as if she were endowed with a life of her own that took no count of men and their beastliness, and as she heeled to the swell all those drunken bodies moved together and all the heads swayed as if jerked by a cord.

That was the way we came into the Old Bahama Passage, a chancy place at the best of times with a crew alert and daylight to see by, and we in the dark and nine of us, men and boys, stiff-faced with fatigue and the worry of the night, to guard the cabin, to steer, to handle the canvas and watch for the milky shimmer of the reefs.

Towards daylight I went with Brady and Dawkins and searched amongst those reeking forms for the least drunken ones, the men who had fallen early and slept off the worst of it, and kicked them into wakefulness. But the day had come, with the evil white breakers of Diamond Cay showing plain off the larboard bow, and Cuba looming to starboard, before we had hands enough to afford us relief.

Lot came, with eyes bloodshot and gray hairs on end, and with that familiar sheep's look of innocence, and took charge of the poop as if nothing had happened. I sent our weary afterguard off to their hammocks. Dolainde sat against the binnacle, sleeping profoundly, and I did not wake him.

As I entered the cabin Lia Dolainde sprang up from her couch, her face pale and mysterious like the faces of women who watch long hours at a deathbed. "Roux!" she whispered, and the old nickname gave me a pang. She had not called me Red in a very long time. I thought of those merry winter journeys in the sleigh, and the days when I taught her to skate on the ice of Gosport River, when she was a child, all eyes and quick legs, and I the young seaman out of a berth and time on my hands. All that seemed very long ago.

"Your father is all right," I said in a voice like the scrape of a shoe, so parched I was, and so forspent.

"I was thinking——"

"Of Brule?" I uttered a hoarse chuckle. "He's well enough, Lia, though he got a bit drunk at the last. You heard his fiddle?

I tell you he was more use to us than twenty bosuns armed with capstan bars, for he kept those madmen dancing till their energy was spent. Ay, he fiddled the legs out from under 'em——"

"And you, Capitaine?" she murmured in that small lost voice. "There was fighting yesterday—I heard the guns and the shouting——"

"Not much of a fight," I said indifferently. "A brush, say, and a piece of luck. Too easy, much. Were you frightened? You've been shut down here a long time, haven't you? You may go on deck now if you want."

I sat on my berth, and in a moment all my bones and sinews went to nothing. I fell over, knowing that now I could let myself go, and finding a delicious pleasure in the thought of it. I felt the girl pull off my boots and loosen my belt, turning me carefully this way and that, as if seeking for sign of a wound, and I seem to remember a hand in my tousled hair; but I was far gone then, and perhaps 'twas only some idle memory of Mrs. Sherring.

After these worries and excitements I had an uneasy feeling that something worse was in the offing, on the principle that it never rains but it pours. And yet, looking back, the three weeks that followed our threading of the Old Bahama Passage were a pleasure cruise. True, we were lashed by the tail of a hurricane off the island of Inagua, and had to run back over our course willy-nilly for several shrieking hours with nothing but a staysail set, a wild black sky no higher than the mastheads, and spray flying thicker than snow in a January storm in Nova Scotia. And we got the flick of another later, and made a mad run past the Hole in the Wall for the open sea.

And true, when we reached our cruising station off Inagua again, hopeful of the Windward Passage, through which so much of the Caribbee trade must pass, we found those waters acrawl with privateers out of the Bahamas, Jamaica, Bermuda—we even spoke two from our own Nova Scotia with letters of marque from Sir John like ourselves—and such a throng of His Majesty's own ships as I never saw in my life. The whole West Indies fleet seemed to have its station there—a very good one for the blockade of Hispaniola and the guarding of Jamaica down to leeward—and we had a lively time of it dodging the deep topsails and very square yards of the men-o'-war. Any of them, given the chance, would have brought us to and pressed half our men into their service, letter of marque or none; and so we fled from them like the plague and were thankful to sink their long pennants under the sea line astern.

Chiefly we found ourselves cruising empty blue seas under a sky of hot brass, for I turned away from Inagua in disgust. What with privateers and warships, that region was like a haunt of wolves; anyone who spotted a prize had the whole pack down upon him before the last gun was fired. We hunted to the eastward as far as the edge of the Sargasso, a vast litter of brown seaweed carried and held by opposing currents and winds, a mighty strange thing to see. This way, I reckoned, the French and Spanish ships must come, running down the trades for Hispaniola and Cuba.

But not a sail did we see, day after day. I was vexed and puzzled. Was our luck out? The men grew restless under the long heat and monotony. I had given Lia Dolainde the freedom of the deck after that night in the Old Bahama Passage, and she made full use of it, roaming about like any of the shipboys, talking and laughing with the men. She spent much time near the main hatch watching Adam Armitage and his mates put the finish on the new longboat and gig—a thin pretense, it seemed to me, for several times I noticed her in deep converse with Brule, standing over against the main lee rigging, where no doubt they thought the mainsail hid them from my view.

She said very little to me and never stayed on the poop when I was there. In the close quarters of the cabin it was the same, seldom a word, never a direct look. Each night at four bells she kissed her father with a dutiful "*Bonsoir, Papa*" that usually was lost on that sodden man, and vanished behind her blanket-curtain. Sometimes I heard her sighing deeply there in the hot dark. Sleep was difficult in that sultry atmosphere, which seemed to thicken when the cabin lamp was put out for the night. I suppose she lay like her father and me, naked to the faint air down the wind sail and gasping for a breath of it.

Our cask water now had a taste and a feel on the tongue, and at last I swung the brigantine up to Exuma Sound and watered at one of the outlying Bahamas. 'Twas a lonely place with a beach of white sand hurtful to the eyes, although the green behind was like a glimpse of heaven. We had a pleasant frolic there. The lone inhabitant was a graybeard Englishman who talked in a slow west-country voice and had a fat jolly mulatto woman and a swarm of lively brats about his palm-thatched hut. We rolled our casks up the blazing beach from the boats and filled them at his well; and the well set our Nova Scotia lads scratching their heads, for the water in it rose and fell with the tide, though sweet as any spring in the woods at home and common enough in the Bahamas.

I left an anchor watch aboard the brigantine and turned the rest ashore, and away they went, larking, tumbling, beating each other with switches and playing leapfrog along the sand like a rabble of boys out of school.

I went ashore in my own gig with Lot Mayes, Dawkins, Black

Boston, Dolainde, and the girl. Boston had charge of the provisions and found a shady place where we could lie looking out on the beach, the land crabs, and the foolish booby birds. There we lay sipping rum and lime juice cooled in one of those porous earthenware pots which West Indians call monkeys and hang in the sea breeze.

But we could not lie still very long. There was too much pleasure to be had in the feel of earth underfoot after the long weeks of sea. We walked with the rolling shipboard gait, even Lia Dolainde, who laughed at us and at herself. In the tight nankeens and shirt, with a madras handkerchief binding her yellow locks against the breeze and sun, she set us all smiling at her imitation of a tar ashore, walking with legs absurdly wide, and swinging her arms athwartships and not fore and aft as landsmen do, and with her palms facing sternward and half opened as if ready at any moment to clap onto a rope.

She chanted our old favorite, "Haul the Bowline," in the deepest voice she could fetch, and hailed a green parrot in one of the trees, calling him a lubberly hooknosed swab and worse, with some expert profanity concerning the furling of the "fore royal." Our laughter fell a little hollow towards the end of this comedy, and Dolainde said with a whimsical lift of brow, "How well my daughter has learned your English language, Capitaine!"

His indifference irked me as much as Lia's oaths, for, as I have said before, I never could forget the sad small girl crying *"Maman!"* on the *Sally's* deck that night at the Cap, or escape a guilty feeling that we had let her drift into womanhood like some she-urchin of the waterfront. It chilled me to hear that stream of blasphemy pouring from her red lips in a kind of merry innocence, all uttered in the musical and charming accent which she had never been able to lose, try as she might. She saw my displeasure in my face and paused.

"You find it very hard to smile, don't you, Roux?"

I replied in French, "You are not amusing, ma'mselle," and added something about one parrot in the tree and another on the ground. She looked puzzled and annoyed, as I suppose any actress would look upon so cold a critic, and shrugged and turned away.

Boston busied himself with a fire and his pots and pans, and presently we dined in a very sumptuous fashion on dried codfish from home, stewed in claret, and rice rubbed to a powder like snow, and some of the old English wanderer's tomatoes and yams and slices of ham fried together to perfection, and coffee sweetened with molasses. Afterwards Lia disappeared, and her father and Lot and Simon lay in the green shade shredding niggerhead in their palms and stuffing it into their clays, while I went off to explore the bush, puffing on a Bahamian cigar to ward off the mosquitoes.

No one but a sailor after many days at sea, especially in those glaring latitudes, can taste the full pleasure of shade. True shade, I mean, the green gloom of massed leaves so dense that an occasional ray of sunshine falls like a sword. It is more than just a refuge from the sun; the living walls give a privacy delicious after the cheek-by-jowl existence of shipboard, and there is a pleasant sound of birds and crickets and suchlike small creatures in place of the wind's whine in the rigging, not to mention the taste of water fresh from the earth, and fruits from the bough, and above all the solid and comfortable feel of the land itself, rooted fast, not to be moved by any whim of the weather.

Precious matters, I tell you, and no wonder many a sailorman has quit his ship and found himself a brown woman and an easy sustenance in those islands where the days go by like hours and winter never comes. The Caribbees are full of such men, Englishmen, all manner of Europeans, and in my voyages I had met an astonishing number of New Englanders and Nova Scotians, settled all the way from Nassau to Trinidad. Was it the soft life of the islands alone that caught them after long weeks of sea? Or was there something more, a sudden distaste for the North, a horror of the stony fields, the gray seas and skies, the passionless woman in the gray wooden house at home? I had never thought on these things before, and now I pondered, and wondered a little at my own curiosity.

These ramblings and musings brought me out of the dense growth after a time. I found myself treading a sandy ridge covered with a kind of pine, spindly things, not like the pines of home, though something in the smell that hung in the hot air under them reminded me of the woods at Gosport in August weather. And it was this, I suppose, that brought my business back to mind. The sun was getting down the sky. The water casks must all be boated off by now, and time to gather up the men and get aboard. The islands about Exuma Sound concealed a swarm of gentry mighty partial to boat attacks by night, and while I felt confident in our own ability to beat them off, still it seemed wise to weigh anchor and stand out to sea by darkfall.

I took my bearings from the sun, and after some hot floundering in the bush I came upon a small lagoon a little to the northward of the watering place. The water was shoal and alive with flamingos, wading to and fro and darting their heads under the surface as a man wields a claw hoe at home. The late sunlight made a fine show of their crimson wings, a handsome sight, and I paused to admire them from the screen of manchineel bushes along the shore.

Something, a scuffle of sand, an exclamation, drew my attention to the right. I saw two men half sitting, half lying with their backs against a great log of driftwood, and locked in what appeared to be a silent and playful wrestling match. The log shut off part of my view, but I saw that one of them, the aggressive one, was Victor Brule. His face was flushed and intent. Suddenly the other broke clear and, rising on his knees, flung out a white-shirted arm. His hand struck Brule's face a slap that rang over the still water of the lagoon like a pistol shot, and all the flamingos rose together and flapped away to the west with necks outstretched and long legs hauled up, like a flutter of bright bunting in the sunshine.

"Ma chère!" cried Brule in a tone of anger and complaint.

The other spoke then. It was Lia Dolainde, of course, crying in creole French, "Hold yourself, Victor! What is it you think I am? One of your herring girls at Gosport?"

Brule crouched, saying nothing. He looked as if he would fling himself at her again, and she put out a hand to stave him off. I was about to break out of the bushes and give Brule a taste of my fist and Lia a lick with the rough side of my tongue, when he spoke in a voice that was half snarl, half caress.

"I think you are Mademoiselle Lia-Marie Dolainde, who has begged me to assist her father in Saint Domingo, where my word as an officer of the republic may go far. Have I, then, made a mistake?"

"No," she said in a mollifying tone. "But Victor——"

"But Victor! But Victor! You know I love you, Lia. Have I not said so many times? And you—have you not promised, not in words only but with your eyes, your manner, that when certain affairs are brought about one may consider himself your husband—since under the republic there are no priests to make marriages?"

I give a poor translation here, of course; they were using the affectionate "thou" and "thy," and certain creole idioms difficult to put in English.

"Ah yes," she answered without relaxing that wary pose. "But this is not Saint Domingo, and there are certain matters to be accomplished before——"

"Lia!" he begged in a lovesick voice, and I longed to kick the wheedling bull calf that he looked. I was filled with a kind of amused anger, regarding Lia Dolainde and remembering Brule's lady-killing tales. He must have felt very sure of her when she strolled with him away from the landing place and out of sight; and I could picture his defeat, for I knew his method. The soulful looks, the careful flattery in the purring creole voice, the gentle kiss, and then without warning or further ado the swift over-running attack that won surrender before the pretty dear could make even a show of resistance. But it is one thing to storm a silly wench in shift and petticoats and quite another with a girl of Lia Dolainde's mind—and clad in a man's nankeens. Brule had been confounded by a novelty, a woman unapproachable.

"A bargain is a bargain," she said firmly, and I had to admire the high fling of her head, and the way she did not move an inch or cry out to the men around the point.

"But surely," he said in a silky voice, "one is entitled to a payment on account? You are very beautiful, Lia, and I am a man, you comprehend, who has not touched a woman in three weeks, four weeks—a very long time."

She nodded slowly, as if this were very reasonable indeed, but she repeated in that resolute tone, "You shall have what you ask, Victor, when you have done what you promised. Until then you must wait." And with a sudden coquetry that set my teeth on edge, "Am I not worth waiting for?"

Brule glowered and brushed the sand from his trousers. "How can one be sure of that, my flower, when you sleep in one cabin with that cursed Nouvelle-Ecossais?"

"And my father!"

"Ah yes, of course. Your father!" His tone conveyed very eloquently his opinion of Monsieur Dolainde.

She rose to her feet and looked at him indignantly, trying to make herself tall, as if there were dignity in inches, when the cambric shirt and cotton pantaloons clung to her figure in the heat and betrayed every line of it, a charming spectacle for Brule—for any man, even for me, skulking in the bushes like a Peeping Tom. Looking at her in this fashion, I had a sudden twinge of guilt, and the reproachful wraith of Felicity drifted into my mind like a wisp of northern fog, so cool, so pale, so very different from Lia-Marie Dolainde.

Brule arose sulkily, and together they walked towards the landing place, Lia stooping now and then to pick up sea shells that lay like tinted jewels all along that beach—to show her father, I suppose, and to account for her long absence.

At a longish interval I followed, and fell upon my idling crew with a volley of orders—Pride's Cockerel to the life. And so in the broad yellow flare of the sunset we took to the boats and went aboard, and sailed for Crooked Island Passage and the coast of Hispaniola.

Chapter 22

THAT night we held council in the cabin, while the girl slowly waved a palm-leaf fan before her face and watched us from her locker-couch. Dolainde with his wig off in the heat, revealing the sparse gray hairs that once had been as golden as her own. Lot Mayes with his unkempt front hair and the queer short tail at the back, tarred stiff and curling upward like the tail of a gray dog, and the unfailing quid in his lean brown cheek, and the habitual motion of his toothless jaws that brought the chin and the long pitted strawberry nose together like a pair of nutcrackers.

Simon Dawkins and his gold-flecked muddy eyes, his hard round face, brown and rough-skinned as a russet apple. Brule with his cropped black poll, his dainty mustache, and his bright blue glance that never was still. And I, of course—Cockerel Cain.

With the roll of the ship the brass cabin lamp in its gimbals appeared to drag the small round shadow of its bottom across and across the floor, giving off a fine stink of whale oil on the way. We sat in our shirts, unbuttoned in the heat, and grateful for the stir of air that came down the canvas funnel of the wind sail, though it was warm and humid as our own breath.

Lot and Simon looked upon Brule with great disfavor, as if I had brought a polecat into their midst, and did not change their looks much when they knew why he was there. I did not love the man myself, but tsha!—whom could one trust wholly in this world? Unless I had misheard that conversation by the lagoon, Brule and Lia Dolainde and Dolainde himself probably were playing with a pretty little conspiracy of their own. And whatever it was I did not care overmuch. A pistol at Brule's back would help his good faith mightily once we were ashore, and until then our interests were one. And that was true of Dolainde also. The planter was in a fever to reach the old *manoir* on the slope of the Morne du Cap—and so was I.

I put the matter before them. "Gentlemen, you all saw what I saw in the Windward Passage and off Tortuga—a swarm of men-o'-war and privateers all watching one another and the land. No room for us in such a company and no chance to get ashore unseen. I propose to come at our landing place from the east—from a long way east."

"Why?" demanded Lot.

"The Spanish side of Hispaniola lies that way."

Brule spoke. "It is all French now. The Spanish gave up their part to France in '95."

"That doesn't mean the French possess it. Their armies are too busy in the west. The French troops, white and black, are massed along the western coast from Cap François around to Jacmel."

"How do you know?" Brule said.

"Because that's where the English armies landed and were driven out, and where His Majesty's Navy still maintains a tight blockade, as we have seen. Mr. Pride told me all this before we left—had it from the governor of Jamaica. His Majesty's ships don't trouble much with the Spanish side of the island—it's shut off by high mountains from the rest, and it's the poor side, not worth anybody's powder. That's why I say we must come in from that way."

"Do you propose to sail your ship over the mountains?" Dolainde cried through his nose.

"No, I propose to sail her under their northern lee, monsieur. We shall take a roundabout course from here, well outside the Caicos—we must make a good offing in any case, the way the winds lie at this season—and then bear down past the Silver Bank for Hispaniola. Once we fetch inshore, it's a matter of stealing along the coast towards the west, around Cape Isabella and the Monte Cristi—the old smugglers' way, eh, Brule? There are prodigious mountains all along that shore, and if we keep close in——"

"Amongst the reefs!" snapped Lot, wide-eyed.

"As you say—why, our sails will be hard to make out from seaward, and we've nothing to fear from the land. Few settlements and no craft of a size to bother us——"

"There is Fort Liberty," Brule snapped. "You must pass that."

Dolainde looked puzzled. "Eh? Fort——"

"The *ci-devant* Fort Dauphin, monsieur," with an open sneer, "has been given another name."

"Ah!"

"Dauphin or Liberty, we'll give it a good berth," I went on. "We can do that well enough—the fort's at the end of the Manzanillo bight, and we can cut across that and still have the shelter of the reefs—by the Seven Brothers, say, and then a run for Caracul Bay."

"And then?"—Lot's voice.

"That is for Brule to say. He's our pilot to the landing place."

"Um!"

Brule sat up very straight, feeling his importance and clearly eager to impress the listening girl. He put a slender snuff-stained finger on the chart.

"Attention, messieurs! This passage inside the reefs from Cape Isabella, it will not be easy, you comprehend. The brigantine draws a little more water than one could wish, for comfort, but it can be done, you may depend on me." A shrug and a comical twist of his olive features. "One is familiar with that passage from old days and nights in the contraband trade, which I put behind me long ago. Now here I am again. How life is strange! Now the affair of landing, that is delicate—delicate. From Fort Liberty to Cap François the coast is one lace of reefs, on the edge of which there is great depth of water. Some of those reefs have passages deep enough for such a ship as this, and one may get inside and anchor in the very shadow of the mountains. For our landing the Caracul passage is best, it is wide, and the shoals show very white and clear, even from the deck, and there is an old lime kiln on the shore which makes a steering mark. *Bien!*

"But because that passage is easy, there is good reason not to anchor where you might suppose. No! For you must leave your ship at anchor while you go inland, eh? So! After that we go on a little farther to the west. There is a cove I know where no one lives, where the brigantine may ride in four fathoms, concealed from the sea except to the north—and that is guarded by the reefs. And where there are no eyes to see, there are no tongues to speak, and what is better, no Negro drums to send a warning to the Cap or to Fort Liberty. *V'là!*"

Brule sat back with an air of triumph and a sidelong glance at the girl. And Lia fanned herself and avoided his eyes and mine, yawning, regarding the lamp with that bored look of a woman who finds the talk of men incomprehensible and dull, and longs for the moment when they will be done and she can go to sleep.

"And then?" Lot demanded.

I said, "We land with twenty men, Dawkins and I—you're to stand by the ship. The men will be chosen chiefly from the Gosport woodsmen. You wondered why I signed them; now you know. There will be a moon if we judge our time aright. Monsieur Dolainde will guide us across the plain where the plantations are, by night you understand, a matter of twelve miles or so."

"And him?" Simon Dawkins asked bluntly, jerking a thumb at Brule. Brule looked at me and drew in a breath.

"Brule goes along with us, of course."

I watched the creole from the corner of my eye, but I could not tell whether this pleased him or not. Lia's fan halted for a moment, that was all.

"And," Lot burst out, "this leaving the ship in a chancy place, taking a good third o' the hands ashore and traipsing about that wild country in the dark—all this hanky-panky—what's it for?"

I leaned across the table with a tight grin on my lips. "For thirty thousand golden louis, left behind in the Manoir Dolainde that night the blacks went wild."

Lot's mouth fell open, a cavern of astonishment. Simon Dawkins whistled. Dolainde's face was a lined yellow mask. Brule, it seemed to me, looked smug. And Lia Dolainde, curled upon her couch in a shapely attitude that made a pretty jest of those masculine clothes, lay back upon her cushions and closed her eyes. The thick lashes lay like shadows upon her ivory cheekbones. Her hair, free of the handkerchief in which, creole fashion, she bound it during the day, was tumbled in a gleaming golden fall about her breast and shoulders. The hand with the fan drooped to the floor. An image of indifference.

Thus we planned and so we sailed, and I for one felt confident. After all, what was our venture into Hispaniola compared to those of time long past in the Caribbee waters, when English, French, Spanish, all manner of men had left their ships not for a night or two but for weeks and months, and fought their way through mountains and forests full of savage tribes, and conquered fortresses and sacked and burned whole cities, and carried off treasures to which Dolainde's careful hoard was nothing?

Simon hummed about the poop. Even Lot was cheerful. There was in all of us, it seems to me, the spirit of lads about to raid the deacon's orchard on some windy night of autumn; the boy's heart in the man's breast, the challenge of the dark or the unknown, the invitation of the night wind in the trees, the magic of a sleeping town gone strange by starlight, peopled with shadows and lurking dogs; and best of all, the sudden heady freedom of walls and boundaries, the wide world yours for a pair of nimble legs and ready hands. Yes, that was it, the silly, restless, romantic heart that beats in all of us, even when bones are old and flesh withered like an autumn leaf that hangs for a time and drops at last, and heart, bones, flesh, and mind are stilled forever. Boy or man, that is the root of it, gold or no gold, apples or none.

And so in high heart we came down the wind between the

Silver Cays and that other great shoal which Frenchmen call the Mouchoir Carré—Square Handkerchief—and saw the tall mountains of Hispaniola blue in the haze ahead, with their heads wrapped in cloud like a row of vast chowder kettles steaming over a fire. We closed with the land to the northwest of Port Plata, exactly where I was not sure, for a mass of dark cloud came rolling down the hills and over the sea. Soon we were bombarded and half drowned in rain, such rain as must be seen to be believed, the drops as big as pistol balls, beating on the sails with the very sound of musketry, and splashing on the deck in such a torrent that the scuppers could not carry it away fast enough.

I went below to scan the chart and was just in time to rescue it from a rush of water down the wind sail like the outpour of an eaves spout. Lia sprang to help me unlash the canvas funnel, and I roared to the deck for someone to close the skylight. The girl set about the pool on the floor with a mop—she had conferred the duty of cabin boy upon herself—and I grumbled, "What a *blague,* this climate of yours!"

"What is wrong with it?"—in a tart voice.

"What's wrong with a country that parches the blood in your veins at one moment and souses you head and heels at the next, like a scolding wife in a ducking stool?"

"If you don't like it——" She bit off the rest and was silent, leaning on the mop handle and regarding me seriously. Then, in an earnest voice, "Roux!"

"Yes?"

"Don't go!"

She had a light blue madras wound about her piled hair such as you saw mulatto women wearing everywhere in Hispaniola, her favorite headgear, and I thought how poor Madame Dolainde would have wept and stormed to see her daughter wearing such a thing, let alone the man's shirt and those elegant yellow tights.

"What!" I said lightly. "Stay by the ship and let Simon and the lads have all the fun?"

She uttered a little cluck of impatience. "I mean all of you. Don't go ashore in Saint Domingo—what do you call it?—Ispaniola. It is very dangerous."

"Oh, come! You're a fine one to talk of danger, Lia—you who stowed away in a privateer—and sleep in a cabin with Cockerel Cain!"

She arched a black eyebrow at that, a trick of hers when something quizzical was on her tongue. But she swallowed the quip, whatever it was, and told me soberly, "Roux, I beg you to set my father and me—and Victor Brule—on the shore, and go away and never come back! If Papa finds this money of which he speaks, he will find some way to pay his debts to Mr. Pride when the war ends. Surely that will satisfy Mr. Pride? And you and your ship and your men—you have other things to do in these seas before you can go home to those you love. Go and do them, and forget this mad affair."

A black suspicion came upon me then and found its way to my tongue.

"Oho! So that's it! How simple do you think I am, ma'mselle? That would be very nice, wouldn't it? —for you and your clever Victor—and Papa, of course. You could go to the *manoir,* remove the money, make your way to the Spanish settlements, and live happy ever after! Ah no! That's not my notion of the game, dear Lia, nor Mr. Pride's. Tomorrow night we shall be up with Caracul Bay if your charming Victor pilots half as well as he woos, and he and I and Papa Dolainde shall go ashore with twenty brisk lads to see fair play and no monkey tricks. And you shall stay aboard, *ma petite,* and pray for all of us."

I expected her to fly into a tantrum, indeed I hoped she would, for Lia in a passion was charming to watch. But she confounded me, saying in a mournful voice, "Red, you make me hate you, but I cannot say the words. Your temper is like your hair, a part of you, and one must take one with the other—especially one who is a woman like me and sees your danger and can change nothing. I shall pray for you, Red, as you say. Surely the Holy Mother who knew the sorrow of women will grant one little prayer!"

She looked me in the eyes, and what I saw in hers was strange and disturbing, something meant to repel that invited instead, like the somber shadows of the Hispaniola hills. We stood for a long minute in silence, and I know not what might have happened then but for a sharp rap on the skylight and the voice of Simon Dawkins crying, "Sail-O!"

Chapter 23

THE sail was difficult to make out, with the upsplash of that furious rainpour hanging over the sea's face like a gray smoke. The wind had fluked and come ahead, a bad one for threading the reefs, and Simon had reduced sail promptly. From the way the stranger loomed astern, forereaching on us hand over hand, 'twas evident that she had a sloop or schooner rig and carried plenty of canvas, and after another turn of the binnacle glass it was clear she intended to overhaul us. Thunder pealed mightily in the shadowy mountains to larboard, and there was a steady flicker of lightning in the gloom. In a brief lull in the rain we saw her clearly, a low-hulled thing with two tall masts, a schooner right enough and carrying an ominous spread of canvas, reckless of the mountain squalls.

We beat to quarters, and the men stood drenched at the guns, each powder boy holding a bit of canvas over his cartridge bucket and the riflemen covering their priming with their hats. Poor weather for fighting, but the stranger's match and powder were no more waterproof than ours, and I was more curious than concerned. I suspected a blockade runner with the same notion as mine, working up the coast from the eastward with supplies from France, and keeping close to the reefs to avoid His Majesty's ships.

By seven bells in the afternoon watch our doubts and questions were solved, for by that time the stranger had drawn abeam to starboard. He fired a shot across our bows and ran up the flag of republican France, a lean black schooner with a main boom of tremendous length and a flush deck black with men. We counted six guns a side. Lot Mayes and Simon looked at me, and I nodded, reading their thought, and saying with a cheer I did not feel at all, "Aha, my bullies, here's a fight!"

A French privateer by every sign, out of old France perhaps, but more likely out of Guadeloupe or Martinique, well armed to all appearance and undoubtedly well manned with whites, mulattoes, blacks—every desperate sort of man to be found in the French West Indies. 'Twas the habit of the Royal Navy to call the French man-o'-war sailor Johnnie Crapaud and rate him mighty low, but that was not true of the French privateersmen, especially those of the Caribbees. The Guadeloupe privateers were famous all the way from ten north latitude to thirty-five.

This was the kind of thing Mr. Pride had warned me to avoid; and 'struth, there was no profit in fighting a privateer of any sort —one wolf against another and the devil sitting by. With our errand in Hispaniola foremost in my mind I cursed the fellow up and down, but there was no help for it. The Frenchman wanted a fight, that was clear. Perhaps he took us for an armed French merchantman running some special cargo through the blockade for the Cap, and fancied a bit of piracy. More likely he was desperate from dodging the warships himself and, knowing us for a privateer, had resolved to attack, seeing in us a capture of some sort anyhow, and worth a few hundred louis at Guadeloupe for our hull and spars alone.

We ran up our red jack with a cheer and let fly with the long brass gun and the starboard nine-pounder. One shot passed over his deck, I think—we never saw it, anyhow—and the other smacked a neat hole through his foresail. Our lads yelled and Pardon looked his pleasure, though such shooting was too good to last. The Frenchman swung off the wind a bit, respectfully, and when we clewed our foresail to clear the forward deck for action he shortened sail also, evidently wanting to keep his distance.

I dallied with the notion of turning seaward, where there would be plenty of room to fight without the worry of the reefs, but gave it up. Out there a cannonade sounding down the wind would bring unwelcome topsails over the horizon sooner or later. I preferred our chances where we were, and so we thrashed on towards the west, with the Frenchman keeping his distance tack for tack, and both of us loosing off our long guns steadily in the hope of some lucky damage. And all the time the rain poured down and thunder rolled in the dim mountains to larboard in a way that made our gunfire seem a yapping of playful dogs.

I had sent for Brule as soon as we made the land, and he stood at my side in his patched and faded blue naval jacket and soiled duck trousers, with a Barcelona handkerchief tied about his round skull, and darting his quick blue eyes from the strange sail to me, and from me to the loom of the coast. He looked worried, and no wonder, for he stood a good chance of having his head knocked off by the fire of his compatriots, and another of foundering with the rest of us if we fell on a reef in our present uncertainty. I felt a dour pleasure in that. The first chance held; but the second faded considerably after an hour of this luffing and popping, when a fluke of the wind tore the clouds apart and we saw ahead and to larboard the huge cape which the creoles call Casrouge, a landmark of the finest kind.

"We shall be out of the rain very soon," Brule said in a relieved voice, and I nodded. Casrouge is the end of a mountain wall that catches the moisture of the trades and nourishes a rich growth of forest on its seaward flank. Beyond lies Cape Isabella, the most northerly point of Hispaniola, and after you turn that corner you enter upon a coast that is hilly but arid, covered with cactus and such stuff, like a desert tipped towards the sea.

But here the *capitaine-de-corsaire* came to a decision. He must have been mighty puzzled by our presence on this lonely part of the coast and by the course we so doggedly pursued; and I suppose a suspicion had come to him that we counted on some sort of help to the west, a consort waiting there, or perhaps another mad English expedition landing at the Cap. At any rate, just as we made out the low point of Cape Isabella in the clearing weather to the west, he set his foresail again and then put his helm over sharply and sent his lean craft racing down as if determined to cross our stern and rake us with his broadside in the passing.

What a beautiful sight that schooner made! I can see her yet. The masts were not raked so sharply as I first thought, but they were very tall and slender, indeed they seemed no stouter than fishing rods, bent and thrumming with that daring press of sail. Her foresail was a big thing, and she carried a large square foretopsail and fore-t'gallant, a fore staysail and jib, a main staysail, a main gaff topsail, and finally that enormous mainsail, set on a boom that looked as long as the mainmast itself. All of this canvas swelled and strained in the brisk wind as if it would fly out of the boltropes any moment, and laid the hull over so that she showed her copper sheathing dully like tarnished gold; and the long rain-beaten seas ran along her wet black side and sprang foaming into the open ports in the afterpart of her waist, and poured a white lip over the afterdeck, where a group of intent figures stood beside the helm.

She rode the long seas like a race horse, swooping down with a plunge that soused her bow to the knightheads and laid her long sprit and jib boom thwack on the sea as a schoolmaster lays a cane on a young sinner's back, and the shock wet the jib foot and sent spray flying sometimes as high as the foremast head and drifting aft in a mist that obscured the whole midships part of her. Then she rose gallantly, eagerly, to the next sea, with a toss of her bow and a settling of her stern as if she were gathering invisible legs under her, and sprang forward so that her sharp forefoot and a good twenty feet of keel shot clean through the crest and over the succeeding trough.

"Ain't she a tearer?" Lot cried, greatly admiring. The words were hardly out of his mouth when the Frenchman let fly with his broadside, or what amounted to that—one port was smokeless, and I fancied the gunners there cursing a wet match or maybe the priming. 'Twas smartly done, and we had little time to flinch and none to pray. The *Fancy* was sharply heeled on the larboard tack and showing all her deck. I heard someone cry a warning in the waist, that was all, and then *pfitt!*—a ball went past my belt buckle and struck the bitt on the weather side of the poop.

A twelve-pounder at a guess. The stout oak of the bitt gave forth a shower of splinters at the impact, a curious thing to see, as if it were a fat brown bud bursting into flower. Our helmsman uttered a dreadful cry and threw up his hands, swinging as if to tell me something urgent but unable to find the words, his mouth gaping, his eyes turned up to the whites. He fell at my feet, and I saw a foot-long fragment of the bitt standing out of his bronzed flesh just above the trouser band, and blood gushing forth as you see wine spurting about an ill-fitted spigot in a cask.

I was aware of the wheel spinning wildly and Simon and one or two others springing to wrestle with it, and the *Fancy* swinging into the stiff wind and the upper sails on the foremast already shaking violently, as if they would tear themselves clean off the yards. I turned away from poor Fowler and looked anxiously along the waist. A shot had buried itself in the mainmast and spalled a ragged white star in the brown polished wood. Another must have crossed the deck between the masts, where three men lay very still and another on his back, writhing and beating his hands and bare heels on the planking.

Call it luck or good gunnery, three hits out of five was a mighty jolting circumstance, and a glance to starboard showed the schooner still coming down very fast off the wind, with a great bustle about her starboard battery as the gunners labored to reload. I was absurdly angry with the Frenchman for taking me by surprise. According to all theory of sea fighting, he should have held his fire until he was passing our stern, to get the best effect. Instead he had loosed off while the ships were quartering. And I had held our own fire in keeping with Pardon Gardner's rule, dinned in my ears the whole way south—"The fust broadside's always the best 'un, Nathan, 'specially with raw gunners like most of ours. Remember that. After the first fire they're excited and they tend to load slovenly and aim wild. Hold your broadside, then, till you're sure. And be mighty sure!"

And so we had missed a chance to rake him as he jibed, and now, with the *Fancy* sweeping blindly up into the wind, no gun of ours would bear but the two six-pounders on the poop. So much for theories and hearsay! It came to me with bitter force then how green we all were at this deadly game, how much we had to learn—and how much that brisk Frenchman knew.

Seeing our broad foresail furled, he had poured his fire on our quarter in the hope of striking the helmsman or smashing the steering gear. That done, with the sail we were carrying our brigantine would very likely fly up into the wind—as she had—and give him all the chance he wanted to rake us from stern to stem. And that is exactly what he proceeded to do, carefully, gun by gun, as his schooner swept past, a bare cable's length astern.

Sometimes I shiver still at the memory of that helpless minute. All hands crouched or lay flat on the deck, awaiting the iron storm, and I bellowed to the landsmen, "Aloft! Get aloft, there! Into the rigging and fire on their gunners, damn your eyes!" But they hung about the deck, casting gloomy looks aloft, where our fore-topsail and t'gallant were all ashake and booming as if the very thunder had come down out of the mountains and perched about the mastheads. One or two cried out that no man alive could keep a musket dry enough to fire in this flood of rain. Maybe they had the right of it; but when one of them, the young Indian, Wokwees, scrambled up the fore rigging with a musket slung from his shoulder I pointed an angry finger, yelling, "There's the only man among ye! Ah, ye lubbers, what's the good of ye?" Whereupon three or four followed him, treading the ratlines with a queer air of doubt and desperation. I turned away with a hopeless flip of my hands as the first shot of the Frenchman's broadside sang over the poop.

In the meantime Simon had the watch hauling manfully to get the main boom amidships, and Lot had run forward to see to the headsails. We were caught betwixt the Frenchman astern and the wind ahead, with the *Fancy's* sails coming aback and likely to take the sticks out of her. The young seaman at the helm looked pretty pale about the chops, and no wonder, with the Frenchmen shooting at his back and that limp bloody form at his feet.

I said to him quietly, "Hard astarboard." When the wheel was hard over, and just as another shot went past my ear, a roar through my cupped hands to the after gang, "Main-tops'l haul!" They heaved on the braces with a will that lost nothing by the sound of the Frenchman's fire. Round came the main yards on the starboard tack. By now the foreyards were full aback and the fore-topmast and royal mast bending like wands. I watched them anxiously, praying *Hold, hold, good spars!* I seemed to see them where I saw them first, in the woods at home, grown tall and slim on the ridge side and toughened by the sweep of winds along the narrow valley. And they held. They held!

I thanked God then for the forest that grew them, and Peter Sargent for his careful shaping of them; and I thought of 'Lisha Riddock's sails, and Dan Stacey's good hemp rigging, with a song at the heart. Now Lot's men got the head sheets over and hauled aft ready for the starboard tack, and stood there waiting, staring aloft, and wondering, and doubtless praying. And I found myself talking to my ship. "Over! Over, girl! Over, my beauty, if ye love me half as much as I love you!"

I had lost count of the Frenchman's gunfire, and I did not take my eyes from those all-important head yards, but I was aware of a commotion all about me on the poop, the two six-pounders banging away and leaping back against their breeching tackles like live things, and the squealing of gun trucks and the heavy rumble on the planking, the quick grunted oaths and cries of the men as they reloaded and handspiked them up to the rail again, and Pardon Gardner yelling in the waist, "Stand by, lar-board gunners! Don't fire till I give the word or I'll have the flesh off your backs tomorrow—if ye live till then! Powder boys!"

I lived a year in those moments. Slowly—ah, God, how slowly! —the brigantine eased over, with everything cracking and thundering aloft, until at last I was able to shout in a voice that shook with relief, "Forebowline, let go and haul!" and the head yards swung round on the new tack. We set the foresail then, and the *Fancy* surged away. Phoo! I was sweating, sweating like a monkey jar in sunshine, and so were we all.

And now both ships were heading down the wind, for the Frenchman's maneuver had taken him well in towards the reefs, and he did not like them any more than we. But we had the outer berth, and I resolved to keep it. Going large like this, with our spread of square sail forward, we had the greater speed, and began to come down on him hand over hand. Pardon's Delight began to speak, and presently our starboard nine-pounder as well. I shortened sail a bit to keep our advantage, for the *corsaire* was not armed for running any more than we, and had nothing better than a pair of carronades aft to answer our long gun and the nines —and the wind and rain were in his gunners' faces.

"Ho!" grinned old Lot to me. "This is a better business, my cock! Why don't ye crow?"

I shook my head, and the motion set my thick locks splattering like a wet dog's. "Too good to last. He'll wear in a moment."

"In this sea?"

"Better a sea or two over the side than hang on and have the spars shot out of him from astern. Get down and watch your head sheets, man, for we must swing when he does."

The Frenchman hung on for a space. I dare say he had expected us to wear full round and make for Cape Isabella again, and was puzzled by this bold pursuit. But now he made up his mind. Round he came, and shipped a sea that must have soused his gunners thoroughly. Seeing that, I put away the rules for good and stood straight on, our stem to his broadside, gambling on the wetting of his guns. I roared once more to the landsmen, trying to whip them into the rigging with my tongue. And this time they went, seeing Wokwees and those faithful others still clinging aloft.

I could not see past the wet gray-bellied foresail to the bow, where Pardon's long brass pet was speaking steadily, but I knew Lot would have all ready there, and Simon was in the waist with his cutlass out, commanding the boys to lay the pikes along the deck, ready to hand. There was no knowing what the Frenchman would do when he saw us bearing down; for the moment his schooner was staggered by that blow of the sea, and now he shipped another. I pictured the drenched and gasping men at his guns, trying to stop the vents against this flood of water, or fumbling for their powder horns to renew the priming, while their match tubs washed about the deck or foundered in the scuppers.

A pretty fancy, only partly true, for as we came on I saw a red tongue leap from one of his waist guns and another farther forward, and a shot came slap through the taut canvas of our foretopsail and knocked a man from the maintop. I saw his dark figure falling and the crew of the aftermost starboard six-pounder scattering out of the way. The body struck fair athwart the gun and bounced, hung on the bulwark for a moment, and dropped in the sea. God knows what the round shot had done to him, but every bone in his body must have been broken by that fall.

But now came a yell of rough-edged voices forward. I glanced forward anxiously and saw nothing amiss. Then I looked at the schooner and saw her mainsail sagging and aflutter. 'Twas hard to tell what had happened, for although the ships were now no more than two musket shots apart the rain was still sheeting down. It seemed too great a stroke of fortune that some skilled or lucky shot of Pardon's Delight should have done the very thing we wished for a perfect revenge, and sheared away the Frenchman's halyards. At any rate he had lost the steady pressure of his mainsail, and the schooner began to pay off rapidly until it was stern to the wind. And at that moment the rain ceased and the sun came through hot—hot as the devil's own kitchen pots, as if all that heat pent up by the hanging clouds had burst on us at last.

Chapter 24

ALL this time, mark you, I had not paused to find what damage we had got from the Frenchman's fire, except to take the evidence of my own eyes that the masts and rigging held. I knew the *Fancy* had been hit hard twice at least, for I felt the quick wince of the hull and heard cries that had no direction, that might have come from anywhere; indeed I only knew my ship was hurt in some unseen way, as a lover knows an illness of his mistress when she is afar. I was excited in the way that any man knows who has tasted battle—now gripped with fear (and a very shaking thing it is, and chilling to the heart) and now all taut with desperation, recklessness, call it anything you like so long as you don't call it courage; and now cold fear again, for my ship, for my men, and not least for myself; and now the warm rush in the veins that passes for courage and really comes from the spleen—anger at being made to shake like this, at being struck at by some foreign fellow, at the damage to the ship; the desire for vengeance overriding all else.

Spleen it was that made me hold straight on when the chance had come to luff and maybe shake the Frenchman off—pure schoolboy anger and no bones about it. The fellow had stung my ship, and he should pay smartly for it. And so we swept down in the burning sunshine, on a heaving sea turned blue and sparkling in a moment, and swung across the Frenchman's stern as he had crossed ours so short a time before.

"The wind will haul in a minute," Simon warned as we closed. I paid no heed except to notice that the pressure on our sails was slackening. My mind was all on Pardon Gardner and his larboard gunners, and I cried out, "Steady, steady, lads! All hangs on this!" Pardon was at the forward nine-pounder with his hooknose over the breech and squinting his eye along the sights. There was a cluster of men in the Frenchman's main rigging and a great bustle aft, as if they were working desperately at the wounded mainsail; but some of that bustle had other ends, for his stern carronades flamed and smoked as our bowsprit drew past the schooner's transom, and again I felt that cruel crash and jar of smitten timbers in our hull.

Pardon shouted, "Fire!" and jumped clear as the gunner's match came down to the touchhole. The gun leaped back in its breechings and spat a gush of flame and thick white smoke. Pardon did not wait to see the result, but ran aft to the next gun until it bore, and the next, until all five had fired. Three had been loaded with ball and two with grape. The long brass swivel had been stuffed with langrage—bolts, nails, scraps of iron, a very wicked medley at close quarters.

Dimly above these mighty sounds I heard a crackling skyward and cast a look that way, half expecting to see some of our top gear broken and falling. And I laughed crazily, seeing those mis-begotten landsmen of mine all aloft, clad in nothing but their leather breeches, crouched about the tops, clinging in the shrouds, some of them sitting astride the foreyard and the fore-topsail yard on the lee side, clutching the footrope with their bare toes as if born to such a perch, and firing their muskets and rifles and striv-ing to reload as the brigantine swept on. They had come a long way from the woods by Gosport River for this moment. I thought how after all was done and past, when they were back in their log camps and brushwood bivouacs at home, they would boast of this adventure in the far southern seas—and in secret wonder how they came to be persuaded into it.

Now we were past, and as our smoke blew through the Frenchman's rigging and whisked away along his deck we could see some pretty evidence of Pardon's work. The schooner was a low thing, and our fire could not help sweeping her deck at such a range, with such an opportunity, but there had been good shooting, too. All down that long narrow deck we could see fallen men, and others bending over them; and while her spars appeared unhurt, that drooping mainsail and the taut foresail were showing blue sea and sky through slits by the dozen, and even as we watched, their main staysail and jib came fluttering down all adrift, the first falling on those scrambling figures amidships and the other dangling in the sea.

Our lads began to cheer, but I yelled, "Stow that and save your breath! Stand by to go about!" For it seemed clear to me that we should luff and thus keep the weather gauge—indeed I had a rosy notion that we might cruise back and forth like that and pound the *corsaire* to splinters at our pleasure. But the *Fancy* came up so slowly when the helm was put down that I knew at last the truth of Simon's warning. The wind had fallen to a breath, and as we came over on the larboard tack Lot Mayes stabbed a horny finger to the eastward.

"Yonder comes the new wind, Nathan—clean about!"

'Twas a condition common enough in the islands, where the land winds and the sea winds alternately flourish and die, but it came at an awkward moment. All around us and the Frenchman and inshore the sea rolled in long steep swells, rippled faintly by the dying breeze from the west. About half a mile in the offing lay a broad band of water where the swells were unruffled, glittering like a mirror in the sunshine, and beyond that again I could see the first cat's-paws of an easterly breeze, the trade itself, coming down at a great rate.

"That'll fetch the Frenchman round, Nathan—and us to loo'ard!"

"Not while this westerly air holds. Helmsman, wipe her off, lively now! Hard up, the wheel!"

"What now?" cried Lot.

"Prepare to board—what else? Larboard gunners, there!"

"Ay, sir?"—Pardon's voice.

"Load all with grape. Mister Brady!"

"Ay, sir?"

"Stand by with your grapplings, Michael, and make fast as soon as we lay him aboard, or yonder wind will part us. Aloft, there!"

"Ay, sir?"

"You landsmen stay where you are and shoot your best as we close. Once we're alongside—do you hear me?"

"Ay, sir. Alongside——?"

"Down with you and join the boarders. Mr. Dawkins! You'll take charge of the forward boarding party as arranged—I'll take charge of the party in the waist with Brady. You, Mister Mayes, will remain where you are and keep charge of the ship. Mister Gardner! Where is Mr. Gardner?"

"Here, sir!"—peering at me earnestly under the foot of the foresail from the forecastle steps.

"Ah! I'm going to lay the ship alongside his starboard quarter, Pardon, if I can. Fire as your guns bear, and once we're alongside you'll take charge of the fo'c'sle with your station at the long gun. Now, lads, is all that clear?"

Silence, then a scattered "Ay!"—"Clear enough!"—"Ay, sir, Nathan!"—and finally a chorus that lifted to a shout.

That was the way we went down to the Frenchman, the sailors cheering all together, the woodsmen in the rigging uttering that wild "Ya-hoo!" which in Gosport sets the tavernkeepers bolting their doors, and the young Indian, Wokwees, perched far out on the fore-yardarm, naked to a clout, yowling the Micmac war cry.

I glanced to starboard, measuring our distance from the white line of the reefs, and saw the clouds shining like silver in the sunshine and rolling up the steep flanks of the mountains in great loose bunts as if Old Harry himself were furling sail. Then I noticed Victor Brule leaning against the tafferel and gazing towards the land.

"Go below," I said curtly. "We'll want a whole pilot when the time comes."

He gave me an odd look. "In that case, Capitaine," he answered coolly, "you had better let me stay where I am. The *goélette* carries three big carronades each side—eighteen-pounders by your measure—and she sits the water lower than your brigantine. Consider what will happen to your hull, and those inside, when you close with her."

"Eighteens! How d'ye know?"

"I saw her in Jacmel, in '94 or '95."

Brule was not a timid man. Did he think it beneath his dignity as an officer of the republic to hide himself below? Or was he trying to frighten me into keeping my distance? Carronades had short range, but at close quarters such a weight of shot was formidable. Well, the deuce with considerations now! The time had come to close and have it out.

"Stay, then," I growled. "But if it's honor that worries you, put your pride in your pocket, man, and lie down on the deck when we join action. You're much too valuable to lose."

A nod and a shrug. I thought with a qualm of Dolainde and the girl, down in the cabin. Still, the cabin should be safe on this approach—'twas well aft of the Frenchman's line of fire except for the two stern carronades, and they would be aimed high to hit our people on the poop.

The old wind at our backs was dying fast. We seemed barely to move. That was my impatience, I fancy. To the eastward the white flecks of the coming breeze were now a quarter mile away at most, with the belt of calm retreating before it, a narrowing stretch of glassy water that reached almost to the schooner. 'Twas a coin's toss whether or not we gained the Frenchman's side before the squall struck.

Their stern carronades began to fire. They made poor practice at first, but as we drifted down upon them the round shot struck again and again, sometimes ahull, sometimes knocking a shower of splinters from the bulwark, sometimes skimming over the hastily ducking heads in the waist. We made no answer, all loaded as we were with grape. Along the schooner's side we saw a splash of bodies flung to the sharks. The resolute *corsaire* was clearing his deck for the struggle to come.

I looked about me then, about my feet, and said sharply, "What! Have ye flung poor Fowler overboard?" Lot Mayes shifted his quid and jerked a thumb. Past the forward edge of the poop I saw a row of upturned feet on the main deck close by the musket racks. My breath sucked sharply at the sight. In such a business as we had seen, a captain must keep his eyes aloft, watching his own spars and canvas, or seaward on the weather and the enemy—he can spare no attention for the men who fall and are dragged away beneath his nose.

"How many?"

"Six dead. The wounded are below."

I noticed some of the men and all the boys glancing uneasily at that silent row between the poop ladders. I called out briskly, "Shanks, there! Master Shanks! A tune if you please—a lively one!" The gaunt schoolmaster whipped the fife from the tail of his rusty black coat, and with the pale fat drummer at his side began to pace the deck on the starboard side, playing with much more industry than music, "All in the Bay of Biscay-O."

The ships were very close now. We could see the French crew swarming aft to meet any attempt of ours to board, screaming defiance at our waiting gunners, a mass of uplifted yelling faces, black, white, and brown, with kerchiefs of all hues bound about their heads in the fashion of the islands, and brandishing a thicket of pikes and cutlasses and musket barrels.

Our long gun fired, and then the larboard nine-pounder, and the landsmen in our rigging began a ragged fusillade that went on and on, and dulled the cries and drowned the music altogether. The air was flat calm now. The schooner had lost her way entirely, and we came down upon her with the last of ours, both ships heaving up and down like pumps on the swell. The sun poured down a cataract of heat that pressed upon our gasping bodies as though it were the piled-up weight of the whole burning atmosphere, and the cannon smoke hung close about the bulwarks and between the ships in thick gray-white wreaths, eddying slowly to the level of the topgallant yards.

There was a dull shock as the hulls came together. I saw Michael Brady and his men fling their grapnels into the smoke—and the smoke suddenly alive with red-hot fireflies where the schooner's bulwark lay. There was a commotion aloft, too. Our fore-yardarm had fouled the schooner's main rigging. The Indian, Wokwees, astride the yard at its tip, uttered a yell and vanished into the smoke. For a moment I thought the fouled yardarm would hold us off. In that case we could not board the Frenchman from the waist. But now our starboard forebrace parted with a crack like a gunshot. The big yard thus released swung in hard against the larboard fore rigging, and the *Fancy* bumped and slithered another two fathoms' length along the schooner's side before she brought up.

All our larboard guns were firing now as fast as the men could reload, and there was no stopping any of them, even had I wished, though I knew the two aftermost six-pounders were not bearing at all, but simply thrashing the sea beyond the Frenchman's stern and adding smoke to smoke. There are no words to describe that din. Indeed after another minute our ears sang so loudly with the clap of our own guns that all small sounds were lost, or gone to a far thin whine like old Lot's voice, shouting through his cupped hands at my ear.

" . . . mischief for'ard . . . dunno what . . ."

The ships were wrapped in a powder fog so thick that I could barely see our mainmast. It stung the eyes and nostrils as burnt pepper stings, and set us all coughing and wheezing. I had a cutlass in my right hand and turned to pick up the pistols loaded and laid out for me on the top of the cabin hatch. One I stuck in my belt and the other was in my left hand as I made for the poop ladder. I saw Brule, pride forgotten, crouched in the doubtful shelter of the skylight coaming. I ran down the starboard side of the waist, stumbling over several men who lay writhing and crying out, and others very still, and noticed vaguely the grouped forms of the larboard gunners hard at work, and the darting powder boys and other dim figures all facing intently towards the schooner.

All this was as it should be, and I went on towards the forecastle and met a figure coming aft, cutlass in hand. My eyes were streaming, and the smoke seemed thicker there, but I noticed the fellow had a furtive crouch, and I thought he was running away from his post.

I yelled, "Hold hard, there! Where are ye going?"

For answer he swerved and made a terrific cut at my head. I struck out with my cutlass to ward off the blow, and the blades clashed.

"You fool!" I said in a fury. "What d'ye mean by——" Then I saw him clearly, a tall mulatto man naked to a pair of cotton drawers, with a small soft-leather purse or poke slung about his neck by a thong, the kind that Hispaniola Negroes wear to hold their witch charms. I had never seen him before. I knew in a kind of wonder that he was one of the schooner's crew. But what was he doing here?

He seemed to know quite well, for he grunted and swung his cutlass back for another stroke as my left hand brought the pistol up. I shot him through the belly, and he dropped his weapon and sat down with a thump, clutching his middle and staring at me with wide astonished eyes. I went on at a run and found the forecastle in an uproar, a mass of fighting, shouting men.

Boarded! We who had planned in such high confidence to do the boarding ourselves! Once more I cursed my ignorance. The Frenchman knew all the tricks of the game, and here he was, with what looked like half his crew, sweeping Pardon's fellows off the forecastle. And there stood the brass swivel gun, ready to be swung, to blast the whole length of our waist—the means of victory within his grasp!

Chapter 25

A BITTER moment, for all the fault was mine. I struck at a strange bearded face that appeared before me widemouthed and yelling. It disappeared, whether wounded or not I cannot say. But there was another face and another and another; the whole fore part of the ship was a whirligig of smoke and enraged faces, some familiar, many strange, that popped before me like figures in a Punch-and-Judy show, mouthing words in unnatural voices, and accompanied always by a fist and a weapon that struck or stabbed, now at me, now at someone to my right or left, and then vanished, face and fist together, making way for the next. Every man sees himself the center of the battle, and that was the way it seemed to me, though I knew I made only one more face and one more fist in all that guignol.

But now there was a surge; the whole frantic struggle moved bodily aft. I found several of my own men about me, and we were borne back and back and finally tumbled into the waist, some by the ladder and some clean off the forecastle deck. I found myself cheek by jowl with Pardon Gardner. He was bleeding from a bad cut on the head and grasping firmly the rammer of the long gun, as if he had determined to save something from the rout. He bellowed in my ear, "Here's ill work! 'Fore God, Nathan, they came over the bow and along the spreet like a swarm of apes flung out o' the smoke. . . . What's that?"

There was a flogging of canvas overhead and from the direction of the schooner. The hanging smoke rushed past our faces as if we stood in a flue. Then it was gone—clean—and all that had been hidden came to light. The wind had struck. Strange how a man's worries change with circumstance; at any ordinary time I would have been most fearful of our spars and canvas, caught in a squall like this with our yards acockbill and the sails all anyhow. But all I thought was *Now we can see, at any rate,* and my greatest concern was lest Brady's grapplings give way and let the ships drift apart. And that is a further measure of my ignorance, or plain stupidity, or my blind anger, call it what you will; for with the ships apart we might have turned our whole attention to those fierce men swarming on our forecastle.

The gunfire had ceased as if by an order. There was a sudden scramble and press of men about me—the boatswain with the boarding party gathered by my hopeful orders in the waist, seeing what was afoot forward and coming to our help. I had a quick fear that the larboard gunners had left their posts—and in that case we should be boarded by the waist as well. I turned to shout a warning, but it died in my throat, for I saw the Frenchman's afterdeck, a frightful spectacle.

From his shot-bitten tafferel to somewhere about the foremast his deck was a crawling mass of broken men and pools of blood that spread and ran in long trickles to leeward, where the scuppers bled like open wounds, all down the side. I had heard old man-o'-war sailors talk of scuppers running blood and laughed at them. I did not laugh at this.

The Frenchman had deceived us completely by that rush of men towards his stern as we closed, for he had concealed another swarm somewhere forward, ready to spring on our bow. But he had paid a price for his deception, deliberately perhaps, knowing full well what would happen when our larboard guns were fired. Grapeshot at close quarters is a fearful thing. Each gun that bore had flung across the schooner's deck a shower of sixty iron bullets large as plums, most of them flying in a cone from ten to twenty feet across. The visible parts of his planking were scored as if a sharp harrow had been dragged across it time and again. The low bulwark and the mast butts were pitted and splintered, the loose folds of the mainsail and the lower cloths of his foresail were slashed and flapping in rags and tatters "like a poor trollop's petticoat in a winter wind," as Simon Dawkins said.

And yet in the midst of this desolation there were groups of men not only alive but working furiously, some at the guns repairing the tacklings cut by our shot, some attempting to make fast their main staysail, which was tangled with a broken fore-topsail brace and flapping violently in the easterly wind and swinging a heavy block back and forth; and right aft was a little knot with pistols and cutlasses gathered about the helmsman, a Negro, a giant of a man—and a mighty resolute lot they were.

They did not seem inclined to board. I turned and saw our landsmen scrambling down the rigging, alarmed by the sudden jerk and uproar of our own sails. I called them about me, together with the larboard gunners, and we leaped upon the schooner's stern, about twenty of us in all, swinging every sort of weapon from a cannon ramrod to a tomahawk. There was some popping of pistols, a futile sound somehow, and then we were at blows, yelling like drunken Indians, and again the whole affair became a whirl of contorted faces and busy hands.

The schooner's men clustered about the helm—she had no wheel but a queer long tiller that fitted into slots in a wide quadrant on the deck—and for what seemed to me an hour or more and probably was less than fifteen minutes we struggled and stamped and struck at hostile heads and blades, with now and then a man going down as if an invisible hand had plucked him through the deck. Although our shouts and clash of weapons made noise enough for fifty drunken blacksmiths, I felt somehow a growing silence behind, and guessed that the French captain and his throng on the *Fancy's* bow, and Lot and Simon and their men, were gazing on our struggle and each other, uncertain of the next move in the game.

This outer silence was pricked at intervals by a sharp crack overhead, that seemed to come from the sky itself, clear above the clamor and rattle of our little struggle at the Frenchman's stern, meaningless and irritating as a shutter banging in the wind at night. Of a sudden there was a parting in our savage dance and I found myself confronting the tall black, who stood at the tiller head sweeping a bloody cutlass about him, roaring strange African words and showing a mouthful of teeth like a shark's, all filed to points in the cannibal fashion. There were many like him in Hispaniola now, for since '93 the French privateers out of Jacmel had gathered into their net a number of English and

Spanish slavers on the home run for Cuba and Jamaica, and turned their cargoes loose in this unhappy island as if there were not beasts enough between the Hispaniola capes.

I faced this dark Goliath, feeling not a whit of Bible David's courage, though I could have used his sling and pebbles very handily. I had fired my second pistol and flung it in a wild grimacing face long since—and the swing of the cutlass in that strong black hand made a mighty awesome whistle at such quarters. But here was the core of our small battle, and I felt the eyes of my seamen on me, and so, a most reluctant champion, I struck at the black man with my navy cutlass; and from then on he gave his furious attention all to me.

His weapon was one of those thick-backed blades the Spaniards call machetes, used about the plantations for mowing sugar cane, hacking out underbrush, and suchlike purposes, a favorite tool of the Negroes and a nasty one, having two feet of razor edge with the weight of a boat ax behind it. I was no swordsman, nor was he, but he knew at a glance that my weapon had a foot more steel than his, and a point besides, and 'twas the stab no less than the slash he had to fear. But fear's a poor word for that man. He had none.

We performed a duel that would have outraged poor Monsieur Galibrand, back home in Gosport, with his dainty attitudes and his talk of *coup* and *flèche* and deuce-knows-what. It seemed to fascinate the men about us, for they shrank away from our wild slashing and chopping and thrusting, and stood about yelling encouragement as though their own quarrel had no more importance. Again and again the big Negro smote my blade a blow that well-nigh sent it flying from my hand; again and again I slashed at his head or thrust at his belly, only to find the cane cutlass sweeping up or down—and always in the way.

He must have had a wrist like a bear's, for he plied the thing with great dexterity, from the forearm as well as the shoulder, and 'twas a heavy thing to wield in such a fashion. I found my own cutlass heavy enough in all conscience, and I was no weakling. Before long every sinew in my forearm ached and burned. Under the fierce sun the sweat ran down my face and breast and back and dripped about my loins as if I stood under an eaves spout in a thunderstorm, and with it I felt my strength running away into my shoes. I saw the black man through a glaze of sweat that magnified him, a huge blurred figure wielding a weapon big enough to cut my body through at a stroke, and strong enough to do it.

Then in some blind way my cutlass point found him. I felt the tip pass into his flesh and threw my whole weight forward in a flush of triumph. I heard a quick "Ah!" from the men behind and to the side. I thought I had the giant and so did they. But the fortune of war is not so certain as all that. 'Twas a little thing that upset me—a ringbolt in the deck. I stubbed my toe against it hard, and my wet hand slipped from the cutlass hilt. I stumbled forward, head down, neck bent, arms thrust out to save myself, seeing nothing now but the naked feet of the black man, splayed and enormous, leaping back, and every moment I expected to hear the downward whistle of his blade—the last thing I would hear in life. One stroke of that thing would whip the head from my shoulders as clean as the guillotine in Guadeloupe.

But now came another bang from that invisible shutter overhead, and the black man fell across me, uttering the high scream of a stabbed horse. Down we went to the deck together, and his weight knocked the breath out of me. Someone dragged him off and jerked me to my feet. I found my lads closing in, and the schooner's men throwing down their weapons, all the fight gone out of them with the big Negro's fall, and crying supplications in every tongue from French to Eboese.

I looked aloft then and saw a ghost perched on the schooner's mainmast cap—Wokwees, the young Micmac, calmly slipping a ramrod down the still faintly smoking muzzle of his musket. I gaped at him for a moment. I had seen him knocked from the *Fancy's* fore-yardarm when we fouled the schooner's rigging, and diving into the powder fog. I thought he had fallen between the ships and gone to the sharks long since. The truth was simple enough. He had jumped into the Frenchman's shrouds, climbed to the cap, and stayed there through the fight, hurling his thunderbolts from on high like a copper-nosed god, unnoticed in the uproar.

Another mystery was revealed—the silence to starboard. The heaving of the ships on the swell had parted our hastily flung grapplings, and the *Fancy,* having more sail to the wind, had drifted a quarter mile to leeward. There we could see a struggle in progress about the forecastle, the sparkle of cutlasses lifting and falling, and small white puffs of pistol smoke, all soundless down the wind like a mummers' play.

The schooner's helm was down, and fixed so in the quadrant, and she moved jerkily under her torn canvas, paying off before the wind and slowly coming up again. We drove those abject prisoners into the hold and clapped on the hatch and put men to guard it. I sent a man aloft to cut away the dangling staysail and brace, and thus rid us of the block that still swung like a murderous pendulum between the masts. Two hands went forward and began to cut away the jib, which was dragging in the water beneath the sprit, but I called to them sharply to haul it inboard. We would need every scrap of the Frenchman's shabby canvas if we were to sail the prize home to Mr. Pride.

Without a word from me the men set about that butcher's yard along the deck, picking up bodies, head and heels, and heaving them over the side. There was life in some, no doubt, and, now that I am old and all the heat and fury of that wild day has passed away long since, there is a plucking of cold fingers at my heart when I think of them, and how I did not lift my voice to save them. Of course, my men were only doing what the French crew would have done—nay, had done in the early stages of the fight.

But that aside, I was still afire with the desperate emotions of the struggle just past, and full of anxiety for my ship and men down there to leeward; I had suffered a pike thrust, painful though nothing to boast, which pierced my left breast slantwise, passed under the muscles there, and emerged beneath my armpit; and I had been on my feet without food or sup for twelve straight hours, all under strain such as no man knows who has not gone through such an experience. There is no give in rope that has been stretched taut for too long, and there was none in me. Dead or living I let them go, and thought so little of it that when one of our seamen cried, "See! There come Davy Jones's pallbearers!" and I swung and saw the swirl of shark fins in that flame-blue sea, I put back my head and laughed like any madman.

But enough of that. I ordered the helm up, and the schooner swung off the wind. We loaded the Frenchman's long gun and a dozen of the muskets strewn about the deck. We found our grap-plings still hooked over the bulwark and in the schooner's main chains, and bent fresh lines to replace those broken when the ships parted, and placed them ready to heave again. And then with that beggar's holiday of tattered canvas flapping and rat-tling in the breeze we came down to the *Fancy* once again.

Lot Mayes's gaunt figure stood alone at the brigantine's helm. He saw us and after a careful stare swung the wheel and set the *Fancy* yawing so we could come up with her. I had a notion of grazing along her side until our long gun bore and then firing a blast of grape into the crowd of Frenchmen on her forecastle.

But I gave that up as we came alongside, seeing our own men and the French all mingled forward and no chance of firing so much as a pistol now without danger to our own.

Six of our party in the schooner were wounded, though not crippled, and I bade them stay and keep the prisoners below—and very uneasy they were, I remember, saying one of those blackies was sure to put a match in the powder when he found all was lost. As I gained the *Fancy's* deck and had the grapplings secured I looked back and saw all six of them clutching their muskets and limping forward, clear of the expected blast.

Simon Dawkins sat dazed upon the *Fancy's* main hatch with his head between his hands and blood dripping slowly from a soaked bandage about his forehead. A number of others crouched or lay about him, the driftwood of that storm about the forecastle. I paused and gripped his shoulder anxiously. He looked at me dully, his eyes glazed with pain, and put a pistol in my hand, without a word. The fight must have moved its slow dance back and forth a number of times since I led my party aboard the schooner, for several fellows, ours and theirs, lay in the forward part of the waist, all dead or mighty close to it.

Simon had kept our men pressing forward, no matter how the fight swayed, to give the Frenchmen no time or opportunity to load the long brass swivel gun. And he had succeeded so far, although Pardon Gardner always claimed afterwards that what saved the disaster was the simple fact in his hand—he had carried off the rammer. At any rate, Simon had fallen out at last with a cut on the head, and Michael Brady led the fight, a mighty figure roaring like a bull moose and swinging a boat ax. We thrust in our bodies and voices with the rest, and our combined weight and clamor burst upon the French boarders with a shock that threw them back . . . back . . . back . . . until several of us were storming onto the forecastle itself.

There the battle ended abruptly. No doubt some of the Frenchmen had noticed us coming down with their schooner a prize and found their situation hopeless. No doubt some had their fill of fighting anyhow. At any rate, first one and then another threw his weapon overboard and fell upon his knees. The mood went through them like a plague. In half a minute all was over, and 'twas curious to see how some of them groveled, begging mercy, and some stood silent, with folded arms, and others crouched on their hams, regarding us with sullen expectant faces, awaiting death with the unhappy patience of cattle in a slaughterhouse. All but the French captain, a tall man with a sallow and dissolute face in which a pair of intense black eyes burned like coals. He made a remarkable figure, even in that motley gathering, with his white paduasoy breeches, white silk stockings, and silver-buckled shoes, his shirt of a pale greenish silk, the tasseled scarlet sash about his waist, the common red flannel nightcap on his head.

In a high harsh voice he cried a stream of malediction on his men, spattered them with all the names of all the filth to be found between Brest and Basse-Terre round by the east, and then turned, ran out on the jib boom, and without hesitation jumped feet first into the sea. I thought the fellow had some mad notion of swimming to shore, sharks or none; but he could not swim, or did not try. In the clear water we saw his gaudy figure going down, deeper and smaller, weighted by the heavy pistols in his sash and the cutlass firmly gripped in his hand. A procession of bubbles came to the surface, and that was the end of him.

So we had come out top dog. But 'twas a very sorry business and a very sorry dog. My ship—my beauty of the Gosport yard—

was hacked and torn out of all countenance above decks, and the carpenter with a long face reported the hull pierced in at least a dozen places, some of which were below waterline as the brigantine lay now on the starboard tack. I called hands to the pumps and soon had evidence of all he said. No thick and oily bilge water but pure Caribbean came gushing from the spouts.

I sent Lot with a dozen unwounded men to take over the prize, and the new batch of prisoners was herded aboard the schooner and battened in the hold with the rest. There were a lot of them —we counted seven-and-thirty living in the morning, when the last of their badly wounded died and was passed up through the hatch. How many others had gone to the sharks in the fight, we never knew, nor were we very curious, but there must have been close on ninety or a hundred men in her crew when the schooner first came up on us.

'Twas our own loss that concerned me, and as soon as we had repaired our rigging enough to stand off the land—we had drifted nigh to Isabella Point—I ordered the roll called. Counting Lot and his dozen aboard the schooner, thirty men were able to answer their names, many of these in stained bandages and their faces gray with weariness and loss of blood, and twelve more lay desperately wounded in the schoolmaster's care below. Forty-two! We had gone into action sixty-nine. One man's body was lost overboard, the rest of that doleful sum lay in a row along the afterdeck covered with tarpaulins against the sun.

The boatswain stood forward, knuckling his forehead respectfully like the old man-o'-war's man he was. "Nathan, sir, the men has a favor to ask."

"What is it?"

"Don't chuck our own poor lads yonder to the sharks."

I nodded slowly. "In the morning we'll stand in to the land somewhere and bury them. Anything else?"

"A sup o' rum all round?"

"I was going to say that. A stiff grog all round—and well earned. Come down to the cabin with me and get the keys."

Brady followed me down the companion, and at the door I paused. "You'll take the mate's watch, Michael, until Mr. Dawkins is fit for duty. Where's that man Brule?"

"Down in the prize masters' berth playing his fiddle—some damned tune called the Carmagnole—as peaceful as ye please."

I opened the door. The air in there was like an oven, for the skylight had been closed and the companion door fastened as soon as we joined action with the schooner. Dolainde sat on his berth with a face like death itself. He was drunk, but he looked ill as well. The air, no doubt.

Sharply I said, "Where's Lia?"

"Lia?"

"Your daughter. Speak up, man, for God's sake!"

I was alarmed, for all along I had thought her safe in the cabin. Dolainde considered deeply. He hiccuped once or twice. At last he muttered, "She went . . . down there," waving a finger towards the trapdoor in the floor which led to the powder room and arms chest—a precaution of Mr. Pride's, built into the ship out of some memory of mutiny in his younger days.

I tossed Brady the keys to the lazaret and spirit locker, pulled up the trap, and went down the small dark steps. The lower door stood open. I thought, *I must lock it, after this*. The place was lit in the usual fashion by a lanthorn shining through a glass in the farther bulkhead, for safety's sake. On one of the kegs sat a small weary figure, elbows on knees, face in hands.

"Boy!" I said, "have you seen——"

Lia Dolainde arose unsteadily from the keg and looked at me with dark staring eyes.

"Roux! You are hurt—there is blood on your shirt!"

"What are you doing here?" I demanded. "Where's the powder boy?"

She gestured with a hand. "He has gone. He was curious to see what had happened—up there." I noticed that the battle door remained open. I would speak to the gunner about that. What was the good of drills and instructions if he failed to close the main magazine door when action ceased?

"And you?" I said curtly.

"I helped the boy to pass out the cartridges. He showed me which were for the six-pound guns and which for the nines. He showed me how to fill the flannel bags with powder from the copper measure—you know, in case the made-up ones ran short—and which barrel had the musket cartridges and which the pistol ones. We were busy a long time, and I am so thirsty. . . . But Roux!—your shoulder!—look at it!"

"My shoulder's all right, it's my temper you should worry about. You have no business here, and I should have the boy's hide tanned for letting you stay. What did you come here for?"

She looked indignant—if a woman can be said to look indignant with her face a patchwork of black powder smudges.

"In the cabin there was too much noise. It was terrible, especially when the guns fired on the deck upstairs, boom-boom-boom, like a stick of wood beating my head. And all the men shouting and running. I heard you sometimes. You sounded very angry. Well, all that . . . it frightened me. So I came down here, where there is not so much noise, because it is safer."

"Because it's *what?*"

"Because it is safer."

I looked at the stacked kegs, each stamped with the broad arrow of His Majesty's dockyard at Halifax, the heap of flannel cartridges for the cannon, the scatter of dropped musket and pistol cartridges underfoot, some of them trodden and burst, with the torn paper spewing black powder grains over the planking. And I sat on a keg and threw back my head and howled with laughter.

The logic—the wonderful logic, the charming logic of women!

Chapter 26

WE ANCHORED in Isabella Bay on the following day, in six fathoms of water, and boated our dead ashore. The place looked beautiful from seaward, a low green shelf beside the bay and the mountains rising blue behind. But afoot we found it eerie, very still and somehow chilling even in the high hot noon, for wherever we turned we found ruins of masonry, of houses all white and burst and strangled in the green grip of queer trees and bushes and creeping plants, a whole town overrun by the Hispaniola bush, and not a living soul.

Someone—Dolainde or Brule; Dolainde, I think—said it was where the Spaniards made their first settlement in the Americas, and told how most of them perished of fever and the rest abandoned it, close on three hundred years before. It astonished me to think that white men had been in these parts so long, but they may well have been, from the look of that dead town at Isabella. I have no head for history, and all I know is that we buried our six-and-twenty Nova Scotiamen under a giant ceiba tree down by the shore, with their feet towards the north, and said what prayers we knew and came away.

We lay at anchor in the bay for two days, a heavyhearted company, stopping the shot holes in the hulls and covering them with sheet lead, and mending rigging and sails. On the second day I went aboard the schooner for a close inspection of the prize. She was not much to look at now. Our fire had only hulled her in a few places, but the decks were so chipped and splintered that every barefoot seaman watched his way like a cat crossing a hot hearth. Her hemp and canvas were old and worn before we slashed them with our shot, and all aloft she was a wilderness of patches and splices where Lot's men had been at work.

"Well enough for this Caribbee weather," observed the old man dourly, "but can ye see her living through a gale in our northern seas? Best scuttle her now and save good men."

"What about the prisoners?"

"Set 'em ashore on our way to the Caracul Passage. Thirty miles from here, say, where it's too far for 'em to come back and molest our lads' graves yonder, and they'll have to climb over the mountains to get to Monte Cristi town."

I considered. "Well enough for them, Lot—but the schooner? No! She'll fetch a price at Halifax, newly rigged and sparred. Mr. Pride——"

"Ah! Mr. Pride to be sure!" in a bitter voice.

"Well, prize money's not to be despised, Lot. Those poor fellows we buried yonder paid a hard price for the schooner—and there's their families at home to think about."

"Um. Something in that. Well, what next, Nathan? Looks to me as if our cruise is nipped in the bud. We've barely enough men left to man the *Fancy* and the schooner, and three of the prize masters are dead."

I put up my chin at that. "What! 'Scape off home with our tails dragging, just because we met a wildcat in the road? We won the fight, didn't we? Besides, we've a mission to perform in Hispaniola, thirty thousand yellow boys under our jib boom's end almost, and d'ye think I'd turn tail on that?"

He looked at the land, all shimmering green and purple in the heat, and twisted his thin lips in a grin that had no mirth in it.

"Nathan, if 'twas me I'd turn tail on all o' that so quick you'd never know I'd been here. D'ye remember that night we left the Cap? I said to myself, Never again, Lot Mayes!"

"And here you are!"

"Ay—for my sins."

We went below and looked in the Frenchman's cabin, a frowsty place with that faint but interesting air which women leave in a place where they have tarried for a time. Lot saw the puzzled look on my face and flung open a locker at the starboard side. It was hung and heaped with women's things, fine gowns of silk and suchlike stuff, and laced petticoats and linen, stockings, shoes, most of them little used if used at all, and stuffed in there all anyhow.

"One o' the prisoners talks a little English. Says the captain—him in the fancy drawers that drowned hisself—carried a couple o' doxies about with him from one out-o'-the-way port to another in the islands—and gathered pretty fal-lals for 'em along the way. A downright pirate if ye ask me, though the prisoners vow they're proper privateersmen sailin' under a letter o' marque from the Committee o' Public Safety—whatever that is, and they weren't jokin'—in Guadeloupe. Not a scratch o' pen to show for't—I searched the lockers top and bottom."

"What's she called?"

"*Hirondelle* in the logbook. What's that mean?"

"Swallow."

"So? Umph! Well, it's not a bad name for her at that. She's a graceful thing in her way, and ye saw the way she skimmed on a wind. Course, she's mighty dirty, a proper hurrah's nest, and chock-full o' cockroaches and them little red Joseph ants. A chimney swallow, say, with a bit o' soot about her wings."

I turned to go. Lot said, "Wait a minute, Nathan. Don't ye think young Ma'mselle Dolainde ought to come over here and pick out some o' those kickshaws in the locker? I mean to say, 'tain't decent for a gentle-born female to be prancin' about in men's nankeens and a shirt—not in front o' the seamen, anyhow." He looked so sanctimonious that I had to laugh.

"I'll tell her, Lot. But I doubt she'll come. She seems quite satisfied with what she's got."

And there I was wrong. Lia went over in the gig and came back with two French sea chests crammed with stuffs, and carrying a pair of modish hats no doubt intended for a French officer's wife or mistress in Hispaniola, and intercepted by the late *capitaine-de-corsaire* for his own. She had in her dark eyes that look of deep happiness which new finery gives to women everywhere, no matter what trouble or sorrow may have gone before. I was astonished, for I had come to look upon Lia-Marie Dolainde as a tomboy who would rather dance a hornpipe to Brule's fiddle than give a thought to petticoats or parasols.

She disappeared into the cabin and stayed two hours, I don't doubt trying on and putting off, and prinking before the looking glass, until she had seen herself in every bit of that flummery. Lot grew uneasy after a time and regretted aloud that he had mentioned the matter at all.

"We should ha' let well enough alone, Nathan. Suppose she comes topside dressed like a hoor of Babylon, and our poor lads yonder scarcely cold in their graves?"

We heard her coming up the cabin stairs and waited grimly in the shade of the awning like a pair of vinegary spinsters at a ballroom door. And Lia confounded us.

She had chosen a somber black gown, a hoopless Spanish kind

of thing, with golden-yellow lace along the flounces, and descending in graceful folds to the toes of her small shoes. The black sleeves came to the elbow, and there a cascade of yellow lace fell loosely to her wrists. She had parted her gleaming blond hair in the middle and drawn it to the back of her head, where a great tortoise-shell comb rose out of it. There was a fine black lace mantilla drawn over the comb and down about her shoulders. Around her neck hung a rosary of a kind common in Hispaniola, the beads made of seeds from the *palme à chapelet,* which grows on the tops of the mountains, and a small crucifix carved from an ivory nut lay in the white fold of her breasts.

Gone was the long-haired boy growing out of his breeches. In his place was a graceful young woman with a quiet beauty in her face and a pair of grave dark eyes that saw us, acknowledged us—and dismissed us—in one look. I heard a gasp behind. That was Dolainde, sitting in his usual place on the breech of a six-pounder in the awning's shade. His eyes were bulging. I felt a twinge of pity for the sot, seeing how Lia resembled her mother in that rig. He must have felt that he was seeing the ghost of his bride of twenty years before.

Lia dropped him a small curtsy and turned away from us all, stepping down to the main deck with that strange new dignity. And Brule emerged from the shadow of the 'midships awning and came to meet her, hands outstretched, with a glad smile and a triumphant glance towards the poop that made the small veins in my temples beat like drums. Thus they stood, hands together, talking eagerly in low tones, as Michael Brady came to me with a pull at his forelock and announced, "All's done aloft, sir, and the carpenter's satisfied with the hull."

I turned to Lot. "And the schooner?"

"We can sail whenever ye say."

"In the morning, then, as soon as the sea wind makes."

"Ay, ay, sir."

And in the morning, in the early forenoon, with the trade wind filling our patched sails and ruffling the hot blue water, the mountains wavering in the haze as if painted on a silken screen, and the Caribbean clouds with clear white tops and murky bellies sailing their eternal procession over the sea's face in the offing, we weighed anchor and left Isabella Bay.

Strange, how in our common voyages year in year out we bury men at sea and say, "Ah well, there goes poor Jack, a good shipmate and God rest him lightly," and think no more about him except to bid a shilling for his clasp knife or a dollar for his chest at the mainmast auction afterwards. The sea is so very wide, so very deep, and every wet acre exactly like another; it is all one from pole to pole, and who could stretch a hand within a month—within an hour—and say, "That's where he lies, poor Jack!" and tell the truth?

But when you bury men ashore there is the mound, the patch of green, the stone, the tree, the things you mark it by, and there's poor Jack, or what is left of him, fixed and forever in foreign earth, under the whisper of foreign leaves, a hundred or a thousand miles from home; and there you must leave him, feeling in your heart a qualm as if you had broken faith with him somehow.

That was the way we left our dead at Isabella, gazing aft in silence while the green of the forest turned blue and slowly dissolved in the haze. The shape of the great ceiba tree stood out for a long time after the rest was only a tinted mass, and that is what I remember best.

Before long we had other things to think about. There was no time or chance for mournful memories as we threaded league after league of reefs along the coast. Brule proved a skillful pilot, and I gave him a grudging admiration as the hours went by. Once or twice my heart failed me, seeing how narrow was the passage between the white grounds clearly visible from the deck, but I swallowed my fears, and the *Fancy* went through gallantly, with the *Hirondelle* following cautiously in her wake. And the end was well worth the risk, for we were well in the blockade region now, with only the reefs between us and the sharp eyes and sharper questions of His Majesty's fleet. We had no fear of the French; they had no ships worth mention in these waters, and the coast was uninhabited, league on league.

Somewhere in the region of Sand Cay we hove to and put the prisoners ashore, a glum lot, staring at the mountain wall between them and the nearest town. Most of them had fully expected to be hanged or flung to the sharks, but we got no thanks for our mercy. Indeed as our armed boat crews pulled away from the beach the Guadeloupeans howled their opinion of us from the safety of the trees, and one or two bold fellows ran out and shook their fists, and danced in a mischievous sort of way with thumbs to their noses and other gestures less polite. Watching their antics through a spyglass, I could think of nothing so like a troop of monkeys. Michael Brady was in charge of the longboat, and when he fired a pistol over their heads it was downright comical to see the way their bare feet made the sand fly as they scampered to cover. Well, those feet would be sore and their bellies mighty hollow by the time they got over the hills, and they would have a pretty tale to tell the commandant at Monte Cristi, not to mention the Committee of Public Safety in Guadeloupe.

We sailed on and gave the port of Monte Cristi a wide berth, using the nearby mountain for a steering mark, a mighty long-backed thing like the roof of a barn and so called by the creoles —La Grange. And as we rounded the high point close inside the Haut Fond shoals I felt a tightness at my throat, for there in the haze far ahead loomed the hump of Cap François, forbidding as a giant in a fairy tale.

Brule threaded a cluster of reefs and low mangrove islands called the Seven Brothers and headed boldly across the bight which makes deep into the coast and leads to Fort Liberty. He assured us we had nothing there to fear—the plantations had been destroyed and the planters murdered or driven out in the slave revolt, like those at the Cap, and there was nothing but a garrison of republican troops, white and black, each jealous of the other and limp with solitude and the heat.

All this way we had come under short sail, first because 'twould have been madness to carry full canvas in such touchy going, and second because I wished to reach the landing place at sundown or not long before. The risk of the venture was very clear to me now that we were on the scene. The cove in which Brule proposed to anchor the ships while the landing party performed its mission was roughly halfway between Fort Liberty and the town of Cap François, and little more than a dozen miles by crow flight from either of those places.

Brule declared, and Dolainde confirmed, that the rough mule track between the towns passed inland from our landing place two miles at least, probably three; and that the ships would lie well screened from any eye to seaward. They seemed to know it well, and I dare say the cove had been a convenient dodge hole for smuggling craft pursued by *guardacostas* in the time gone by.

When we eased in cautiously to the land at last, the sun had gone down behind the distant Morne du Cap, and night itself came out to meet us, loud with insects and the shrill piping of tree toads and laden with those strangely mingled scents of the

Hispaniola forest that range all the way from spice to carrion, dank, mysterious, forbidding—and inviting. I found myself shivering a little, and blamed it on the night breeze off the hills.

There was no time to be lost. Many of the landsmen I had brought so far for this adventure had been wounded in the fight, and so I chose my twenty men from the fittest of our battered crew. One was Simon Dawkins, vowing his wound was nought but a slit in the scalp, and healing already. Another was Wokwees, the young Indian, whose senses, keen as any dog's, made him the perfect scout for our advance into the land.

Dolainde had gone below to bid his daughter au revoir. He was a long time about it, and I did not like to break in upon them. When he came at last I dived below to get my pistol and cutlass. The cabin lamp was lit and the curtains drawn across the stern windows. Lia stood beside the table wearing a cool yellow thing that left most of her breast and shoulders bare and gleaming like beautifully carved and polished ivory in the lamplight. I picked up the weapons and thrust a fistful of paper cartridges into one pocket and my tinderbox into another. I turned to go, saying lightly, "Well, Lia, here goes for your father's fortune!" and saw her eyes strangely bright.

I paused. The fine nostrils she had inherited from her mother were drawn and quivering, her short upper lip caught between her teeth, and she held her slim brown fists at her sides, clenched so that the knuckles were white.

Gently I said, "My dear, there's nothing to worry about. It's really very simple. Your father—yes, and Brule—will be in far less danger ashore than they've been any time these past few days at sea."

"And you?" she said, sinking upon her locker and bursting into tears, her face all awry like a child's in pain. My men were waiting. And when a woman weeps—really weeps—there is no beauty about her, only a pitiful kind of ugliness. Yet I went to her swiftly, as if tugged by a cord, and sat beside her and put my arms about her. She laid her face against the open breast of my shirt, and I felt the warm tears running down my skin. If there was any notion in my head it was that I must comfort her, as many a time I had comforted a young and leggy Lia in the old days by the river.

I had one arm about her shoulders and a hand upon her waist; and suddenly, without warning, without thought at all, a sensation swift as fire passed from that warm and pliant flesh to mine and flared all over me. Notions, plans, resolves, all these were nothing then. Brule was a shadow, Dolainde a name. Mr. Pride, yes, and Felicity ceased to exist. I only knew that inside me somewhere a vague long-gathered yearning, nameless and unrecognized all this time, suddenly had burst forth and filled my heart with warmth and my head with light.

Love? The poets call it that. I was only a young redheaded seaman, scornful of sentiment, none too intelligent. Hunger and thirst I knew, and suchlike simple things, but this was a new need, strange and insistent like a question that demands an answer—and the answer was in my arms, warm and alive—and weeping. Lia! Of course! How could I have been so dull, so very blind? She belonged to no one in the world but me, she was part of me, and I had not guessed until this moment, as if I had gone to a looking glass and seen her face and not my own.

I put a fist beneath her chin, tried to tip it back, and she resisted firmly, keeping it tucked against her breast as if she did not wish to show a face so woebegone. Then she gave way and turned her face upward, eyes closed, tears in the long dark lashes, and gave up her warm moist mouth to my fierce kisses.

How long we remained in that embrace I do not know, and did not care. But after a time I was aware of the impatient stamp of feet on the deck above. I rose from Lia's side reluctantly. She did not try to hold me, but sat with her golden head tipped back against the bulkhead, breathing in a deep disturbed fashion and regarding me with eyes still bright with tears, still haunted by mysterious fears and doubts all overlaid with a passion that stirred me to the bones.

"I shall come back," I said, drinking in the look of her and groping the table top for my pistol and cutlass.

She did not answer. I turned and went up the stairs.

Lot put us ashore in the longboat, and I had a last word with him as we stood amongst the mangrove roots.

"Keep all quiet on board. Show no lights by night nor smoke by day. Strike the topmasts if you think they show above the trees—they shouldn't. If all goes well we shall be back tomorrow night. Towards morning, probably."

"And if ye don't come, Nathan?"

"Stay here two days—three days, and be sure. If we're not back by then, or send no word, something's gone amiss. Up with your hook and make an offing in the brigantine. Leave the schooner at anchor and a boat on shore, in case some of us make our way back here."

"And once I'm in the offing in the brigantine?"

"Be off with you! Water in the Bahamas somewhere and make for home."

"Damme! And leave you and the lads?"

"If we're not back in three days we'll all be dead as turnips, like as not—and what good can you do us then, hanging about here, an easy prize for the first picaroon? You've Ma'mselle to think about. Do what I say!"

He turned and spat in the dark as if he did not like the taste of my instructions. Then, "Ma'mselle? What about Ma'mselle —with you and Brule and Dolainde dead as turnips. Eh?"

I answered slowly. "Take her back to Gosport, it's the only thing to do. Tell Mr. Pride that she's to have my full share of the Spanish prize—in hard money, mind—and that her life's her own. And tell her . . . tell her . . . no, that's all."

"There's Miss Felicity, Nathan."

"There's nothing more to say," I answered roughly. "Why should I fill your head with messages you won't remember half an hour? Begone, man, and hold faith in my luck, for all our sakes."

Simon Dawkins was waiting with Wokwees, Brule, and Dolainde at the head of the line of seamen. Every man carried strapped to his shoulders a stout canvas pack or haversack made by the sailmaker on the voyage south. These for the carriage of Dolainde's fortune. Each had a cutlass at his belt. There were no firearms but the pistol in my hand. If all went well, a slash or two of the cutlasses would be all the force we needed; if things went wrong, firearms would only make a noise.

Off we went, picking a way through the dense growth in a darkness spangled with fireflies.

Chapter 27

OF ALL evil journeys I give you a journey through tropical thickets at night. We might have waited for moonrise, but I was impatient to start, seeing our passage to the mule road as an hour's stiff walk, no more, and reckoning that the moon would do us no good in any case there in the black shade of the trees.

Often we had to hack a way through the undergrowth with

our cutlasses. The air was hot and humid, the darkness hummed with mosquitoes, there were owls and other nocturnal creatures that fled away from us, setting our teeth on edge with their cries. The seamen had a great fear of snakes, though none of the Hispaniola snakes are poisonous, and ever and anon I found some fellow crying oaths and laying about him with a cutlass when 'twas nothing but a creeper dangling from a tree. Again and again we had to pause while some nimble lad shinned a trunk for a sight of the stars. Again and again we stepped into a bit of open and thought it was the road, only to find the dark vegetation closing in beyond.

Altogether we were four hours in this black and choking maze before Brule and Wokwees and I, with Dolainde stumbling at our heels and the long line of seamen crashing along behind, emerged into a dusty alley in the bushland. The moon was well up by now, and the narrow roadway gleamed like water in the shine of it, far to the right and left. We paused there for a time to catch our breath, Dolainde wheezing like a foundered horse and all of us dripping sweat.

We pushed eastward along the road and after a time crossed a stream on a rickety wooden bridge that Dolainde recognized. At the crossroads beyond he took the left fork without hesitation. He panted and lurched—he seemed tipsy, but I knew that could not be, for I had kept the spirits locked away from him for twenty-four straight hours. I gave him my arm and he clutched it readily. As we went along I became suspicious of the unending black bush on both sides of the road. I knew we should now be amongst the old plantations. I thought Dolainde was lost. But suddenly he halted and stabbed an accusing finger, crying, "There is the Habitation Evremont—see what those *canaille* have done to it!"

Clear in the moonlight now I perceived the brick walls of what had been a considerable mansion, gutted and roofless, the doors and windows mere black caverns. It stood off the road a little way, almost submerged in a growth of bush and palmetto. Before long we passed another ruin. This had been of wood and was burned to the ground, nothing left standing but the naked chimneys, the very ashes swallowed up in the flourishing undergrowth. So it must have been with the next, but there even the chimneys had been razed, as if the spirit of destruction had determined not to leave one brick upon another. Only a pair of tall stone gateposts stood, and even these were half hidden in a growth of those strangling vines which had given us so much trouble on the way.

So it was all along the road, the sugar and coffee fields grown up in a tangle of bushes, creepers, and palmetto, with here and there the shell of a mansion half drowned in the crowding vegetation like a half-tide rock, its dead face gleaming in the moonlight; and sometimes the tumbled ruin of a cane mill, or a boiler and silent machinery festooned with vines, all that remained of a busy stillhouse. Most of this destruction had been done in '91, and in the years since the whole Plaine du Nord had fallen into a wilderness that astonished me, though I knew how quickly this greedy thronging greenery must have closed in when the slaves were no longer there to fight it back.

A ghostly sight, all of it. I had a quaint whimsy that we were back from the dead after centuries, not years, especially when we emerged into the King's Way, the great avenue from Cap François into the heart of the rich plain, made and maintained by gangs of slave labor in the past. It had been wide enough to pass four carriages abreast and was lined with stately palms and the handsome villas and mansions of the rich planters—all gone now. This was the way I had come with the *Sally's* crew to rescue Dolainde and his family. There was little to recognize; even the road had sunk from sheer neglect, gullied and broken by the violent rains of the country, and all the ditches choked. The slaves in their mad fury had left nothing—even to chopping down the palms along the way.

Had I been any sort of philosopher I suppose I should have seen a just retribution in all this, for although there were easy-going planters like the Dolaindes, in general the fine gentlemen and ladies of creole Hispaniola had treated their blacks with a cruelty beyond a northern imagination. I remember once hearing Dolainde boast that some of his slaves had been with him twenty years, and I had asked idly how long they lived as a rule on the other plantations. "Seven," he had said casually. Blacks were cheap, and 'twas reckoned profitable to work them to death while they were in their prime. That was why the slave traders had a constant market in Hispaniola down through the years. Murder? Ay, call it that. But I was young then, and no philosopher, and all my thrifty Nova Scotia sense was offended by this present spectacle of waste and destruction. I found myself muttering, "Savages! Savages!" and thinking of the blacks alone.

I knew from the stars that Dolainde was heading well to the southward of the town of Cap François, and presently we left the Chemin du Roi and plunged into the half-gloom of an old plantation lane. Suddenly Wokwees pulled up, snuffing and whispering, "Moke! Moke!" We paused for a full minute. I caught a faint whiff of wood smoke myself. Then Dolainde said in his strained voice, "Go on. There is nothing to fear." We pushed on past a huddle of grass huts surrounded by small plats of maize and manioc on what once had been the broad lawn of a mansion. Wisps of dying cooking fires rose straight up in the moonlight. Evidently a few of the blacks, not liking the prospect of military service or weary of lounging half starved about the streets of Cap François, were clinging to the old scene, growing what food they needed, and content. Whoever they were, they did not trouble us. If any of them peered forth and saw our silent file go past, he must have withdrawn in a fright and buried his head in the bed, thinking doubtless we were zombies, the living-dead, who walk about at night in search of souls.

The ground was rising now, and before us loomed the great ridge of the Morne du Cap. We could look back upon the plain, stretching miles to the south like a moonlit sea. We had crossed the narrow neck of it, and the Manoir Dolainde could not be far. I watched eagerly for the familiar white pillars of the portico facing on the plain. Dolainde let go my arm and broke into a shambling run, and we followed him, sweating and blowing up the long incline of the old estate road. For a time nothing was visible except the same dark mass of vegetation we had seen the whole way through the plain. Then appeared a line of staggering wooden shanties, choked with bushes and vines. Dolainde cried triumphantly, *"V'la!"* Dimly I recognized the old slave quarters, though the paths were gone and all seemed dead and deserted.

We trotted on, but in a short space Dolainde pulled up and cried out as if stung. We clustered about him, staring. The moonlight was very bright on the road, but it made the shadows black and deceptive. Slowly I recognized a line of slender trees that stood in the forefront of the mass, and a faint shimmer as of water or grass beyond. It came to me in a dull surprise that these must be the lemon trees that grew along the roadside before the *manoir*. Then the grass beyond must be the lawn, and—yes—there were the massive gateposts with their carved and once-gilded balls, each post and ball made from a single piece of guaiacum, the wood we call lignum vitae, hard as rock and well-nigh as enduring. The wide wrought-iron gate with its delicate tracery was gone—no doubt carried off in '93 to be made into pikes at some primitive forge.

"What's the matter?" someone said. I did not answer, nor did

Dolainde. Slowly I walked between the posts, feeling the old carriage drive beneath my shoes. On both sides stretched the lawns, now a rank growth of grass as deep as a man's knees. In one place someone had planted a manioc patch, but even that was nearly swallowed in guinea grass and must have been abandoned after a season.

But where was the tall house and its wide white wings, all built of cedar and mahogany as durable as the very mountains, and finished inside with mahogany floors and paneled in satinwood and rosewood and suchlike stuff? It should be standing before me now like a white cliff in the moonlight. I heard the cautious feet of some of the seamen following me and moved on, anxious to solve the mystery myself.

It did not take very long. The dark mass of shadow before me retreated steadily as I advanced, and it came to me that I was seeing only the gloomy forest on the steep slope of the Morne behind, and where the *manoir* had stood was only space. A few steps more. A row of trees, leafless and wild-armed, emerged from that shadow and stood naked in the moonshine. The genipa trees before the house. How well I remembered the rustle of their leaves in the mountain breeze at evening! In those days they had an appearance very like the cherry trees of home, though more luxuriant, and bore a queer ashy-colored fruit as big as a man's two fists. Now they were skeletons, killed by the fire that destroyed the big house, and guarding nothing but a mass of greedy vegetation that had sprung up in its ashes.

A fit of anger shook me, anger at the destruction of that beautiful home where Lia was born, and a dark and growing anger of suspicion. The stark trees, the rank growth where the house had been—all this was old, as old as '93. The slaves must have put torch to the *manoir* the very night we left. I had expected to find it standing. Hadn't Brule said . . . Brule!

I turned to the whispering seamen at my back. "Pass the word for Victor Brule!"

One of them trotted away towards the road. I noticed then a group of men stooped and busy at the side of the old carriageway. I walked back to them. Simon Dawkins spoke. "It's Mister Dolainde, Cap'n. Seems mighty sick."

I knelt at the old planter's side. They had laid him in the guinea grass with one of the canvas money sacks rolled and tucked beneath his head. In the moonlight he looked a corpse, but he was breathing faintly and his fingers twitched.

"Monsieur!" I said.

He opened his eyes and stared up at me a long time. His lips twisted as if he were trying to smile, but all they achieved was a kind of sneer, diabolical in that light.

"So!" he uttered in a harsh whisper. "It is gone, the Manoir Dolainde."

"But Brule said——"

Again the sneer. "He lied, of course. I knew he lied. He deceived you, but not me. Yet it stabbed me to see it gone, really gone." His voice became stronger, though he looked like death itself. "In Halifax I met a creole prisoner, one of the *petits-blancs,* taken in the fighting at Gonaïves by the British troops and sent north to the prison hulks. He had seen the *domaine* sometime in the rainy season of '94 and talked to one or two of my old servants still living in the quarters. The house was burned that night, you comprehend. Not of intention, they said. The field blacks were pillaging the place . . . they found the wine . . . you know what it was like. Well, a candle or two upset . . . the hangings torn and lying on the floor—the woodwork dry as tinder in the summer weather . . . that was the way of it."

His eyelids drooped. A spasm shook him. His lean face was convulsed with pain. I caught up one of his hands and chafed the wrist anxiously.

"You are ill, monsieur. What is the matter?"

"It is nothing."

"Surely there is something we can do for you?"

"Nothing. Let me lie here, and rest yourselves. You can do nothing in the dark. In the morning . . ."

"Yes?"

"In the morning I shall show you where it lies . . . my treasure . . . my treasure that I have come all this way to find."

"It is buried, then? We shall have to dig?"

"Yes . . . yes, Capitaine . . . you will have to dig."

A seaman trotted up, panting "Brule, sir—Brule's gone!"

"What! Gone where?"

"Nobody minds seeing him after we turned off the highroad. He must ha' stepped aside in the bushes and let us go past."

Simon uttered a bitter oath. "I never trusted that grinning fiddler-man. Here's trouble!"

I stood up and scraped my jaw. No use hating Brule. He had made off, as doubtless he had planned to do all along, and natural enough. Four hours along the King's Way would put him in the town. What then? Warn the French officials, of course. But it would take him some time to pass the sentinels and more to convince the commandant of his truth. And none of them, commandant or staff, would stir themselves before morning if half the tales were true. According to Mr. Pride's information the French staff at Cap François was sunk deep in sloth and women, not to be moved except by earthquakes.

"Trouble?" I said. "Ay, but we needn't look for it till tomorrow—noon at the earliest."

"What's your mind?" Simon said.

"Dig up this money of Dolainde's as soon as daylight comes and start across the plain at once."

"In the broad day?"

"Who's to stop us?"

He nodded and put a hard fist on his cutlass hilt. "Ay, who?"

Chapter 28

THE night was long. Under the cool breath of the mountain a chill mist rose out of the plain and eddied slowly in the moonshine. In those latitudes the sun turns a man's blood thin somehow, so that when the night mist comes it rattles the teeth in his head and sets him shivering as though he stood naked in the icy fog of the fishing banks at home. The *domaine* was a healthy place compared with the dank plain below, but there was ague and fever in this air—the breath of Yellow Jack himself. There was no sleep to be had, what with the chill and the infernal whine and prick of mosquitoes. I would not permit a fire. Hour after hour the seamen stirred and muttered, flogged their arms, slapped at mosquitoes, or tramped up and down the carriageway, munching the ship biscuit we had taken in our pockets for the journey.

'Twas worse when the moon went down. Then the night went solid black. The stars were hidden in the mist. We huddled together for warmth, ay, and for comfort in this dismal place. Dolainde lay very still for hours on end, with spasms of agony from time to time that set him writhing in the grass with his knees drawn up and his teeth grinding terribly. But he uttered no complaint.

When the first touch of daylight smeared the darkness in the east I shook him gently. "Monsieur, it is morning. There will be full light in half an hour, and then we must work quickly."

"Ah! True! Give me your hand. Now lift me . . . *doucement* . . . *doucement* . . . so!" He stood, swaying, with my arm about his thin shoulders. I sent two of the seamen to rummage the old slave quarters for digging tools. As the light grew they came back with a rusty hoe and shovel, crying that, ecod! there were spiders in those cabins big as crabs, and long ugly things that ran about the floor with fifty or a hundred legs—they had not stopped to count or to look for more tools.

Simon took one of Dolainde's arms and I the other, and at his direction we walked slowly towards the thicket where the house had been. His feet moved, but it seems to me we really carried him, and his body had no more weight than one of those straw images that boys in Gosport tote about the streets on Guy Fawkes Night. His cheeks were sunk against the bones as if they had gone to skin, and his blue eyes burned deep in their sockets. I remember thinking, *We shall have to carry him all the way back to the ship, he can never walk.*

We found the flagstones that ran along the front of the *manoir,* half hidden in weeds and creepers, and followed them to the point where they turned towards the rear.

"Now," Dolainde said in a strong voice, "let us walk straight towards the last of the genipa trees . . . that one over there . . . slowly . . . slowly . . . it is somewhere between . . . you will find a heap in the grass . . . you comprehend, the servants were in great fear and there was not much time to conceal . . ."

"Ha!" Simon grunted and stopped. He let go Dolainde's arm and bent over, parting the grass. There was a long and narrow mound. With a cry Dolainde tore himself free of my grasp and flung himself upon it, arms spread, his lean hands clutching at the sod. The seamen stood about, astonished. Simon raised his brows at me over that prostrate sobbing figure. The planter lay with his face against the grass of the mound, babbling all manner of things—prayers, endearments in the creole Spanish of San Domingo, curses on republicans white and black, and a repeated, "Alone . . . so very long . . . so very long . . ."

When he turned his head at last and said to me, "You understand, Capitaine?" there were tears in my eyes.

"Yes. It is her grave—Madame. How did you know?"

"The creole prisoner at Halifax. Some of the servants, the faithful ones, came out of hiding in the cane fields after the fire, after the others were gone. They found what was left of her, lying here on the *pelouse* where those savages had flung it, and made a grave . . . this . . . here. Ah, my God, if you knew how often I have cursed myself that I did not die with her that night! She was everything to me, you understand, everything! There was nothing else when she was gone. Luz! . . . I did not know the meaning of her name until the darkness came . . . Light! . . . Light of my life blown out . . . blown out . . ."

He spoke in creole, and the seamen could not understand his words, but the import of it all was plain enough, and there was sympathy in all their faces—and a growing uneasiness. The sun had burst over the mountains beyond the plain and was eating up the mist. They kept glancing towards the north, towards Cap François, and stirring in a restless way that could not be ignored.

"Monsieur," I said gravely, "the time is short. Brule must have reached the town long since. We must get what we came for and return at once."

Dolainde rolled his head and regarded the ring of sober faces. Then he looked at me with a very intent gaze.

"*Monsieur le capitaine,* I ask your indulgence. The time is very short indeed for me. You wish to know the truth? I am a dying man. I have known it a long time, ever since the Fulani man put the wanga in my hand that evening in Barrington Street. You remember? I recognized him, though he ran away so fast—one of my field slaves, a troublesome fellow, the Fulanis were too intelligent to make good slaves; I had him beaten once or twice. I made inquiry of the prison agent there in Halifax. The Fulani man was captured when the British defeated a black regiment of the French at Port-au-Prince. I said no more. The damage was done. I felt it soon after, a little gnawing low in my belly, as if I had swallowed a snake. It became worse as the months went by, as if the snake were growing.

"I went to your doctor at Gosport, that simple man, who told me, 'Inflammation of the bowel,' and gave me medicines. And the gnawing went on. I visited doctors in Halifax. They said, 'Inflammation of the bowel,' and gave me other medicines. That is what doctors always say when there is something inside they do not understand. Poor devils, what do they know, after all? They cannot see inside a man. Listen, Capitaine, when these Negroes of Saint Domingo hate a man they make a charm, a wanga, and do certain things . . . and certain things will happen to that man. He cannot escape. Do not smile. I have seen it happen many times in the old days. So . . . it happened to me. Since then my one fear was that I should die up there in your cold North, so far from my beloved Luz. The war . . . the blockade . . . there seemed no way of getting back. I continued to mingle with the *émigrés* at Halifax, hoping for news of home. I drank, to quiet the snake. I played cards to pass the time. At last I saw a chance—when Monsieur Pride began to build the ship and talk about a cruise in the West Indies. You know the rest. And now . . . now I am beside her, my Luz. Before the sun is very high I shall be dead, and then the snake will leave, and I shall be here with Madame whose side I never should have left. Do not look so incredulous, Capitaine. There is a kind of wisdom one learns in hot climates that you do not understand. I ask one thing."

"And that, monsieur?"

"Bury me beside her . . . here. Begin to dig, for, as you say, the time is short."

I hesitated.

"Dig!" he said violently.

And so we dug the grave, a ghoulish business with that living wisp beside us watching us with those feverish eyes. The soil was black and soft. There was little work to it, although the seamen sweated freely in the morning sun and took turns with the shovel. When the hole was three feet deep or so, Dolainde cried out "Enough!" and threw his head back and lay very still. I had a strange impression that he was trying to give up the ghost by an effort of will.

I said to him quickly, "Monsieur, where is the gold?"

The eyelids quivered. "Gold?"

"Thirty thousand louis d'or—you told Mr. Pride, remember? That is why we came."

"Ah *oui!* I ask your forgiveness."

"I do not understand."

His lips curled in that painful snarl. "You do not understand! No—you could not understand, because you are one of Pride's family, his heir, one learns, the affianced of his daughter—that cold she-fish. All you understand is money. Learn, then, there are more precious things than money in the world. One of them is love between man and woman that does not end at the grave. Love that is forever."

As he uttered these words his face fell into a repose like death itself, a look that never left it, as if fixed in yellow wax, and although he talked much more the lips barely moved, and I had to bend over him closely to catch a high thin voice that seemed to come from afar.

"Love . . . it is not to be bought, my friend. Your foster father tried to buy it from your mother . . . did you know? And when he failed he set himself to ruin them—she and the man Cain she married. It was simple. Cain was a fisherman, it seems, and suddenly he could not sell his fish. He tried this one and that. They would not buy. Life is hard in your cold country. When a fisherman cannot sell his fish he must eat it or starve—or try his hand at something else. Then the man Cain found that no one would employ him. But suddenly, yes—there was a friend, there was Monsieur Pride who had ships and wanted seamen—who wanted the man Cain. And so Cain sailed for Saint Domingo as a hand before the mast. He was a man of spirit with hair like yours and a pair of fists. With a man like that it is easy to pick a quarrel, and the master and the mates had their instructions. I do not know all that they did to him. I only know I met him long after on the beach at Port-au-Prince where they had flung him ashore, a wreck of a man, living from hand to mouth, and drunk whenever he could gather a few sous. I pitied him, I heard a little of his story—when he was very drunk, you understand. And finally I gave him money for a passage home to Nova Scotia.

"I did not know what followed his return—not until I came north to cast myself upon the charity of Monsieur Pride. Then, amongst the people of the town, I heard the tale. In his absence Cain's wife had perished, giving birth to a son—to you, it seems. Cain lingered for some years. Then one night he broke into a tavern and drank three bottles of brandy, one after the other. They found him dead in the morning with the empty bottles at his side. The boy—that was you, of course—he was put in the hands of those grim people in your country who look after orphans. That was how you came to Pride's hands—to a home in that great wooden tomb the people call Pride's Fancy. A strange whim of his, but perhaps you see the working of his mind. It does not matter.

"I first met Amos Pride in the old days, in the islands, when we made two of a band of outcasts, adventurers, seamen who had quit their ships for the easy life to be had here forty or fifty years ago. I was eighteen or nineteen. Pride was a few years older. Pride was one of us, but never one *with* us, you comprehend. He had little use for drink or women, he dreamed of wealth, he talked of nothing else. He had come here with his head full of old tales of riches gathered in these waters by the Brothers of the Cays, but of course those days were past. The wars . . . the navies of four nations swarming in the islands . . . the old game was finished. There was only petty robbery, a trading sloop here and there, a raid upon some village in a lonely part of the coast—for wine, for food, for mere excitement sometimes. We were a shabby crew. At last I went into the land and began the respectable life of a planter. That was when I met Luz.

"It was some years before I met Pride again. I was doing well by then, and he was captain of a little brig he owned himself, carrying salt fish and timber to the islands, taking back to Nova Scotia a cargo of rum, sugar, molasses—you know the kind of thing. So . . . we struck up a trade. Soon after that we went into the smuggling trade as well . . . Monte Cristi . . . the Spanish in America . . . like finding a silver mine. You know all that. Perhaps you know all this I have told you . . . I have wondered, sometimes, why . . ."

The voice trailed off. I shook Dolainde. "Go on!" I said, as if I could hold him to life with my own urgency. The far thin whine began again, although the face was lifeless, like someone whispering behind a mask.

"You want the gold? Capitaine, there is none. There never was. We spent our money, Luz and I, as fast as it came. Why should we save? The lands, the blacks, the sugar mill, the distillery where we made the Rum Dolainde, famous everywhere—there was our wealth. We thought it would go on forever. Who in Saint Domingo did not? We lived in Paris half the year . . . the hot months . . . lived like a king and queen . . . everybody envied us

. . . the rich creoles. Finished. All finished now. You must forgive me if I lied. It was the only way I could get back to Luz. You . . . you will return to your ship as you came . . . an easy journey after all . . . with nothing on your backs to slow your steps . . ."

Again the thin voice died away. I shook him gently, though my wrath was very great, seeing how he had plunged us all into danger for his sick man's whim. The thin lips were parted, showing the yellow teeth, but no sound came.

"What's it mean—all that gibberish?" Simon said.

"It means there is no gold. He was dying and brought us here to bury him."

At once they all broke into voice, cursing Dolainde and Mr. Pride, and crying that they had not shipped for any of this tomfoolery, and it was like to be the death of them. Simon turned upon them in a rage, shaking a hard fist under the nearest nose; but it was something else that stilled them. Dolainde's eyes opened wide. His lips writhed as if struggling for speech, and suddenly he uttered, "Lia!" in a voice that rang in the hot silence like a trumpet. That and no more. He did not move again. The eyes remained open, staring, unwinking, straight into the burning Hispaniola sun. I tore open the rumpled white coat and shirt. There was no heartbeat and no breath.

For a time we stood about him, silent. Then I motioned two of the seamen to lift the body into the grave. They obeyed, touching it reluctantly, as if they expected the open mouth to yell a malediction on them any moment. I laid my handkerchief over Dolainde's face, and they shoveled the earth and clods slowly until the corpse was covered, and then quickly, hastily, eager to get it done. When the second mound was level with the first, Simon Dawkins muttered unexpectedly (for he was no pietist like old Lot Mayes), "There'd ought to be a prayer, like. 'Tain't decent otherwise, and bad luck'll come of it."

I nodded and took off my faded old three-cocked hat. Most of the men had nothing for headgear but a kerchief wrapped and knotted. Some knuckled their foreheads out of reverence. Most stood impatient, glancing away towards the road.

"God rest this man and woman . . ."

"And have mercy on us all," added Simon.

"And have mercy on us all, amen."

We turned away, and as we did so one of the seamen, a great rough fellow from Gosport Head, cried out and sprang aside, tugging at the cutlass in his belt. I was not superstitious then and am not now. I know that people sicken and die as Dolainde did, people in our own far country who never saw Hispaniola and some who never saw a Negro. The doctors call it inflammation of the bowel or a consumption of the liver or some such thing, and surely they must know. And yet—and yet we saw there, clear in the sunshine, a small gray snake gliding away in the guinea grass that stood about Dolainde's grave.

In a moment it was gone.

Chapter 29

WE SET off in a mighty hurry, the seamen throwing off those worthless knapsacks and growling their opinion of the whole affair, Simon jeering at them for a lot of cowards, and I bringing up the rear in a high-nosed fashion—as if I were not running just as fast as they. The sun was high. I reckoned the hour at nine o'clock. Traveling like this, in broad daylight and the deuce with caution, we should be far across the plain in three hours' time. I clung to my notion that Brule's alarm at Cap François would bring no danger this side of noon, picturing a company of French infantry marching languidly down the King's Way in the forenoon heat and stopping to rest at every shady water hole.

This pretty dream was shattered suddenly. A hard drumming of hoofs sprang out of the hot silence ahead. We were passing the last of Dolainde's old slave quarters, but there was no time to jump aside and hide. There was time for nothing, not even the drawing of a cutlass. I heard a single shout of alarm from someone at the head of our hurrying file, just where the road made a sharp turn in its drop towards the plain, and then we were overrun and shrinking away from the hoofs and flashing sabers of a troop of Negro cavalry. They were mounted on fine-looking horses, the former property of planter-aristocrats, I fancy, a little shaggy now, galled with hard spurring and blown and lathered by the gallop from the Cap; and the men looked enormous, standing in the stirrups with sabers uplifted to strike, and crying out to us in creole to surrender.

The seamen obeyed readily—there was nothing else for it—and no blows were struck; but one of the riders, an officer by the gold embroidery on his scarlet cuffs and collar, spurred his horse over to me and aimed a terrific cut at my head. I fired my pistol at his sweating black face—I think the most brutish face I ever saw—more from instinct than from any hope of killing him; but I was swerving to avoid his saber, and the shot went wide. I suppose I was as near death then as I shall ever be this side the grave.

A voice down the road cried sharply, "Dessalines! Dessalines! *Halte-là!*" and a most extraordinary creature rode up to us on a tall brown horse—a small and very ugly Negro well past middle age, gaunt about the face, with high cheekbones, a broad flat nose, and a pair of enormous lips. His skin exactly matched his polished black cavalry boots. His trousers were sky-blue with a broad gold seam, and the sky-blue coat had scarlet cuffs and lapels, richly embroidered with gold lace, and two immense gold epaulets whose dangling tassels twinkled in the sun. He carried a cocked hat at the saddlebow and wore about his head a handkerchief like the others, except that his was of yellow silk. His saber was not drawn. He sat his horse lightly with his left arm at his side, and I noticed a queerly deformed finger on the hand that held the reins.

He regarded "Dessalines" and me with a pair of large black eyes, intelligent, imperious, a little ferocious, and motioned the black officer away. There was a profound silence. Our seamen had taken the cutlasses from their belts and thrown them on the road, obeying the fierce gestures of the horsemen. I dropped the smoking pistol and began to slip my cutlass out of the sheath, holding it by two fingers under the guard lest there be any mistake about my intentions. The small Negro put up his left hand and said in a calm reedy voice, "Keep it, monsieur. I am not afraid of you. You are the leader of these men?"

"I am their captain, yes."

"Ah! So it is true that you speak creole well! You have been in this country before?"

"In trading ships, yes."

"*Bien!* And these are your men. Are there others?"

"No."

"Now tell me—what do you here?"

I told him. There was nothing to conceal, for obviously he had talked to Brule. I added what Brule did not know—that Dolainde was dead and we had buried him. With a curt command to the rest of his company he left us under their guard and rode up the lane with the savage man Dessalines and a pair of troopers. All the horsemen were dressed in the uniform of French dragoons, with white trousers tucked into polished black riding boots, blue tunics unbuttoned in the heat, with the broad lapels turned back and exposing the scarlet lining; and every man except the little leader had a blue pullicate handkerchief tied about his head. Their more formal headgear, a stiff and very tall hat of black glazed stuff cocked fore and aft, was fastened to each saddlebow. And each man had a pair of heavy pistols in his saddle holsters.

There were forty or fifty of them, and as we stood with glum helpless faces at the roadside they entertained us with blood-curdling suggestions, twirling their bright sabers and clearly enjoying themselves. I was thankful when the little officer came back. Apparently he had satisfied himself of the truth of my story. I dare say the new grave on the plantation lawn and the scatter of abandoned knapsacks along the carriageway had told their own tale.

I was convinced that our lives were not worth twopence in the hands of this fierce crew, and I addressed the little Negro boldly, saying, "I demand that we be taken before the commandant at the Cap." A cackle of laughter from the dragoons. The little man said solemnly, "Why, *monsieur le capitaine?*"

"We are white men, prisoners of war. He will hold you responsible if any harm is done to us in his *arrondissement.*"

The officer called Dessalines uttered a wild laugh at this. The small black man was unmoved. *"Bien,"* he said in a mild voice. "You shall see him." He turned and cried a command. A trumpet blared and gave us a nervous start. At once the horsemen arranged themselves and their beasts in a long double file and sat like statues, each with his saber held erect from the waist and tipped against his right shoulder. A motion of the small Negro's hand sent us scrambling into file between the lines of dragoons, and he and Dessalines spurred their beasts to the head of the column. Another blast of the trumpet and off we went, the horses at a walk and ourselves making an easy pace of it down the middle of the road.

In the next three hours I had opportunity to study and also to admire this sample of the black army the French had raised in Hispaniola. The men were tall muscular fellows with a precision in all their movements that I had never seen equaled, not even by Prince Edward's own regiment of fusiliers at Halifax. Their saddles, arms, equipment, and uniforms were of the best. Every bit of metal shone, to the last brass button on their tunics, and except for the dust of their brisk ride from the Cap their uniforms were spotless. They sat their horses with the ease of veteran cavalrymen. Perhaps they were part of a *corps d'élite,* but even so I saw very clearly now what I had suspected long ago—that black troops properly trained and equipped, and fighting in this hot green hell, were more than a match for any European army. And I wondered what the French thought of this, now that the British had been driven out.

All along the King's Way we found the same succession of ruined mansions and choked fields that we had noticed in our moonlit journey across the plain, a melancholy spectacle. I wondered how many of the owners and their handsome languid women were now living, and where. I was no pietist, but when I thought of the bygone days, the dancing, the drinking, the gambling, the extravagant wives, the lively mistresses lolling in smart carriages between the palms along this very road, all borne you might say on the whipped shoulders of the blacks, I could not help seeing it all as a kind of Caribbean Sodom and Gomorrah, five years, say, after the wrath. But chiefly in my thoughts, recurring again and again, was a gloomy wonder about Lia and our people at the landing cove. Had Brule betrayed them, too? I comforted myself with the knowledge that old Lot Mayes, uneasy man, would be keeping a sharp watch, and at the first sign of trouble would cut cable and make off.

On our own prospects I was glum. I had a dim hope that if we reached the Cap alive we might convince the French commandant of our right to be considered prisoners of war. In that case, through Mr. Pride's influence in high places, we might be liberated by exchange, or at worst by the end of the war.

But in my heart I knew how poor a case we had. We were not man-o'-war's men or simple merchantmen, but something between that the French knew only as *corsaires*. They would judge us by their own, who were little better than pirates. And what would they say of our strange errand in Hispaniola? A likely story!

As we emerged from the Haut du Cap and saw the bright blue water, and the white town wavering in the heat haze at the foot of the long green slope, the trumpet pealed once more and the column came to a halt. I was alarmed to see the little officer and Dessalines spur off and gallop away to the town. What did that mean? Why were we not being taken to the commandant? I watched the dragoons unfasten the black cocked hats from their saddlebows, blow the dust off carefully, and put them on over the kerchiefs tied about their heads. The cockade of republican France made a gaudy flower at the left side of each hat. In addition the hat of the black *sous-officier* bore three tall plumes, red, white, and blue, waving gaily in the sea breeze. Each dragoon dismounted and flicked his boots, saddle, and weapons with a cloth, and, this done, at a trumpet signal all sprang into the saddle, and at another the column resumed the steady walk-march down to Cap François.

As we started down the slope the town looked pretty much as it had when I first saw it from the deck of the *Fair Wind* years agone. I could not believe my eyes. Was that night in '93 a dream? But as we drew into the outskirts I saw that the haze had distorted and concealed the truth. The gleaming white stone houses were in most cases nothing but burnt-out shells, some of them roofed over crudely with a scatter of boards, some with a thatch of bundled grass after the fashion of Negro huts, but most of them gaping to the sky. There were black spaces littered with charred rubbish where the wooden shops had stood in long shady arcades, with their tall posts supporting the overhanging upper stories.

In the streets the sun fell like a bludgeon, and the remembered stink of slops and human filth arose and fairly shimmered in the strong light; but perhaps that was only the flies. A swarm of ragged and half-naked people poured from the ruins to cry insult at us as we passed. Most of them seemed to be plantation blacks living a hand-to-mouth existence in the town; but I noticed many *petits-blancs* amongst them, and others in the shabby remains of fine clothing who must have been whites of the old ruling class, now one with the blacks and jeering as loud, ay, louder than the rest. Such was the progress of liberty, equality, and fraternity in five years. I felt a certain smug sorrow for the whites, thinking how far they had come down in the world, and a certain revenge for their insults in knowing how far they yet had to go.

Most of the public buildings stood as I remembered them. Apparently they had been garrisoned by republican troops that night Macaya's blacks went wild in '93. We saw the big church in the Place d'Armes, the Bureau of Marine, the customhouse, the infantry barracks. There was a queer wooden structure in the square, hung with torn bunting and withered fronds of palm, which the *sous-officier* informed me was the Altar of the Fatherland, erected by the republican commissioners from France and used on public occasions as a kind of pulpit from which the people were addressed.

We arrived at last before the governor's palace, a grand affair, dazzling white in the sunshine and surrounded by well-tended gardens and well-armed sentinels. A smart Negro guard turned out at our approach. Their long bayonets glittered. The trumpet halted our little cavalcade. The *sous-officier* dismounted, exchanged tremendous salutes with the officer of the guard, and passed inside. An hour went by. We prisoners stood hot and dusty in the blazing square, weary to death with the long march in the sun. The horses shook their heads and stamped and swished their tails against the multitude of flies. The black troopers sat like statues, as if every lattice in the palace were a jealous commander's eye. And all about us the rabble of Cap François, black, white, and brown, shook its fists and howled for our blood, without knowing a thing about us except that we were "Inglismum" caught somewhere in their island in time of war.

Simon Dawkins muttered to me, "Ecod, Nathan, if ye can't get us into the hands of a white officer mighty quick, we're dead men all. Yon mob would pull us to pieces in a minute."

"Not while the dragoons are here," I said uneasily.

"They're black as the rest. Turn us over to 'em quick as wink."

But now the *sous-officier* appeared and beckoned to me from the steps. I went to him, and we walked inside at a smart pace, passing a pair of blue-clad sentries under the portals and another pair at an inner doorway. Then we crossed a spacious marble-tiled and pillared hall filled with people dressed in the best French taste, many of them Negroes in gorgeous uniforms, some sitting, some standing and chatting politely with ladies of every complexion from white to black. Tall Negro lackeys in scarlet coats and tight white breeches passed amongst the throng with trays of wine glasses. An animated scene. I wondered if it was part of the daily life of the palace. There was a matter-of-course air about the lackeys. One thing I remember particularly. Although all these people talking together produced a great buzz, the individual voices were subdued, and when one handsome young Negress in a green silk gown laughed shrilly, a number of the black officers turned such severe looks her way that she fell silent, poor thing, and seemed to shrink down in her chair.

We passed another pair of lackeys and left the sounds of the anteroom behind. The *sous-officier's* heels and spurs rang on marble tiling in a cool shadowy passage where the sea breeze blew through the lattices. Another pair of lackeys and another door, a whisper from the *sous-officier* to an unseen someone just inside, and a respectful voice saying, "*Mon général,* the English captain is here."

A sharp voice barked, "*Entrez!*" and in we went.

The room was hung with gold brocade. The floor was of black marble. Several Negro officers stood to one side, regarding me curiously. One white officer stood amongst them, a middle-aged man with a thin sickly face and bearing on his scarlet tunic collar the gold acorns and oak leaves of a general of the French staff. He gave me an indifferent glance and had in his eyes the queer lost look I had noticed in some of the white ladies in the anteroom.

At a long mahogany desk at the head of the chamber sat a man busily signing papers. He read each quickly and now and again dipped his quill and scrawled a footnote in addition to his signature. I could see only the top of his bent head, a brushed mat of graying black wool gathered in a short queue and tied with a sky-blue ribbon to match the color of his coat. A Negro!

There was something oddly familiar about the set of the shoulders with their vast epaulets, and then I noticed the deformed finger on the right hand. He threw up his head and looked straight at me with an amused gleam in his eyes. The ugly little man of the plantation lane, of course. But what was he doing here, in the presence of these respectful officers, the one man seated in the room?

I could see that he relished my amazement.

"So you see, *monsieur le capitaine,* you have your wish!"

I stammered, "You . . . You are the commandant here?"

He sat up straight in the chair and said in his high mild voice, "Monsieur, you see before you the commander in chief of all the armies of the republic in Saint Domingo."

"But the commissioner . . . Monsieur Sonthonax?"

"You are behind the times, monsieur. Monsieur Sonthonax went back to France nearly a year ago. I sent him." He turned briskly to one of his aides.

"Send for the witness Brule."

He regarded me silently for a full minute, playing with the quill in his dark fingers.

"Monsieur—Monsieur Cain, is it not?—you have been taken in arms in the territory of Saint Domingo, in the company of the *ci-devant* planter Dolainde, an enemy of the republic. Dolainde, it seems, has cheated the guillotine. But you—we have you and your band of rascals. What have you to say?"

"I am captain of a private ship of war, sailing under letters of marque signed by the colonial governor of Nova Scotia, in the name of the King of England."

He was not impressed. Indeed he looked puzzled.

"Nouvelle-Ecosse?" he repeated. "Where is that?"

"A British colony in North America."

He raised his grizzled brows. "You are, then, an American?"

"Of a kind, yes."

"And this Nouvelle-Ecosse, this colony of which you speak, it makes war on us in Saint Domingo?"

"It is part of the empire of England, which is at war with France."

"Ah! So! And you have this document, no doubt, this so-called letter of marque?"

"It is in the cabin of my ship."

"And where is that?"—sharply.

I felt a great rush of relief. So Brule had not told him everything! Lia and the others were safe, for the time being at any rate.

"I do not know," I said. "We were landed by boat upon the coast. She may be anywhere by now."

He frowned, knowing I lied. But he did not press the point.

"We come now to your presence in Saint Domingo. The King of England gave you permission to land in this island?"—with a sardonic smile.

"No."

"Ah! That is better. You speak the truth sometimes. Go on, monsieur!"

"I have told you before, the planter Dolainde wished to recover something of value in his *manoir* on the Haut du Cap. He persuaded us to land, to go with him and carry it away. We found the *manoir* destroyed and nothing left, and Monsieur Dolainde fell ill and died next morning. We buried him beside the grave of his wife and——"

"So I have seen. One has heard of these Dolaindes. They had a reputation of kindness to their slaves—a very rare thing, monsieur, in Saint Domingo. That is a point in their favor in the next world. It is, even, a point in your own favor now. *Bien!* And so you and your men were returning with disappointment to your ship—this ship whose whereabouts you do not know—when you were arrested by Dessalines and his dragoons?"

"That is correct."

A twitch of annoyance. "I address you as monsieur. Have the courtesy to do so with me."

"Monsieur."

There was a commotion at the door. The aide rushed into the room, crying, "*Mon général,* he is gone—the man Brule!"

Chapter 30

THE little general leaped out of his chair. I thought he would leap at the aide's throat. The mild, almost benign expression had fled from his bony face, and in its place was a look of the utmost ferocity.

"Imbecile! Where?"

The aide was in a palsy of fright. He had a handsome and intelligent face, of Fulani blood probably, and doubtless was a devil with the ladies in his idle hours, but now his smooth ebony skin had a grayish tinge and his large eyeballs rolled and gleamed with terror.

"Excellency," he stammered, "it was your own wish that the citizen Brule should go free until called upon. Your Excellency said——"

"I said! I said! Dolt, I ask you where he is, the citizen Brule!"

The aide swallowed hard. "Excellency, one learns that he left the town, in the company of certain other *petits-blancs* and mulattoes, about fifty of them, three hours ago."

"How?—simpleton!"

"In a *chaloupe* stolen from the fishermen, *mon général.*"

His Excellency stared at the wretch. A muscle twitched in his gaunt cheek. At last he made a gesture of dismissal, saying in his old voice, "It is not your fault, of course, Damas. It comes of trusting the *petits-blancs* like Brule. Dessalines would kill them all, and all the mulattoes as well. Sometimes I think . . . but no . . . we must not think of that."

He sat down and gave me a gloomy attention as the aide melted thankfully into the silent group standing by the wall.

"What do you know of him, this man Brule, *monsieur le capitaine?*"

I was in such a rage that I could scarcely speak. "I met him when he was a prisoner in Nova Scotia," I said thickly. "He had been taken in a small French warship somewhere in these waters. He was a creole of Saint Domingo, one of the poor class, the little-whites, as you say. He wished to return. He offered to pilot our ship into this coast in exchange for his freedom. We took him at his word."

"Ah! And now he has his freedom well enough. Have you any idea where he has gone?"

"Yes, monsieur. He has gone to seize my ship."

"Then he knows where it is—and you do not?"

"I lied, monsieur. The ship is anchored in a cove not twenty miles from here."

"So close? Dieu! You are bold, you Nouvelle-Ecossais. What then?"

"I suppose he intends to sail her with these men he has picked up in Cap François. As a *corsaire*. There are many like him working out of Guadeloupe, Martinique—but there is something else."

"And that?"

"A young woman, daughter of the planter Dolainde. He will take her with the ship."

His Excellency raised his brows. "So? And that does not please you, one can see. This young woman—she is something to you, *monsieur le capitaine?*"

"She is all the world, monsieur. Without her there is nothing."

He leaned back in the great polished chair. "So you love, you English! One has heard that you are like fish, who produce young without touching one another. Forgive me if I smile. Your expedition to our island does not seem to have been a success, monsieur. You—and the *ci-devant* planter Dolainde—and the money that did not exist—and the renegade Brule—and the ship—and now the girl. There is a saying amongst us—'When whites fall out, the black man has his due.' Now perhaps you see why it amuses us, this war between the English and the French in Saint Domingo. What do you think of the English attempt to take our island?"

"I knew it would fail, and said so from the first."

"*Bien! Bien!* You are angry and you speak the truth—I see it in your face. It is a pleasure, monsieur, to see a white man in the mood for truth. You will forgive me if I observe that it does not happen very often. That has been my experience. While you are in that mood, monsieur, permit me to show you something." He called out sharply, "Carbet! The seeds, if you please!"

There was a little scurry behind us, the sound of a drawer pulled open, the faint hiss of something poured. One of the aides came forward and placed on the shining mahogany a glass jar three-quarters filled with grains of maize. There was something odd about the grains. Whether natural or dyed, I cannot say, but nearly all of them were black; the rest, a thin layer at the top, were white.

The little Negro took the jar in his hands. There was a childish pleasure in his face. I had an impression that this was a favorite trick of his.

"Regard, *monsieur le capitaine!* Here is our Saint Domingo as you knew it in the time gone by—the whites on top, the blacks beneath. Now in '93 something happens—so!" He gave the jar a single shake. Some of the black grains appeared on top, some of the white had vanished into the black mass below.

"Here, monsieur, is Saint Domingo now. The top is part white, part black, as you see. *Bien!* That is the way I wish to keep it. Do you know why? Because our island must have the brains of white men, the knowledge they possess, the knack of doing things that is born in them. You saw the old plantations on the Haut du Cap—it is so all over Saint Domingo. Our black folk have their freedom now, but they are confused about cultivation. They cannot see the difference between work and slavery, and so they have destroyed—destroyed—and there is hunger all the way from Tiburon to Cabo Engaño. That must be corrected. We shall need the whites to do it. I wish to see a country, one country in the world, where whites and blacks work together for the good of all. But there are obstructions. Many of the planters ran away. Then came the English armies at the urging of the *émigrés*. I have thrown the English out, with some assistance"—he gave a curt contemptuous nod towards someone in the group behind me—"with assistance from the troops of the republic, of course. I have my gratitude to France. But now, you comprehend, I am in sole command of the armies of Saint Domingo, and I intend to keep it—for the good of all."

His voice had taken on a harsh note. His hard black gaze looked past my shoulder, and suddenly I knew he was not speaking to me but to that unhappy white general standing amongst the silent Negro aides.

"If all goes amiably, all goes well. But if there is interference with my plans—from any side—from France, let us say, now that the English have been driven out——" He took the jar in both hands and shook and shook the thing with such violence that beads of sweat stood out on his skin. One hand dropped to his side at last. The jar stood poised upon the outstretched palm of the other. There was a great change in the grains. Here and there a speck of white showed far down the jar, and several had settled to the very bottom. The top was solid black. He held the heavy jar thus for a full minute at arm's length, without a waver, as stout a test of strength and nerve as I ever saw in my life. Then, abruptly, he put the thing down and stood looking me in the eye and drumming his fingers on the mahogany. There was no sign of arrogance in his face, only a very great resolution that would stop at nothing to achieve its ends.

"Monsieur, you may go—you and your seamen. When the man Brule came to me with his story I thought perhaps the English had made some new descent upon us. That is why I went to see for myself. I believe you are what you say. In any case you are too few to do much harm. Go away, then, go back to your Nouvelle-Ecosse, and tell your people what you have seen in Saint Domingo."

"You—you mean——"

"I mean you are free, monsieur. I have given half a million black men freedom, it would be strange if I could not free a score of whites. You and your men will be conducted to the *embarcadère* and given a boat—I cannot have you wandering about the roads. You may pursue the renegade Brule—you may go to the devil if you wish—but you must go. If you are found with a foot to shore in Saint Domingo afterward you will be killed without mercy."

He paused, and a faint smile softened the ugliness of his bony black face.

"You are a bold young man or you would not have come here on this mad affair. You deserve well. I wish you well—you and the young woman. It is something to be a young man and in love. There are no seas, no mountains, only a distance to be crossed. That is a miracle we all share, black and white alike. Go!"

In my haste to get away I barely uttered a word of thanks. He had turned to his papers and taken up his quill, and if he heard my mumbled sentiment he gave no sign. But as the *sous-officier* of dragoons fell in beside me, marching to the door, the voice of the little general came sharply.

"Monsieur!"

I turned. "Yes—Excellency?"

"When you tell your people in the North about our Saint Domingo, tell them also the name of the black man who spared your life. You have good cause to remember it. I am called Toussaint —Toussaint L'Ouverture." He bent to his papers again, quill in hand; and that was the last sound I heard as I passed through the doorway, the busy scratch, scratch, scratch of the pen.

The boat was a pinnace left behind by the frigate *L'Indien* last year, when Sonthonax and his mulatto mistress and friends packed off so hurriedly to France. So the *sous-officier* informed me gravely, adding that it had been kept with care as "property of the republic." We looked upon it with the rueful eyes of seamen anywhere who come upon a good boat ruined by landsmen's care. Fortunately it was too big a thing to haul easily ashore, else no doubt they would have dragged it high and dry after the fashion of landsmen and left it to fall apart under the full blaze of the sun. As it was, the pinnace lay uncovered at a mooring off the foreshore. At the quayside a Negro soldier, guardian of the republic, abandoned his fishing line hastily, found his musket, and presented arms as our little cavalcade came down to the water.

There was little ceremony. The *sous-officier* uttered a sharp command, and four dragoons rode up from the rear of the column with our cutlasses, bound with cords in bundles of half a dozen or so and carried on their saddlebows. They flung them in the dust at our feet.

"By the order of His Excellency," said the officer, and saluted reverently at the mere mention of that strange little man. I pulled off my shabby hat and bowed. We picked up the bundled weapons and waded out to the boat. The water was breast-deep at the mooring, and the feel of it on our skins was a touch of heaven.

We were exhausted after the sleepless night and the long march in the heat, ay, and by the long hours of anxiety when it seemed to all of us that we would end in the Place d'Armes, kicking our lives out at the rope's end or butchered under the guillotine, or more likely beaten to blood and bones by that howling mob still beating like a sea against the outer line of dragoons. Now by a miracle we were free, and the warm embrace of Mother Sea received us and awakened in our veins a tingle of hope. Here was the long road home.

Four pair of oars, cracked and warped in the suns and rains of an idle year, lay tumbled upon the thwarts. The bottom looked sound enough. Above waterline the woodwork had a look and feel of dry rot through and through. The tiller ropes had rotted to a bleached gray stuff that parted at the first tug. We rowed away in a deep silence, and I put an oar over the stern and steered towards the outer anchorage where the trade breeze stirred the surface of the water. The mob had lost its voice in wonder at this strange turn of events. The afternoon was far gone, the sun sitting on the crest of the Morne behind the town, full in our eyes as we looked back to the soldiers on the quay. In that painful blaze the figures of the horsemen stood facing towards the sea, black and monstrous like figures in a nightmare, half man, half beast, and tall as giants, with the mob and the town lost in the glare behind. Of all my memories of Hispaniola that is the one which seems the most significant—the sun, the mountain, and the line of monsters, strange and watchful, ranged along the *embarcadère* between that cataract of sunshine and the glitter on the sea.

The trade wind died as we drew away from the empty anchorage. When the sun was down behind the mountain there was a sharp clap from the foot of it—the sunset gun at Fort Picolet. In a moment we heard the bugles, very clear across the water, a romantic sound that had in it a note of warning and farewell. I thought of Negro buglers sounding that call in all the posts and camps of Hispaniola, and the dark night coming down. If Toussaint's voice by any chance was stilled, and some other took charge —that beast-faced brigadier of his, Dessalines, say . . .

Simon Dawkins put it best, I think. He jerked a thumb towards the sound of the bugles.

"Some night they'll sound the trump o' doom for every white left in the island."

For a time the sunset hung a screen of red and gold across the western sky with the mountain hard and black against it, but already night was creeping out from the shadowy east flank. Small yellow pricks of candlelight appeared in Fort Picolet and from the more distant town. Then it was dark, and hot, and very still. We rowed three oars a side and worked them in three watches, changing every half hour as near as we could judge. The boat leaked like a fish basket now that it sat deeper in the water, and two men bailed, using my hat and a gourd found under the stern sheets. She was a crazy thing. As the men changed places at the oars you could feel the bottom rippling with their movement. I had a queasy notion that a sharp stamp of my foot would plunge it through.

After each spell at the oars the men sank down and slept at once, all huddled on the bottom like weary children, regardless of the slopping water there and the hard lying. After a time we felt the first breath of the land wind. Simon Dawkins dragged forth the mast and unwrapped the sail, a kind of dipping lug, quaintly fashioned and full of holes gnawed by the rats of Cap François or perhaps some canvas-eating insect. The sheet lines were rotten, but we made new ones with cords the dragoons had tied about our cutlasses, and with a belt cut into strips. As the wind increased, the sail made itself felt, but although the pinnace moved in a livelier fashion, I ordered the men to keep on rowing for the sake of speed. Speed! We seemed to crawl.

About an hour of this and a somewhat harder puff of the night wind snapped the mast short off where it passed through a forward thwart. The stick was dead with sun rot like everything else about her. After some jackknife carpentry and a crude reef in the sail, we got it to the wind again and tended it more carefully, letting the sheets go when the fluky breeze came hard down from the mountains.

I reckoned the distance to the cove at fifteen miles, keeping fairly close inshore, but 'twas difficult to say, sheering amongst the reefs as we were. Twice we touched ground, and I thought the bottom would go out of her, but we shoved right off, and she did not seem to leak worse than before. Now and again a small mangrove island loomed out of the dark like some vague bulky creature risen from the sea, and I had to heave hard on my steering oar to clear it. Once, in such a passage, one of the seamen reached out and grasped a mangrove root and cut his hand on something hard and sharp. He howled his surprise, and I told him harshly to pipe down—it was not every man could say he had found oysters growing on a tree and show the scar to prove it.

My great fear was that I should overrun the landing place, for there was nothing to distinguish in the dark mass of the land, and as we dragged the slow miles past our gunwales hour on hour I had a growing dismay, thinking we had gone far up the Manzanillo bight towards Fort Liberty. But after what seemed all the night, and must have been a good five hours at least, someone forward cried, "See there! A light!" I stood up and made out the red eye of a fire upon the beach, and to the east of it the loom of a long point of the land. There was no other point like that between the Cap and Manzanillo Bay.

We had opened the cove at last.

Chapter 31

I THOUGHT, *What now?* Brule had many hours' start of us, but whatever his plans he must have waited for nightfall to carry them out, knowing old Lot's watchfulness. I pictured Brule and his crew of *petits-blancs* and mulattoes in their stolen sloop coming down upon the *Fancy* in the darkness, the bump alongside, the swift rush to overpower the anchor watch, the ship in their hands in two minutes. I had left Lot with twenty-two men, most of them wounded in the fight with the schooner—fully a dozen of them at death's own door. Brule had fifty cutthroat fellows of the kind that swarmed at the Cap, the riffraff of the colony, ready for any desperate enterprise. If they succeeded in boarding the brigantine the end was certain, though given half a chance Lot's men could blow them to perdition with a blast of grape before they reached the side.

We took in our sail, and I steered cautiously towards the fire. Presently we came in range of a familiar yellow gleam—the stern windows of the brigantine. They had a peaceful look. I tried to assure myself that all my fears were whimsy. No doubt Brule had gone the other way, towards Tortuga, say, where the old sea thieves used to congregate in Mr. Pride's time. Lia was sitting in the cabin, sewing on her new finery by the light of the hanging lamp, and wondering how we fared. And the fire? Lot had sent one or two men ashore to kindle a few sticks of driftwood, a mark for our party returning through the forest with the moneybags.

Then doubt again. I had left strict orders that no lights be shown, and Lot was not the man to break so sensible a rule. If Lot remained in charge of the ship, then somebody else was ashore. Who? Not Brule, at any rate—he would not be such a fool.

I was all impatience to board the *Fancy* and have out my doubts, one way or the other, but Simon growled, "Hold hard there, Nathan! If Lot was aboard the cabin lights wouldn't be shinin' out like that—he'd have the stern windows covered. Somethin's wrong. I smell it. And we'd only make it worse, barging in—a handful o' tired men with a cutlass apiece ag'in Brule and a crowd o' lively rogues with all the arms o' the ship at their hands."

"Pooh! The scum of Cap François!"

"Ay, and if they're anything like the scum o' Guadeloupe that fought us in the schooner, why, they're not to be despised. I say first let's find out who's on shore. It can't be Brule's lot."

"Humph! Suppose it's a company of French troops. Thought of that?"

"Well, sir, s'posin' 'twas. Why'd they light a fire within gunshot o' the ship? It don't make sense."

"None of it makes sense," I said testily, but I knew he was right.

We edged in carefully, hugging the west shore of the cove to avoid passing between the firelight and the ship. As we drew in towards the landing place we made out the dark hull and spars of the *Hirondelle* stark against the glow of the *Fancy's* cabin windows. Our prize was still there, then. Amongst the feverish thoughts in my mind was a notion that Brule might seize the unguarded *Hirondelle* and make off with her, rather than risk a fight for the brigantine.

In my anxiety to make the most of the gloom inshore I steered too close to the mangroves, and the boat grounded. The men pushed stoutly with their oars, but I bade them give over—there was no floating her in that fashion without making noise enough to wake the very mountains. We had fetched up on a large mangrove clump within two musket shot of the fire. I resolved to risk the boat no farther. I whispered to Simon that I was going ashore for a close look, and taking the young Indian with me. Wokwees rose at once, and we stepped out on the slimy mangrove roots with some distaste—they felt like snakes underfoot. Wokwees had eyes like a cat, and could move like one, so I nudged him ahead and followed in his steps, feeling carefully with each foot before putting it down lest the crack of a stick ruin everything.

We had not far to go for a clear view. The mangrove clump stood out a bit from the line of the shore, and after twenty steps or so we emerged into the open and looked straight towards the fire. Several indistinct figures lay about it. Once a man walked up to it from the shadows and threw on more wood. A flutter of sparks went up, and in this added light I made out a man sitting hunched to one side, with his hands clasped about his knees, and staring into the blaze. For a moment his face was outlined sharply, like those shadow pictures the profile makers cut out with scissors and paste on blocks of wood for a shilling a head. There was no mistaking the cut of that jib or the upturned pigtail at the back. Lot Mayes was sitting by the fire.

Was he a prisoner of those others? His attitude was glum enough. We watched, and presently one of the prone men stirred, and Lot arose and went over to him. They talked in low voices impossible to catch. Then I saw Lot raise a pannikin to the other's mouth. Someone sick or wounded, evidently. If they were prisoners there was no sign of a guard. The other figures sprawled about the fire in postures of indifference. I nudged the Indian to go on.

It took us half an hour to cover the rest of the way, creeping amongst the mangroves. At last I reached a place in the shadows well behind the fire itself. I felt about for a stick and tossed it at Lot's feet. He put his head up and looked over his shoulder, frowning in the firelight.

"Lot!" I said, not loudly. "Lot Mayes!"

He turned slowly and faced towards the darkness, turning his head to and fro in search of someone in the rim of the firelight and seeing nothing.

"Lot!" I said again, in the same voice. "Come this way. Slowly. Say nothing."

He came, sauntering, with thumbs in his belt. At the edge of the trees he paused and uttered an incredulous whisper. "Nathan! Nathan, boy—is it you?"

"Ay, Nathan as ever was! Come closer. Come out of the light."

He stepped into the gloom, and in a moment we were together, our arms about each other, and the old man weeping. "Nathan! . . . Nathan, boy . . . this is what I'd hoped for . . . prayed for . . . ever since that schemin' rogue got the best of us . . . but we . . . the lads . . . had just about give ye up . . . he said ye was all took and good as hanged."

I shook him fiercely. "The ship! What's happened?"

"Don't ye know?"

"Brule?"

"Ay, Brule, damn the day we ever set eyes on him. He come out o' the woods about here—alone—clo'es all torn—along about sundown, 'twas—stood at the waterside hailin' the ship—shoutin' that Capitaine Cain and his party was in trouble, up towards the road—said Meester Mayes was to take all the men that was fit to use a cutlass—no firearms, Meester Mayes was to make sure o' that—and bring 'em up to the road—Cap'n Cain's orders. So we put off in the longboat, ten of us—all that was fit to move—and rushed up into the woods the way he pointed. Follered your path well enough for a mile or so—bushes broken, creepers cut away—then we lost it. Wandered about for a bit—couldn't pick it up again—wondered why Brule hadn't come along to show the way. Gettin' dusk—got 'spicious—headed back for the shore. Come out on the point below here—just in time to see Brule and a lot o' wild-lookin' strangers in a crazy little carvel-built sloop runnin' alongside the *Fancy*. They swarmed aboard, howlin' like a pack of Indians, and disappeared below. They'd took the longboat—we could see it fast to the stern o' their sloop. There we was—stranded—stranded and gammoned proper, like the booby birds we were—and not so much as a pistol amongst the lot of us."

"Lord, man—didn't you do anything at all?"

"What could we do? We moved along the shore to the landing place—and we watched the ship. After a time some of 'em come on deck, laughin' and singin', and hove three of our lads overboard. They was dead, I think—they never moved—and o' course the sharks—well, it got dark pretty quick, so we lit a fire in hopes to guide ye back—comin' with the gold, like."

"But Lia, man! Lia Dolainde!"

"I left Black Boston aboard to look after her and the wounded men."

"But have you seen or heard anything—any sign of her—since Brule's men went aboard? Speak, man, for God's sake! What have they done to her?"

He was silent for a space. Then he said grimly, " 'Tain't what they've done to her, Nathan—it's what she's done herself. I don't like to say this—knowin' how 'twas with you and her—but for the past two or three hours she's been singin' and dancin' the *chica* for 'em, right up on the poop, by the light of a couple o' lanterns, and Boston beatin' that queer little drum o' his."

"You lie!"

"Gospel, Nathan. I couldn't believe my own eyes, first. But ye know how thick she was with Brule, in Gosport and aboard the brigantine."

"There's more! Out with it!"

"There was no sign o' the girl at first, mind. Brule came off in the longboat with some o' his cutthroats, each man with a 'unnin' alongside the *Fancy*. They swarmed aboard, howlin' ike a pack of Indians, and disappeared below. They'd took the ongboat—we could see it fast to the stern o' their sloop. There ve was—stranded—stranded and gammoned proper, like the ooby birds we were—and not so much as a pistol amongst the ot of us."

"Lord, man—didn't you do anything at all?"

"What could we do? We moved along the shore to the landing lace—and we watched the ship. After a time some of 'em come n deck, laughin' and singin', and hove three of our lads overoard. They was dead, I think—they never moved—and o' course ie sharks—well, it got dark pretty quick, so we lit a fire in hopes guide ye back—comin' with the gold, like."

"But Lia, man! Lia Dolainde!"

"I left Black Boston aboard to look after her and the wounded en."

"But have you seen or heard anything—any sign of her—since ule's men went aboard? Speak, man, for God's sake! What have ey done to her?"

He was silent for a space. Then he said grimly, "'Tain't what ey've done to her, Nathan—it's what she's done herself. I don't e to say this—knowin' how 'twas with you and her—but for the st two or three hours she's been singin' and dancin' the *chica* 'em, right up on the poop, by the light of a couple o' lanterns, d Boston beatin' that queer little drum o' his."

"You lie!"

"Gospel, Nathan. I couldn't believe my own eyes, first. But know how thick she was with Brule, in Gosport and aboard brigantine."

"There's more! Out with it!"

"There was no sign o' the girl at first, mind. Brule came off the longboat with some o' his cutthroats, each man with a

I was all impatience to board the *Fancy* and have out my doubts, one way or the other, but Simon growled, "Hold hard there, Nathan! If Lot was aboard the cabin lights wouldn't be shinin' out like that—he'd have the stern windows covered. Somethin's wrong. I smell it. And we'd only make it worse, barging in—a handful o' tired men with a cutlass apiece ag'in Brule and a crowd o' lively rogues with all the arms o' the ship at their hands."

"Pooh! The scum of Cap François!"

"Ay, and if they're anything like the scum o' Guadeloupe that fought us in the schooner, why, they're not to be despised. I say first let's find out who's on shore. It can't be Brule's lot."

"Humph! Suppose it's a company of French troops. Thought of that?"

"Well, sir, s'posin' 'twas. Why'd they light a fire within gunshot o' the ship? It don't make sense."

"None of it makes sense," I said testily, but I knew he was right.

We edged in carefully, hugging the west shore of the cove to avoid passing between the firelight and the ship. As we drew in towards the landing place we made out the dark hull and spars of the *Hirondelle* stark against the glow of the *Fancy's* cabin windows. Our prize was still there, then. Amongst the feverish thoughts in my mind was a notion that Brule might seize the unguarded *Hirondelle* and make off with her, rather than risk a fight for the brigantine.

In my anxiety to make the most of the gloom inshore I steered too close to the mangroves, and the boat grounded. The men pushed stoutly with their oars, but I bade them give over—there was no floating her in that fashion without making noise enough to wake the very mountains. We had fetched up on a large mangrove clump within two musket shot of the fire. I resolved to risk the boat no farther. I whispered to Simon that I was going ashore for a close look, and taking the young Indian with me. Wokwees rose at once, and we stepped out on the slimy mangrove roots with some distaste—they felt like snakes underfoot. Wokwees had eyes like a cat, and could move like one, so I nudged him ahead and followed in his steps, feeling carefully with each foot before putting it down lest the crack of a stick ruin everything.

We had not far to go for a clear view. The mangrove clump stood out a bit from the line of the shore, and after twenty steps or so we emerged into the open and looked straight towards the fire. Several indistinct figures lay about it. Once a man walked up to it from the shadows and threw on more wood. A flutter of sparks went up, and in this added light I made out a man sitting hunched to one side, with his hands clasped about his knees, and staring into the blaze. For a moment his face was outlined sharply, like those shadow pictures the profile makers cut out with scissors and paste on blocks of wood for a shilling a head. There was no mistaking the cut of that jib or the upturned pigtail at the back. Lot Mayes was sitting by the fire.

Was he a prisoner of those others? His attitude was glum enough. We watched, and presently one of the prone men stirred, and Lot arose and went over to him. They talked in low voices impossible to catch. Then I saw Lot raise a pannikin to the other's mouth. Someone sick or wounded, evidently. If they were prisoners there was no sign of a guard. The other figures sprawled about the fire in postures of indifference. I nudged the Indian to go on.

It took us half an hour to cover the rest of the way, creeping amongst the mangroves. At last I reached a place in the shadows well behind the fire itself. I felt about for a stick and tossed it at Lot's feet. He put his head up and looked over his shoulder, frowning in the firelight.

"Lot!" I said, not loudly. "Lot Mayes!"

He turned slowly and faced towards the darkness, turning his

head to and fro in search of someone in the rim of t
and seeing nothing.

"Lot!" I said again, in the same voice. "Come this w
Say nothing."

He came, sauntering, with thumbs in his belt. At the
trees he paused and uttered an incredulous whisper
Nathan, boy—is it you?"

"Ay, Nathan as ever was! Come closer. Come out o

He stepped into the gloom, and in a moment we we
our arms about each other, and the old man weeping
. . . Nathan, boy . . . this is what I'd hoped for .
for . . . ever since that schemin' rogue got the bes
but we . . . the lads . . . had just about give ye
said ye was all took and good as hanged."

I shook him fiercely. "The ship! What's happenec

"Don't ye know?"

"Brule?"

"Ay, Brule, damn the day we ever set eyes on hi
out o' the woods about here—alone—clo'es all torn—
sundown, 'twas—stood at the waterside hailin' the sh
that Capitaine Cain and his party was in trouble, up
road—said Meester Mayes was to take all the mer
to use a cutlass—no firearms, Meester Mayes was
o' that—and bring 'em up to the road—Cap'n Cai
we put off in the longboat, ten of us—all that was
and rushed up into the woods the way he pointed.
path well enough for a mile or so—bushes broken
away—then we lost it. Wandered about for a bit—
it up again—wondered why Brule hadn't come alor
way. Gettin' dusk—got 'spicious—headed back f
Come out on the point below here—just in time to
a lot o' wild-lookin' strangers in a crazy little car

cane cutlass at his belt and armed with pistols and muskets from the ship. They came right inshore here below the fire, and Brule sung out for us to come and take our wounded out o' the boat. 'Three of them were foolish enough to resist when we went aboard,' he says, very cool, 'but here are the rest.' So we carried the lads up careful to the fire—they weren't fit to be moved at all, and four ha' died since, here upon the beach. Brule said, polite—oh, he was polite as the devil, I tell ye—'It is very nice, the fire, Meester Mayes, but you had better sleep, you and your friends. Capitaine Cain will not be back. None of them will be back.'

" 'Why?' says I.

" 'Because,' he says, 'they are to die in the square at Cap François tomorrow. It is very sad.' And off they went to the ship.

"While this was goin' on, another party o' the scoundrels went over to the *Hirondelle* in the jolly boat and fetched two kegs o' tafia—we could see 'em in the light o' the boat lantern. By the time Brule got back aboard they were at it, and for the next three hours and more there was a fine hey-my-nonny about the *Fancy's* deck. 'Minded me of our passage down the Nicolas Channel—even to Brule's fiddle for a time. But they didn't seem to take to his fiddlin' like our own lads—a lot o' wild shoutin' and argument—till finally Boston appeared, squattin' on the cabin hatch and beatin' his drum—and the girl, laughin' and callin' out to 'em, and singin' bits o' songs in their own tongue, and dancin' the *chica* for 'em—on and on and on—and all those wild men clappin' their hands and screechin' fit to wake the dead. They've been quiet now an hour or more—not a soul movin'—no sign o' life but the cabin lamps. But you—you, Nathan—what about you and the others?"

"Along the shore a bit. We've got a boat——"

"What!"

"Hish! Go down and tell your men—easy now—easy does it! The badly wounded will have to stay where they are, for the time being, anyhow. The others are to move back into the trees, quietly, one at a time. They're to join me here."

"What ye goin' to do, Nathan?"

"Board the *Fancy* and have it out with 'em. How many are they?"

"Hard to say. Three dozen anyhow."

"Go and tell your men."

That was a night I shall never forget. A thunderstorm was brewing in the mountains, and the land breeze had unfolded a great mat of cloud that shut off the stars. We moved and breathed in a black and muggy void. Nothing stirred aboard the brigantine. We pushed the boat off and began to row, with kerchiefs wrapped about the oar looms to keep them quiet, and dipping the blades with a caution that had no real worth because each plunge set up a phosphorescent swirl that blazed like fire. Even the drip of the wet blades as they swung produced a sparkle like a powder train, and as we drew into the deeper water I could look over the side and see the moving shapes of large fish—sharks, no doubt—glowing with a pale and ghostly light below.

Every moment I expected to hear a loud challenge from the *Fancy's* deck, and a blast of musketry and cannon on the heels of it. There was something ominous and waiting in the silent bulk of her as we closed. I steered for the bow to avoid the broad gleam of the cabin windows and because the watch most likely would be sitting on the main hatch—if indeed the whole crew were not at stations and awaiting us. Nothing happened. We slipped off our shoes for quiet and the better footing. Simon Dawkins in the bow stood up and caught the brigantine's bobstay. One by one we went up, each man in turn leaning from the sprit to give a hand to the next, and all of us dripping sweat with the simple effort of it, there in the dark oven of the night.

Still not a voice, not a sound aboard. We unsheathed our cutlasses and went about our business swift and silent as a parcel of wharf thieves. Lot Mayes and I led the way. Outside the forecastle door we stumbled over a man. He did not move. I stooped and sniffed. He stank of tafia. Lot stirred him, not gently, with a foot. The fellow grunted in French, "Yes, yes, boatswain," and began to snore. I put my head inside the forecastle and found a solid reek of tafia, of sweating unwashed bodies, the very smell of Cap François, and a chorus of drunken snores.

I posted Michael Brady and three men there with cutlasses to strike down any who attempted to come out. The rest of us scattered along the waist in a quick fumbling search. Half a dozen more of Brule's rogues lay about the deck in drunken attitudes, all sodden with tafia. We could hear others in the hold, snoring and muttering beneath the open fore hatch. We put the hatch on quietly and posted men to guard it.

"Now for the cabin," Simon muttered, looking aft to the yellow glow of the skylight. My heart was in my throat. I was wild to go on, yet dreading what I should find. All this had been too easy—much too easy—after our long hard road. I felt a prickle not so much of danger as of evil, and whispered hoarsely to Lot and Simon, "Stand back, you understand? If there's a rush that man may kill the girl—he may do anything. In any case this part of the affair belongs to me. Remember that. I have a reckoning with Brule."

I crept upon the poop. The wind sail was still rigged for a breath of air in the cabin, useless on this still and sultry night, but the skylight stood full open to receive it. I put my head into the glow and peered down, and my heart leaped. There was Lia within a few feet of me, still wearing the thin yellow gown and crouched with an air of unutterable weariness on the familiar locker. Beside her stood Black Boston with his big arms folded across his chest, and both gazing towards a part of the cabin beyond my view where the voice of Brule was speaking softly and easily. I could not catch all he said, but what I did astonished me. The fellow was talking in a pleasant, dreamy way of life in Guadeloupe.

Chapter 32

FOR what I did then I make no excuse. Call it stupidity if you like. I can say only that my red hair got the better of my judgment, as it has so often in my life, and I put my free hand on the skylight coaming and vaulted down into the cabin. The flimsy table gave way under my weight and went down in a tremendous crash of wood and glass, for a carafe of wine and some tumblers stood at Brule's end of it. I heard Lia scream, but I had no attention for her at that moment, clutching the cutlass in my right hand and springing very nimbly to face Brule.

He sat in the maplewood armchair which was mine, the captain's chair, resting an elbow on its polished arm and pointing a cocked pistol at my breast.

I think I was far the more astonished of us two. Brule apparently had made free with the wardrobe of the late master of the *Hirondelle,* for he made an elegant picture in white tights and Hessians, a white shirt whose lace wrists and frilled jabot had wilted somewhat in the heat, a rich green coat cut away very sharply at the waist, its silver buttons all opened for comfort, and drooping a pair of long tails over the chair seat. All this I took in at an amazed glance, but chiefly my gaze was held by that familiar cropped black poll, the sleek mustache gleaming as if oiled, the sardonic smile that showed a little of his small white teeth, and beneath the half-shut lids a glitter of bright blue eyes.

"Don't move!" he said. "You are clumsy, my friend, and you may break something more. Drop your cutlass! That is better. So you escaped! I might have known you would—the lucky Capitaine Cain who falls always on his feet! And so you left your men to hang?" I could see the speculation in his eyes.

"That is my affair," said I.

"Ah! A painful subject, no doubt. I respect your silence, Capitaine. And what is the affair which brings you so rudely into our midst? You might have knocked—there is a lady, my betrothed——"

"Liar!"

"Your manners go well with your looks, monsieur. Suppose you ask the lady."

I turned to Lia, sitting bolt upright on her locker, one hand at each side clasping the edge of it. The knuckles were white. She had a strange frozen look upon her face and would not look at me. She looked at Brule.

"It is true, Nathan. I promised Victor long ago, in Gosport——"

"I don't believe it!"

Brule laughed. "What can one do with a man who does not believe his own ears? You see, my friend, that we have been at a merry game of purposes, all of us. Monsieur Dolainde wished to return to Saint Domingo. So did Lia. So did I. Monsieur had a delusion of money hidden in the old *manoir*. I knew there was none, I knew the *manoir* was destroyed. But I knew something else. I knew there must be someone in authority in Saint Domingo who would wish to see some of the old planters return, and to restore to them some part of their estates, for the good of the island. I am a good republican, I have served as *enseigne-de-vaisseau* in a ship of the Saint Domingo squadron, and what is more important I am a creole of the colony, one of the *petits-blancs,* the poor whites who fought in the insurrection. Was it not reasonable to suppose that I could return and plead the cause of the Dolaindes? This I told to Ma'mselle—to my dear Lia, who wished to get away from those cold Prides and their charity, and to see her father happy on his lands again. *Voilà!* In gratitude she promised me her hand. It only remained then to persuade you and your *beau-père,* the amiable Pride, to grant us passage to Saint Domingo. As you did, in your unwilling fashion."

I was still watching her face. "But," I cried, puzzled and outraged, "this fellow cannot do what he promised, Lia! The estate is a ruin, even the land cannot be restored without the labor of an army of slaves, and your father——"

"Where is my father?" she asked in that rigid voice, and watching Brule.

I hesitated. There was no good in lying. She would have to know. "My dear," I said gently, "he is dead."

A bitter cry came from her lips, but there was no emotion in her face.

"Suppose you explain, Capitaine"—Brule's mocking voice. "Monsieur Dolainde left here in your charge, did he not?"

"There is no need, Victor," Lia said wearily. "My father was dying when we left Gosport. I suspected it. Now I know." A spasm shook her, half shudder and half sob. "Oh, my God, Nathan, why did you have to come back here tonight?"

"Yes, why?" Brule said. "In the morning we should have been on our way to Guadeloupe in the brigantine, Lia and I—do not move, monsieur—and everything would have been so simple—no sad good-bys—and no regrets."

I looked at Boston, standing there with a face carved out of ebony.

"You!" I said in English. "What have you to say for yourself —taking Mr. Pride's pay and my orders, and playing this man's game?"

He rolled his eyes at me. "Nathan, sah, I jus' done what Miss Lia asked me."

"Ah, don't reproach him, your faithful Boston," Brule said in an amused tone. "He has taken good care of our Lia, I assure you—a perfect duenna, a veritable *cafard* who came out of the wall at the lightest tap." He chuckled at his own wit. "Tonight when those drunken rascals of mine kicked up their heels, demanding a share in everything—in everything, you comprehend —I thought we should be hard put to defend our Lia, he and I. But it was she who suggested the bold thing to do—that she go on deck amongst them, to sing, to dance for them, to be all things to all of them and nothing to any one of them. Do you see? Perfect equality and fraternity and no chance for liberties. How they are clever—women! I had my doubts, but I remembered that night in the Nicolas Channel and I let her go; and Boston played the drum. How she danced! How she sang! And how they shouted for more, the *coquins*—and toasted her in tafia, again and again and again. Dieu! I thought they would never drop. Monsieur, applaud her courage, as I do. She was magnificent!"

He was talking to fill time, of course. Behind that glib tongue was a mind mighty disturbed at my appearance, wondering what had happened on deck, and hoping any moment to hear the voices of his men. All this I knew, and he saw it in my face. A change came over his countenance. He uttered a short laugh.

"*Allons donc!* Let me put the cards before you, monsieur. Your clothes are dry, so you did not swim. You have a boat, then, and no doubt someone with you. The old man Mayes, I suppose, and those others I left on shore. I could have kicked them to the fish as my men wished, but no, I listened to Ma'mselle and let them go. So you have a dozen men, perhaps, on deck at this moment, I do not doubt, while my crew sleep off their tafia. Yet some of the drunken fools must be stirring even now, and they are forty-seven to your handful. What follows?" He shrugged his fine green shoulders and went on. *"Comme ci, comme ça!* All that is certain, my dear capitaine, is that we are here in the cabin together, you and I and the pistol in my hand—and Ma'mselle, of course. I ask you to think especially of Ma'mselle. She is sensitive, she is fatigued, she has sorrow for her father. Let us spare her another brawl and bloodshed. There has been enough, you will admit. Let us argue this matter like sensible men."

"Go on," I said.

"Capitaine, you are the heir of Monsieur Pride, one understands, the chosen husband of his daughter. Someday they will be yours, that great house in Gosport, the stores, the warehouses, the ships, the money he loves so much—and Mademoiselle Felicity, of course. Those are the things to which you belong, then, up there in the North—in that cold country where the word freezes on the lip, where one is drowned in snow for half the year and lost in fog the other half. In Nova Scotia, yes. You do not mind, you are accustomed to a wind that today is sad and a little chilled, like a woman weeping, and tomorrow is like a whip on the naked skin. No doubt you love that sky which is gray always, and that sea always cold, and that land which is nothing but melancholy trees and stones, and those people who have a lean and starved look all the time, and rush about doing this and that because Meester Pride says they must."

He raised his black brows and opened his eyes very wide. "On the other hand, she belongs here—our Lia—in these islands where the air is always warm upon the skin, where the sea and sky are blue always, where the leaves do not fall from the trees and the birds do not fly away, and the people have time to sing, to dance, and to make love—which is very important to a woman. Have you thought of all this, Capitaine?"

He gave me that candid blue gaze, but he was talking to Lia, of course, and offering her not merely a contrast of two ways of life but of two lovers present in the flesh, himself very elegant in his borrowed plumes, soft-voiced and debonair, the picture of a creole gentleman in the new republican manner, and I the rough red-haired seaman from the North, filthy and unshaven, a lean and scowling figure in soiled duck trousers and a torn shirt. I held my hot tongue lest I make it worse. I glanced at Lia, wondering what was in her mind. The old flush of high spirit was gone from her olive cheeks, and her dark eyes had a haunted look. The fine nostrils quivered. Her long yellow locks lay tumbled about her bare shoulders, where I suppose they had fallen during that endless dancing on the deck. Her body drooped as if she were faint, and yet she had that attitude of a woman on guard, her knees pressed together in the thin silken gown that clung about her in the heat, the body bent slightly forward, the hands clasping the locker edge, her eyes watchful and somber, the breast alive in slow deep movements, and all the rest of her motionless.

"So you have nothing to say!" Brule exclaimed. "But after all, monsieur, what could you say? If you told the truth you would have to say this: 'I never gave Lia-Marie Dolainde one thought when she lived under the same roof with Felicity Pride. If I noticed her at all I gave no sign of it—not a kindly word, not even a smile in all the time when she was desolate and lonely in that desolate and lonely house. I cannot blame her if she turned to her fellow unfortunate, the prisoner Brule, an officer of the republic forced to earn his bread with comb and scissors in a foreign land, who shared with her his longing for the beautiful islands in the sun. But when I found her in my ship, when Monsieur Pride and his daughter were so far behind—yes, then I regarded Lia-Marie Dolainde. She was beautiful, she had passion, she would make a charming toy for the long months of the cruise—do not move, Capitaine!—and now, even now, when my cruise is a failure and I must go home with the sad news to Meester Pride, still I wish to have her, the pretty creole. Perhaps—perhaps I could keep her somewhere quietly—in Halifax, where I have kept women before, *hein?*—and marry that cold Felicity and her fortune and be the king of Gosport——' "

"Victor!" cried Lia Dolainde.

"The truth, *ma belle*. This is no time for pretty words."

I broke my silence then. "Brule, you have a dirty mind. It smells like those hovels at Cap François—where you came from, I suspect. It is true that I did not regard Lia much in Gosport, as you say. I am a simple man, I looked upon her as a child—and she kept herself to herself. I admit that it was not until this voyage that I saw her as she really was. It was not until I left the ship to go on that journey to the Manoir Dolainde that I knew what she meant to me. But now that I do know these things, Brule, I am not prepared to give her up so easily as you seem to think. Certainly I do not believe Lia really loves you now, or ever did, or ever will."

Brule waved the pistol airily. "You hear, Lia? He talks well, this red fox, eh? Almost one might think he believes what he says."

He darted one of his quick glances towards the skylight. His position was safe enough. I dare say he had chosen to sit just there, beyond the line of any shot from above, because on this night of nights he could not trust his own rogues. And now his caution was rewarded. He saw my upward glance and smiled.

"No, *monsieur le capitaine,* I cannot be reached from up there, whoever has the deck. That is unfortunate, eh? There is only one key to this affair, and it is in my hand. I warn you that if we should receive any more unwelcome visitors through the *tabatière* I shall kill you where you stand."

A silence in which he seemed to be listening intently. He shrugged at last.

"You interrupted me a minute ago, monsieur. Let me go on with what I have to say. I wish to give you credit for your true thoughts. I do not believe that you love Mademoiselle Dolainde any more than you love Mademoiselle Pride. More than that, I do not believe the great thing in your life is the fortune of Monsieur Pride any more than I believe you really hoped to get your hands upon the mythical fortune of poor Monsieur Dolainde. No, none of that, monsieur. You are a strange people, you Nouvelle-Ecossais, a little tribe of Yankees who still acknowledge the king George, lost in the wilderness halfway to the Pole. You scurry between the forest and the sea like a little multitude of beach birds who must seek for food every moment of their lives or perish. A bitter existence, but it has given you one thing I admire—your ability to hew ships out of the forest, to launch them on the sea and sail them anywhere.

"It is something, that. Your land is hard, your skies are cold, you cannot love your unlovely women, and so you love your ships, for they alone are beautiful. Monsieur, I watched you gather the timbers for this ship. I saw you hover about the carpenters as they put it together piece by piece. When she was launched I saw the worship in your eyes, and felt a warmth in my heart for you. For I could understand. This, then, is the one thing you truly love—this ship in which we sit. I come to my point. She is now mine by possession, this brigantine, by a proper act of war which will be recognized by any marine court in France or her colonies.

She belongs to me—Victor Brule, *capitaine-de-corsaire* in the service of the republic!"

He rolled this off his tongue in a magnificent way, as if he really believed it, and set me wondering how much of my wine he had swallowed before I dropped through the skylight. But the pistol was steady, his eyes alert.

"Possession," I said coldly. "That is a matter I am prepared to dispute with you, my friend. Suppose I told you that we got away from the ruins of the Manoir Dolainde, all of us, and that the deck above is held at this moment by thirty of my Nouvelle-Ecossais, armed and ready to strike at any head that appears."

He shrugged. "Suppose you are lying, monsieur. Probably you are. I feel quite sure you are. I suspect that you stole aboard alone, past those drunken seamen of mine, and think to frighten me by your own boldness. But there is room for doubt, I admit. And we have the lady to consider. That is why I am in a mood to bargain with you."

"Oh?"

"An agreement between gentlemen, monsieur. I remove to the captured privateer *l'Hirondelle* over there, with Lia and my men and certain stores which we shall need for our affairs in these waters. The brigantine, I give it you—this ship which is the one thing in the world you truly love. You can sail home then and make your peace with Monsieur Pride for this unfortunate voyage, and all will be well. You will marry Mademoiselle Felicity, and Lia and I will rejoice in your good fortune."

"An Indian's bargain. Have you nothing else to offer?"

"Yes!" His voice went hard as flint. "Your life, which I hold now under my finger! Make up your mind, monsieur. We have talked long enough."

"And who—forgive me if I seem distrustful—who is to see that it is carried out, this bargain between gentlemen?"

"Ah! Well said, monsieur! It must be someone we both respect, no? And who commands our wishes more than the charming person in the cabin here with us? Lia, *ma belle,* tell our young friend what is best for his own good."

The girl spoke quickly, in a hard breathless voice, not looking at me but at Brule—always at Brule.

"Victor is right, Nathan. I love him—no one else in the world. He can give me the kind of life I want, here in the islands where I was born, where I was happy. You must take what is offered you—this ship which you love—and go back to Gosport, to the Prides."

"You see?" said Brule.

The words were plain enough. They chilled me to the soul. Yet I was puzzled by that strange intent look of hers. I thought of the small bird and the snake, but that was absurd in the light of Lia's vigorous mind and passions. Beside her Brule was a weakling, a scoundrel right enough, but too merry a man, too fond of ease and pleasure, especially the pleasure of women, to spoil his love-making with an overbearing manner, even if there were some hope of success that way. I knew that lady-killing vanity of his. I could see him now in the little shop at Gosport, waving his comb and scissors and boasting of his conquests, talking of love as a game that must be played by certain rules if one would have its sweetest relish in the end.

Then why was Lia watching him so carefully? It came to my thick mind slowly that perhaps there was nothing subtle about it after all. In my search for a meaning in this queer three-cornered battle of wits that left so many things unsaid, I had failed to place myself in Lia's shoes and overlooked the simple thing, the one fact that might explain all else—her attitude, her fascinated stare, that cold avowal of her love for Brule.

She was looking at the pistol in his hand, at the hard round eye of it staring straight at my breast. Just that, and nothing more.

Chapter 33

IN AN awakening of happiness I cried out to her, "Lia! Oh, my dear girl——" but there was an interruption. A voice from nowhere startled us all, so absorbed we were in this play of wits and passions that made the cabin a small world of itself. It was the high twang of Lot Mayes. I looked up and saw his gray-stubbled face in the glow of the skylight, peering past the wind sail.

"Nathan! There you are! Um!"—seeing Lia—"Beg pardon, miss. Well, you're all right, then, you and Nathan—and there's Boston, too, I see. Nathan, there's work to do. The lads think we should go below while those rogues of Brule's are still half-seas-over, and make sure of 'em with belaying pins. So do I. And besides——"

He could not see Brule, of course. My skin seemed to feel the cold kiss of the pistol's mouth as though the thing had grown two fathoms' length across the cabin. I cried up to him with a dry mouth, "I've a matter to discuss here first. Get back to your post, man. Go!"

I knew what ailed him. Lot was thirsting for a sup of rum, poor man, and could scarcely wait to be about it, though he had to kill Brule's whole crew with his bare fists first. His face hung above us for a moment in the soft haze where a cloud of moths and smaller insects fluttered in the upflung light of the lamps, a ghost of a face twisted in disapproval of me, of Lia, of the whole parched world. Then it was gone, and presently we heard his distant complaint and the unmistakable voice of Simon Dawkins in reply, and the low grumble of the men.

"So!" Brule snapped, and I saw a flicker of desperation in

his eyes. "It is true, then! The luck of the devil! If one had time it would be interesting to know how you contrived it, monsieur. I saw Toussaint himself ride off with a troop of Dessalines' dragoons—and black patrols kicking up the dust towards the bridges in the plain—have you wings, you Nouvelle-Ecossais? *Eh bien,* it does not matter now. I made you an offer, monsieur. What is your answer?"

He was sweating in his borrowed finery, his round olive face and cropped black hair shining as if with grease. I answered slowly, with a conviction I did not feel—let me be honest, with my heart in my mouth.

"I do not like your bargain, Brule. You offer me my ship, which is in the hands of my men in any case, as you have seen. You offer me my life. But consider—if you killed me, how could you escape? You suggested a few minutes ago that Lia be the judge between us in this bargain, yet you sit there with a pistol in your hand."

He snarled, "What would you have, monsieur?"

"Surely the judge should hold the only weapon in the court?"

"Bah!"

"You say that Lia loves you—she has said so herself. In that case, what have you to fear? Come, my friend, let us put this matter to the proof. Let Lia take the pistol. After all, her person is the matter in dispute between us, is it not?"

Silence. Silence long and terrible, with my heart thumping out the measure of the minutes, and Brule turning a wild blue glare from Lia to me and back to Lia again. His easy confidence was gone. There was hatred in his eyes, and it seemed to me something of despair. I turned my head to Lia. She was looking at me, and for the first time since I entered the cabin our eyes met. And then . . . and then for the space of a moment the mask was gone. For a moment I saw in her eyes the look she had given me that night I left the ship for Manoir Dolainde. For a moment only. Then it was gone. We looked away to Brule.

And he had seen. In that moment of revelation my poor Lia had betrayed the whole fabric which her own wit had spun about her in defense these long, long hours. I expected Brule to leap and scream, I expected a shot—I expected anything but the look on his face then. The man looked bewildered and lost. He even looked old, as if upon the thirty years he had lived another thirty had been flung.

I felt almost sorry for him then. He wanted her, he loved her very much. There was no doubt about it. I loved Lia so much myself that I could feel the very pang that must have pierced him when he saw that confession in her eyes.

It is strange. The world is full of women, many of them beautiful, more beautiful than Lia Dolainde as worldly standards go, and most of them open to a wooer who can strike some chord in them; and yet for any man, saint or libertine, there is one woman, one alone who has meaning, who has the answer to the question that is in his soul. He may pass an hour, a year, a lifetime with some other, but the question remains and he is not complete, he must go through the world like the lost dog he is, taking what he can by the way but seeking—seeking always—and unsatisfied.

He spoke at last, clutching the pistol firmly and crying, "No!" in a strange hoarse voice. And then in a dogged sort of way, with something savage in his tone and in his face, "Monsieur, at first I only wanted her in the way that any man wants any woman, and I had too the contemplation of a certain revenge—I do not know what else to call it, but that is not the word—I, the poor *petit-blanc* and she, the rich planter's daughter—you understand? The justice of the thing. You do not know what it was to be a poor white in our Saint Domingo of the old days. The very blacks despised us. I used to watch men like Dolainde driving through the streets of Cap François with their pretty wives and daughters, or their mistresses, with a black on the carriage box in better clothes than mine, and all the pleasures of the world theirs for a wave of the hand. I envied them, I hated them—who of the *petits-blancs* did not?—and thought how someday . . . someday . . . you understand?

"That was the way I thought of Lia Dolainde when I first saw her grown-up, in Gosport, all those miles from Saint Domingo. But after I talked to her once or twice I knew that she was like me after all, a creole, lonely and longing for the island we both knew. We became comrades then. I made love to her, of course; that was the natural thing to do; but she would talk only of her father—'Papa'—Papa Dolainde—and how they longed to go back to Saint Domingo. So—you see? When Monsieur Pride fitted out this *corsaire* for the southern seas we thought the way was clear. Dolainde put out a hook, and your greedy *beau-père* swallowed it. This I knew from Lia. So I went to Monsieur Pride myself—and he swallowed me. The difficult matter was Lia herself. We knew—she and I—that her father would never permit her to go on the voyage, nor would Monsieur Pride. So we called in the aid of our good friend Boston here and smuggled her on board. The rest of that you know. What you do not know perhaps is that Lia promised herself to me if I saw her father settled again on his old *domaine*. That I promised readily. I was not lying. I thought I could. But of course all that was hopeless, as I found in Cap François. The blacks were in the saddle, and in any case the old estates were ruined.

"And so I returned to this place, to the brigantine, with a crew of *petits-blancs* and mulattoes as hopeless as myself. I explained to Lia the affair, not all of it, but enough. I wished to take the ship and go to Guadeloupe—with her, you comprehend. I think

I could have persuaded her if you had not appeared. But—here you are. And now you want her—you, who have everything in the world—while I have nothing. Is it just? I ask you, is it just?"

I made no answer. There was nothing to say. The man was working himself to a passion, and I wondered what would come of it. The eyes he turned from Lia to me were the eyes of a lunatic, and every time he mentioned her name he swung the pistol towards her as if to aim his very words with the thing. I could hear Boston breathing heavily at my shoulder. Did he understand a tenth of all this?

"Life?" Brule shouted, though none of us had said a word. "What is life to a man like me? Half my friends in Cap François are dead or gone. The rest will have their throats slit someday, any day, when the blacks decide the time has come. With Lia—yes, with Lia I could have gone to Guadeloupe and made a new life for myself and her. But no, that is not to be. She is still the daughter of the Manoir Dolainde, while I—I am Brule the smuggler, the barber, the fiddler, the *petit-blanc* of Cap François. I see it in her face—her face that deceived me all this time, that desires nothing but to give itself to your kisses, Capitaine Cain. And you? What have you done to deserve her? Nothing! Nothing! *Bien!*—then you shall not have her, Capitaine. Not I, not you—that is just, I think."

"Brule!" I cried.

"Do not move, Capitaine, for if you do I shall kill you—and why should you die before the rest of us? Boston, pull up the trap door, if you please. Move, black man!"

Boston gasped, "Mistah Brule, sah!"

"Pull it up or I kill you, Boston."

The cook's eyes bulged, but he stood his ground. Brule turned the pistol full at Lia.

"The trap door—pull it up, black man, or I pull the trigger——"

Boston uttered a queer sound, part whine, part groan. He stepped forward and slid the brass bolt in the flooring and slowly lifted the door by the ring.

A dry sharp smell of powder came up from the darkness below. Brule snuffed. A wild pleasure lit his face. He seemed to me then half drunk, half mad. He stood up and with his left hand unshipped the nearest of the cabin lamps, giggling in a thin high cackle like a half-witted lout on a Halloween prank, and watching us, watching us always, with the heavy pistol aimed at my poor girl.

"My friends," he chuckled, "you are privileged. You are about to witness Lucifer descending with the lightning into hell—by the private entrance. You will not appreciate the spectacle, of course. The moment I pass below you will run up the cabin stairs—as if you could save yourselves, imbeciles! By the time you reach the deck I shall be in the magazine, and—pouf!"

He began to descend the steps, facing us and wearing on his round sweating face that terrible smile. The hinge of the trap was towards our little group, and the three-foot length of the thing, held open by Boston's trembling hand, stood like a shield. When his shoulders barely showed above the top of it, and with the pistol raised, Brule paused.

"Lia," he said in a passionate voice, "I loved you. Put me in your prayer." He passed from our sight in a leap, and I sprang and kicked the trap door shut and slid the bolt with trembling fingers, crying to Lia and Boston, "Run! Run!" I cannot remember the cabin stairs at all. We seemed to fly. In a moment we were running along the deck and I heard my own voice shouting, "Take to the boat, all hands! The powder!" Magic words! A company of shadows sprang from the pitch-darkness and raced with us to the forecastle head. A patter of bare feet and the quick *tic-tac* of Lia's shoes and then we were dropping into the boat. I had my arm about my darling's waist, and stood on the sprit and swung her down to Simon Dawkins's arms, every moment expecting a swift and terrible convulsion which would end us all.

There was no counting of noses. Someone cut the painter, and we rowed away in a most furious haste towards the land. The dim form of the *Hirondelle* loomed out of the darkness, but I ignored her. My one thought was to get Lia ashore and carry our wounded up into the woods away from the blast. As we rowed, stroke on stroke with those rotten oars, to safety, Boston gabbled out the story of that mad scene in the cabin, and I remember the exclamations of the seamen as he talked, and the loud voice of Lot Mayes praying in the bow.

And still no explosion.

Michael Brady murmured, "Cap'n, what's happened, d'ye think?"

I laughed, shakily. "Brule is trapped between decks for the moment. He knew the trap door led to the magazine, but he didn't know there was a lower door, which lately I've kept locked, with the key in my pocket. A flimsy thing, matchboard stuff—he'll have it down by now."

A minute passed, and another. We could see the embers of the fire on shore, a red dot in the solid blackness of the land. Behind us remained the pale yellow glimmer of the *Fancy's* cabin windows, peaceful as ever.

Suspicion came to me. I said, "Lay on your oars!" in a voice like the rustle of dry leaves. Tricked! Tricked, of course! Old seamen tell tales of ships blown up in a moment of battle by some fanatic in the powder room, just as they talk of mermaids and sea serpents and Flying Dutchmen and the rest. But who really believes them? Think of it—the dim room full of wicked little kegs, the broached one ready for the first demand, the powder black and glistening like the devil's own table salt, the match, the lantern, the pistol in the hand to touch it off—what man could have the courage, the cold and bitter courage—eh? What man? Not that pleasure-loving man Brule, at any rate.

I could see it now, the plan spawned in that cunning mind whilst we three stood or sat like dreamers under his pistol. To scare us all overboard, neck and crop, by a shrewd bit of play-acting and a threat—that was the first accomplishment. The rest was simple. He had broken down the matchboard door below, passed through the magazine, and opened the main door that led to the after hatch, the cockpit, and the landsmen's quarters in the hold, where half his scoundrels were sleeping off their carouse. He was kicking them awake even now, and in a few minutes they would be on deck, ready for any deviltry.

Instinctively I shifted course towards the *Hirondelle*. We would make sure of the schooner anyhow. And then? There was no wind for running even if we wished. We would have to fight it out, ship to ship, there in the dark. But as the boat swung—as the seamen murmured in surprise—as old Lot stopped his prayers and rapped out, "What the devil!"—then it came. A dull thud first, not so much heard as felt, as if some water giant had smitten our own boat's bottom with a hammer. A distinct pause of one or two seconds, in which we gaped towards the ship, and then an ear-splitting clap and a spout of bright orange flame that tore apart the silence and darkness in a single terrific stroke. The flame shot two or three times the height of the mastheads in an instant and sent the cabin hatch, the binnacle, and skylight spinning far up into the immensity of the night, all mingled with bits of beam and planking and God alone knows what.

As boys we had made "lightning" in the summer dusk behind the wharf sheds, sifting a handful of stolen powder down to a lit candle on the ground—a sport that cost us sore skins when our elders caught us in the act. It was like that, this flame, but multiplied beyond all count. Still the result was not what I had feared. Powder is a thing you come to respect, seeing the effect of it in a pistol, a fowling piece, and then in cannon fire, so that you regard a keg or twenty or thirty kegs with a very great awe indeed. In that wild scramble along the deck in the dark I had flinched from an explosion that would blow the whole ship to flinders and ourselves to dust.

What happened was something less, though terrible enough. The brigantine remained, with the whole poop deck blown out of her and the stern windows breathing smoke and flame like the nostrils of a dragon. The mainmast, scorched to the truck by that great gush of flame aft, burned like a torch in the night, and presently tall tongues of fire rose out of the hull where the cabin should have been. Behind us in the dark heart of the land the echoes of that great blast rumbled in the mountains, peal after peal, and going on and on until it seemed all Hispaniola must be ringing with the sound, and broad awake and wondering. We looked in each other's weary faces, our eye whites gleaming in that bloody light, awed and silent, like a clutch of sinners caught in some guilty secret by a light from heaven and the voice of God.

I sat on the stern sheets with the steering oar in one hand and Lia held close in the other, her face against my breast, sobbing her heart out. The rest of us watched the ship. For a long time the fire was entirely aft, or so it seemed, and then Pardon Gardner cried, "See there!" and a flicker appeared at the fore hatch, went out, appeared again, and rose and spread. I thought to see Brule's rogues appear, first one and then another and finally a mad rush over the side where their stolen *chaloupe* was fastened to the starboard fore chains. But there was not a man, from first to last not so much as a cry, no sign of life, only the hiss and flutter and crackle of the flames. Within two hours the whole ship was afire, burning in one wide flame that climbed the masts and went on to the sky in a tower of lit smoke as tall as the night itself. The fire cast a bloody orange glow upon the water all about her, so that in the midst of the darkness she sat lonely and magnificent on a great tray of burnished copper, like a sacrifice. And not a breath of wind, no night breeze off the mountains, nothing, as if the very mountains held their breath at the spectacle.

And all the while I sat there with a dull ache at the heart, watching the death of my ship, my lovely brigantine, and holding Lia close against me, not for her comfort but for mine. A man is a weak creature after all. We rant and swagger and put forth our strength and think upon ourselves as gods on earth; but when our dreams are shattered, when we see the work of our hands and minds all gone to pieces in a moment or a night, then we must turn to a woman after all.

One by one the yards fell; the topsail yards first and then the topgallants, but for some reason the royals hung on to the last, when the masts themselves trembled and came slowly down, aflame from end to end, the main first, then the fore, and plunged into the sea. Lot Mayes said quietly, "There they go—the best sticks that ever came down Gosport River. Nathan, d'ye remember the Spanish coins Dan Stacey set 'em on—for luck?"

"Ay. We should have known better, Lot. The Spaniards never had much luck of all their silver, did they?"

"And d'ye remember how Amos Pride cut his hand that morning of the launching? A bloody omen, that's what I said, and wasn't it the truth? Here we are six-and-thirty men all told, that sailed from Gosport eighty-four."

There was no reply to that. I held my tongue.

Once the masts had gone the fire dropped back upon itself as if it lacked a guide towards the sky, and slackened steadily. The gutted hull remained afloat, giving off more smoke than flame, and the circle of lit sea about it shrank and lost its glitter. I looked over my shoulder and saw the faint light of morning in the east. I stirred then, and asked Lot to steer, and ordered the men to take up their oars.

"What now?" the old man said.

"We must get aboard the schooner, pick our wounded off the beach, and make sail as soon as the trade wind blows. The blacks must have heard that powder clap and seen the glare in Fort Liberty, maybe in Cap François."

"Sail where?" he said.

"Home to Nova Scotia—where else?" I felt Lia stiffen in my arms.

"In that riddled thing?" Lot cried.

"Men have sailed farther in worse."

"Ay, ay, God help us, so they have."

The men began to row, and Lia turned her face up to me and pushed herself a little away.

"Red . . . Red . . . You are going back to them . . . the Prides?"

"Never!"

"But where?"

"There are many places we can choose. The province is nigh empty still. Somewhere we shall find a village by a river, you and I, where there are trees to fell and float down to the sea, and ships to build—for that is what I want to do. They are beautiful, ships."

She turned her head and gazed towards the somber mass of the land, and the tops of the mountains stark against the dawn. I guessed the anguish in that look.

"Lia, my dear," I said gently, "all that is darkness and best left behind. There's terror in it, all of it, for people like you and me. He talked of warmth and sunshine, that man Brule—but all I ever saw in Hispaniola was that everyone but the slave folk stayed indoors away from it, they shut the sunshine out with jalousies and blinds and lattices and stayed in darkness to be cool. Darkness—always darkness, night and day; and not just the shadow cast by sun or moon, but something more that seemed to me to come out of the earth itself. Look at it now—over there —the sun is up and still there is the black shape of the mountains —and when the sun stands overhead at noon there will remain a gloom in the forest and in the houses where every man or woman with a drop of white blood must creep and stay and gasp for breath till nightfall. Prisoners—prisoners always—prisoners of the sun and prisoners of that black multitude about them."

"Not all the blacks are cruel, Red. Some of them I loved."

"True. But what are most of them but savages a few years out of Africa, with nothing but a memory of cruelty there and here? Someday they may work out their destiny in Hispaniola, and then life may be safe for other folk amongst them, but that won't come in your time, Lia. It will take a century. Two, perhaps."

She did not answer. The oars rose and fell. The slim shape of the *Hirondelle* seemed to swim towards us in the half-light of the anchorage. A voice hailed from the shore, one of our wounded crying out to us not to leave them, a cry drawn out and melancholy, like the voice of the land itself. The girl shivered in my arms. I put my lips to hers but she turned her face away. Her eyes were closed, her skin as white as alabaster in the first pallid gleam of morning.

"Lia," I said passionately, ignoring the seamen, ignoring the watchful face of old Lot, worn and gray and haggard, like a prophet in the wilderness, "Lia, where we are going the sun is a lover, not an enemy. It is a pleasure to be outdoors, to walk about in the full shine of it, to feel it on the skin. Even the earth is greedy for our sun—there is no monstrous mass of green to shut it out, the trees stand tall and clean, and there is a pleasant smell under the branches. Do you remember the smell of the pines? And there is the rocky shore and the cool smell of the sea, and the brown sails of the fishing boats, and the sound of the calkers making music in the shipyards——"

"There is winter," she said, without moving.

"Ah yes. The snow comes, and all the countryside is white as a fine tablecloth—ay, whiter than that, and sparkling brighter than all the diamonds of India. The stuff creaks underfoot, and the air tingles on the cheek—you want to run and wave your arms and shout, because it is like wine, our air in winter. That is the time for the sleigh and the nimble pony and the bells; for the skates and the fur cap and the frozen river like a road that waits to be traveled—don't you remember, Lia? Don't you remember how we laughed and sang and were happy in the wintertime?"

She turned her face and looked up at me, her eyes dark and mysterious, her rich mouth quivering as if she were about to weep, or smile.

"There are storms," she murmured, "and then there is no sunshine and no sleigh bells and no skating on the river, only the wind and the snow and the darkness—those nights, so long, so very cold—and you have not said the word my heart is waiting for."

"Eh? Storms and nights! There must be a time to shut out the world and turn to each other, Lia. There must be a time to love."

* * *

Do you remember, Lia my darling? Do you remember?